Advance Praise for *Scarlet Music*

"In this fictional biography, Ohanneson firmly anchors Hildegard of Bingen's life and prophetic witness in the historical events, both religious and secular, of twelfth-century Europe yet weaves for us a remarkable portrayal of a woman, deeply steeped through her visionary insights and mystic experiences into the numinous feminine divine which expresses itself as Wisdom and Love. With creative imagination and profound insight into the mind and heart of Hildegard of Bingen, Ohanneson evokes for us an intriguing yet deeply moving characterization."

— Miriam Schmitt, OSB, co-editor of
Medieval Women Monastics: Wisdom's Wellsprings

"In a culture that hungers for depth, *Scarlet Music* is food for the soul. A good story wakes us up, provides fresh alternatives, consecrates our sufferings, offers meaning. *Scarlet Music* is a *good* story. The hours spent with this music will enrich the heart and mind."

— Robert F. Morneau, Auxiliary Bishop of Green Bay,
author of *Ashes to Easter* and *The Gift*

"Joan Ohanneson succeeds in revealing more of the woman behind the mystic, the visionary, and the prophet — a woman who saw herself as 'weak' but who could make corrupt clergy and kings tremble, a woman who suffered severe bouts of illness but who could expend her energies in monumental accomplishments. We see the strength and weakness of her human attachments, her anxieties and her fears, but also her daunting courage and her compassion for ordinary folk. *Scarlet Music* is an admiring, sensitive, and richly detailed walk through the life and times, in the footsteps of Hildegard of Bingen."

Madonna Kolbenschlag, author of
Eastward toward Eve and *Lost in the Land of Oz*

"*Scarlet Music* will rivet the modern reader with its masterly evocation of times and peoples past, of saints and sinners, abbots and popes, and the shadows of great monasteries spreading across the landscape. Joan Ohanneson breathes life into the statued choirs of the Middle Ages so that they stand vividly before us debating far more seriously than we the questions we think of as our own bold inventions. Soon the pages and binding fall away and we find ourselves eavesdropping on all that is human in Hildegard and all that is divine as well. It lacks only Russell Baker offering an introduction to seem an episode of *Masterpiece Theater* at its most arresting and enlightening."

Eugene
Queen Bee a

D0204781

SCARLET
MUSIC

SCARLET MUSIC

HILDEGARD OF BINGEN

- A NOVEL -

JOAN OHANNESON

A Crossroad Book
The Crossroad Publishing Company
New York

This printing: 1998

The Crossroad Publishing Company
370 Lexington Avenue, New York, NY 10017

Printed in the United States of America

Acknowledgments will be found on pp. vii and viii,
which constitute an extension of the copyright page.

Library of Congress Cataloging-in-Publication Data

Ohanneson, Joan.
    Scarlet music : Hildegard of Bingen : a novel / Joan Ohanneson.
        p.   cm.
    ISBN 0-8245-1646-X (pbk.)
    1. Hildegard, Saint, 1098–1179 – Fiction.   2. Civilization,
Medieval – 12th century – Fiction.   3. Christian women saints –
Germany – Fiction.   4. Women mystics – Germany – Fiction.   I. Title.
PS3565.H29S3   1997
813'.54–dc21*
                                                        96–47125

CONTENTS

OPUS DEI —
THE WORK OF GOD
The Benedictine Liturgy of the Hours

- **Matins** — *Between 2:30 and 3:00 a.m.*

- **Lauds** — *Between 5:00 and 6:00 a.m., ending at dawn.*
  To give praise for the day ahead.

- **Prime** — *Between 6:00 and 7:00 a.m.*
  Asking for a blessing on the day ahead.

- **Terce** — *Around 9:00 a.m.*

- **Sext** — *Noon. The hour of the midday meal.*

- **None** — *Between 2:00 and 3:00 p.m.*

- **Vespers** — *Around 4:30 to 6:00 p.m. At sunset.*

- **Compline** — *Between 6:00 and 7:00 p.m.*
  The prayer signifying the day's "completion" before retiring.

ACKNOWLEDGMENTS

I am deeply grateful for the initial help and encouragement I received in Germany from Sr. Adelgundis Führkotter, OSB, and Sr. Ancilla Ferlings, OSB, of the Abbey of Saint Hildegard in Eibingen. The gracious hospitality of Ehrengard and Hans Lothar von Racknitz of Disibodenberg remains a cherished memory that never dims. I recall, as well, the kind assistance of Christina Kress.

Through the years, I have been nourished and inspired by the scholarship of Barbara Newman, Peter Dronke, Anna Silvas, OSB; Kathryn Kerby-Fulton, Matt Fox, Bruce Hozeski, Sabina Flanagan, Ann Kessler, OSB; Heribert Breidenbach, George Kohles, FSC; Barbara Jeskalian, and Sr. Imogene Baker, OSB. The generous counsel and spiritual friendship of Benedictine scholar Miriam Schmitt, OSB, were invaluable.

From the start, Mitch Kincannon's devotion to Hildegard was a joy to me, as were the nurturing and steadfast friendships of Susan McCarthy, Scott Scherer, John Hubner and Jill Wolfson, Freda Taylor, Pat Helin, Eileen Walsh, Alice Pratte, Sandra Conley, and Pamela Jekel.

My gratitude to my dynamic agent, Roslyn Targ, abounds; her faith in this book never once wavered. And to my daughters, Kim, Beth, Jill, and Erin, my deep appreciation for their belief in this book and their years of endearing encouragement.

But most of all, this book is dedicated to my husband Greg, who held back the flood while his love urged me on.

Grateful acknowledgment is made to the following for permission to reprint: Bear & Company for excerpts from *Hildegard of Bingen's Book of Divine Works,* edited by Matthew Fox; copyright © 1987 by Bear & Company, Sante Fe, NM, and from their publication *Hildegard von Bingen's Mystical Visions,* translated from *Scivias* by Bruce Hozeski, copyright 1986, Bear & Co., Sante Fe, NM. Cambridge University Press for excerpts from *Women Writers of the Middle Ages,* by Peter Dronke; copyright © 1984 by Cambridge University Press. Paulist Press for excerpts from *Hildegard of Bingen: Scivias,* translated by Mother Columba Hart and Jane Bishop; copyright © 1990 by the Abbey of Regina Laudis: Benedictine Congregation Regina Laudis of the Strict Observance, Inc., used by permission of the Paulist Press. University of California Press for excerpts from *Sister of Wisdom: Sr. Hildegard's Theology of the Feminine,* by Barbara Newman; copyright © 1987 by The Regents of the University of California. Cornell University Press for excerpts from *St. Hildegard of Bingen Symphonia: A Critical Edition of the Symphonia armonie celestium revelationum,* edited and translated by Barbara Newman; copyright © 1989 by Cornell University. Routledge for excerpts from *Hildegard of Bingen — A Visionary Life,* by Sabina Flanagan; copyright © 1989. *Tjurunga: An Australian Benedictine Review* (published in Arcadia, Australia), for excerpts from *Saint Hildegard of Bingen and the Vita Sanctae Hildegardis,* translated by Anna Silvas, OSB, and published in four parts: 29 (1985), 30 (1986), 31 (September 1986), and 32 (May 1987). Crossroad for excerpts from *Hildegard of Bingen: Mystical Writings,* edited and introduced by Fiona Bowie and Oliver Davies; copyright © 1990.

Excerpts from Hebrew and Christian Scriptures reprinted from the Jerusalem Bible, copyright © 1986 by Dartman, Longman, and Todd, Ltd., and Doubleday and Company, Inc., and the New American Bible, copyright © 1970 by the Confraternity of Christian Doctrine, Washington, D.C.

PROLOGUE

Four decades had passed since the rift between the Eastern Church in Constantinople and the Western Church in Rome. The First Crusade, which had bypassed the Rhineland, was three years old.

Germany stood on the threshold of the twelfth century with a sword in each hand. One hand brandished the sword of the empire; the other, the sword of the papacy. Both pope and emperor were fierce in their claims that their power to rule came directly from God.

This struggle coalesced around the issue of investiture, the ceremony during which the king invests a bishop with his official insignia: his episcopal ring and his pastoral staff. The significance of these symbols was so great that, when King Henry IV struck down Pope Gregory VII's edict forbidding lay investiture, the pope excommunicated him from the Church. This act exploded into a scandal at Canossa in Tuscany where the pope subjected the repentant German king to humiliation by forcing him to stand barefoot for three days in the alpine snow. Only then did the pope grant the king absolution and allow him to kiss his papal toe.

As the two swords clashed, the faithful flocked to the abbeys across the land for sustenance. Monks and nuns fed the faithful in almshouses and hospices, healing them in their infirmaries, sheltering them in their leper-houses.

The two estates were the aristocracy and the peasantry. The lords of the land — princes, dukes, and barons — claimed noble roots in knighthood and property, ever greedy for still more land to live off by the sweat of their peasants.

The ranks of the peasantry, however, were growing more forceful, though memories of serfdom continued to haunt them. All feared that they and their families would be condemned to live in servitude again for generations.

Yet the most fearsome battle of all, the battle between God and the Devil, hung like an ominous cloud over all the people, rich or poor. No one could escape it. And as the new millennium neared, all dreaded the terrors to which this spiritual battle might subject them. If God cast down his wrath, who could defend them? All would be lost!

It was into this world, plagued by violence, dread, and uncertainty, that Hildegard of Bingen was born.

Part One

1098–1136

✠

Wisdom teaches in the light of love
and bids me tell how I was brought into
this, my gift of wisdom.
When I was in my mother's womb,
God, by a breath of life...,
impressed this vision in my soul.

– Vita Sanctae Hildegardis

The birthing room in the Castle of Bermersheim was like an oven. The midwife grew more desperate as she stood by the birthing bed and watched the womb waters seep out drop by drop. Lady Mechtilde had been in labor since dawn. By now, her voice had grown hoarse from gasping as each labor pain lifted her hips and ripped through her, exhausting her with false hope. She felt as though a hundred horses' hooves had been trampling on her belly, thrusting her into yet another battleground where she searched in vain for the face of her husband, the count.

Twisting from side to side on her pillow, she cried out the count's name again and again, pleading with him to return for the birth of their tenth child. The midwife sighed in frustration because both women knew such pleas were folly. Battle was the count's only passion now. The lust for land had become insatiable as men reeled in their efforts to wrench it from one another. It mattered little if the clash was between brothers and cousins, the Welfs and the Hohenstaufens, the Church and the Crown. Like his peers, the count cared only that the wheel of war kept turning. "It will never end," Mechtilde groaned.

"Drink this, my lady," the midwife urged, hoping the sugar water would strengthen her. Mechtilde slumped forward and took a sip, then collapsed back on her pillow. In the heat, the sheets on the birthing bed had grown fetid and were streaked with vomit and urine. The midwife began humming to distract herself from her fears. She had already rubbed the birthing woman's flanks with oil of roses to hasten the delivery and placed agrimony root on her belly again to soothe her pain. But by now, not even the jasper stone Mechtilde clasped could give her the energy she needed.

Through the haze of her pain, Mechtilde clung to a single consolation: her tenth child would be spared from every strife. In its life, there would be no wars to fight, no blood to spill, no anguished screams on the battlefield. For custom decreed that the tenth child must be tithed to the Church.

By sunset, the air was unbearable, black with a thousand flies. The countess of Bermersheim had still not delivered. Each clang of the church bell fell like a hammer on Mechtilde's soul. Why had the Virgin abandoned her? Fixing her eyes on the single candle flame that pierced the darkness, Mechtilde prayed to die. Her scream split the room as the waves of her pains surged faster and faster. Haggard with agony, she gave up her soul and reached for Death's arms. Then she heard the child's cry.

"Praise God, my lady. There is a new daughter."

"Is she alive?" Mechtilde gasped. "Am I?"

The midwife reached for her mistress' hand and kissed it. Once again, the women had passed through the door between life and death together. In the agony, both knew they had labored in the womb of God.

But now, lest the Devil have time to snatch her soul, the infant was whisked off to her christening, exchanging the watery cradle in her mother's womb for the spiritual waters of baptism.

"Rest now, my lady," the midwife crooned. "At the end, the babe came so easily; it was as though the Virgin herself drew her from you and placed her in my hands."

At five years, the child was taller than her peers, and, except for sudden bouts of illness, she seemed to be everywhere in the castle at once. The grooms moaned when they felt her tug at their tunics, knowing she would not relent until they brought her to see the falcons or crouched with her at the castle pond to watch the flashing fish. Because she was the youngest of ten, her siblings indulged her whims shamelessly, as did every kitchen maid and stable boy.

Only the count remained aloof. Yet, whenever he rode into the castle courtyard, Hildegard dashed to him, clasping his leg when he dismounted so he could not escape.

"Where is her nurse?" the count would shout impatiently as he pried his daughter's arms away from his leg.

The count studied his children with detachment: the straightness of Roricus' back as he sat astride his mount, his lance perfectly positioned; Druitwin's uncanny instincts when he hawked or rode to the hunt and practiced killing; Clementia's beauty, glowing through her shyness; the sway of Odilia's hips that elicited glances each time she glided past the men in the great hall. Hildebert saw it all and stored it away. His heirs were pieces on his chessboard, pawns to be skillfully played in ways that were sure to maximize his fiefs. What land grants would ensure his sons chances of knighthood in the service of Church or Crown? How best to sweeten his daughters' dowries to attract the most brilliant marriages?

But the tenth child's future needed no scrutiny, since her dowry had been determined before her birth. A wise decision, the count knew now, for as Hildegard grew, it was clear that this daughter was different. Her will was too strong, her acts too bold, traits that would surely prove troublesome later.

These same fears nagged him now as he sat before a sputtering fire in the hall and realized that Hildegard had appeared at his elbow. When he turned, the depth of her violet eyes startled him, as did the steadiness of her gaze. She reached out silently, and her finger began tracing a battle scar that ran the length of his cheek. As she did, tears filled her eyes.

"The blood covered your eyes that day and ran into your mouth and you swallowed it," she said. *"You thought you were dead."*

The count froze. What was she saying? How could she know?

"Why do men go into battle, my lord?" she asked calmly.

He stared at her blankly for a moment. "To protect their land and possessions," he replied distractedly. "And to prove who is the strongest and bravest, for only the strong and the brave survive."

"And what becomes of the others?"

"Some become prisoners; others fall from their wounds. Many die."

"Were you ever afraid in battle, my lord?"

"Fear has no home in the heart of a warrior," he muttered.

"I must be brave, too, then!" she cried. "So I can fight at your side."

"No, Hildegard," he said briskly. "The only battle you will need to fight is with the Devil, the enemy we can neither hear nor see. He crouches nearby in dark corners, ready to snatch our souls when we grow weak. But you, my child, will be protected."

"By you, my lord?"

Her question stabbed him. His only answer was to turn away.

For days, thoughts of Hildegard stalked him. How could the child know his fears on the battlefield and the fact that he had swallowed his blood? When he mentioned the incident to Mechtilde, she looked stricken but quickly reassured him that their decision would safely place Hildegard's future in God's hands.

Yet each time he recalled how Hildegard's eyes had searched him, a chill ran through him. In an instant, she had thrust him back to those moments of terror on the battlefield when he had groped in the air before he staggered and fell. The question pricked him again: How could she know? He had no answer. Daunted, he rested his mind on his triumphs as a warrior and on how a single command from his lips could reduce an enemy's ranks to oblivion. Yet, without any stealth or cunning, this child had disarmed him as no enemy could.

Though he remained aloof, the count now searched first for Hildegard's face when he entered a room or returned from his travels. When he met her gaze, however, the fears taunted him. *She had not even been born then. There was no way she could have known.*

Hildegard rarely approached him now. Did she sense his discomfort? The hope calmed him. Still he greeted each sunrise with relief, knowing it brought him one day closer to the day when his fears about Hildegard could be put to rest.

Hildegard's nurse was despondent. Though her knees were numb with cold, she knelt to pray in the castle chapel as Hildegard wiggled beside her like a frisky pup. "Help me to understand this child, Holy Mother," she pleaded with the Virgin. "Tell me what I should do!"

A hand on her shoulder startled her. Looking up, she saw Lady Mechtilde. "Hildegard told me you were weeping," she said.

The nurse flinched. "My lady, I beg you to relieve me of my duties as Lady Hildegard's nurse," she said, curtly. "I have failed in my efforts to discipline her."

"In what way?" Mechtilde began tugging nervously at the ring of keys hanging from her waist. "The child adores you."

The nurse looked grim. "I fear not, my lady. No matter what plans I make, Hildegard eludes me. When I think she's at my side, I find her lagging behind me, where she can escape at will." She threw up her hands. "Indeed, where is she now?"

"But does she disobey?" Mechtilde bristled.

The nurse flinched. "If anything, she endures me with a patience that I find unnerving. Sometimes I don't know which of us is the nurse and which is the child."

"Nonsense!" Mechtilde muttered, jangling her keys again.

The nurse's eyes flashed. "My lady, at Hildegard's birth, the midwife agreed that she had the eyes of an old soul. The child is aware of things we do not see. It frightens me."

"What are you saying?" Mechtilde drew closer, bracing herself for yet another revelation about Hildegard's strange behavior.

"Two nights ago, she pulled me awake in the dark of night and

dragged me across the freezing courtyard to the stable...," the nurse
uttered.

"But why?" Mechtilde interrupted.

"'I must go!' was all she would say. But at that moment, I felt something more than the child's hand pulling me forward. I felt compelled
to follow her." The nurse caught her breath. "In the stable, the grooms
were bending over a mare trapped in thwarted labor. The animal was in
torment, its coat drenched with sweat and its head twisting wildly as its
mouth sprayed foam across the straw. Yet Hildegard approached the mare
calmly and placed her cheek against its heaving belly. Stroking it tenderly,
she began to sing to it, as though to comfort the unborn creature within."

Mechtilde was aghast. "She could have been killed! Did no one
stop her?"

"We were too stunned! Even the grooms gaped at her, amazed that
though the mare's shudders shook the stable, the child kept stroking it.
Finally it dropped its foal. And even as it spewed out water and blood
on the straw, the child kept stroking it." The nurse's voice broke in a sob.
"When it finally lay calm, the child held up her arms to me and asked to
be carried home. Until that moment, no one had moved."

Mechtilde stiffened. "Why wasn't I told of this?"

"I dared not speak of it, nor, I suspect, did the grooms who feared that
the count would punish them."

Mechtilde sagged with relief. "Thank God no harm came from it. I
am sure that once the child knew that a mare was due to drop her foal,
her curiosity tempted her. Nothing more."

The nurse hung her head. "The grooms swore on the Virgin's soul
that the child had never seen the mare before, my lady. Hildegard had
not been allowed in the stables. His lordship had forbidden it, lest she
meet with an accident. But when I reminded her of his rule, she became
anxious to leave and would have run away without me."

"The time has come," Mechtilde informed the count. "The castle is
full of whispers. We can wait no longer. The child must be told."

"You need not remind me, my lady!" he snapped. "I know my duty."

Mechtilde winced, though she did not envy him. "It is best for a child
with such...uncommon ways, my lord," she ventured softly. "She will be
protected from prying eyes in her new home."

The count found Hildegard perched on a mound of straw outside the stables as her eyes followed the groom's rhythmic strokes as he brushed the coat of the count's favorite mount.

"Hildegard, come ride with me," the count called out as he approached the stable.

The child stood at once, wiped her hands on her shift, and ran to him. She is so small, the count thought, as he lifted her in the air and placed her on his mount. As they rode out through the gates, her legs were trembling, though her hands rested gently like two white flowers on his leathery fists.

Hildegard seemed mesmerized as they rode through the underbrush surrounding the castle, her face filled with wonder at each new discovery. The count realized the child had never been outside the gates. As he watched her, a spreading sense of contentment filled his body. He had been wise to trust his impulse to invite her to ride. His task would be easier now.

The day was sultry. The count headed for a grove of trees nearby where they could seek shelter. As they leaned against a tree trunk, Hildegard's eyes came alive as she glimpsed the gnarled roots of the tree that were visible around them. She touched them with such reverence that, for a moment, the count thought she would cry. Her eyes feasted on the forest around her, and she was filled with wonder. It was as though the beauty she saw was too much to bear. Looking up, she pointed to a sapphire-winged butterfly that had alighted on a leaf just above her head. She stared at it for several moments, then turned her attention to a patch of ferns on the forest floor. As she parted the lacy stems, she saw something gleaming. Reaching in, she withdrew a small stone covered with an emerald shimmering.

"It's called moss," her father explained.

"But how can something so soft and green grow on something so cold and hard?" she asked him.

"Perhaps it's God's way of teaching us that what may appear to be cold and hard can still produce something beautiful," the count replied. "Remember this stone whenever your heart feels cold, my child," he said with a sudden urgency. "Remember that God is all-powerful."

Later that day, as Mechtilde strolled on the castle crosswalk, the sound of laughter rose from the courtyard below. Looking down, she saw that her husband and daughter were returning. Their laughter relieved her. Clearly, all had gone well.

That night, as they lay in their bed, Mechtilde turned to the count, anxious to hear Hildegard's reaction to the news of her future.

"I never told her," the count said, turning his face away. "She will learn soon enough."

On the eve of Hildegard's seventh birthday, Father Wolfram, the village priest, arrived at the castle, hat in hand, with the official documents. He had taken great care to brush the dirt and straw from his robe and to scrub his face until it shone. Since inheriting the position of village priest from his father, this was the first time he had been summoned to transact a church matter on the count's behalf. He could barely contain his excitement.

But any hope the priest had for a chat and a cup of wine was soon dashed. Once the count examined the documents, he signed them quickly and affixed his seal. Standing, he handed the documents to the priest and dismissed him.

There was no turning back now. The tithe of the tenth child was due.

As the travelers advanced, the forest grew silent as the birdsong and the scampering sounds in the underbrush ceased.

The count's horse led the way. Hildegard rode with him. After three days, the travelers' bodies were so cramped with fatigue that every move caused pain. To make matters worse, they had slept fitfully last night at the Castle of Kauzenburg in Bad Kreuznach. As they pushed ahead, the count's thoughts kept returning to the scene of their departure in the castle courtyard. He could not recall a time when the whole staff had gathered to say farewell.

Again, he saw Hildegard's nurse hopping about as she made certain that the child's traveling bag was securely fastened on the squire's horse. The nurse had wondered aloud how soon the child would outgrow the new woolen cloak she had just woven for her and, indeed, whether, in the child's new life, she would need a cloak at all.

Squinting back tears, Clementia had hugged her smallest sister tightly, pressing her favorite blue ribbon into Hildegard's hand to remind her of the times they had sat for hours combing each other's hair.

"Why was Clementia so sad when she hugged me?" Hildegard had asked him earlier. Remembering, the count looked down now as his daughter dozed against his chest. For the first time, he patted her head gently as they began their ascent of Mount Saint Disibod.

Behind him, Mechtilde's horse stumbled, its whinny ricocheting through the forest like a nervous scream. Steadying herself, Mechtilde shifted her hips again, hoping to dispel some of the numbness that weighted her limbs. For the hundredth time, she wrapped herself in the mantle of Father Wolfram's words.

"You have more cause to rejoice than weep, my lady," the priest had assured her. "What better way to honor your tithe to the church than by placing Hildegard with the holy anchoress, Lady Jutta of Sponheim. Few oblates are offered the gift of a teacher so skilled in the riches of the Psalter and Holy Scriptures. I assure you, in such a setting, your daughter's future will be secure."

"It is not the future that worries me, but the present," Mechtilde had protested. "Hildegard's health is often delicate, and she is unusually ...*sensitive*, as well. Should such a child be confined to a lifetime in a hermitage as the sole companion of a holy recluse?" The prospect still chilled her. But what other choice did they have?

The priest had begun pacing nervously. "Yet I would remind you, my lady, that you and the count are twice blessed. As Lady Jutta's oblate, the child will reside there under the protection of the Abbey of Mount Saint Disibod. She could not ask for a more tranquil home."

Surely the priest would not deceive her. Pressing the fingers of her left hand against her forehead, Mechtilde began to pray to the Virgin again.

Halfway up the mountain, Hildegard awoke and saw the first signs of the stone wall. Above it, a huddle of white clouds crowned the mountaintop as the sound of church bells floated down to greet them.

"Where are the bells coming from?" Hildegard asked, tugging at her father. But the count had turned to inform the grooms that they were nearing their destination.

When they reached the mountaintop, two stone posts loomed up, marking the abbey's entrance. A chubby, white-haired monk emerged from the gatehouse to greet them.

"Deo gratias!" he intoned, greeting the travelers with a formal bow. "Welcome to the Abbey of Saint Disibod! I am Brother Porter."

Behind him, a young, red-haired novice appeared from the gatehouse bearing a pitcher of water and a linen cloth. As he poured the water over the travelers' hands, Hildegard saw the sweat trembling on his upper lip, but when she smiled at him, he looked away quickly.

"Father abbot has instructed me to bring you to the reception hall where he will meet with you. He is at prayer in the chapel now," the novice stammered, finally hazarding a glance at the child.

As he led them across the abbey grounds, Mechtilde frowned at the noise surrounding them. Shouts soared and hammers pounded while a lusty curse arose when a cart crashed nearby. Meanwhile, the fragrance of freshly baked bread wafted from the abbey ovens, and smoke rose from an open courtyard where spits of pork were crisping in the noonday sun.

As they walked, the novice pointed out the abbey church at the north end of the complex, then the quadrangle that comprised the cloister with its covered walkway. Lining the cloister were bays with stalls to provide the maximum light for the monks to illumine and copy manuscripts. Adjacent to the cloister was the chapter house where the brothers met daily to conduct the abbey's affairs. Just beyond were the monks' dwelling and the abbot's house.

The abbey's reception room was spacious. "Many auspicious gatherings have taken place here," the novice announced solemnly. Wooden benches lined the walls, which had been coated with the smoke from countless candles. Dominating the room was a large trestle table topped with a linen runner, embroidered with scrolls of silver and gold.

"The runner is a gift from the hands of our anchoress, Lady Jutta, your new mistress," the novice announced to the child.

But Hildegard's eyes were drawn to a tall, ivory cross on the table that contained a relic of Saint Disibod, the abbey's founder. Flanking the cross were two bronze candlesticks in the form of graceful angels with uplifted arms.

The count was drawn at once to the far end of the hall where a row of banners lavished the harsh granite walls with brilliance. "The family insignia of our members and benefactors," the novice explained.

Moments later, a spare, silver-haired monk appeared in the doorway.

"I am Abbot Burchard," he announced graciously. As he bowed, he glimpsed the father's clenched fists and the mother's anxious frown. Then his eyes glided to the child.

"I welcome you to Mount Saint Disibod, Lady Hildegard," he said, smiling. "You are as blessed to be Lady Jutta's oblate as she is to be your magistra, your teacher."

As Hildegard curtsied, the abbot was struck by the confidence that streamed from her eyes. Not surprising, he thought, noting her high forehead and slender neck, all hallmarks of the wellborn.

Looking up, Hildegard noted that the abbot's skin was crinkled like parchment. His eyes were tired and red-rimmed, and her nose twitched from the odor of incense that clung to his robe.

"With Lady Hildegard's entry, we celebrate a new spiritual wedding between the noble houses of Sponheim and Bermersheim," the abbot said. For the first time, Mechtilde beamed.

The abbot congratulated himself. His decision to encourage Count Hildebert's proposal to Lady Jutta was fortuitous. He must take care to place the Bermersheim banner in a visible place in the silken parade.

"Had you met Lady Jutta before she went on pilgrimage?" he asked the count.

"No, my Lord Abbot, though our families are related through land and blood. But we were aware that she chose to become an anchoress upon her return from her pilgrimage to Santiago de Compostela. How soon afterward did she settle here?"

"Her father, Count Stephen II von Sponheim, endowed the hermitage for her three years ago," the abbot said, clasping his slender hands contentedly. "Since then, her presence has showered this abbey with countless blessings. Like many, her guest and cousin, Margravine Richardis von Stade, has traveled here to be near her prayers and seek her counsel. Indeed, she has become one of our most devoted benefactors. What's more," he brightened, "to honor Lady Hildegard's entry...," he cleared his throat, "into our community, both the margravine and the anchoress will grace us with their presence at the midday meal."

"Truly?" Mechtilde asked, smiling. "Then Lady Jutta is not confined to the hermitage?"

"Yes, indeed!" the abbot replied as he turned to the child and added, "but she has agreed to dine with us this one time to honor Lady Hildegard's arrival."

Hildegard met his gaze, and he felt a strangeness. It was as though the child looked through him. He gestured for them to leave the reception hall and begin walking to the hermitage.

"We will see your new home at last, *liebchen*," the count said gruffly to Hildegard, as the travelers began walking. Despite his brusqueness, his eyes lingered on his daughter, luminous now in her long, white dress whose fine lace sleeves were embroidered with tiny pearls. Her head was crowned with a circlet of blossoms, her blond hair tumbling past her shoulders. Around her neck, Mechtilde had placed her prized possession: the sapphire locket that had passed from mother to daughter for generations.

As they strolled, two monks hurried past them, but like the novice, when Hildegard smiled at them, they lowered their eyes and hurried on.

Puzzled by this second rebuff, Hildegard lifted her chin as her mother had taught her to do when she felt afraid. Everything was so different here. Where were the children? Where did they keep the animals? Was her home, the castle, far from here? Last night, she had missed sharing her bed with Clementia. Her head began to ache again as it had when they had left the courtyard at home and the maids had covered their faces with their hands and wept. Why had they been sad? Hadn't Father Wolfram announced at Mass that day that she would be traveling to a mountaintop where she would live with a holy lady in a little house that was attached to a chapel?

"You'll see!" Father Wolfram had promised her. "Lady Jutta will be the best surprise of all."

But now Hildegard was not sure. When she smiled at this lady, would she look away as the monks had done? Without thinking, she reached for her father's hand.

The servant, Herzeloyd, pushed back her strands of gray hair as she opened the hermitage door and curtsied to the visitors, her eyes widening visibly at the sight of the child. Good God, she thought, how will this wee thing survive here? Stepping aside, she gestured to the parlor, an arm's length away.

The resemblance between the two women sitting there was striking. Each was graced with the fabled attributes of the Sponheim women: the burnished copper hair, the cinnamon freckles, the blue-green eyes.

"Welcome, Lady Hildegard." The woman in the plain, gray, woolen gown came forward. "I am Lady Jutta." The anchoress had long auburn braids, and her smile had the warmth of a summer day. Above her heart, she wore a small cockleshell: the pilgrim's badge from Santiago de Compostela.

"And I am Margravine Richardis von Stade." This woman's voice rippled like a melody, and she smelled of lavender. Her bearing was as elegant as Lady Jutta's was simple.

"How stylish you are, dear child!" the margravine enthused as she studied her. "You were born to wear sapphires. They match your eyes." The woman's ivory dress seemed to rustle all around her, providing a foil for her lustrous coils of red-gold hair that were interlaced with pearls. The girdle at her waist was embellished with buds of scarlet and gold and violet, its tasseled ends falling in graceful folds to her hem.

"See how our jewels agree?" the margravine exclaimed, first placing her ring beside Hildegard's sapphire locket and then next to the child's eyes. "We are quite alike, you and I," she glowed.

The child stared back foolishly.

"Hildegard, are you really here?" Lady Jutta's voice asked eagerly. "For weeks now, I have watched for you at my window. Thank you for coming to live with me." The woman's warmth drew her forward.

The anchoress took the child's hands in hers. "How special they are," she said, examining them. "What's your favorite thing to hold in them?" she whispered.

Hildegard drew closer. "My rabbits," she whispered back, agreeing to the secret.

"Why is that?"

"They're soft and white, and they like me to stroke them when they're frightened."

"And what else do you like to hold?" the anchoress' voice was lower still.

The child's eyes sparkled. "Once I held the reins of my father's horse when I rode with him. And I like to search for stones covered with shiny moss in the forest." Their heads were together now as though no one else was in the room.

Watching them, the count sighed as he shifted in his chair.

"Have no fear, my dear count," the margravine murmured. "Your child will be secure here with Lady Jutta." She moved closer. "You are aware, I'm sure, that she forfeited a brilliant marriage to one of the noblest houses in the Rhineland to devote her life fully to God." Pursing her lips, she added, "But then, she could seek no greater esteem than the fame that surrounds her here."

Her words fell on deaf ears. The count's eyes were riveted on his daughter. For the hundredth time, the question taunted him: "What does my child see?"

The abbot could barely contain his delight when he arrived at the hermitage to escort his guests to the special meal.

Though the guests rose to leave, the anchoress remained seated.

"Father Abbot," she announced, "in my joy at my oblate's arrival, I fear I took leave of my senses. To depart from the hermitage to dine with you is to revoke my vow." Smiling, she rested her hands on Hildegard's shoulders. "My oblate will represent me at table today, on the eve of our enclosure."

The abbot twitched as if to shake off her words. "I don't understand. You had agreed, my lady!"

The anchoress sat back and thrust her slippered feet forward. "A folly I can only undo by remaining here."

The abbot's stare was fierce.

"I trust you will honor my decision, Father Abbot," the anchoress added calmly.

Thwarted, the abbot glanced at the margravine, but she seemed intent on examining her sapphire ring.

"As you wish, my lady." The abbot spit out the words. "I will convey your regrets to the brothers."

"The regrets are yours, my Lord Abbot," she replied swiftly. "I have none. Indeed, I would hope that some of your brothers would bow to my need to honor my vow."

The abbot bowed stiffly as they took their leave. He was livid. How could she do this to him? He could never forgive her. So offended was he by Lady Jutta's decision that it was only when they stood at the refectory door that he realized that the margravine was not with them either. The double insult stung him, burdening him now with having to explain and defend the absence of two guests.

As they stood there, Hildegard shrank back against her father's knee, the column of solemn monks ambling past them. Closing her eyes, she heard the crunch of their sandals on the newly laid straw in the refectory, then saw how they folded their arms as they took their places at the long wooden tables.

Inside, she felt their stares trailing her as the abbot escorted them to his table. He stood at his place with raised arms as he invoked the blessings of Saint Benedict, their founder, and Saint Disibod, the abbey's patron. Then the count and countess were toasted, after which the monks raised their winecups for the third time to a bewildered child whom they had hastily placed on cushions of straw. She could barely reach the table. Surrounded by the river of black robes that flowed around her, the child appeared like a small, white pebble cast up on a midnight shore.

At dawn, the clang of the church bells seemed to split the stone walls of the hospice, jolting the count and countess awake. Their eyes flew to Hildegard, still slumbering, her small arms outflung. Bending down, the count tapped her chin, feeling her sweet child's breath graze his finger. A few more hours.

Pulling on their clothes quickly, the trio splashed their faces with water from the bucket that had been placed outside their door. Mechtilde felt dazed as she combed Hildegard's hair for the last time and tied it with Clementia's blue ribbon.

They left the guest house and hurried to the abbey church. The prior looked relieved. "The brothers are waiting," he said nervously.

Hildegard could feel the sweat in her father's palm as she stumbled across the threshold. The church was dark inside and huge, like a forest, except that everything in this forest was made of stone. Huge stone trees soared up on either side of her, their trunks entwined with thick vines laden with strange-looking fruits and flowers. Grinning animals with sharp pointed teeth and horns and human faces peered out at her from the branches. The sweep of the arches seemed like arms stretching out to one another along the ceiling. Far ahead, the altar blazed so brightly in the darkness, she wondered if it might be on fire. She clung more tightly to her father's hand.

Now the sound of chanting voices began soaring around her. The new sound embraced her, lifting her off the ground as she floated past the rows of monks who stood in their stalls on opposite sides of the altar. First one side would chant, then the other would answer, like partners in a graceful dance. The sound had such beauty and power, it held her aloft. She felt ecstatic. The voices rose even higher now, ever more glorious....

The grip of her father's hand startled her. Beside her, she felt her mother shiver.

As the trio neared the altar, Mechtilde could scarcely breathe. Her heart plunged at the sight of the funeral torches lining the steps of the altar while the chants seemed to wind around Hildegard like a burial sheet. For a moment, Mechtilde longed to seize her child and flee.

Two monks came forward to escort Hildegard to the altar. One walked beside her while the other walked ahead to cleanse her path with incense. Feeling a gush of relief, the child saw Lady Jutta smiling at her from the altar where they would make their promises to serve God as magistra and oblate.

The promises to embrace their sacred roles were uttered. Suddenly, the child felt dizzy, now overpowered by the incense that rose from the golden censer, uncoiling before her eyes like a twisting serpent.

One by one, each candle was extinguished as the chapel fluttered into darkness. Hildegard groped for Lady Jutta's hand.

Now a sudden crackling sound filled the air as the first funeral torch was ignited. As each one was lit, the flames sucked at the dry rushes, filling the chapel with an ominous hissing. Overhead, the bells tolled slowly like cries for help, mourning the symbolic passage from life to death as the anchoress and the child left the outside world for a new life of enclosure in the hermitage.

Two monks appeared at their sides now, urging them first to kneel, then to lie prostrate before the altar, extending their arms so that each of their bodies would form a cross. Then they covered each body quickly with a heavy black pall.

Around them, the monks' chanting voices rose like a cresting wave.

"Placebo et dirige." The Office of the Dead had begun.

"Go forth, O soul, out of this world in the name of the Father Almighty, who created you."

Out of this world . . . Remembering Hildegard's birth, Mechtilde bit her knuckles until they bled. Their tenth child would disappear from the world now. Drab, woolen shifts would cover her now, never pink damask. Her budding body would flower and wither, untouched, with no child at her breast to hush its first cry.

"Hear, O daughters, and see, bend your ears and forget your people, your father's house."

"What have we done?" Mechtilde whispered, shuddering. "She is too young, too innocent. Never again will she run free down sloping vineyards covered with goldenrod and bluebells or search for moss-covered stones in the forest."

"Dead to this world, may they live in Thee. . . . "

The chapel collapsed into emptiness, the monks standing like specters now, their heads lowered, their faces lost in the hollows of their cowls. The silence seemed to stretch into aeons. Then came the quickening, the new birth.

"In the midst of death, we are in life," the chants rang out.

"I will enter the place of the wonderful tabernacle!" the voices sang, as the pall was removed. The child looked terrified as she felt someone lift her to her feet. Her cheeks were flushed, her white-gold ringlets matted against her sweating forehead. Stricken with fear, she locked her eyes on

her father's face, begging for comfort as he walked toward her, pleading with him to run with her from this terrible place, which choked her with smoke and had smothered her as she had lain on the cold stone floor.

Though his heart broke at the sight of her, the count dared not respond. Steadying his hands, he placed a circlet of ivy leaves on her head, ignoring the tremors from her quivering chin and her desperate whimpers.

Instead, he handed her the shining gold plate that held her dowry: the deed to his vineyards.

As he guided her tiny hands, the child lifted the gift, offering herself in exchange for the crushed grapes, the scarlet wine that would be poured into chalices and be transformed into blood at Rhineland altars, recalling another sacrifice, remembering the Christ.

Leaning down, the abbot received the offering. As the small arms trembled from the weight of the plate, a light in the child's eyes pierced him as he received it.

"Lady Hildegard, you have left your old life behind you. Your new life of enclosure begins now with your new magistra."

Removing the flaming torches from the altar, the monks held them aloft as they led the procession to the hermitage. Dipping a green bough in holy water, the abbot blessed the hermitage doorway, then each tiny room, then the door to the courtyard, whose gate would open now only to visitors.

When the moment came, the count knelt and held out his arms to Hildegard. Once he embraced her, she felt safe again, secure as before. All would be well now, and they could go home again. But she then felt her father's body shuddering around her, like a log filled with red-hot embers, collapsing in the fire. As he wrenched himself from her, she felt her mother's cheeks, wet with tears as she held her child's face in her hands and bathed it with kisses. Now there was only an eerie sob as Mechtilde stepped back and, turning from her child, joined the count and the abbot as they walked out the door and closed it behind them, leaving Hildegard on the other side.

As the parents watched, the workmen stepped forward, tools in hand. With swift, deft strokes, they plastered the hermitage doorway with mortar, covering it over until every sign of the entrance had disappeared. The enclosure was complete.

Inside, Hildegard ran back and forth, confused and fearful. Turning to the anchoress, she saw the woman struggling to fold her arms, while her eyes were wide with pity. Beside her, the servant sighed loudly, her eyes filled with tears. Shouting her parents' names, Hildegard raced from room to room, sure they were hiding, then pounded on the door as the women stood by silently. Gasping for breath, the child began pummeling the anchoress.

"Let me out!" the child screamed, as the anchoress knelt beside her. Clasping the small fists in her hands, Lady Jutta tried to kiss them as the small sobbing body flailed in her arms.

On the mountain road, far below, the parents paused to take one last look up at the hermitage.

High above them, they glimpsed two small arms reaching through an iron grill in a window, the hands fluttering wildly like the wings of a frightened bird.

"My lord!" a quivering voice called out to them. "My lady! You forgot me. You forgot to take me home!"

At first, the child heard only the silence, the hush of it, like breath issuing from every crevice in the hermitage. Then she disappeared into the silence, pulling it over her head like a coverlet as she knelt by the window each day to wait for her parents' return. Within a week, her eyes were so swollen from crying, she could barely see the food in her bowl. When the anchoress tried singing to her, she covered her ears. And when the servant tried to tempt her with sweet treats, the child pushed them away.

Why had her parents left her here with these strangers? And why wouldn't these people tell her when her parents were coming back? She was so confused and so frightened! She missed her sisters and wished she could hold her rabbits. There were no children here, only monks. Yet whenever a monk appeared at the courtyard gate, she ran and hid, fearful that he had come to take her to the chapel again where he would make her lie down on the cold stone floor and try to smother her.

When would her parents come?

As the days passed, Jutta grew desperate. All her efforts to distract the child had failed. Hildegard's eyes were clouded with wariness. At night, they would hear her sob so hard, they feared she would choke.

"How soon will they come back?" she asked them again and again, but they had no answer except to say how much they loved having her there.

"We must find something to fill her emptiness," Jutta whispered to Herzeloyd. "Something she can draw comfort from, like a friend."

"This hermitage could not hold another child, my lady," the servant cautioned.

Jutta nodded. "But there are other things we might try. We could plant a small tree in the courtyard."

"You can watch it grow and tell us about the ways it changes," they told her. "The tree will be your special friend and belong to you alone."

It was then that they saw her first smile.

In time, the tears were replaced by flickers of joy when she raced to the window to greet the tree each morning and return to watch its shadow lengthen in the courtyard each night.

As the days passed, the women began to notice that the thing that calmed Hildegard the most was the sound of the bells. She began to listen for them every three hours when they rang to call the monks to prayer. They became a kind of comfort, something she could look forward to, something that was predictable and never changed.

"Why do they ring?" she asked the anchoress.

"The monks call the bells *vox Dei*, the voice of God," Jutta explained. "They ring to remind us to stop and give praise, for God is a poet and everything in creation is God's song. But they also ring to remind us to ask God for the things we need for ourselves and for others."

"Does God hear everyone?" the child asked.

"God's heart is so big and so open, there are plenty of places for him to put our prayers," the anchoress said, smiling. "I know that it's true because before you came, I prayed to God to send me an angel, and the song that God sang back to me was you."

Hildegard stared, still too cautious to trust. "Truly, my lady?"

When Jutta nodded tenderly, Hildegard placed her head in the anchoress' lap for the first time. As the child's spun-gold hair fanned out across her lap, Jutta breathed a prayer of thanksgiving. This moment had finally come.

As she stroked the silken locks, she whispered, "Remember, dear child, that when we are born, God gives each of us a guardian angel. That angel not only cares for us but can turn our prayers into bread for the hungry and cloaks for those who are cold. Our angels bring our prayers first to those whose hearts are broken, for they are the ones who need our love the most."

So that's why the monks stopped to pray so much all through the day and night! Often, Hildegard would wake in the dark and hear Lady Jutta chanting the Psalms with the monks at Matins as she sat at her window closest to the chapel. Through her grille, she could see the monks' candles flickering like stars in the darkened chapel. This window was one of the three windows in the hermitage that served as their eyes to the outside world. Lady Jutta sat behind a second grilled window in the parlor when she counseled pilgrims, while a third window in the kitchen opened to receive food and supplies. Hildegard would listen for the first creak of the cellarer's cart as it lumbered down the path from the abbey kitchen, dashing to that window to guess what Brother Cellarer might be sending them that day. Would it be newly picked apples or turnips and cabbage or almond cakes sweetened with honey?

"Guess!" Herzeloyd teased the child at first, but after a week, she realized that Hildegard always guessed correctly. The child then lost interest in the cellarer's cart and no longer came to the window.

By spring, Hildegard seemed at home in the hermitage. She and Lady Jutta spent the mornings sewing, their needles darting like hummingbirds as they embroidered vestments and altar linens for the abbey and the anchoress told the child endless tales of her pilgrimage to Santiago de Compostela. In time, she began to teach the child to sing, gently coaxing the first, shy notes of Hildegard's "Alleluia" until the child's sweet song of praise filled the room.

In the afternoons, Hildegard watched as the anchoress sat at her grille and counseled her visitors. It could be a serf with rag-bound feet or a duke confessing the sins he hid beneath his fur-lined coat. Knights often appeared on the eve of a battle, or widows seeking counsel, or itinerant monks who had lost their way. No one was turned away.

Day by day, the child watched her mistress' shoulders lean forward, straining to hear the halting questions and the fears that grew into sobs. "Pray for me, my lady. I beg of you!" And when they were gone, the child would watch the anchoress fall to her knees to keep her promises.

But the child loved dusk the most; it was the time of surprises in the parlor. Day after day, passionate prophets stepped from the pages of holy writ and dazzled her. It could be Moses, describing the thunder and lightening atop Mount Sinai. Or the prophet Isaiah, alive with extravagant promises that streams would burst forth in the desert and turn burning sands into pools of cool, clear water. Or breathless Jeremiah, insisting that he was too young to be called to bleed for the needs of his people. "Is there no balm in Gilead for the daughter of my people?" he begged.

"Is there no physician there?" Awed, the child sat at her mistress' feet as she was introduced to each of them. At times, she forgot to breathe.

Later, before she went to sleep, she would stand at the window, scanning the night-sky, searching for the eyes of the prophetess Deborah, the judge chosen by God to reawaken the soul of Israel. Or would listen for Sarah's throaty laugh at her discovery that she had conceived a child in her old age. Is anything too wonderful for God?

And with the first snow, she would plead with Jutta to tell the Christmas story again, finally drifting into sleep in the arms of the Virgin, she whose womb cradled the sun and the moon and the stars and her Son, whom she birthed but never understood.

Sometimes when she lay awake, Hildegard thought back to her first night in the hermitage. She had been so frightened that she had crawled into Lady Jutta's bed, curling up to her warmth, imagining that she was back in her bed beside Clementia again. Lady Jutta had held her then, smoothing away the trembling. After a week, however, she told her that she must sleep in her own bed now, but also that she would not be alone.

"You have only to ask and the angels will come to you," the anchoress had told her. "They will hold you tenderly. Listen to them," she said, touching Hildegard's ear. "They have beautiful secrets God wants you to hear." It was then that Hildegard learned to love the silence in a new way.

At sunrise and sunset, the anchoress taught the child to pray by listening for the whispers of God.

"In the silence," Jutta began, "I heard the wind sweeping the trees: first the pines, then the oaks, then the apple leaves. *Deo gratias!*"

"The crickets are clicking in the dark now, and I see the sparks of the first fireflies," Hildegard answered. "And earlier, I heard the bees buzzing as they flew into the hearts of the flowers, searching for honey. *Deo gratias!*"

"I hear the sound of the doves cooing and cows mooing like soft thunder. *Deo gratias!*"

Slowly, an ever-deepening awe drenched the child's senses. This awe, Lady Jutta taught her, was what had inspired the first psalms of praise.

Hildegard began each day by peering at the courtyard, eager to see if her tree had changed during the night and to see what color the world had chosen to wear that day. She decided that winter was usually sad and gray or suddenly white, and sometimes the sky shook its fists with thunder and lightning. The clouds wept on and off through spring and frightened the sun away until, bit by bit, the world turned green as the earth preened itself and her tree shook out its leaves and stretched its limbs, gliding into the gold of summer. When the chill returned in autumn, she watched as her tree burst into flames and its leaves drifted to the ground like crimson petals.

A year had passed.

Daybreak. The bells were ringing for Prime. Leaping up, the barefoot child ran to the kitchen and felt the rush of wind from the open window.

But when she looked outside, Hildegard screamed. The anchoress was standing outside the gate on a grassy knoll, her arms outstretched, her face lifted like an offering to the morning sun.

"My lady, what are you doing?" the child cried in alarm. "Why have you left the hermitage?"

The anchoress spun around. Her face was radiant.

"Hildegard, today is your anniversary! You have been enclosed for a whole year now. You must come and run on God's green earth again and breathe in the air. Come, child!" she cried.

But the child remained stupefied. She hovered anxiously on the threshold between the two worlds, confused and uncertain. *Once you enter, you must never leave!* If she did, what would become of her? Yet Lady Jutta's arms were beckoning.

Slowly, the barefoot child crossed the courtyard and paused at the open gate. Seeing her hesitation, the anchoress ran to her. Scooping her up in her arms, she twirled her, first one way, then the other, until they grew so giddy that they lost their footing and tumbled to the ground. As the anchoress fell back on the earth, she uttered a deep sigh and flung her arms wide again, turning her face from side to side as she bathed it in the morning dew.

"Oh, Hildegard, my little one," she gasped, "This is your chance! Breathe in the clouds, drink the sun!"

The child lay back, her tousled hair spilling out on the ground like golden honey. The warmth of the world made her dizzy. Within moments, the sun's glare closed her eyes.

Rolling over, the anchoress propped herself up on her elbow, and in a moment of joy, she bent down and kissed the child's forehead. It was the first kiss the child had received since her parents departed. Instantly, the child felt a ripple of fear. What did the mistress' kiss mean? Did coming outside mean she was saying good-bye?

For a long time, the woman and child lay on the ground in silence. Around them, a bee flirted with a patch of buttercups. Breezes glided across their skin like invisible feathers while the autumn sun warmed their bones. Wherever Hildegard looked, there was nothing but green surrounding her! The beauty astounded her. Turning on her side, she saw ringlets forming on her mistress' forehead. Though Lady Jutta's eyes were closed, she was smiling. She had never seen her mistress so happy. Hildegard's body felt warm and light as she began to doze.

"Why are we lying here?" she heard Lady Jutta cry.

Hildegard sat up, blinking her eyes. "We have the whole world to see today!" the anchoress tugged at her. "The sun is over our heads and we haven't even begun."

Hand in hand, the woman and child climbed to the edge of the hill. In the valley below, the Glan and the Nahe Rivers met and unfurled like silver ribbons in the sunlight. High above, the blue sky was a boundless seascape, the clouds drifting across the sky like foam.

Was this day a dream? Hildegard squeezed her mistress' hand to re-assure herself. Strolling downhill, the child was intrigued with the feel of the soft, lumpy earth beneath her feet. She paused to blow dandelion puffs in the wind as ants crawled on her feet and tickled her.

"I had forgotten how many shades of green there are in the world," the anchoress sighed, as Hildegard pulled on her arm, restless with questions.

"Was this hill always here? And those vineyards?" she asked excitedly. "And that orchard of apple trees? And those cows? Did they always graze there?"

"Let's ask them!" the anchoress cried. Picking up her skirts, she ran toward them.

Squealing with delight, Hildegard streaked beside her. As she ran toward the herd, she saw herself sitting again at her milking stool at the castle, dipping her finger in the foaming bucket of new milk, creamy with sweetness.

As they stood aside and examined the cows, Hildegard pointed to one whose udder almost dragged on the ground.

"Its calf will be born any day now," said the anchoress.

"*Tomorrow*," Hildegard nodded. "*It will have four black spots on its white skin. One will be over its eye and another beneath its chin.*" She patted the cow and kissed it before she walked on.

The day passed in a soft glow of glory. When they returned to the knoll, Hildegard's eyes crinkled with delight when she saw that

Herzeloyd had spread out a cloth for them and a basket of bread and apples.

Watching them from the gate, the servant clapped her hands as Hildegard tried to capture a butterfly, noting the lithe young body beneath the thin linen shift. The child had sprouted up fast this past year, always standing on tiptoe at the window, anxious that nothing escape her gaze.

All through the day, the woman and child wandered, breathing in the world until the air grew chill and the bells for Compline began ringing.

With a last, sweeping glance across the star-studded night sky, they sighed as they reentered the hermitage only to find that the servant had filled every room with blossoms and branches from the world they had just left behind.

The next morning, as they took turns carding the wool, Jutta began speaking carefully.

"Hildegard," she said, "you recall the cow we saw in the pasture, the one whose unborn calf you described?"

Hildegard smiled and nodded.

"Brother Cook mentioned to Herzeloyd that the calf was born early this morning. It was white and had four black spots where you said they would be."

"Yes, my lady."

"Hildegard, when you looked at the cow, how did you know where the spots would be?"

The child seemed surprised. "I saw them, my lady. I saw them on the calf's skin." The child's face was a mirror of trust as she looked up at her mistress.

"Hildegard, have you seen such things before?"

"What things, my lady?"

"Things like the spots."

"Yes, my lady," she said, lowering her eyes.

"Why have you never spoken of them?" Jutta asked softly.

"I feared you would scold me, my lady, as my nurse in the castle had done. She was so distressed, I felt it was best not to speak of these things again."

"What else have you seen, my child?"

Hildegard paused and bit her lip. "Once, long ago," she began uncertainly, "I saw a light so bright, I could not move for the trembling. But I couldn't speak of it then." She hurried to say, "I was a little child and had no words." Swallowing, she looked up anxiously. "My lady, are you angry with me?"

Lady Jutta shook her head. Gathering Hildegard in her arms, she held her, rocking her slowly, forgetting time. But her mind was whirling. *Why has God sent this child to me?*

And though she felt comforted by her mistress' heartbeat against her cheek, Hildegard felt anxious. She thought it best that she never speak of these things again.

Hildegard lay in her cot, unable to sleep. Six years had passed since she first came to the hermitage. Those early days had been so tranquil. Everything had begun to change two years ago when Lady Jutta was summoned to leave the hermitage to meet with the bishop of Mainz and his councillors in the abbey hall.

When she returned, she sank into her chair by the grille with a great sigh. Her eyes were glazed.

"It appears that our life in the hermitage is over," she whispered. "The bishop has dispensed me from my solitary vows as an anchoress." Her hand shook as she reached for her cockleshell.

"Over?" The child froze.

"The abbot has received an offer from my family to endow a monastery here, on the condition that I agree to guide it as magistra." She was still in shock.

"A monastery?" the child asked anxiously. "What does that mean?"

"Other women would come to live with us. Like the monks, we would live in community and follow Saint Benedict's Rule for a life of work and prayer."

Other women? That meant that she would no longer be alone with Lady Jutta and Herzeloyd. She could not imagine it. Fear began to pinch her.

"You won't be alone anymore." Jutta's smile was brave. "You will have sisters now."

Sisters? Hildegard thought. Sisters were what she had left behind in the castle. These would be strangers. What would they think of her? Her head began to ache as though a band of steel was tightening on her forehead.

"Once this hermitage is enlarged, we can accept the ten new entrants," she heard Lady Jutta say. "Until then, I have much to do." Her voice sounded hollow.

"Ten strangers, my lady?" Her voice was like a wisp of smoke. "What will become of me? Must I leave and find another cell?"

"What are you saying?" Jutta cried. "You will be more important to me than ever!"

But Hildegard could already feel herself swaying as her field of vision began to shatter into prisms of light. She gripped the arms of her chair as the prisms were cracking into shards of glass with jagged edges. Waves of nausea coursed through her body.

"Herzeloyd, come quickly!" she heard Lady Jutta shout.

Two sturdy arms lifted her, then lowered her onto her cot. The clasp of Lady Jutta's hand steadied her.

"Never forget that you will always be my first and most dearly beloved daughter," the anchoress had reassured her then.

Hildegard had clung to those words again and again over the last two years. So much had changed since the others had entered. She watched them come one by one, descending like birds into the nest of the hermitage. The twins, Gertrud and Gisla, entered first, sweeping in like hawks caught in a fowler's snare, raw from their father's relief to be rid of them. Both were short and sturdy; their long black braids fell to their waists like rope. Yet when they spoke, the twins seemed more like mother and daughter. Gertrud's jutting jaw defied intrusion while moon-faced Gisla not only hung on her sister's words but felt compelled to echo them.

Ilse alighted next, dainty and smiling, cooing like a dove as she fluffed her skirts and smoothed her sleeves, instantly impressing them with her vast repertoire of sighs. In contrast, Kunigunde chirped like a mocking-bird. As the youngest of six daughters, she had learned to interrupt or go unheard. Except for Bertha's tapping fingertips, the rest brought only the sounds of their confusion: the dragging footstep, the hiss of rebellion, the noisy yawn.

Hiltrude, Lady Jutta's niece, was the youngest at twelve and clung to Hildegard like a newly hatched chick. Apple-cheeked, she nodded more than she spoke but seemed eager to please.

As each one came, Hildegard grew more uncertain. At fourteen, she was a head taller than the others, a fact she deplored. She envied their natural ease and self-assurance, mindful that it flowed from life in a world she had barely known. Intrigued, she studied the ease with which they lifted their skirts to climb the stairs or lounged back in chairs or moistened their lips with their tongues as they whispered secrets or signaled each other in ways she could never decode. As they processed into chapel, Hildegard memorized the sway of their hips and their utter confidence as they dismissed others' thoughts and comments with a flick of their hands.

More and more, Hildegard ached with awkwardness, certain that her arms dangled like poles from her shoulders and her hands flapped at her sides. Have they discovered how different I am? she agonized, feeling impaled by their curious stares or stifled giggles. *And always the fear: What would they of me think if they really knew the things I see and hear?*

The questions tormented her as she twisted in her bed in the darkness. By now, fear had invaded every bone in her body. Her first prayer was always for vigilance. She dare not let down her guard.

"I am impressed with the dedication of your noble benefactors," Bishop Otto of Bamberg admitted to Abbot Adelhun as the visiting prelate toyed with his wine flask in the abbot's quarters. Outside, the grounds were teeming with guests who had come to glimpse the former anchoress and new magistra, Lady Jutta, and to witness the promises of her new entrants.

"If all your guests have been half as generous as the Sponheims and Stades, your new monastery's endowments should comprise a third of the Rhineland," he smiled.

Abbot Adelhun shrugged, feigning indifference. They left the abbot's quarters and went into the hall draped with flags.

"I am told that Margravine Richardis has endowed a chapel for Lady Jutta's new monastery," the bishop probed.

"One certain to nourish the deep roots of the Sponheim family here. It will be the first of many endowments, I am certain. They have been most generous," the abbot smiled, folding his hands.

"The margravine's path is littered with sparks of excitement, is it not?" the bishop smiled suggestively. "No doubt she will join with Lady Jutta in bringing even more fame to this abbey."

The abbot was stung by the double insult. Why was the abbey's success always laid at the feet of the anchoress? he fumed. Would he never be credited? Every flag that crowded the walls of this hall was the fruit of his years of ceaseless strategies and careful planning.

To be sure, once news of Lady Jutta's foundation spread, dowries had flowered at his feet like spring meadows. Families raced to place their women here, aware that no land grant or forest could equal the graces flowing from Lady Jutta's tutelage.

Yet of late, the abbot had begun to dread his meetings with her. Each one left him with feelings of shame and envy. He both resented and craved to receive the praise that she lavished on her oblate, Lady Hildegard. He found himself chafing when she inquired if he had heard the latest chants Lady Hildegard had composed or knew of her great success with a healing salve she had concocted with herbs from the abbey garden. Even after all these years, the abbot still regarded Hildegard as an intruder. She made him anxious, as though she possessed some power that allowed her to look through him.

"My Lord Abbot?"

Looking up, he saw the bishop at the open door, scowling. "The bell has rung a second time," he growled. "Must I proceed without you?"

Lady Jutta's eyes were glistening as Hildegard knelt before her at the altar.

"What do you ask?"

"To discern my calling as a Benedictine nun."

The words of commitment followed. The candle in Hildegard's hand began to tremble. Horrified, she watched as wax spilled like hot white tears down the front of her new black robe.

As forgivable as her blunder was, Hildegard was still stunned by it. Moaning softly, she lowered her eyes as her beloved mistress placed the novice's white veil on her head.

The moment was in ruins; Hildegard felt hot with shame. Steadying her candle, she rose and turned, defending herself internally against her sisters' gasps at the wax cascade that blemished her robe. *Another reason for them to whisper.* When she finally sank to her knees at her prie-dieu, she could hardly breathe.

Why had this happened? For six years, her one consuming desire had been to emulate Lady Jutta. As her oblate, she had inhaled every note of plainchant, every psalm of longing, every prophet's plea.

Yet on this cherished occasion, her mistress would be forced to present her to God as a clumsy virgin in a spotted gown.

The blunder sealed her in a membrane of shame. For weeks afterward, when her sisters discussed the day, Hildegard demurred, claiming that she remembered little.

"But Hildegard, how could you forget? Surely you prepared longer than any of us for the promises. And surely you memorized the Rule long before the rest of us," Gertrud said.

"Why would I?" Hildegard replied. "I was an oblate then and…"

"But you were the first to know that a monastery was being endowed for Lady Jutta," Kunigunde interrupted. "You must have begun to prepare."

"I did not!" she replied firmly.

"Not even when Lady Jutta was named magistra?" Gisla said, frowning. "Surely, she explained the Rule of Saint Benedict to you in great detail."

"And the promises." Bertha tapped out the words. "Obedience, conversion of life, and stability to this abbey."

Hildegard stiffened. "The Rule was mentioned, of course, but only as it was lived by the monks."

"But you must have known what to expect."

"Unlike the rest of us," Gertrud chided.

"Things like the haircutting," Ilse challenged.

"I knew nothing of it," Hildegard pleaded. But she knew from their pursed lips that no one believed her.

Why was it always like this? Why were they always testing her? On that bleak December morning, hadn't she crouched on the same wooden stool, awaiting her turn to be shorn with the rest of them? Hadn't Lady Jutta's hand grasped her hair just as tightly as the knife blade sawed through her long, blond braids? And when the sawing stopped, hadn't she also clasped the back of her naked neck in disbelief, straining to see where her hair had dropped in the basket on the floor?

"Come now, Hildegard, you could scarcely forget repeating your promises at the altar?" Ilse challenged.

"Of course I remember that!"

"Nothing more?" Ilse insisted, casting a quick glance at the others.

"What could be more important than the promises?" Hildegard asked.

"To be sure." Ilse's voice was flat. "Lady Jutta would be the first to agree. She taught you well."

Hildegard swallowed, forcing herself to recall Lady Jutta's mandate. "The others will look to you for guidance. I have every confidence that you will inspire the faith of your sisters."

God knows, she had tried. She recalled how, masking her shyness, she had bravely guided her newly arrived sisters on a tour of their home: the workroom where they would meet and sew, the alcove where they would eat, the magistra's room, and the newly enlarged space for the copyists and scribes. It had pleased her to see Hiltrude's eyes brighten at the sight of the two wooden carrels and the array of inkhorns and quills. She had been unprepared, however, for the whisper: "It's all so cramped! How will we manage?"

Hildegard's surprise had turned to shock upstairs when her sisters recoiled from the neat rows of cots with their straw pallets, and the small chests beside each bed.

"Impossible!" Ilse had sniffed, pointing to the trunk she'd brought from home, a trunk twice the size of the chests next to the cots.

Hoping to reassure her, Hildegard had quickly opened a chest and displayed its contents: a long-sleeved black robe, a pair of felt slippers to wear inside, two sets of white underwear, and a sturdy pair of work shoes.

Ilse's hand had flown to her mouth. "No silk?" she had gasped.

"Silk? For us?" Hildegard had winced. "Only the priests wear silk and then only for Mass in the chapel. Everything we need is here in this chest."

Nostrils had flared and lips had clamped; another door had slammed shut. Panic had swept over her. How had she failed? What had she left undone?

Behind them, she saw the glow beginning, then the soft explosion of Light. The radiant Woman appeared dressed in a hyacinth robe and a necklace of emeralds.

"Beloved, because your intention is pure, God will grant your desire in time, for your will to do good is the most fragrant of all aromas.

"Recall: No warmth goes to waste!"

Sighing, she yearned toward the Woman as she faded. "Not yet!" she cried.

"Hildegard? What are you saying?"

Startled, she had blinked and had seen Hiltrude's alarm. "You were mumbling again!" she had said nervously. "You looked so strange!"

What had she done this time? What had she said?

"Stand up straight, my lady!" Herzeloyd scolded as she bent to lengthen Hildegard's robe. "And hold your head high, as well."

"Why can't I be small?" Her voice was petulant. "Why can't I be more like them?"

"Because this is the way God made you."

"It's not enough," Hildegard moaned.

The old woman sat up. "You must be patient, my lady. Things will become easier in time."

"When?" Hildegard demanded. "Even Hiltrude is beginning to look at me oddly now. And Lady Jutta has only crumbs of time to toss to me."

Herzeloyd sighed. She could not deny that the magistra now spent more time out of the new quarters than in them, either swept into conferences with the abbot or meeting with benefactors.

"She has no time to visit until after Vespers," Hildegard complained. "And by then, she's so tired, she can hardly see."

"Try to be strong, my lady," the servant said. "Time answers every question."

But both their hearts ached for her. The transition from their life in the hermitage had been too abrupt and, coupled with the demands of her changing body, had thrust Hildegard into utter confusion. Though Hildegard rebelled at her height, the servant could see a certain grace emerging: her oval face now more refined with its wide brow, slender nose, and full lips. In the last year, though her white-gold hair had darkened a shade, her ivory skin had paled even more in contrast to her violet eyes, ever more intense, still searching for a safe place in this new world of surprises.

"Be patient, my lady. You must leave Lady Jutta to God now," the servant advised her. "And you must learn to love the sisters she has given you."

"I try," she sighed. "But it is I who am the stranger now, always fearing that I may say things that will cause them to laugh or whisper."

The servant's eyes narrowed. "What kinds of things, my lady?"

A sadness clouded Hildegard's eyes as she shook her head and turned away. "The bells for Vespers will be ringing now," she said.

A moment later, they sounded. As the servant drew back, Hildegard hoisted up her skirts and raced to the stairs, her hem unfinished. She must not be late; she must not stand out; she must not be noticed.

The year of testing was over.

Within the hour, they would take their final vows as brides of Christ. As the novices lined up outside the church, Hildegard glanced from face to face, reveling in her sisters' delight. As they adjusted their coronets of violets and lilies of the valley, each of them looked to her for reassurance. "Is it all right? Is it on straight?" Nodding, she smiled to herself, recalling how they had seen the coronet she had fashioned for the statue of the Virgin and how they had begged her to make one for each of them for this day. Their compliments had thrilled her.

Over the past year, the ice of her loneliness had begun melting. By the sheer force of her will, she had learned to bite her tongue when the Light began and to bury her face in her hands when she received a vision so that no one could tell from her eyes. Throughout the day, though she listened well, she seldom chatted. Yet when she chose to share her thoughts, her sisters listened carefully, often asking her advice and valuing her judgments. In spite of her emerging confidence, however, Hildegard took care never to let down her guard. She made certain that her chants never rose above those of her sisters. She took care to acknowledge every kindness and to safeguard every secret. And when the day came when her belly was wracked with cramps for the first time and when the blood appeared between her legs and startled her, her sisters came to her aid with explanations, hovering over with care and concern. The blood was only the tears of her disappointed womb, they reassured her, putting her fears to rest. That night, as never before, she wept in gratitude for the gift she had longed for but dared not believe she could have: the gift of belonging, the gift of sisters.

Warmed at the memory, Hildegard looked around her, feeling one with the flurry of the day's excitement. Today, the past year seemed like a miracle. It was as though a dozen rivulets had merged into a flowing stream whose shores were bound by the Rule. Day by day, each of the girls struggled to find a way to navigate past the rocks and shoals of her sisters' humanity, for the Rule had its demands.

Night after night, Hildegard rose in the darkness and stumbled with her sisters to Matins, then scurried back to bed for what seemed like moments before rising again to celebrate the day's first light at Lauds and, moments later, the office of Prime. Thereafter, they stopped every three hours through the day to pray, completing the circle at Compline as the sun set and the Great Silence fell like a hush across the abbey.

And now today, by the grace of God, they would make their final promises as nuns.

The bells rang a second time. Inside the chapel, the voices became subdued as the men paused to smooth their velvet tunics and the women's jeweled fingers adjusted their veils. At the third bell, there was a stirring as the procession of novices filed down the aisle and entered the sanctuary, each face radiant beneath a fragile crown.

Now every eye turned as Lady Jutta, the new magistra, followed, her skin as luminous as a precious pearl above her white robe. Around her neck, having refused all offers of a jeweled cross, she had chosen to wear a small wooden cross as a sign of her office.

The abbot, spare and solemn, followed. Turning from side to side, he nodded to the benefactors as his eyes avoided Margravine von Stade, resplendent in a vermilion gown and matching cloak, her long hair drawn back and entwined with a rope of diamonds and pearls.

Hildegard heard Bishop Otto before she saw him. The rasp of his labored breathing preceded him as he lumbered down the aisle, weighed down by his burden of damask vestments. His eyes were set like jet beads in his jowled face, marbled with veins. Squinting, his eyes flitted over each girl as she knelt to receive the black veil of a Benedictine nun.

Hildegard had rehearsed the moment a thousand times, dreading another blunder with her candle. For weeks, she had practiced gripping the wrist of her candle-holding hand in order to strengthen it. Yet when she knelt before the bishop, her hand was steady as her thoughts soared.

"On this, my wedding day, I offer my heart to my Divine Bridegroom," she prayed fervently, filled with an indescribable bliss.

Their vows completed, the new nuns now knelt and prostrated themselves, their foreheads pressed onto the marble floor as an act of oblation before the altar, invoking, one by one, those martyred saints who had died for the faith.

Agnes, a consecrated virgin, stabbed in the throat, a martyr at thirteen.

Felicity, the pregnant slave girl and her mistress, Perpetua, both mauled by wild beasts in the arena, their hearts pierced by a sword during their last breaths.

Lucy, a virgin thrust into a brothel, condemned by her faith to death by flames.

Cecilia, whom they failed to suffocate, then partially beheaded and left to suffer and bleed.

Name after name, until the throbbing in their heads became unbearable.

"Holy Virgin martyrs, be with us! Hold us in the promise of heaven this day!" Hildegard prayed.

In her mind's eye, she could see herself and her sisters lying there, arms outstretched, their bodies like a circle of human crosses, their cheeks like crimson petals on the marble floor.

Now, in a sweep of memories, Hildegard recalled the last time she had lain in this place on this floor beneath a heavy pall, unable to breathe. Remembering the hiss of the funeral torches, a long-buried sob rose in her throat, choking her, as she groped once again for her father's hand.

"My lord, you forgot me! You forgot to take me home!"

Never again, for her parents had passed from this life since she had lain here last, both victims of a raging fever.

The singing began again as she joined with her sisters, crying out three times: "Accept me Lord, as thou hast promised, and I shall truly live! Having seen him, I love and trust him. He is the love of my choice until death calls us home."

At day's end, Hildegard had never felt so full or so joyful or so alone.

Joyful, because she had embraced the challenge and was a vowed nun now. Alone, because there was still no one with whom she dared share the triumph of her spotless robe and steady candle. There was still no one to care that the blood on her hand came from a grip on her candle so fierce and determined this time that her nails had pierced her skin.

The summer of Hildegard's twentieth year was ending. Even before Lauds, the August heat had begun to creep into the dormitory with the first glimmerings of light. Hildegard slipped her hand beneath the sheet to release her nightgown, which was twisted between her legs and torso. Her thighs were damp with sweat.

A fly droned nearby, circling endlessly. Even with her eyes closed, Hildegard could recognize each of her sisters by the sound of her breathing: Gertrud's short snores, as though sleep was a duty; Gisla's soft, hissing whispers; Ilse's occasional moans and shallow breaths as though she was gasping for air.

Raising herself up on her elbow, Hildegard then looked about at the mounds of bodies surrounding her, some with arms akimbo, others flat on their bellies.

Finally, her glance rested on Hiltrude. She lay on her side, clutching her pillow, her lips parted, her breathing steady. The coverlet had been kicked aside, exposing the sweep of her slender legs and small feet. Hildegard sank back and sighed, "My best and most trusted sister. How dear she is to me, even in sleep!" While Hiltrude was clasped in dreams, her skin seemed to shimmer; her limbs were so graceful, they seemed to float.

Hildegard rose, dressed, and went downstairs, where her peaceful thoughts of her sleeping sisters were quickly shattered as she pushed through the crowd clustered at the door of the hospice. The air in the main hall was heavy with the sour smell of sweat and the stench of festering flesh from the bodies crouched on the floor or moaning on the pallets. Hiltrude had also now come downstairs, and as Hildegard stepped carefully through the maze of bodies to reach Hiltrude, she was stopped by a chilling moan. Looking down, she saw a heap of rags matted with dirt and leaves and clumps of vomit. When she bent down, the rags stirred, revealing a small, birdlike body beneath the filthy tatters. The creature lay on its side, its knees drawn up and held together by two spindly arms, while the small pointed chin was pressed into the chest as though it hoped the body would disappear.

"Is it a boy or a girl?" Hildegard puzzled, covering her nose against the rising stench.

"Both: a girl in boy's clothing," Hiltrude replied. "No matter, the poor creature is ravenous. She snapped at the bread crusts and stuffed them in her mouth so fast, she choked on them and vomited."

"How long has she been here?" Hildegard asked, peering at the lice in the girl's matted hair.

"Brother Porter said a crone from the village was gathering herbs in the forest when she heard a clawing and found this poor creature trying to eat the bark of a tree. The crone carried her on her back and left her here at the gates, wide-eyed and babbling. When I tried to examine her, she cringed like a trapped animal," Hiltrude reported. "I think her wrist is broken. She screeched when I touched it."

Kneeling, Hildegard turned the young face toward her: beneath the grime, she saw a half-closed eye and blue-black skin surrounding it. At her touch, the girl began flinching and her legs trembled uncontrollably.

Placing her hands on the girl's knees, Hildegard gently eased the legs down onto the pallet. It was then that she saw the dark red patch spreading from her groin and staining the thighs of her dirt-caked legs. Some of the blood was still moist.

"What is your name, child?" Hildegard whispered, stroking her grimy brow. "Where are you from?"

The small face was shriveled with terror. As Hildegard lifted the girl's hand, she could feel the throbbing. Loosening the fingers, she saw that her palm was encrusted with dried pus. Looking closer, she saw an object embedded in it. It looked like a small ring.

Brushing the matted hair back from the young face, Hildegard whispered, "Where did the ring come from, child? Why do you cling to it?"

The girl sucked in her breath. "It's mine, the ring of my troth," she choked, "though I was left for dead after the lord of the manor had finished with me on my wedding night."

"The lord of the manor?" Hildegard drew back.

"She speaks of the bride's price," Hiltrude muttered, "the right of the lord of the manor to have the first coupling with any bride who dwells on his land."

"No, no, you must be mistaken!" Hildegard cried. "Where is your husband, child?"

The girl's whimper was pitiful. "They said he went mad with grief when he found me. Thinking me dead, he ran away." The girl tried in vain to lift her head. "I'm certain they killed him."

"Rest, child," Hildegard whispered. "No harm will come to you here." Rising, she drew Hiltrude aside.

"Burn her clothes and bathe her, then come to the herbarium. I'll prepare a lotion of woundwort and sanicle to clean her wounds and blend some betony and chickweed wintergreen for the dressing."

"Sleep now," she whispered to the girl. "You're safe here."

When Hildegard stood up, she was sure her hands were on fire. The pain was incredible. She staggered through the maze of pallets, deaf to the cries of the babies she had always stopped to hold. By the time she stepped outside, the heat in her hands had become unbearable.

"You took her fear from her when you touched her," a Voice whispered.

Frantic, she ran down the path to the herb garden, kicking open the iron gate. Sinking to her knees, she thrust her hands deep into the dark, moist soil.

"Viriditas, the green breath of God, heal my hands," she prayed, pressing her forehead against the earth. "Free them from this girl's terror, lest I impart it to all I touch! And whisper your healing secrets to me that I may use each seed and root and vine to heal in your name."

A sharp October chill had invaded the chapter room, and Jutta welcomed it. If nothing else, it would keep her daughters alert for today's reading on humility, a reflection she prayed would bear fruit.

The day's business was brief. Hiltrude announced that Brother Cellarer was impressed that the apple orchard had yielded twice the usual harvest this year. Hildegard caught Hiltrude's wink.

"If you want a tree to flourish, you have to hug it," she had informed Hiltrude earlier in the year. "Trees have hearts, too, you know," she had said, smiling. Apparently her advice and Hiltrude's work had now resulted in a fine harvest.

Seeing their delighted exchange, Jutta uttered a prayer of gratitude. The bond of friendship that had developed between her niece and her oblate was a blessing for both of them. Hildegard sat more erect now, her shoulders squared, her hands at ease in her lap. She appeared to have made a truce with her body and spirit. Once Jutta appointed her as herbalist, she became absorbed in the world of salves and ointments, quickly wearing a path between the hospice and herbarium. Even Brother Infirmarian had noted her dedication.

"Sister Hildegard touches the herbs with a reverence one usually reserves for holy things," he confided to Jutta. "I see it in the way she brews a cup of tansy tea for a dying elder or applies an aloe and marigold potion to a child's fire-blistered feet." Jutta smiled to herself. No wonder Hildegard's sisters teased her about spending more time on her knees in the herb garden than she spent in the chapel at prayer.

The chapter reading for the day had ended.

"My daughters, I have one last announcement," Jutta said. "The sheriff has asked us to watch for a runaway serf who belongs to our benefactor, Count Ulrich. Father abbot requests our vigilance, knowing it would bode ill for the abbey if the girl were ever found inside our gates."

Hildegard stared straight ahead. Across the room, Hiltrude cleared her throat as Jutta went on to read the necrology: the names of the abbey's friends, now deceased.

Hildegard kept staring. A second cough from Hiltrude. Then a third.

In a glance, Hildegard saw the anger in Hiltrude's eyes: Will you speak of the girl in the hospice or shall I? But Hildegard only turned away.

The confession of faults began, familiar and dreary.

"I spilled candlewax on my Psalter at Matins."

"I scolded Sister Ermintrude for only half-filling my ale cup at breakfast."

"I broke the Great Silence: I sang aloud in my bed."

"I dozed at my carrel."

Hiltrude thrust her hand in the air.

"My lady, I tended an ailing girl in the hospice," she sputtered. "She might well be the runaway serf. She was so battered, I barely touched her. She was wild with fear, all bloody and bruised, screaming with pain. I calmed her. . . . " Her voice dropped to a whisper, "Until help came."

"Sister Hildegard, after chapter please examine the girl and determine if she might be the suspect. Then report your findings to me at once."

"I attended this girl well into the night, my lady," Hildegard called out clearly.

"Truly?" Jutta snapped. "Then why weren't you the first to speak?"

"My lady, the child is gravely ill in body and soul. As a bride, she barely escaped death after the lord of the land had . . . had his way with her. I have begun treating . . ."

Jutta's glare silenced her. "Sister Hildegard, her presence must be reported at once. She is the property of her lord and is bound in allegiance to him. She must be returned."

"If she lives, my lady," Hildegard replied.

"Even if she dies," retorted Jutta.

"But until then, my lady, surely the Rule requires that we provide hospitality for such a poor one," Hildegard reminded her.

The challenge was palpable. Every eye was on Jutta's face.

"The Rule does not require that we harbor a criminal, especially one who fled in rebellion against the rights of her lord."

"The rights of her lord or the Lord God, my Lady Mother?"

"My daughter, are you confessing a fault or reveling in one?" Jutta thundered.

Reddening, Hildegard fell to her knees. "I confess that I did not come forward at once, my Lady Mother. I accept my penance."

"You will take your meals on your knees at the back of the refectory for ten days." Jutta rose. "Chapter is dismissed."

One by one, the nuns filed out after the magistra, and none looked back. Hildegard sat alone in the chapter room, not amazed at what she had done, but wondering why she had done it.

Hildegard prayed for the gift of tears as she crossed the monastery courtyard. Her eyes felt as though they were filled with sand. Exhausted by doubts, she felt like a sleepwalker. Why had she chosen to defy Lady Jutta?

Standing before the magistra's door, she raised her hand three times, praying for courage. Finally she knocked.

"*Deo gratias*," Jutta's voice was quick to respond.

"*Benedicite*." Eyes lowered, Hildegard entered and knelt for the blessing.

Jutta's hand on her shoulder startled her. "Rise, Sister Hildegard, and sit beside me." Obeying, she averted her red-rimmed eyes lest the tears begin.

But there was only silence. Lady Jutta's eyes were closed. Was she praying?

Outside, footsteps crunched past Jutta's window, fading quickly. As she waited, Hildegard watched a bug braving its way along the edge of her veil. As she flicked it away, she risked a glance at the magistra. For the first time, Hildegard noticed the cobweb of hair-fine lines that were etched on the woman's cheeks. And she saw that the furrows in the woman's brow had deepened so much that her wimple must chafe.

Seeing the changes, Hildegard felt her heart drop. Lady Jutta was growing old. Her eyes fled to Jutta's cockleshell for reassurance. It, at least, remained untouched by time.

The magistra stirred. "Sister Hildegard, why did you hesitate before reporting the runaway?"

"The question haunts me, my lady, just as do her eyes, which follow me, and the fear that blankets her like winter frost and chills my soul."

Jutta's voice was firm. "Daughter, by what authority do you defend her? Has pity blinded you to the offense she has committed against her lord?"

"My lady, if you had seen her, as I did, her body purple with bruises, her face distorted with swelling. Two of her teeth had been knocked from her jaw: the gums were festering. Would you have denied such a wretched creature pity?"

"And what would you say to her lord?"

"That it is not she who is criminal, but he."

"How dare you!" Jutta blazed, her mouth twitching with alarm. "This woman is bound to the land of her lord; without his protection, her family would starve. Though we may loathe what he did, her lord would argue that he took what was his, by law."

"By custom, my lady," Hildegard insisted.

"I repeat: by law!" Jutta shouted. "A law that grants a lord the right to all that dwells on his land, including the maidenhead of every virgin." Her hands were shaking.

"Even unto death, my Lady Mother?"

Jutta's sigh became a shiver. "What passion compels you to pursue this, my daughter? Why is this serf so important to you?"

"My lady," she cried, thrusting her hands forward, "These hands caught fire the moment I touched her. I heard the spiraling scream still trapped in her body. I felt her choke when he thrust his wine-soaked fist in her mouth to silence her pleas, then slapped her as he plunged his knee between her legs to stop the struggling. And most fearsome, I heard her shriek as she cried out to the crucified Christ as her flesh was ripped raw, her hymen slashed, splashing her thighs with crimson rivers of tears and centuries of blood."

At her revelation, Jutta looked stricken, unsure. "I insist: the matter is between the lord and his God. It is not for you to judge."

Hildegard bit her knuckle, sobbing now. "My lady, can these words truly be yours?"

Jutta's eyes were filled with pain. "They are not now nor never will be, my daughter! But they are the words of a law that the church itself also upholds, as you well know."

"Know, my lady?" Hildegard's eyes flashed. "When did you ever speak of such things to me?"

Stabbed by her defiance, Jutta blanched. "The world beyond these walls is full of evil, my daughter. There was no need until now to speak of such horrors."

"You forget that the wounds of the world overflow into the hospice, my lady; I bind those wounds night and day. Even now, before it's too late, I beg you: teach me all that I must know of the world that inflicts them. At the very least," she pleaded, "teach me things such as this, things I am ignorant of, an ignorance that gives my sisters cause to pity me."

A small voice whispered to Jutta, "The days are long past when she will cup her hands to catch your every word. You must accept that she is a woman now." The time has finally come, Jutta thought, as I knew it must, one day.

Hildegard had returned to the hospice after Compline to attend to a woman who had given birth to stillborn twins. Even though she had toiled in the hospice for two decades, she still wept when she told a mother that her children were dead. Would it ever get easier? she wondered as she headed for the monastery. As she shivered in the damp night air, she wrapped her cloak tightly about her. Her chapped hands ached from hours of pounding her mortar in the herbarium, but the need for syrups and poultices had increased with the recent rains. Pausing, she arched her back and stretched her arms. She was exhausted.

Ahead, she saw splashes of moonlight on the roof of the monastery and, beside it, the towering outline of her beloved tree. In the decades since they had planted it as a sapling in the hermitage courtyard, she had sought out its shade again and again after a daunting day in the hospice. She often hugged it and even climbed up into its branches to weep in its arms.

There had been so many births and deaths in her work since then, so many cures and near-miracles, all challenging her to delve even deeper into the healing power of the earth's mysteries, like the healing power of gems and minerals that had intrigued her of late. With each revelation, she was flooded with awe. With such abundance, how could there not be a God?

Blue-gray storm clouds were foaming overhead as Jutta watched the two monks approach the monastery. Abbot Adelhun's head was bent and his shoulders hunched while the stride of the younger monk was relaxed, his glance sweeping across the length of the enclosure walls. She studied him closely since he was to be their new provost and chaplain.

Once inside, the abbot was quick to apprise Lady Jutta of her good fortune in his selection of Father Volmar.

"I would hope so, my Lord Abbot," she replied firmly. "Our benefactors have grown impatient with their daughters' complaints concerning the last two chaplains, who proved so unsuitable."

"A memory that Father Volmar will quickly erase," the abbot retorted, as his hands quickly disappeared in the folds of his sleeves. "Under Father Volmar's guidance, our scriptorium has flourished. The brothers value his counsel and trust his judgment."

"It will be my privilege to serve you, my Lady Magistra," Volmar said, bowing, but not before Jutta saw the deep frown that cut a path across his brow. Praise unsettles him, she noticed: a good sign if he's humble, a bad sign if he's unsure. Of medium height, Volmar had a spare frame, an aquiline nose, and skin pitted with acne. From the way he bore himself, she could see there was tension in his shoulders. At thirty, his hair was already flecked with gray.

"We welcome you, Father Volmar," Jutta said warmly, smiling. "And I can assure you that your gifts will hardly lie fallow here. Our monastery is blessed with the talents of gifted women who will, I am certain, inspire you, in turn. They have a keen appetite for challenge, as you will learn."

"I shall welcome it," Volmar replied quickly, "and do all in my power to deserve your trust."

"And to ensure that your new chaplain is not deterred from his monastery duties," the abbot purred, "I am relieving him of his duties in the abbey scriptorium."

Volmar was clearly surprised. Was this appointment a reward or a punishment? Jutta wondered. And for whom: the monk or us?

In fact, distressed by the magistra's unhappiness with two confessors in a row, the abbot had begun scanning the faces at the midday meal in earnest. As the brothers ate their stew and passed the bread, few showed interest in the day's reading from Clement of Alexandria. Only Volmar's eyes darted with speculation as he weighed the merits of what was being read. Encouraged, the abbot began noticing Volmar's patience as he bent over the carrels in the scriptorium, his instructions helpful and clear. "His mind is keen," the brothers agreed. "He challenges us by answering a question with a question." Could this be a sign?

"Help me, Holy Lady!" the abbot had implored the Virgin. "I must not fail this time!"

Yet as Jutta glanced at her new chaplain, a far different prayer to the Virgin arose in her. It was a mother's plea for her daughter: "Holy Mary, give me the wisdom to know if I dare speak to him of Hildegard. The time grows short."

Part Two

1136−48

Wisdom herself spoke:
"Hear these words, human creature,
and tell them not according to yourself
but as taught by me.
Speak of yourself like this. . . . "

—Vita Sanctae Hildegardis

The afternoon sun was still strong when Margravine Richardis von Stade reined her palfrey to a halt at the abbey gates. Despite the brisk autumn air, the horse was streaming with sweat from the steep ascent; the margravine had been intent on arriving in time to be greeted by the bells for Vespers. Now she was rewarded. The chanting voices drifted toward her, filling her with feelings of peace. But the greatest comfort of all was the knowledge that her Sponheim family roots were so deep here; when she arrived at the abbey, it was like coming home.

Yet a single glance across the abbey landscape jolted her. Scattered beneath the trees, clusters of tattered pilgrims tried to hush the cries of moaning children, while others hung atop their crutches, vacant-eyed like specters lost between two worlds. The greatest shock of all was the new hospice. It dominated the compound, dwarfing everything in sight. Its looming walls were ringed with still more pilgrims, begging entry. The paths between the bakehouse and brewery were cluttered with people waiting their turn to receive food from Brother Almoner. Overwhelmed by the clamor, the margravine reached for the gate and steadied herself. Had she stumbled into the wrong place?

"Welcome, my Lady Margravine!"

Looking down, she saw Brother Porter's round face staring up at her. "The abbey extends its sympathies for the loss of your lord. We pray for his soul."

A wave of comfort warmed her. "I rested my soul on the abbey's prayers," she said softly. Slipping down from her mount, she handed the reins to her waiting groom.

"There are so many strangers here, Brother Porter! Where have they come from?"

"The news of the hospice spread quickly, my lady. And since the harvests were scant this year, many are hungry."

"So it appears," she replied curtly.

"But we are able to feed and heal many more now, my lady. Indeed, your generous heart has made much of this possible."

How ironic, she thought, as the monk led her to the guesthouse. As she passed the pilgrims, she felt assaulted by the noisy shouts and foul smells and quickly covered her nose and mouth with her glove. As she did, a cart rumbled out from behind the hospice, almost knocking her down and drowning out the last sounds of Vespers.

After closing the door to her room, she pounded her fist in her palm. She had hardly expected to find this chaos when she had received Lady Jutta's invitation to spend her days of mourning here. Since the invitation had included two urgent requests for a reply, perhaps there was another concern beyond the magistra's natural solicitude for the margravine's bereavement. Could it be her distress at the incredible disruption that had been caused by the hospice? But of course! For the first time since her arrival, the margravine relaxed.

Hildegard squinted in the morning light as she opened the monastery door to the margravine. She had not seen her since their first meeting in the hermitage. Her one indelible memory of the meeting was that the margravine's presence had filled the room. Time has been kind to her, Hildegard thought now, though she is not as tall as I remember. The margravine smiled, and Hildegard felt the same charm flowing from her that she had felt when they had first met.

"A hundred welcomes, my lady!" Hildegard enthused. "I am Sister Hildegard von Bermersheim."

Startled, the margravine drew back, appraising her.

"But of course! Except that the child has exchanged her sapphire eyes for amethysts," she said charmingly. As she leaned forward, the fragrance of lavender rose from her coat's silky marten collar as it brushed Hildegard's cheek, but beneath it, the tautness in the woman's body reminded Hildegard of the strings of a lyre stretched too tight.

Hildegard smiled. "Come," she said, leading the guest to the magistra's room. "Lady Jutta is sure to recognize your footsteps."

How fragile she has become, the margravine thought as she glimpsed her cousin upon entering the room. When their eyes met, however, the color rose in Jutta's cheeks, filling her guest with a deep sense of blessing. The magistra's arms reached out to her cousin eagerly, though she made no effort to rise.

"We offer prayers for you several times each day, dear cousin," Jutta sighed. "Though I only saw Margrave Rudolph once, I remember the fire in his eyes when he looked at you."

"Never again," she replied, weeping. "They said the blood gushed from his heart like a fountain on the battlefield, and within the hour, snow covered his body like a great white shroud."

A knock on the door interrupted them.

"Your medicine, my lady," Hildegard said as she offered her mistress a small flask of dark syrup. As Lady Jutta drank it, Hildegard crouched down and rearranged the cushions beneath the woman's feet. "The swelling is less today, my lady," she smiled. "A good sign!"

"Hildegard's devotion to you is touching," the guest noted after the young nun had departed. "But there are so many daughters now who must share that devotion."

Jutta looked away. "With blessings come duties. And with duties, demands. Since our land grants are scattered, they require constant attention. Careful accounts of the harvest must also be kept and the rents collected. And yes," she brightened, "Sister Hildegard, my prioress, is a great help to me in these matters and excels in her efforts in the hospice and herbarium as well. We would have lost one of the twins to lung-sickness had it not been for her diligence. Now both work at Hildegard's side in the hospice."

"Amazing! I still recall her as a shy child in the hermitage," the margravine said. "Have you ever wished to return to it? Have you any regrets that we burdened you with this monastery?"

"Never." Jutta reached for her cousin's hand. "Look at the joys and challenges it has brought to my life!"

"Clearly," the margravine agreed. "And fame, as well."

Jutta flinched. "Our new abbot, Kuno, would hasten to remind you, as must I, that the abbey was flourishing long before I came here." When her cousin looked askance, she added, "As for your claim, what are the real fruits of fame, after all, my Lady Cousin? Only that our names will be spoken with kindness. In the end, love is the only legacy, that love that offers hospitality."

The margravine shifted uneasily. "Tell me, my Lady Magistra, how can you dedicate your life to prayer with so many strangers milling about, moaning and shouting at every turn?"

Jutta looked up quickly. "Hospitality is the heartbeat of our life here. We are reminded each day that every guest must be received as another Christ."

The margravine shrugged. "So you consider the work of the hospice to be a fair exchange for the shattered peace and silence?"

"Our work is our prayer, my Lady Cousin. We do have islands of silence all around us: we keep silent during meals and from the close of Compline to the beginning of Prime. As you well know, we pray in silence day and night for those who have no hope. If I find the noise distracting me, I seek the silence of my heart."

"I envy you, my lady." The margravine's voice was strained and lofty, her head beginning to throb.

Jutta leaned forward anxiously. "What you must understand, my Lady Cousin, is that the hospice does not belong to us. It is the symbol of your trust in us. We sought nothing yet were given much by hearts such as yours. Once we embraced that trust, it could only flow through us to feed and comfort others."

"Including your benefactors? Or are they to be denied a portion of the peace and comfort you lavish on the pilgrims who hurry here?"

Jutta sighed. "Would you trade places with any one of them? Do you envy them their rags and rotting teeth and stunted bones?"

"Certainly not. But I am a pilgrim soul, too, and have every right to ask for the gift of peace and silence."

"You ask us to choose? . . ."

"Is that so much?" the margravine countered. "We, after all, send you our dowered daughters clothed in terraced vineyards and fertile fields bursting with grain. And when fortune discards us or drapes us in widow's weeds, may we not reap a part of the harvest that we believed awaited us in the fields of silence we've sown and nourished over the years?"

"We need only trust that there will be enough for all," Jutta replied evenly. "The Son of Man taught us that when he fed the multitudes."

"How many gifts of mills and toll fees and granaries must we offer you then in exchange for peace and silence?" the guest asked bitterly. "Tell us, and we will gladly do your bidding, so great is our need to fall back on those pillows of solace we long to find here."

Jutta's hand reached out, her eyes pleading. "Please understand, my Lady Cousin."

"Ah, but do you understand? Do you truly believe that our jewels console us when we twist in the night in our empty beds or when stillborn babes are placed in our arms or when our men are gone so long we've forgotten the sound of their laughter? I speak truth when I say that we have wounds that bleed unseen beneath the folds of our satin and velvet and have a need for the peace and silence we once found here."

"I grieve that you feel so betrayed by the hospice," Jutta said sadly.

"Only the one you chose to build. A small one would have served the abbey as well. Surely some of the endowments might have been just as well spent to enlarge the library or assist the scholars in their translations of the Arabic texts that are of such interest now. And what of the guest house? How can the abbot hope to offer hospitality to the royal court or to papal legates with such small quarters?"

"The abbot would be the first to agree with you," Jutta said calmly. "Indeed, the concerns you have expressed have been his for some time. He will be pleased to know that you agree."

"Especially now that I am newly widowed and my husband's estate has yet to be settled," the visitor seethed.

The magistra was aghast. "Surely my ears deceive me, my Lady Cousin. You cannot mean what you imply!"

"You feign surprise, yet it is clear to me now that the urgency of your invitation had as much to do with the abbey's current needs to feed the swarms here. A generous endowment, perhaps, in the margrave's name, or in mine, in his memory?"

Lady Jutta drew back as though her cousin had slapped her. "God forgive me," she pleaded, "if that was what my words conveyed to you. Never, never, did I intend that. I had an urgent need to confide in you, to share a secret that..." Her words slurred. "You were the only one I dared trust...."

She clutched her throat, writhing as a spasm of pain choked her. Gurgling, she clasped her belly and, with a smothered screech, fell forward at the margravine's feet.

The margravine's scream still echoed as Hildegard flew to the magistra's room. The margravine was frantic at her failure to stop the abbess' bleeding and was sobbing with pleas for her cousin's forgiveness. Seeing them, Hildegard seized the back of a chair to keep herself from fainting.

Lady Jutta lay sprawled on the floor where she had fallen. Hildegard moved forward to examine her, kneeling blindly, bravely, in a pool of the magistra's blood. But it was when she held her beloved mistress and felt the woman's limp arms dangling that she felt her heart crack in two. These were the arms that had rocked her again and again in the hermitage, then led her day by day, prayer by prayer, from sleet to sunshine.

Hildegard felt a crushing pressure in her chest as she lifted her hand for the first time to bless her mistress. Then holding the magistra against her heart, the daughter began rocking the mother as the margravine gasped and dashed from the room. In that instant, Hildegard's field of vision cracked again into jagged prisms of flashing light, and she was unable to see. Feeling for Lady Jutta's cheek, she kissed her beloved comforter, rocking her until the others came and took Lady Jutta away.

Volmar rang the bell at the nuns' monastery gate to announce his arrival. Above him, a crescent moon hung like a slender silver scythe in the heavens. Its beauty calmed him as a novice hurried to unlatch the gate. As they crossed the courtyard, his chest felt tight and his palms were sweating.

Inside, the nuns took turns keeping vigil at the magistra's bedside. Her collapse earlier that day had left everyone stunned.

The nuns had barely managed to mumble their prayers during Mass that morning, their faces buried in their hands to avoid seeing Lady Jutta's empty chair.

"How fares she, my lady?" Volmar whispered to Hildegard at the magistra's bedside.

"I have given her poppy syrup to ease her pain," she replied. "But when I touch her hand, it is your name that she calls."

In the candlelight, the woman's skin looked ghastly except for the patches of vermilion that stained her cheeks with an unnatural glow.

"The flesh near her heart is badly scarred," Hildegard said, *seeing through her closed eyes. "Yet some flame still flickers."*

"Confession, perhaps," the monk advised. "When she stirs, we will anoint her."

"As she has anointed so many," Hildegard said, looking over Volmar's shoulder.

They had started to come, legions of them, streaming to her, filling the room, all the souls she had loved back to life from the beginning.

Volmar puzzled at the slow, spreading smile now erasing Hildegard's sleeplessness and the grayness beneath her eyes.

"I will be in the chapel if you need me," she told him. When he looked down, Lady Jutta's eyes were opening.

"Closer," she rasped. Bending down, he felt her hand on his wrist: her grip was intense. He felt as though every drop of strength had fled to her fingers, though her veins stood out like knotted blue threads on the back on her hand.

"Listen well! Hildegard..." Exhausted by the few words, she closed her eyes again. Beads of sweat moistened the edge of the linen cloth covering her head. Still, her grip was fierce.

"My son," she began again, her eyes watering. "Since childhood, Hildegard has seen and known things hidden to us, though she dares not speak of them. Her visions are truly of God but fill her with dread." She clutched his hand even more tightly now. "Promise me that you will never desert her," she pleaded. "I place her in your care." Her hand went slack as though it was melting. "My son, pray for me when I am dead," she whispered.

Volmar felt dizzy. Lowering his ear to her mouth, he was relieved that her breath, though faint, was still steady. She slipped into sleep.

Within the hour, Volmar brought her the Eucharist. Then, bending down, he placed a crucifix at her lips for her to kiss. "Before Christ, my lady, I promise to do what you asked of me," he heard himself whisper.

Closing his eyes, he knelt by her bed as he joined with her daughters to chant the Miserere, the ancient psalm of the heart aching to begin the journey home: "Sprinkle me with hyssop, and I shall be cleansed; wash me, and I shall be made whiter than snow."

The abbot approached now to anoint her forehead and hands and feet with the holy oils and to bless her for the last time.

At midnight, Hildegard suddenly awoke in her stall where she had been sitting alone, praying.

Looking up, she saw a wave of golden light hovering, flaring three times before it faded.

The new chants rose in the chapel and flowed down the mountainside. Hearing the heights to which the voices soared, the cooks cocked their ears in the bakehouse, and the scribes looked up from their pages of vellum. The melodic leaps and rippling melismas dazzled them. When had a chant's syllable been embellished with so many notes? And what composer dared risk flights to such exquisite heights, believing the human voice could succeed in reaching them?

Hildegard had first heard the notes in her soul as she lay trembling in her new bed one morning after her election as magistra. On that morning, her election still seemed to be a dream. She had scarcely had time to step back from Lady Jutta's death when she became her successor. It had all happened so fast; it still seemed unreal. Like a surging fountain, the sounds had risen and overflowed in her, encouraging her to embroider the simple plainchant she had learned at Lady Jutta's knee. Within her, the notes became a kind of soaring, as though her voice was climbing a ladder of light to a certain height, then plummeting gently, only to rise again.

The first time she sang the new chants in chapel was when she had remained to pray after Vespers with a few others. The music seemed to be pouring through her and could not be contained. She was filled with awe. Was she inside the music or was it inside of her? Gertrud and Gisla had gaped in amazement, while Hiltrude had leaped to her feet. Yet Hildegard had sung on, unable to stop, aware as never before that she was clasped in a mystery.

She began to see the colors of the sounds as she sang them, as she had as a child when the monks' chants at Disibodenberg had first lifted her.

Now, she, as magistra, was singing those notes with her sisters, the notes floating down the mountainside. Yet even as she sang, a new truth overwhelmed her: after all the years of dismantling the barriers between herself and her sisters, now, as a thirty-eight-year-old magistra, she must learn to embrace a new loneliness. Looking out at her daughters, she acknowledged the chasm: the three small steps between their separate worlds. In chapel, her chair rested alone on a velvet-cushioned island. Never again could she whisper secrets or empty her pockets with the others to share all the straw and pebbles of their day. Lady Jutta, do not leave me, she implored.

Now, like an ebbing tide, her inner song receded, her voice blending again with those of her new daughters: "Look to him so that you may be radiant with joy, and your faces may not blush with shame."

Though she had sung those words a thousand times, her throat closed on them now, stunned by a truth she could not have imagined: Lady Jutta was dead, and she was the magistra.

Glancing up from the ledgers on her desk, Hildegard was relieved to see Father Volmar. He was their legal adviser, and she needed his signature on a document for their newest land grant. His presence was as calming as his counsel was indispensable. When a benefactor asked her to describe him, she was quick to praise his thoughtful ways and unfailing patience but found herself at a loss to provide a physical description. He was simply there to say two daily Masses, one for the nuns and one for the benefactors. And twice a month, he heard the nuns' confessions.

"Though I see him every day, have I ever looked at him?" she puzzled.

"You must be relieved to complete this transaction, my lady," Volmar said now, dipping his quill in the inkpot. Her eyes studied him as her ears trailed the slow scratch of his quill on the parchment. "The tasks are unending, are they not?" he said, smiling.

"The demands of the tolls and harvests alone could easily consume me," she agreed. "Now I understand why it's said that magistras cherish the rule of obedience the most, else they would never stop long enough to pray."

"Yet look how much you've accomplished already," he enthused. "The village rents are collected, the bridge tolls levied, and most of the mill fees have been paid. And judging from your careful accounts," he said, pointing to the open ledger, "I am certain that all is in order here."

"And if the brothers in the northern grange have the yields they expect," she said, brightening, "the wheat harvest will be the best in years."

The provost laughed. "You'll see: life will be calmer after the first snowfall," he reassured her. "Besides, the land needs rest."

"As do we all," she sighed. "As do you, Father Volmar."

Nodding briskly, he smiled and rose, their business finished. Yet he lingered, unwilling to leave.

"You have my admiration, my lady. You have kept your secret well."

"Secret?" Hildegard was startled. "What do you mean?" She tensed. What had he seen or heard?

"Your gift for music, my lady. Your compositions."

"Ah, yes. Of course!" She was relieved. "For my daughters."

"And for your brothers as well," he said. "Brother Wilhelm, for one," he added.

Hildegard looked askance. "Spare me your jest, Father Volmar. Brother Wilhelm has refused to acknowledge that nuns can speak, much less sing."

"With all due respect, my lady, Brother Wilhelm himself requested the abbot's permission to secure copies of your new antiphons to the Blessed Virgin. He hopes to combine the abbey and monastery choirs at Michaelmas when our new lord chancellor of Mainz makes his first visit here."

Brother Wilhelm? Hildegard thought. Surely not! As precentor, he had strongly opposed their monastery's founding.

Volmar's grin was infectious. "It appears, my lady, that your chants have disarmed him."

For the first time, Hildegard saw the gray flecks in Volmar's black hair and recalled now that he always stooped when he entered her doorway and that his voice was as calm as the warmth of summer. Revelations, indeed.

As Hildegard picked her way along the frost-crisp pathway to the abbey reception hall, she wondered if dining with benefactors at the abbot's table could be considered work or penance. Abbot Kuno's requests for her presence had increased as news of his largesse spread. Since he had served as abbey cellarer prior to Abbot Adelhun's death, Kuno had spent years accounting for the abbey's resources. Now he had the power to spend them. Though he stood at medium height, he appeared to be much taller due to his stocky build and thick neck and the way his arms swung from his shoulders like sturdy oars, propelling him forward.

Today, as always, the abbot would introduce her as both the magistra of Disibodenberg and the former oblate of Lady Jutta von Sponheim.

Stepping from the daylight, Hildegard adjusted her eyes to the dimness of the reception hall. The row of silver goblets glinted on the table, alerting her to the guests' importance.

As she braced herself to greet another room full of strangers, the abbot approached, his face flushed with too much wine, the neckline of his robe already dark with sweat.

"An auspicious gathering, my lady," he confided in a whisper as his sour breath overpowered her, "and important guests you must meet."

Hildegard sighed. Since becoming magistra, she had struggled to defend herself against Kuno's demands lest she become his pawn.

"In a moment," she said, easily spotting Volmar's black robe beneath the silk parade of standards at the far end of the hall. He appeared to be captive to a red-faced count who was shaking his fist, no doubt insisting that his serfs were packs of lazy thieves.

But the abbot would not be deterred. "By your leave, my lady," Kuno said, steering her to a cluster of guests nearby. As they approached, the circle parted.

"Your Grace, may I present our magistra, Lady Hildegard von Bermersheim," Kuno announced hoarsely. "My lady, his excellency, Lord Henry Moguntin, our new archbishop of Mainz."

Hildegard looked up into the blue eyes of a giant. His white-gold hair and beard were a foil for his lapis velvet tunic edged in ermine. He wore a gold cross set with a blazing ruby. As he drew close to her, Hildegard felt the heat of his body.

"I am honored, my lady." He moistened his lips slowly. "I understand that your daughters are twice blessed: you not only guide them but inspire them with your music, as well." When he drew even closer, she stepped back, unnerved by the way his eyes glided over her face and body.

"Your Excellency," she murmured.

"I have also been told that your antiphons to the Holy Virgin are exquisite," he said, peering into her violet eyes. "How soon may I hear them?"

Taken aback, she turned to Kuno.

"At Michaelmas, as scheduled, Your Grace," the abbot said nervously.

"Michaelmas?" he frowned.

"For your official visit, Your Grace."

"Splendid!" he exclaimed, his eyes still fixed on Hildegard. "I look forward to such a singular celebration." Turning casually to the woman next to him, he added softly, "I trust you will grace us with your presence there, as well, my lady."

Hildegard turned to meet the eyes of Margravine von Stade.

"My Lady Magistra," the woman said as she made a mock bow. "I had hoped to surprise you. Have I succeeded?"

Hildegard blinked. She had not seen the margravine since Lady Jutta's funeral. She had stood apart, swathed in black veils, and had disappeared soon after. The contrast was startling. Today, every eye in the room was drawn to her. She looked regal. Her glistening copper hair was drawn back and was coiled at the nape of her neck and crowned with a headband of opals. Her almond dress rippled with every breath, enhanced by its low neckline and wide, trailing sleeves bordered in hyacinth velvet. The girdle at her waist was embroidered with golden leaves. Hildegard recognized the scent of lavender.

"We are neighbors now," the woman crooned. "Since I have taken up residence in the Nahe Valley, I will be near to this dear abbey that I have always regarded as my second home." Her eyes crinkled prettily. "We will surely see more of each other now that you are magistra. How splendid to know that you have succeeded Lady Jutta, my dear. It helps soften the pain of her passing."

Hildegard shivered, hearing again the margravine's scream when Lady Jutta fell at her feet.

The guests began seating themselves at the table, lured by the fragrance of saffron-laced stews. The steaming tureens were being placed on the table beside platters of currant-spiced dumplings and game pies spiced with pepper and cinnamon.

As the wine flowed, so did the conversation at their tables. Archbishop Henry sat at the same table as Hildegard, and she studied him, trailing his restless eyes as they swept across the room. Yet when he met her gaze, his eyes explored her face so brazenly, she looked away. Her tongue felt thick in her mouth, and she was unable to swallow. When she risked another glance, his eyes were back again, studying her intently as he inquired in detail about the families of her noble daughters. Beguiling her with a half-smile, he asked probing questions that unsettled her. Yet she also saw that he could barely tear his eyes away from the margravine, and she watched their interaction intently. Without once acknowledging him, the margravine drew Henry to her with consummate skill, simply by noting that her daughter Luitgard was a former queen of Denmark and that Hartwig, her son, was the current cathedral provost in Bremen. As his guest unfurled her credentials, Kuno slouched back in his chair, ballooning in utter contentment, oblivious to the fact that his robe was spattered with grease and his hand seemed stuck to his wine cup.

Hildegard's head was spinning. Archbishop Henry's attentions had flustered her, and seeing the margravine again had distracted her in ways she could not name. She felt caught in some mysterious web that was beginning to form. The thought frightened her. The world from which they came was too strange, too ominous.

"What's troubling Lady Mother this time?" Ilse squinted over her embroidery, wincing as she pricked her finger for the second time.

"Please," Hiltrude begged, "remember that she's our magistra now. Everything is different. We can no longer expect..."

"We all know that," Ilse interrupted. "I mean the way she's been pacing up and down in chapel while we're rehearsing the music for Michaelmas. Yesterday, she snatched the monochord from Sister Chantress in the middle of a phrase, insisting that she play it herself. I can't understand why she's so anxious. By now, we could chant those antiphons in our sleep."

"I expect the abbot is pressuring her, demanding perfection for Archbishop Henry's visit," Gisla suggested.

"I've heard that His Grace is wonderfully handsome," Ilse purred, re-threading her needle. "Two of the maids saw him mount his stallion at the gate and said that the muscles in his shoulders fairly rippled beneath his tunic."

"Truly, Sister Ilse?" Gertrud sneered, raising her eyebrows. "I daresay it was the sight of a man's shoulders that heightened the curiosity of a certain nun of Watton. And look what fate befell her!"

Ilse gritted her teeth. As usual, Gertrud had snapped at her words like a dog snapped at bones. "Spare me your suspicions, Gertrud. Must you always be so quick to judge?"

But the others, seizing on Ilse's morsel of gossip, urged Gertrud to regale them again with the tale of the English nun.

"A true story," Gisla reminded them, clearing her throat. "Witnessed by Ailred, the abbot of Rievaulx."

"A four-year-old girl was dropped on the doorstep of the Watton monastery by Archbishop Henry of York," Gertrud intoned, relishing the moment.

"For reasons unknown...," Gisla took care to add.

"But as she grew," Gertrud hurried on, "It was evident that she lacked a nun's vocation. If anything, the girl flounced about like a whore, seducing a monk at the first opportunity. The pair indulged their lusts until suspicions arose and sent the monk fleeing. The guilty nun confessed, and she was cast into prison and hobbled with chains when her outraged sisters learned that their sister was pregnant. In their fury, the nuns contacted the monks in the adjoining house, and together, they captured the guilty brother. Flinging him to the floor, they handed him a knife and demanded that he castrate himself before his pregnant mistress."

Gisla shrieked, and Kunigunde covered her mouth with her hands while Hiltrude looked stricken. But Ilse's cheeks were flaming, her lips parted in a smile.

"See what you started!" Hiltrude accused her.

But Ilse would not be denied.

"Their crime was love," she insisted. "It could have happened to any one of us."

"But not here, and not to you," Gertrud mockingly lamented.

"How cruel you are, Gertrud," Ilse whispered hoarsely. "And how unforgiving."

Every eye lowered.

Hiltrude could feel her stomach knot. It had happened again. Why did Gertrud seize every chance to humiliate Ilse, always picking at the scabs of her weakness? The others indulged Ilse's romantic flights of fancy as a diversion. Why couldn't Gertrud? Why did she always lie in wait to pounce on her? And why in God's name did they relish that vile story so much, knowing the anguish it was sure to cause?

The air was heavy now except for Gertrud's shuffling feet and Gisla's sigh. But Ilse, crumpling with tears, swept her embroidery from her lap and kicked it from her path as she flew from the room.

Michaelmas. Overnight, the gray granite walls of the abbey church were festooned with newly cut pine boughs and sprays of bright red berries, while the sharp fragrance of pine sap mingled with the spice of incense in the chilly winter air. The guests in the church came to rapt attention when His Grace, Archbishop Henry Moguntin, stood in the doorway and took his place in the procession.

At the sight of him, Hildegard tensed, and her heart began pounding. Had this day really come? Was he really here? As his eyes flitted over the crowd, she froze and prayed that he would not look at her. He was even more handsome than she remembered. A fear gripped her. What if she opened her mouth and was unable to sing? What if she couldn't remember? All those weeks of rehearsals, all her demands for perfection that had driven the sisters mad. Why had she told His Grace that her chants to the Virgin would be sung at Michaelmas? What was she thinking?

As he proceeded down the aisle, Hildegard stared straight ahead, not letting herself look at him. Of late, even in chapel, she found herself blushing as thoughts of him that were something less than holy scaled the fortress of her prayers. As he processed past her stall now, only an arm's length away, her heart pounded wildly.

Dear God, how could she live if he found her chants uninspired?

Over the weeks, the possibility had become unbearable, magnifying her fears, crowding her soul. What if the novices lost their places, or someone coughed or sang off-key? And worst of all, what if her compositions were mocked because her notes dared to leap beyond the confines of plainchant?

The next thing she knew, the Light was consuming her, lifting her as she began to sing.

Afterward, she remembered nothing. All she could recall was the bliss.

From the whispering around her, she realized the Mass must be finished. When she looked up, the abbot's eyes were shining. "My Lady Magistra, the music was sublime."

Where had she been? Dazed, she heard the abbot's cough as he touched her elbow, a signal for her to join the recessional. As she walked, she saw only light rise from the choirs and crowds on either side of her as she glided into the blinding whiteness of the snow and winter sun.

And the next thing she knew, Volmar was standing at the door of the hall, buoyant with joy.

"Your chants left them breathless, my lady," he gasped as a crowd surrounded her, at once marveling at the purity of her music and draping her with garlands of praise. She felt herself nodding. She remembered nothing.

The guests were departing now. The hall was empty, except for the novices who were clearing the tables and returning the benches to their places along the walls. At the far end of the hall, Volmar saw the magistra bid the last guest good-bye and then sink into a chair. This was the moment he had waited for.

"Brother Wilhelm came forward at once and told me his brothers had never sung with such joy," she announced, as he approached her. "His gratitude humbled me."

"As your gift has humbled us, my lady. How could it not? Your chants parted the curtains of heaven today!" the monk exclaimed. "And the news will be carried quickly."

"By some," she murmured, looking away.

"By all who heard, my lady," he insisted.

"Except His Grace, Lord Henry."

Volmar sighed. "A pity he had to leave for Mainz before the chants. Still, he sent his regrets."

"Nothing more?"

"Your music was celestial, my lady," Volmar replied, evading her question.

But Hildegard only stared. She knew now that Archbishop Henry had no interest in her antiphons. He had come for other reasons.

"My lady?" Volmar frowned, aware that her lips were trembling and her teeth were chattering.

Leaping to her feet, Hildegard stifled an urge to pound the walls, even to scourge herself. Anything!

"Fool! Fool!" she cursed herself. Pushing her provost aside, she stumbled from the hall, her tears scalding her, her throat choking with the taste of ashes.

The snow had been falling steadily for four days. Only the tops of the abbey gates were visible, like black fingertips reaching through the snow. It took the strength of seven men to slice through the ice-crusted drifts in order to push the gates back. All the while, the wind was merciless.

The nuns shivered through Matins, then raced back and sank into their beds, still wrapped in their woolen cloaks.

It was just after Terce when they found her. Hildegard was lying face down on the ground in the cloister, her wimple twisted to one side, covering her left cheek while her right cheek was bruised and swollen.

Though mute with pain, Hildegard heard the footsteps rushing toward her, then the cries of anguish as they lifted her and Hiltrude's hands cradled her head. Lying in her bed, she heard the murmurs of concern, but she was too numb to speak.

"No wonder she can't stop shivering," Gisla cried. "Her bones must be numb after lying on those freezing stones."

"But her hands are so hot, they could be on fire," Hiltrude puzzled. "If only she could tell us what happened."

But Hildegard knew that even if she could, they would not understand. How could she explain the sudden appearance of her visions, descending without warning, anytime, anywhere, stunning her with words and images that staggered her. It had happened again that morning as she was applying a flaxseed poultice to a pilgrim's leg. Her head was seared with pain as though someone was pushing a sliver of glass through her forehead. Reeling with nausea, she left and got as far as the cloister, only to be overwhelmed by a vision of a huge and marvelous star exploding before her eyes, almost blinding her. It was surrounded by a shower of falling stars, all blazing as they plunged into a dark abyss, draining her, leaving her faint with weakness.

In Christ's name, was what happening to her? What did the vision mean? And why had it seized her with such violence? After that, nothing.

Two days passed before she opened her eyes. Volmar had volunteered to stay with her while Hiltrude went to the herbarium to fetch more salve for her bruises. Hildegard touched her left cheek: it was completely numb. When she looked up, she saw Volmar's smile, but shining behind him, bathed in the Living Light, was Lady Jutta. Tears spilled from Hildegard's eyes, but her lips were so cracked, she could barely speak.

"Am I going mad, my Lady Mother?" she cried out frantically to Lady Jutta, who stood over Volmar's shoulder.

The monk drew back.

"When I fell into the wind," she whispered hoarsely, *"my ears melted with the roaring, and my eyes shattered into prisms of light."*

Her fingers kept pulling on the coverlet.

"Then as the heavens opened, I saw my skull parting like the petals of a flower and a Blinding Light came and flowed through my brain..." she wept. *"And the brilliance flowed into me, warming my breasts and heart like the sun warms the earth with its rays. And in the midst of the brilliance, I understood all the books of Holy Writ: the Prophets, the Psalter, the Old and New Testaments."*

Her jaw went slack, her eyes transfixed as she strained to listen. Then she began turning her head from side to side.

"But, my lady, the Voice in the Light insisted that though I was weak and corrupt and would return to dust, still I must do what was commanded of me. 'Write what you hear and see,' it thundered at me three times. I hear it still!"

She choked on a sob. Her eyes widened as she shrank back on her pillow.

"No, no! I cannot, my lady!"

Her scream split the air.

"I dare not! Why did you leave me to bear this burden alone?"

Her fear came in short breaths now as she tried to raise herself up on her elbow, only to fall back with a pitiful thud.

"My lady?" Volmar asked gently.

But her eyes were darting wildly as she looked above his shoulder. "Where has my Lady Jutta gone?" She began to weep.

Volmar froze. "I do not know, my lady." His reply was calm. "Perhaps if we pray together, she will return. Until then, you must rest."

Volmar's mind was racing. Thrusting his hands in his sleeves, he gripped his elbows in an effort to steady himself. Was Lady Jutta truly in the room or was the magistra feverish in her need for Lady Jutta's help? Why, then, had her "conversation" with Lady Jutta been so contentious and her demands on Lady Jutta so unyielding? And why, in God's name, was he privy to this? What could he do?

Hildegard tugged at his robe. "How did I come to be here?"

"Your daughters found you in a faint on the floor of the cloister."

"But Lady Jutta was here, I saw her, *I told her*..." She gulped back her tears.

"I believe you, my lady. I heard your words."

"My words?" Her stare defied him.

"You spoke of the Voice in your vision, the Voice in the midst of the Light."

"No! You heard nothing!" she screamed. "Nothing, swear to me!"

"My lady, listen well," he said firmly. "As Lady Jutta lay dying, she spoke to me of your visions and begged me to nurture your gift in every way. I swore to her that I would do what she asked of me, assuring her that I would honor her wish."

Hildegard recoiled as though he had slapped her.

"Her wish?" she flared. "And what of me? Now that I've been abandoned, are my wishes of no concern?"

"Abandoned, my lady?" Volmar sputtered. "Do you mean...," pausing, he glanced over his shoulder, "by disappearing as she did now?"

"And as she did the first time, when she left me without warning. I was alone, bereft, with no one who understood my visions, my secrets. I had no one but her." She began to sob. "She did not prepare me: she just left me behind."

Volmar prayed for the grace to calm her. "Forgive me, my lady. I never meant to offend, only to help."

"Never!" she turned her face away. "Leave me!" Jamming her fist against her lips, she twisted her knuckles until she spit out blood.

For twenty-one days, the magistra appeared to barely breathe. The nuns shivered when they bathed her, alarmed that her skin was like a thin veil on her body. She gagged on food, even refusing the honey-sweetened porridge prepared for her in the abbey kitchen. Finally, Hiltrude succeeded in feeding her crumbs of bread and sips of ale, but she still looked like a phantom. Day after day, she lay with her knees drawn up and her face to the wall.

"Where has our lady gone?" Gisla whispered as she blotted Hildegard's brow and wrists.

"And when will she come back to us?" Ilse whispered, giving voice to their greatest fear.

Outside, Volmar kept pacing in the courtyard. He was frantic. "Where is she now?" he kept wondering. "What does she see?" He dug his fingertips into his forehead; beneath them, his eyes burned with fatigue. How long would these visions imprison her? When would they end? Her moods exhausted him, her outbursts igniting like flames in midair. What would he say or do next that would enrage her? He was still reeling from her strange rebuke after the Mass at Michaelmas. For days afterward, she prowled about restlessly, snapping at every distraction, fasting mercilessly until she collapsed. What had he said then that had provoked such a tirade? And why did she resent his promise to Lady Jutta or accuse him of spying on her? The questions tormented him. He was sure that her faith in him had been shattered.

Unlatching the courtyard gate, he headed for the chapel. Only prayer could restore his sanity.

Hiltrude jumped when Hildegard's hand touched her. "Holy Communion," the magistra whispered hoarsely. "I will need it now."

When the message came, Volmar felt a burden slide from his shoulders. The magistra had finally asked for the one gift he longed to bring her. For weeks, she had refused the Host, so weak that she feared vomiting it. But Volmar suspected something more.

When he arrived at her bedside, the face on the pillow was so gaunt, it could have been mistaken for a death mask. The bones in the abbess' cheeks and chin seemed to pierce her skin. Sensing his presence, Hildegard turned her face to him, but her eyelids felt weighted with lead.

"My Lady Mother, I have brought you the Eucharist." His voice was a hush. "Do you wish to confess?"

Moistening her lips, she attempted to answer. "My friend, God has punished me with this sickness for refusing to write down what I hear and see in my visions." Her voice cracked. "The blood has dried in my veins, and the moisture has gone from my flesh and from the marrow of my bones." She groped in the air to find his hand. "Before God, I confess my sins of arrogance and disobedience and accept my penance."

Absolving her, he placed the Host on her lips.

"For your penance, my lady, you must embrace your terror. Only then can you obey the command to write what you hear and see."

Her moan chilled him. "Dare I?" she whispered.

"I will be at your side, my lady. I will never abandon you." The words gushed from the monk as at the same time his heart swelled and apprehension seized him. He would do anything to keep his word — he would even brave his own vow of chastity for her sake.

Abbot Kuno straightened his shoulders and brushed off his robe as he hurried up the steps to the chapel. He was out of breath, as much from haste as from excitement. The trio of guests had arrived: Margravine von Stade, accompanied by her son Hartwig, and her daughter Richardis. The latter had come to join the monastery, and the abbot was intent on welcoming the three of them before they met with the magistra.

As he peered in the chapel, he saw their bowed heads at the altar where the relics of Blessed Jutta were interred. The family was in mourning following the death of the margravine's oldest son, Rudolph II. Since he left no heirs himself, doubts were raised as to who should inherit the vast Stade holdings, which stretched from the lower Weser to the Eider in northern Germany. Rudolph's sister Luitgard would be a logical choice. After divorcing King Eric Lam III of Denmark, she had married Count Palatine Frederick of Sommerschenburg. Her holdings now reached far beyond the Rhineland.

The prospects for expanding the Stade endowment from this new source excited Kuno as he glimpsed the remaining heirs walking toward him.

Hartwig, the margravine's son, was the current cathedral provost in Bremen. He was a lean man in his thirties; his pale skin and auburn hair identified him as a Sponheim, though the hair around his tonsure was thinning and his beard was scant. His flitting glance betrayed the kind of wariness that expected trouble. Next to him, his youngest sister, Richardis, was like a sunbeam beside a cloud. Her mother's namesake, she was endowed with thick flaxen hair that fell in waves to her slender waist. Her blue eyes were searching and curious. But Kuno's hope that her ready smile implied naïveté was quickly dispelled by the confidence of her willowy stride and her unblinking stare.

After greeting the margravine effusively, Kuno turned at last to Richardis. "On behalf of the Abbey of Mount Saint Disibod, I welcome you," Kuno assured her, aware that the young woman's eyes were narrowing. He smiled and went on: "We are delighted that you will be continuing the Sponheim legacy here at Mount Saint Disibod, an illustrious one that Lady Jutta inspired and Sister Hiltrude nourishes."

"But one we must credit to our illustrious great uncle, Count Stefan, who endowed the hermitage for Lady Jutta," Richardis replied, smiling thinly.

"Indeed," Kuno nodded, "a date that the abbey commemorates each year with a Mass of thanksgiving on the anniversary of his death."

"I have yet to attend," Hartwig announced crisply. "But I shall make every effort to do so now that my sister has chosen to be vowed to this community."

Richardis stepped forward. "I am anxious to meet the lady magistra of Mount Saint Disibod," she said abruptly. "Where may I find her?"

Kuno cleared his throat and pointed to the women's monastery, feeling strangely like a novice who had failed to respond at the first sound of the bell.

It was not until the margravine appeared with her children that Hildegard realized with a mild shock that she had never thought of her as a mother. An arresting presence, to be sure, but more like a crimson flame casting a glow than a woman who put a child to her breast.

Bowing low, Richardis rose slowly from her curtsy. "Am I truly entering the gates of Paradise, my lady?" Her gaze was direct, her face radiant.

Hildegard settled back in her chair, aware that a new set of wings was descending into the nest of the abbey. But these wings were strangely muffled and thicker. The sound of a swan.

"Paradise?" the magistra asked, smiling. "That will depend on what you bring inside these gates and who you become when they close behind you," she said. "There will be many surprises."

She is her mother's daughter, Hildegard thought. The folds of Richardis' cornflower blue dress fell softly over her body. She was only sixteen, but it was clear that she had inherited her mother's charm, and her words flowed with the same rippling eloquence.

"The notion that abbeys are inhabited by angels is quaint, if not amusing," Hartwig cautioned, thinking of the tensions at his cathedral house in Bremen.

"If not here, then where?" the margravine shrugged. "It is the reason our family has taken great care to safeguard the peace of this holy cloister."

"So I will be in Paradise after all," Richardis mused. "Will I find angels here?" she asked brightly.

"If your heart is humble," the magistra replied evenly, "but even the days and nights of angels are filled with work and prayer."

"I have prepared myself for both," the girl assured her, flinging a glance at her mother. "The decision to come here is mine alone."

Hartwig coughed noisily. "Even as a child, we saw my lady sister's hunger for knowledge. My lady mother and I are grateful that her appetite will be nourished here."

"But I did not choose a setting. I chose a teacher," Richardis was quick to clarify. "I did not choose an abbey. I chose Mount Saint Disibod because you were here, my Lady Hildegard. And I have much to learn from you."

Hildegard saw the margravine's graceful fingers clenching, releasing, her eyes shuttered with pain.

When in the glowing presence of her mother, Richardis was clearly a fresh light, bravely flaring. Yet Hildegard wondered how much of this new wick could survive trimming in the days ahead, and how brightly her flame would burn after stumbling night after night through the darkness to Matins.

Yet the words hung in the air: "I have much to learn from you." Looking at the creature of sunshine standing before her, Hildegard was filled with a sudden poignancy. This entrant was so self-assured, so elegant.

"Mother of God," she prayed. "Help this swan to find a nest here in this restless abbey of sparrows."

The carrel and stool had been placed beneath the single window to catch the slivers of daylight that filtered into the magistra's room. A second stool stood a short distance away. The sloping lectern was bare except for a small spray of apple blossoms that had been placed there, their fragrance the first soft protest against the musty months of winter.

Running her hands along the wood, Hildegard peered at the shelves where she had stored her stylus, wax tablets, and rolls of vellum. Above the lectern, the gallery held inkhorns and goose quills, a ruler to mark out the pages' margins, and a pumice stone to scrape the vellum.

All was in readiness. After a lifetime of secrecy and vigilance, she would open the floodgates and reveal her visions. The command had forced the decision on her. She had no choice.

Lady Jutta had accused her of arrogance in assuming the visions were destined for her eyes and ears alone. Yet at this moment, she longed to escape, to run, but to what safe place and to whom? Bracing herself, she leaned forward and wrapped her arms around the carrel.

"Help me to trust!" she implored the Virgin.

Outside her door, Volmar had also paused to pray, but his plea was to Lady Jutta: "Do not desert us, my lady!" Deep within, he understood that his promise to the magistra was fraught with peril. If something went wrong, the abbot would hold him responsible. In disclosing her visions, would she become like those seers whose visions had left them blind or speechless? And what if she lost her way in some shadowy labyrinth and could not return? Worse yet, as her scribe, what fate awaited him if he failed to record her words correctly?

Yet when he entered her room, his fears were submerged in hers.

"Why should others trust me?" she cried.

"Why did God trust you, my lady?" he replied, calmly. "The visions were given to you to be shared, not hoarded."

"You repeat Lady Jutta's words...." Yet he could feel that his confidence steadied her.

"If nothing else," she sighed, "I pray that, one day, your faith in my visions will be justified in the eyes of your abbot and brothers."

Volmar's heart sank. Her concerns were valid. As it was, the monks still deeply resented the nuns' presence. Brother Librarian, for one, was still grumbling, stoutly refusing the nuns' pleas to read his precious texts. "Let their rosaries suffice. They have no need of Augustine." Others joked about the nuns and mimicked them, while frail Brother Sacristan was still aghast when a nun strolled past him. "What are those women doing here?" he railed. "This is an abbey. They must leave at once!"

"How do you think my brothers will respond when they hear of your visions, my lady?" Volmar asked patiently.

"They will think I am mad or vain or prey to fantasies."

"There will be questions, of course," he granted. "And doubts. However, in time..."

"And will you defend me against your brothers' disdain, Father Volmar?" Her eyes flashed in a sudden panic.

"My lady, I would hardly have offered my help..."

"And your loyalty? Do you offer me that as well?" she demanded fiercely. "Otherwise, how can I open my soul to you? How can I trust you with things I see?"

"My lady, it saddens me that even as we begin, you have so little faith in me," Volmar groaned.

"You will stand with me against your brothers, then?"

The monk folded his arms, defending himself against the terror that was descending on her like an ominous cloud.

"Must you go to these lengths to test me?"

She tried to speak but a sudden quivering defeated her.

"I feel you are asking for my soul, my lady."

"No," she whispered. "My terror is that I am entrusting you with mine."

Volmar's body sagged with fatigue.

The abbess sat motionless on her stool, wax tablet and stylus in hand. As the time passed, Volmar quieted his thoughts with prayer, asking the Virgin to protect them lest any evil spirits invade the room. As the silence lengthened, the monk began to doze, only snapping awake when his quill clattered to the floor. As he stooped to retrieve it, he realized that the magistra was leaning forward, her jaw slack, her nostrils flaring.

He heard a soft moan, then a mumbling.

"What is it, my lady?" he ventured softly.

"The Light has come," she nodded thoughtfully. *"A Woman's Voice calls out to me, pointing to One who sits atop a mountain blazing with unbearable brightness. Soft shadows fall from its shoulders like great sweeping wings.*

"At the foot of the mountain, two Virtues gaze at me. One Virtue symbolizes Fear of the Lord, that awe and humility that are the beginning of Wisdom. Her human form is covered with dozens of eyes to aid her in her quest.

"The Woman's Voice explains to me that the second Virtue at the foot of the mountain symbolizes Poverty of Spirit, the first beatitude. Her form is that of a young girl wearing a pale tunic, but she streams with so much Light, her face is obscured.

"Now a waterfall of sparkling rays flows down from the One atop the mountain, bathing these Virtues with Light, as the faces of people appear, surrounded by stars."

Hildegard paused and strained forward as she steadied herself. "Listen well," she cautioned Volmar. She then continued:

"The Woman explains to me that the brightness that crowns the mountain is the Divinity issuing orders to the world, even as its soft, sweet wings protect it.

"Now the One on the mountain calls out to me, 'O humanity, you who are fragile like the dust of earth, cry out about the corruption that rises all around you. Condemn the indifference and carelessness of all who ignore that corruption and silence all warnings against it. O fragile human, become a fountain of abundance so that those who would revile you may be inspired by your flowing waters. Arise now and cry aloud all that has been revealed to you here by the power of the Divine.'"

Stillness.

Hildegard sat erect on her stool as a sigh spiraled through her. When she turned to Volmar, the monk felt a sudden chill. Her face had a feverish flush, and the violet in her eyes had darkened. Her wimple was matted to her forehead with sweat.

"Take care, my friend. We have entered into another realm now," she said softly.

Like stones cast in a pool of fathomless waters, her words rippled out, urging him to brave the undertow, knowing they could not turn back.

It had been six months since Richardis von Stade had become a novice at Mount Saint Disibod. Despite her efforts, she began harboring grave doubts about coming here. The worst time was at day's end, at Compline. Even as she chanted each antiphon and responsory, she found herself plotting ways to avoid the midnight stumble to chapel for Matins and Lauds.

She kept reminding herself that she had not been naive in coming here; she fully expected that her life would be turned upside down. There would be difficult moments, of course, like exchanging her fur-lined cloak for a dull black one and relinquishing her amber ring and her favorite girdle embroidered with scarlet blossoms and pearls.

What she was not prepared for was the daily dreariness: the ceaseless prayers and unyielding schedules and rules. Everything was so maddeningly predictable! Sometimes she wanted to stand up in chapel and scream. The hair cutting shocked her. She realized that the scraggly patches that were left would be hidden beneath a married woman's wimple. But unlike a wife, she would have no long hair to spill across the pillow at day's end as a feast for her husband's eyes. In the sewing room, she studied her sisters' faces. She wondered how many memories of curls and waves and braids still slumbered beneath their wimples, as their hair turned from gray to white. Then, the sudden truth: for the rest of her life, only her face and her hands would distinguish her from the others.

Yet one stubborn hope still clung. There had to be some way that she could challenge her mind and exalt her spirit here. There must be something that could dispel the feeling that she was disappearing. She must find it! She choked on the thought that she had fed too long on her mother's idyllic tales of this abbey. She was convinced now that her mother had come to believe that Mount Saint Disibod was her private domain, one over which she fancied herself presiding, as her daughter Luitgard had done as the queen of Denmark. Those tales seemed like a cruel joke now. Had her mother been deaf to the ferocious clangs of the blacksmith's anvil that always drowned out their voices at Lauds? Did she never cringe as she passed the muttered curses of tenant serfs, bent over beneath their tithes of grain and wood as they stood at the abbey gates? And what of the unceasing bells, cutting the days and nights into little pieces, disrupting dreams and snuffing sleep?

Lady Jutta's holiness was surely the spiritual elixir that had sustained her mother here, quenching her fears, soothing her sadness, sending her home renewed. Or had she only imagined her mother's tenderness on her return, her arms reaching for her as they curled up together beneath the soft fur on the big bed curtained with emerald velvet, memories now engraved on her soul.

It was in those moments that the mountain began to dominate her dreams, challenging her to plumb the secret of Lady Jutta's holiness. How could her silent life as an anchoress have brought her such fame? Intrigued, she began invoking her name, calling to her in every prayer. By her fifteenth year, she had made her decision.

"As a nun at Disibodenberg, I will be free and safe at last," she said boldly when she announced her decision.

"Free from what and safe from whom?" her mother had asked tersely. "There are no such places outside of heaven, not even at Disibodenberg."

"Then why did you always find a way to stay there for weeks at a time, year after year?"

"To be with Lady Jutta, of course, who remained unfailingly humble despite her fame. Because of her, the Sponheim name has spread far beyond the Rhineland. Since our roots flourish there, we must take care that our endowments are well spent. News at the abbot's table is invaluable, as well, and the guest list impressive. Guests from the royal court visit there in greater numbers now, and the library is one of the best in the Rhineland." She sighed longingly. "Yes, there was much to commend it."

"And after she died?"

"She reached out to me in far deeper ways through the faith-filled letters of her successor, the lady magistra Hildegard. Her gifts are exceptional. She also sees visions."

"If the abbey at Disibodenberg has brought such comfort and joy to you, why aren't you pleased that I've chosen to spend my life there?"

The margravine reached for her daughter's hand. "Why languish there when arrangements can proceed at once for a brilliant marriage of your choosing?"

"Was it Luitgard's choice to marry the king of Denmark?"

"She was . . . content. And it suited her temperament, so high-strung and excitable."

"Heightening your appetite, perhaps, for yet another crown to embellish the Stade pantheon?"

The mother shrugged off the question as she plucked a piece of lint from her daughter's sleeve.

"Heed me well, my Lady Daughter," she whispered, her eyes intense. "As I watched you grow, my heart swelled. Your appetite for life is matched only by your beauty. It glows like an opal's fire, burning beneath the surface. Men sense it. I see desire cloud their eyes when they glance at you. You must seize the moment. Wherever you look, the fruit is yours to pluck: lands stretching to the sea, dotted with castles, forests teeming with game. Nothing you ask would be denied. I am certain of it."

But inside, Richardis was screaming. She knew more than her mother imagined about the beckoning hunger in men's eyes. Often enough, growing up in the castle, she had sensed men's lust as their eyes undressed her. She saw, as well, the sweet, aching stares of the awkward young pages, gaping as they stumbled past her in the great hall. What's more, she had chanced on too many captive serving maids, moaning with pain in the shadows of castle ramparts or stifling their screams as they were flung on the straw in stinking stables. Then week by week, she had watched their slender bodies swelling, their young legs slowly purpling with veins until the day their screams blended with those of their newborn babes. Life held more promises for her — she was certain of it.

"Trust me," her mother had crooned, stroking her daughter's hand. "The monastery would be too insular a life for a spirit as vibrant as yours."

"Would you have uttered those words to Blessed Jutta as she lay dying?" the girl inquired, as she slowly withdrew her hands from her mother's clasp.

The margravine paled. In that instant, Richardis began composing a letter to her brother Hartwig in Bremen, requesting his aid on her behalf.

Looking back now, it seemed to Richardis that a decade had passed since that day she had ascended this mountain, breathing the air crisp with the fragrances of the forest, listening to the horses' hooves slipping on the rain-soaked autumn leaves.

And having come so far, it still came as a shock to learn that novices could not enter the library until they had taken their final vows as nuns, a full year away. She prayed for patience. Until then, she must content herself with embroidery, a skill that had soon become her favorite name for penance.

When the spring rains finally subsided, the first sunny days produced an epidemic of giddiness.

Hildegard saw it in the wandering eyes and restlessness as the chapter meeting droned on. Did Gertrud's downcast eyes mean that she was sleeping or only dreaming awake? What fantasy was Ilse indulging in as she wiggled her feet in her felt slippers? Did anyone remember what business had been conducted the last few days and what duties she had just assigned? And surely the abbot's visit today would provide yet another distraction.

Abbot Kuno entered the room, smiling broadly.

"My lady," he announced, "I bring you and your daughters warmest greetings from the Abbey of Cluny." His words were quickly rewarded with a loud hum of interest.

"It was my privilege to be a guest there for a fortnight," he enthused. "It is, of course, a most successful...and blessed enterprise. Indeed, I was impressed to learn that the abbey has recently extended its mission by installing four leper-houses in the countryside."

"But nothing less could be expected of Cluny," Hildegard replied, "with its thousands of monks and hundreds of abbeys. Would you not agree, Father Abbot?

"Indeed, my lady," he agreed loudly. "But I bring you news from Cluny that requires an even deeper generosity. The abbey risked sheltering an outcast who had been condemned for heresy by the Councils of Sens and Soissons. His books were burned, and the pope forbade him to teach and write. Accepting his fate, he wandered from place to place, until Abbot

Peter threw open the doors of his heart to shelter him and honor his greatness."

The nuns were astonished.

"Two days before I departed from Cluny, the abbot announced that this outcast had died, no doubt from a broken heart. His name was Peter Abelard. I come asking for your prayers that this brilliant scholar may not be forgotten."

Hildegard nodded. "What portion of his legacy would you have us remember, my lord?" she inquired.

"The heart of his teaching: that everything depends on the education of the conscience and on an inner conversion that flows from the purity of one's intentions rather than the number of one's good deeds."

Dangerous words for an abbot to repeat, Hildegard thought. Would he dare proclaim them to a benefactor whose land grants served as burial grounds for his sins?

"I beg your prayers for him," Kuno repeated earnestly.

"My Lord Abbot," a clear voice called from the back of the room, "may I ask that you would request prayers, as well, for his widow, Heloise, the mother of his son and now the cloistered prioress of the Paraclete? Her heart was also cleft in two when her husband accepted a monk's tonsure and she, the enclosure of a nunnery. Surely you recommend our prayers for her, as well."

"How could I not, Sister Richardis?"

"My Lord Abbot, is it possible that you agree as well with Abelard's teaching that since women's souls are more refined, they are more capable of greater intimacy with the Holy Spirit, and therefore, the 'New Man' of which Abelard wrote has much to learn from women?"

The abbot blanched. "My respect for women has always been reflected in my devotion to the Queen of Heaven, Sister Richardis!"

"And includes, I am certain," replied Richardis, "those women whom Peter Abelard called Christ's apostles, notably Mary Magdalene, whom Christ revered so much that he chose to appear to her first after his resurrection, remembering that she and the other women had not, like the men, abandoned him at the cross. Thus, Abelard would maintain, women are closer to Christ than men."

Kuno threw open his arms but remained silent.

Turning, he thanked Hildegard abruptly, his face flushed and his jaw grinding as he edged toward the door.

Volmar waited patiently outside Kuno's door.

Finally the prior appeared. "The abbot will see you now," he said. Lowering his voice, he winked and tapped his ledger. "He's in good spirits today. All the rents have been collected."

The abbot, his back turned when Volmar entered the room, called out his greeting over his shoulder. Volmar was grateful that the abbot was positioned across the room, thus decreasing the intimacy of the meeting. "Father Abbot, a matter has arisen that needs your sanction. It concerns the magistra."

Kuno spun around. "Well, what is it now?"

"While you were at Cluny," Volmar began, "she asked me to record a text, which she then dictated to me. At the time, it appeared to be a simple matter. It is clear now that the task will require a great deal more time. May I have your permission to continue assisting her?"

"How much time will it add to your duties as provost?"

"Two hours each day, Father Abbot."

"Two hours?" He drew back. "I think not! What task could possibly justify that much time?"

"Father Abbot, the abbess sees visions that she's been told to record."

"Visions!" he exclaimed. "What next?" He threw up his hands. "Surely you jest."

"I do not, my lord." The firmness in the monk's voice startled him.

"If you regard this as serious, what made you proceed without my permission?" the abbot growled.

"I felt it wise to test the claim before I dismissed it," Volmar said, as his hands fled to his sleeves.

"Are you saying that you have been persuaded?"

"Not yet." Volmar shook his head. "At times, the visions the magistra describes are so intense and shrouded in mystery, I fear she is overwhelmed by her senses. Yet, at other times, I feel the truth of them in the depths of my bones. The messages and images she relates could only come from God."

Volmar's anguished face gave Kuno pause. He turned his away. If he agreed to let Volmar continue and the visions proved false, he would be the laughingstock of the abbey. The benefactors would be embarrassed, and Blessed Jutta's reputation might dim. Yet if the visions were true, there would be revenues, pilgrims, benefactions....

"An abbot must remember to whom he must give an account of his stewardship," the Rule reminded him. More to the point, if the visions contained important messages, dare he risk stifling them?

When he turned back to look at Volmar, he saw his eyes were closed. Kuno knew his brother was praying: for courage, if the visions were true, and for mercy, if time proved them false. Can I do any less? Kuno thought.

"You may proceed," the abbot murmured. "But two conditions must be met. The content of the visions must be kept in the strictest confidence. And a nun must be present at all times to assist the abbess with any need that might arise." Stroking his beard, he added, "Advise the magistra that my choice would be Sister Richardis. The daily discipline would be good for her soul."

When Volmar related this discussion to Hildegard, she was furious.

"How dare he presume to interfere!" she shouted. "What's more, his choice of Richardis is preposterous. She's a novice! She's been here barely a year. Clearly, this is another ruse to sweeten the margravine's purse."

Volmar shrugged. "Then whom would you choose, my lady? Which of your daughters would bring the needed skills to the task?"

Hildegard frowned at his question. Why was he so sanguine about the abbot's suggestion? Couldn't he see that having a novice in such a position might prove disquieting? Granted, her duties would merely be those of a scribe, and Richardis' talents were obvious. Indeed, Hiltrude had noted her scrupulousness: "No sooner does she hear than she obeys," she had remarked about the novice. And Hiltrude claimed that Richardis always raced to chapel as though the bells were rung by God alone, even if she left the threads of her loom dangling and her copyist's quill in the inkpot.

"Her defense of Peter Abelard was impressive," Hildegard admitted aloud to Volmar, "and her challenge to father abbot was bold."

"A spirit as fiery as hers bores easily," Volmar added. "It will only be a matter of time before she seeks new challenges. The abbot's suggestion might prove wise, after all, my lady. A third set of eyes and ears and another keen mind would both enrich our work and challenge her talents."

"Then you would agree with the abbot's choice?"

The monk shrugged. "I would be willing to test it."

But *was* it a risk worth taking? Hildegard wondered. The girl's unbridled confidence both thrilled and disturbed her in ways she could not explain. When she glanced at Richardis in chapel, memories of her life at the window in the hermitage began to surface. How different it might have been if she had explored the same world that had given Richardis such confidence. Even when Richardis arrived, she approached the life at the abbey as a great adventure, one that she alone had chosen. How glorious to be so free and fearless! She could only imagine the wonders Richardis had already seen and heard and smelled and touched.

Dangerous thoughts.

Closing the monastery door behind her, Hiltrude feasted her eyes on the blossom-rich courtyard. Outside the wall, the apple trees swayed in the breeze like masses of billowing lace, and their fragrance caressed her. Sinking to the ground, she closed her eyes, feeling the coolness of the stone wall on her back, surprised to feel tears rolling down her cheeks.

Since becoming prioress, blissful moments like this were rare. Hildegard's pace was daunting, the demands consuming them both from Matins to Compline. The weeks whirled past as Advent flowed into Christmas and Lent into Pentecost. Even on days like this, when the magistra was ill with a pounding headache, she conducted business from her sickbed. No detail escaped her. Yesterday, she had inquired repeatedly about Richardis' progress: Was the novice performing her duties willingly and without grumbling? Was she humble among her sisters, careful not to exalt herself in any way? And most importantly, did she pray the Divine Office reverently?

"Yes, on every count, my lady," Hiltrude had assured her. "And she has endeared herself to the sisters by her readiness to help when they find themselves in need."

"Thank God," the abbess had replied, patting Hiltrude's hand in gratitude. The gesture had touched Hiltrude. Since Hildegard had become magistra, there had been few such moments. But Hiltrude never doubted their mutual devotion, especially as the burdens increased and Hildegard came to depend on her even more.

But this past year, she had sensed that something had changed. The magistra appeared distracted, often looking past her when she spoke. Is this why yesterday's casual gesture brought tears to her eyes? For a moment, she was back with her dearest friend again, hugging trees in the orchard. Why did she cling so fiercely to those memories? Was it because life was so simple then?

A flurry of soft breezes lifted her veil. She straightened up. The bells for Sext would be ringing soon. As she reached for her basket, the courtyard gate clanged. Looking up, she saw Richardis.

"The magistra sent word that she wanted to meet with me," Richardis said, breathlessly. "I ran all the way from the cloister."

"But she's unwell today," Hiltrude said. "Has some urgency arisen?"

"If so, I was not told." Pausing, she looked at Hiltrude directly. "But in truth, I care only that she asked to see me." Swallowing, she added plaintively, "In the year I've been here, this is only the second time."

What could it be? Hiltrude wondered. Recalling the magistra's queries about Richardis earlier, Hiltrude felt a knot twist in her stomach.

"This is an honor indeed, my lady," Richardis gasped.

But the eyes that looked back from the mound of pillows were unsmiling.

"Before you begin," Hildegard said, "you must know that many things will occur that you will struggle to understand but must not question. The work that stretches before us is endless. Your patience each day will be sorely tested."

"Yes, my lady." The words blurred in her ears. Her heart was fluttering.

"We will work two hours each day; the task will...unfold."

"So I might be better prepared, may I ask the nature of the task, my lady?"

"If you were not already prepared, I would not have chosen you," the abbess replied crisply. "The work will be simple. Father Volmar will record my words, and you will assist him. No more than that."

Why wasn't this task assigned to me in chapter? Richardis wondered. And why is she so elusive?

"One thing more," the magistra declared. "You may not discuss the nature of this work with anyone at any time. Do you understand?"

"I do, my lady."

Lifting her chin, she peered at the girl through half-closed eyes. "Have you any questions?"

"Only one, my Lady Mother. There are so many here whom you know so well and trust dearly. Why did you choose me?"

"Because I believe you can carry the burden."

Richardis drew back, surprised. "Those were the words she spoke yesterday."

"She?"

"A village crone with snow-white hair. Brother Porter said she appeared at the abbey gates and told him that unless he fetched me, his soul was in jeopardy. When I arrived, she studied me carefully. Her eyes were like blue pearls."

"I have heard of her," Hildegard whispered, subdued. "Some swear that she is one of the far-seeing."

"She made me promise to give you this," Richardis said, opening her hand to reveal a small object wrapped in gray wool. "And she bid me tell you not to fear, for you can carry the burden."

Hildegard's hand shook as she parted the wool. Inside she saw a small round stone, shimmering with moss.

The effects of the foehn had been devastating. The humid, southern alpine winds had spread sickness throughout the Rhineland. The infirmary beds, normally filled with nuns taking their turn at bloodletting and purgation, were filled instead by those complaining of that strange weakness that the foehn produced.

As she bent over Ilse's sickbed, Hildegard closed her eyes and seemed to be listening.

"Take heart; your lungs are clearer now. You'll soon be back at your post of chantress again."

"But not tomorrow," Ilse whimpered.

"I know. After rehearsing for weeks, you'll miss tomorrow's dedication of the Mary chapel. But Richardis has assured me that the choir is superbly prepared."

"Richardis is generous, as always," Ilse replied, nodding.

"Sleep now," Hildegard whispered. "I am certain that in your absence the Virgin will hover over your stall tomorrow and bless all the work you've done in preparing the sisters for the ceremony."

"But Richardis must come and report to me the moment it's over," she pleaded. "Only her words can reassure me."

As she closed the infirmary door behind her, Hildegard paused. *Only her words.* Another compliment for Richardis, who had persuaded her sisters to forfeit their midday rest to rehearse for the dedication. Even now, Hildegard heard the voices chanting her "Responsory for the Virgin," the notes floating toward her on the warm spring air:

Priceless integrity,
Her virgin gate opened to none. But the Holy One
flooded her with warmth
until a flower sprang in her womb,
and the Son of God came forth
from her secret chamber like the dawn.

Sweet as the buds of spring, her
son opened Paradise
from the cloister of her womb. . . .

Hildegard recalled how Richardis had wept when she first heard the chant and had knelt impulsively to kiss her hand. Though a year had passed since that scene, Hildegard was still taken aback at the ease with which the girl expressed her feelings. Another luxury she had never known.

The next day, the sky was bruised with slate-blue clouds while mist hung in the air like uncertain tears.

After Terce, the procession for the chapel dedication began its journey through the chilly cloister, as the tap of the prelates' staffs accompanied the rustling of silks. Kuno was last in line. Again and again, he glanced down at the elaborate gold reliquary he was carrying, its four corners guarded by winged lions, its rim bordered with doves. Each beak flashed with a sparkling diamond. The reliquary contained Lady Jutta's mortal remains, which were being transferred today from the crypt in the abbey chapter house to the altar of the new chapel, where they would remain on display.

The relics crowned Kuno's cherished dreams for a Mary chapel, a promise he had made when he became abbot and pledged his life to the Virgin. Since then, devotion to Mary had swept over the land like spiritual wildfire. Today he could finally rest, knowing that this chapel joined with every church in Christendom bearing Mary's image on its tympanum.

From her chair in the oratory, Hildegard searched among the prelates for Lady Jutta's brother, Hugo von Sponheim, the archbishop of Cologne. Looming above the others, his craggy face looked like it had been quarried, yet his eyes were full of fire. His nephew Hartwig stood at his side, his smile more relaxed since he had become archbishop of Bremen.

Finally, Hildegard's eyes returned to Richardis, her face dappled with freckles, her lithe body alert, her eyes busily exploring the exquisite new reredos. The carved altar screen had been commissioned by her mother as a gift to the abbey and was lavished with an elaboration of lilies to symbolize the Virgin's purity.

A sweep of whispers. Turning, Hildegard was surprised to see His Grace, Lord Henry Moguntin. Because he had earlier sent regrets, they had not expected him. Mounting the steps, he greeted the abbot with a nod and turned to address the assembly.

A year had passed since she had seen him. His face looked tired, and he appeared much thinner, but he still was a striking presence. His sapphire cape, bordered in marten, matched his blue eyes.

Seeing him now, Hildegard blushed at her memory of Michaelmas and the runaway thoughts and unfamiliar sensations that had flooded over her. Since then, those sensations had been quenched by disturbing reports of the archbishop's mercurial behavior, forcing her to accept that his ardent interest in her antiphons was social chatter, nothing more. She swallowed when she saw his brows arch at the sight of the margravine, but she was determined not to be taken in again. No. She was wiser now.

Extending his arms, Henry greeted the congregation: "As we begin this dedication," he said, "I beseech Lady Jutta to bless the life and work of her successor, the lady magistra Hildegard, whom she cherished as a daughter."

Unbidden, Hildegard rose and walked to the altar, placing herself serenely between the abbot and the archbishop, undeterred by Kuno's gasp and Henry's surprise. Raising her hands with theirs above the reliquary, she blessed the dust that was once Lady Jutta's heart.

Later, she would tell Volmar that she did not remember joining them. She remembered only that a cold wind had swept over her and lifted her to her feet.

The air in the reception hall was heavy with the scents of saffron and mustard, while whiffs of garlic and pepper rose from the platters of geese and venison being delivered by the novices for the feast following the dedication.

"You must invite the venerable Bernard to bless your Mary chapel soon, Father Abbot," Archbishop Hugo advised Kuno as they settled into their places.

"You flatter me," Kuno demurred. "Of late, he is far more likely to be at the court of King Louis VII. Indeed, the king was at Bernard's side when he sounded the pope's call for a Second Crusade at Vézelay on Palm Sunday."

"Queen Eleanor of Aquitaine and her nobles have taken up the cross without hesitation...," the margravine added.

"The Rhineland will follow," Hugo thundered. "Our King Conrad has already been moved by Bernard's call, which now resounds within our borders."

The news was sobering. As landowners of vast estates, the guests flinched, recalling bitter tales of the First Crusade, when swarms of serfs in other parts of Europe had answered the call, leaving countless harvests behind to rot in the fields. Now that the Seljuk Turks had captured Odessa, the Holy Land was in danger again. But this Second Crusade, unlike the First, would not pass the Rhineland by.

Glancing up to gauge Hildegard's reaction, Volmar was alarmed to see her fingertips grasping the edge of the table, her knuckles white with strain. Her eyes had the same stare he had come to know so well in the scriptorium. For a moment, he panicked.

Mercifully, the moment passed unnoticed.

But as the monk would later learn, it was in that moment that Hildegard was shown, in a downpour of Light, what she must do.

For the next few days, Hildegard wrestled with her plan. Should she risk sharing it with her two assistants? What if they tried to discourage her?

Richardis, she was certain, would not. She thrived on excitement, creating it at every turn. She waited on her like a maidservant, filling her needs with dispatch. When they began their work each day, every quill was sharpened, every sheet of vellum scraped and smoothed with chalk. Her keen mind and diligence reassured Hildegard at every turn.

Volmar might balk at her plan. Thoughtful and quiet, he was like a sheltering tree. His attention rarely faltered, nor did his interest dim. But would her provost's loyalty falter at this decision? Would he argue that her plan was audacious?

When she began her dictation, Volmar's eyes never left the page.

To Bernard, the Abbot of Clairvaux, from Hildegard, Magistra of Disibodenberg:

As you wave your banner bearing the holy cross of the Crusade, in the name of the living God who strengthens you, I beg you to hear me!

Since my childhood, the spirit of God has flooded me with great wonders to inform my belief. Yet, because I dared not speak of these wonders, they lie like a weight on my soul.

In my visions, a Light illumines my heart and soul, enabling me to comprehend in an instant the inner meanings contained in Holy Writ. Yet though this knowledge resides in my soul, I withhold it, for I am not a scholar and can only read in a simple way.

I have only shared my visions with a certain monk and a young nun who consider my visions trustworthy. But knowing of your holiness, I reach out to you for consolation.

Long ago, I saw you in a vision as a man looking fearlessly at the sun. Seeing your bravery, I wept, longing for your courage to speak, for the visions I do see fill me with torments. My silence has confined me to my bed and subjected me to terrible sufferings. At times, my despair takes the shape of a gnarled and twisted tree.

By the sacred sound of Creation with which every creature re-sounds, I entrust my soul to you and beg your counsel. Should I share these things that press like a weight on my soul? Help me, so I may know God's will.

Hildegard slumped in her chair, and, burying her face in her hands, she began sobbing.

"God be with you, my lady," Volmar whispered softly. Richardis slipped from her stool and crouched at her mistress' feet, her eyes glittering.

"The time has come for the abbot of Clairvaux to honor the magistra of Disibodenberg!" she announced with a certainty that Hildegard both feared and longed to embrace.

The mountain still shivered beneath the chills of an uncertain spring as Lent descended with its baptism of ashes and forty days of penance. The refectory was filled with bottomless yawns and groaning stomachs. Glancing at the somber faces, Hiltrude knew which of her sisters shared her dread of the weeks ahead with their daily portions of porridge, made from mashed turnips and peas. The season's solemnity had settled in, as though the air was draped with mazes of gray gauze.

"If I hadn't learned to convince myself that Lenten fish was roasted chicken," Gertrud had once grunted, "I would have starved to death the first year." Though she smiled at the memory, Hiltrude also sighed; she missed those moments. As prioress, she knew now that her sisters feared she would hear those quips as complaints. In a way, they were right. She now noted who was tardy for meals or who dozed at Matins or who complained too often of illness. Now, at her approach, conversations drifted and eyes strayed. Lent merely stretched the threads of a tapestry whose edges were already frayed.

Yet, as Hiltrude prepared for her monthly confession, it was not her sisters' whispers that burdened her but a shadow that had fallen across her heart.

"I confess to the sin of envy, Father Volmar." Her spine felt like a coiled spring, and her legs were quivering.

"Whom do you envy, my daughter?"

"Sister Richardis, who is under my charge."

The same words of her last two confessions. "Have you prayed for the grace to overcome this weakness?"

"Daily, hourly, since my sin is deepened by the fact that Sister Richardis shows only kindness and obedience to me."

"What is it about your sister that you envy?"

A deep sigh. "She seeks nothing, no one, yet everything flows to her. The sisters are mesmerized by her knowledge of Scripture and intrigued by the songs she learned from the minnesingers in Sponheim. Even in chapel, the nuns' eyes rest on her with such devotion, it is as though she invented prayer."

"Your words describe a saint, Sister Hiltrude."

"Who better to be privy to the magistra's innermost thoughts each day in the scriptorium?" she stuttered. "Besides you, of course, Father Volmar."

"Yet, as prioress," he replied, "it is to you that Mother Hildegard has entrusted the office of greatest trust: care of the household. You must approve of the chantress' music schedule and the sacristan's requests. The cellarer plants no seed in the garden nor orders ale from the abbey without your knowledge. And since you assign the tasks, no one meets with the sisters more than you." Pausing, he asked gently, "Is this not true?"

"Yet no matter how many people I speak to each day, I feel alone."

"Is it because your thoughts and feelings hover over the scriptorium?"

She stifled a cry. "Why wasn't I chosen to work at Mother's side rather than one so young and newly entered here?"

"My daughter, the Rule asks us not to understand but to obey."

"Then I confess to the sin of pride as well," she whispered, resigned, defeated. "And I will pray for the grace of humility."

"As will I, my daughter," Volmar said, blessing her, as he ached with the same questions. As she left, he was heartsick that, as her confessor, he could repeat none of her words to Hildegard.

The abbot of Disibodenberg was exhausted. As he lay down to rest after the midday meal, he groaned at the knock on his door.

When Volmar entered the room, his brow was glistening with sweat. "It all happened so fast, my Lord Abbot," he gulped, waving the scroll in his hand. "They came and went before there was time to summon you."

"Calm yourself, Brother Volmar," Kuno said. "What are you talking about?"

"Brother Porter said that it was just after None when the two white-robed monks appeared to deliver a message to Lady Hildegard."

"And?" Kuno asked wearily, folding his arms.

"Sister Richardis and I were in the room when the magistra received them and was presented with a vellum scroll whose seal was unknown to me. After she thanked them, they knelt to receive her blessing, then begged her leave and were gone."

"And all was well?"

Volmar blinked in surprise. "But of course, my lord!"

"Then why are you in such a state of alarm?" he asked testily.

The monk appeared confused. "Alarm, my lord?"

Kuno cleared his throat. "Brother Volmar, I respect your regard for the magistra, but the messages she receives do not concern me."

"With all due respect, Father Abbot, she felt she would be remiss if she withheld this one," the monk said, handing him the scroll.

To his beloved daughter in Christ, Hildegard, magistra of Disibo-denberg, from Brother Bernard, called Abbot of Clairvaux:

A multitude of tasks has delayed my reply to your generous letter and I regret that these words are more brief than I would wish.

We salute the Grace of God which is in you. Respond to it with all possible humility and devotion, knowing that God rejects the proud and gives grace to the humble.

As for our counsel, my daughter, since you have been anointed with inner learning, what more can we teach or advise you? Rather, we humbly request that you remember us before God and all who are joined with us in spiritual fellowship.

A stiff November wind skidded over the Moselle River as shafts of sunlight turned the icy surface into frozen silver.

Archbishop Henry Moguntin of Mainz, riding along the shore, patted his straining stallion as foam streamed from its jaws. The journey from Mainz would soon be over, and there would be time to rest in Trier before the bishops' synod began.

Though his neck was stiff from twisting against the wind, deep within, he purred with delight. *I had only to wait and, in time, the opportunity fell in my lap, as I knew it would,* he thought, smiling.

Waiting was a game Henry had learned early in childhood. Crowned with a tousle of white-gold curls above a cherubic face, he had had a shy smile that proved irresistible. Even the grizzled falconer succumbed, slipping his time-worn glove on Henry's young hand, then guiding it to the perch of the lord's prize peregrine, aware that he risked death to please the lad. The knights risked no less, letting him brandish the kind of razor-edged javelin that would give even a grown man pause. And when the knights sat sprawled before the fire in the great hall, they let the boy creep into their circle as they drained their cups and boasted of rapes and sword-thrusts.

As he grew, Henry quickly learned to go to the women first: the serving maids, their breath warm on his neck as they pressed him into the softness of their hips and bellies, tweaking his cheeks, rewarded with his boyish kisses. And always, his mother, caressing the golden stubble of his sprouting beard while marveling at his broadening shoulders. "My golden son, my firstborn," she crooned to him. He learned well that he need only wait and the world would come to him, his path lit with stars.

Ahead, the steeples of the cathedral of Trier came into view as Sigmund, his chancellor, waved him on. Henry fastened his glance on Sigmund, who sat astride his mount, his shoulders hunched like a hawk, his blue eyes scanning the landscape, his sharply beaked nose jutting from his face. His curly black beard and hair provided a smoldering contrast to Henry's fair-skinned coloring. But Henry prized him far beyond his swarthy looks and agile mind. His preparations for this trip had been impeccable. No detail had been left to chance. Watching him now, Henry felt a rush of excitement. They were inseparable, each accepting the other's strengths and weakness, needing no words. Sigmund knew both the risks and rewards, and Henry did not disappoint him.

Nearing the city, Henry recalled time-worn tales of Celtic tribes who lived here before time began, followed by the mighty Romans: Julius Caesar, Caesar Augustus, then Constantine.

The footsteps of giants are all around me, Henry mused, and the opportunity awaits me here. I cannot fail.

Passing through Trier's city gates, they headed for the huge cathedral. Around them, throngs of pilgrims pushed and shoved, having waited all night to enter and view the priceless relic reputed to be the seamless coat of the Savior. But Henry and Sigmund hurried on.

Almost a year had passed since Kuno had informed Archbishop Henry of Lady Hildegard's visions. It had been during one of the prelate's official visits to Mount Saint Disibodenberg. Kuno had been tense, both delighted and frightened that they were dealing with something momentous. Henry had been bored. Kuno had begun by mentioning that Hildegard had had visions since childhood.

"Visions since childhood, my Lord Abbot?" Henry had chided Kuno.

"So she claims, Your Grace," Kuno had replied. "Like Father Volmar, I tended to dismiss them as the pious fantasies of a child recluse. I instructed him to tell no one but assigned him to record the visions as the magistra dictated them, assisted by Sister Richardis."

Henry's lips had slid into a smile as he said to Kuno: "A clever choice, my lord. The margravine will applaud, of course."

"No harm can come from it," Kuno had shrugged.

"Was it trust or indulgence, then, that informed your consent?" Henry had murmured, stooping to pluck a sprig of mint from the garden.

"It was a simple choice, Your Grace. Had I denied her, and her visions proved to be inspired, it would be my soul's burden. I choose to believe that good will come from it."

"On what grounds?"

"Brother Volmar's counsel. He has been privy to her visions for a year now and has subjected them to careful discernment. He is a prayerful man and cautious, and he has been exemplary as a monastery provost. Like the brothers, I hold him in great esteem."

"And is Lady Richardis held in the same high regard by her sisters?"

"In some ways she has emerged as one of their teachers. As the magistra has learned, she arrived well versed not only in Holy Scripture but also in the writings of Clement of Alexandria and the Venerable Bede."

"Indeed," Henry had replied tonelessly. "But the magistra's visions are of more interest to me, as is her provost's belief in them."

"He swears that he would put his hand to the fire regarding their veracity."

"Charred limbs will do us little good, my Lord Abbot," Henry had grimaced. "The Church would need more proof than that."

"Surely the approval of the abbot of Clairvaux should suffice," Kuno had replied, with a note of triumph. "Bernard has written, encouraging her and begging her prayers."

"But of course!" Henry had retorted. "Bernard is borne aloft on the prayers he begs from all who encounter him. His humility, I'm told, is twin only to his passion." Clasping his hands behind his back, he had yawned noisily. They had continued their stroll in silence, to Kuno's growing dismay.

"I will not be joining you at Compline," Henry had said abruptly, stifling a second yawn. "I must rest now. I'm expected at the Abbey of Eberbach on the morrow and must ride at dusk."

Bidding Kuno farewell, Henry had turned toward the guest house, quickening his step in his eagerness to exploit the riches of the treasure chest that Kuno had just placed in his hands.

Remembering his first contemplation of that trove a year earlier in that guest house, Henry now neared the cathedral of Trier.

As the prelates from Belgium and France and Burgundy began to assemble for the Synod of Trier, all glanced up at the three-storied dwelling newly built to house the papal court. It was early, and Henry's head was pounding from last night's wine and the sound of church bells thundering from every tower in Trier.

Seeing his peers from Magdeburg chatting heatedly, Henry joined them, noting how quickly their discussion dissolved into grins tinged with bemused respect.

"My lords, we must advise the archbishop of Trier to begin the procession now that the great Diocese of Mainz is represented," the chancellor of Magdeburg quipped.

Damn them! Henry thought, fuming. They pat me on both back and head.

Henry dozed through most of the synod's opening session. At its conclusion, he quickly muttered to Sigmund, "We must seize the moment and proceed at once with our urgent business now at the papal reception."

The huge room was stifling and so densely packed they could barely move; shouts and laughter drowned out any hope of being heard. All had come to pay their respects to the pope, and the guests jostled shamelessly to reach the ear of the papal legate, hoping to gain a private audience with the pontiff.

"Be mindful that, as archbishop of Mainz, I come here as the lord of my land with all its privileges," Henry reminded his chancellor. "Remember that without our support, the pope is powerless."

He kept thinking of that boast as he attempted to navigate through the whirlpool of languages and the touch and smell of political power, with its sweet seductions. Sigmund, too, reacted strongly.

"Take care, my lord! Remember that you have come here to seek one face and to kiss one hand," Sigmund reminded him sternly. "Remember our plan."

"Where is he?" he hissed in Sigmund's ear.

"There, my lord, straight ahead," Sigmund whispered.

Were it not for the drape of white silk above the dais, Henry might have passed by the man he had come to see. Clothed in the simple robes of a Cistercian monk, Pope Eugenius III sat staring out from his massive oak throne, eyes watery with fatigue. His long, pointed nose seemed out of place in his full face and triple chin. His curly black beard and hair were dusted with strands of silver. He was barrel-chested, his belly spilling over the sides of his throne, hiding all but a glimpse of the magenta cushions surrounding him. Wedged in his chair, he shifted with the anguish of a man imprisoned.

Looking up, Henry saw the chancellor of Trier motioning to him as he stepped down from the dais.

"By your leave, Your Grace," the chancellor said to Henry, "my lord Alberon, your host, wishes to present you to His Holiness, Pope Eugenius."

A trail of curious glances followed them. As they neared the papal throne, the bystanders stirred, then scattered like a flock of birds.

- PART TWO -

Pope Eugenius' face was gray with exhaustion. He had just come from Paris where a council had been convened to discuss the erroneous teachings of Gilbert De la Porrée, the bishop of Poitiers.

As he knelt at Eugenius' feet, Henry noted that the pontiff wore only a simple gold ring, devoid of the customary jewel.

"Our blessing on the Diocese of Mainz, my son. Conrad, your king, remains in our prayers," the pope said soberly. Henry tensed, aware of the pope's deep disappointment at King Conrad's choice to go on Crusade rather than to aid him in his papal struggles against the Roman rebels and Roger II of Sicily. Looking up, he saw the pope's eyes narrow.

"We have been advised of unusual news you bring that might prove of interest to our reign, my son."

Caught offguard, Henry blanched.

"Your Holiness, with all due respect, I request permission to discuss this matter with you privately," he replied.

But the pope only gestured to him to move closer. He had no choice.

"Your Holiness," Henry began softly, "I have been informed by the abbot of Mount Saint Disibod in the Nahe Valley that a magistra dwells there whom God appears to have blessed with extraordinary visions that enable her to prophesy."

The pope sighed, then smiled. "Visions are not uncommon among cloistered women," he said patiently. "I trust she shares what she sees with her confessor."

"Indeed, Your Holiness, and it was he, in turn, who convinced his abbot that the visions were truly inspired."

"She is in ecstasy, no doubt."

"No indeed, your holiness. She is in full possession of her senses, and she dictates the words and the images in obedience to a Voice that commands her to reveal what she hears and sees."

"And the nature of these visions?"

"She is able to see backward in time to the first creation and forward to the present and future, including the last days."

"Ours is an age of visions, is it not, my son?" The pope seemed resigned. "One can seek and find them in ordinary places as reminders that God has not forsaken us."

He humors me, Henry thought.

Shifting in his chair, the pope signaled to his cardinal secretary that the audience had ended.

Steadying himself, Henry leaned forward to kiss the papal ring, then rose and retreated, soon disappearing into the crimson sea of prelates that ebbed and flowed around the papal throne.

Within moments, Eugenius summoned his cardinal secretary. "Instruct Bishop Albero of Verdun that we wish him to assemble a commission to meet with this magistra and question her. See to it that they depart in haste and return without delay."

The travelers from Trier peered through the morning mist at the cluster of buildings. "The Abbey of Disibodenberg appears modest, at best," Bishop Albero reported. Jerking on his reins, he halted his stallion. "I am certain we will make quick work of this and turn back toward Trier at dusk."

Behind him, the red-eyed grooms whistled softly, their limbs still wobbling from the punishing journey. Even the bishop's deputy had swayed in his saddle as he struggled to stay awake.

"You seem surprised that Henry Moguntin chose the synod to reveal the news of his far-seeing abbess," the deputy had probed as they pushed through the freezing forest.

"More amused than surprised, since news of this nun has been drifting to France for some time," the bishop countered. "But considering the speed with which the pope dispatched us, it's clear that whatever Henry whispered in the pontiff's ear intrigued him."

"Henry's luck never ceases to amaze me," the deputy sighed. "Even blindfolded, he can turn straw into gold. It falls at his feet, unbidden, time after time."

The bishop shrugged. "But if one depends solely on luck, one can grow careless. Fool's gold shines just as brightly in the moonlight as it does in the noonday sun."

"Not, it appears, for Henry Moguntin."

"Would you change places, then, with this deft alchemist from Mainz?"

The deputy hooted. "You jest, Your Grace! I've ghosts enough of my own, God knows!"

As Kuno stood at the women's door, his cough threatened to strangle him.

"I must see the magistra at once," he sputtered to Hiltrude. "Where can I find her?"

"She is in her room, Father Abbot," the prioress assured him. Hiltrude had never seen him so distressed.

Hildegard looked up from her ledger to see Kuno's eyes bulge as he thrust his hands in his sleeves.

His nod was curt. "My lady, I came to prepare you to receive some distinguished visitors. They are delegates from the bishop's synod now in session in Trier. It appears that His Holiness commissioned them to question you," he coughed again, "regarding the nature of your visions."

Hildegard looked away. "And how would His Holiness know of my visions, Father Abbot?"

"From His Grace, Archbishop Henry, I suspect," Kuno sighed. "You will recall that, as abbot, I am compelled to inform my bishop of any matters concerning the unusual spiritual life of those in my charge." Coughing again, he added, "Especially matters that might cause him concern."

"Or subject you to embarrassment," Hildegard said, lifting her chin.

"It is a risk I took after conferring with Father Volmar," he sniffed.

"And since all appears to be in order, you have nothing to fear," she concluded.

He turned his back to her.

"Yet you still appear troubled, my lord."

"I had no warning!" he shouted. "Visits by papal delegations are extremely rare!"

"I shall do my best not to disappoint you," she said softly.

"Your best?" he frowned, then reddened. Then blessing her quickly, he dashed from the room.

Soon after, Richardis ushered the visitors into the room and seated them. She lingered, clearly loathe to close the door on such a momentous spectacle.

Hildegard rose to greet her guests, her smile quickly closing the distance between them, her violet eyes fathomless beneath her honey-gold brows and lashes. She is in midlife yet has the blush of a maiden, the bishop noted. But there was something else: a quality he could not name but found disarming. Beneath her amazing eyes, he saw the dark gray circles. She prays more than she sleeps, he surmised. Graceful and tall, she seemed ageless. She carried herself with the natural grandeur of a highborn woman, her slender waist defined by her cincture, a symbol of purity, its sturdy knot like a small, determined fist. Her breath came quickly.

"I bid you welcome, my lords," she said. There was a hush in her voice that made the bishop feel awkward. He regretted that he not taken more care to refresh himself before meeting with her.

Easing into his chair, he heard his deputy thanking the abbess for receiving them.

"We bring you greetings from His Holiness, Pope Eugenius, and the synod of bishops," the bishop declared, adding, "and greetings from your archbishop, Lord Henry Moguntin, whose news of your visions sent us hurrying here."

"I am honored, Your Grace." Her gaze was serene. "What is it that you wish to know?"

"We are told that you see certain things in your visions and receive certain messages..., instructions, if you will," the bishop began.

"Indeed. Though what I receive, I never seek." Her eyes became clouded with a puzzling sadness. "What comes to me is from another realm, bathed in Light."

"As from a candle flame?"

"More like a glow, Your Grace. Though it dims at times, it always shimmers when I am meant to see or hear a Voice or view an image."

"Does it glow both day and night?"

"Indeed. It has attended me for as long as I can remember."

"So you are not surprised or blinded by this Light, my lady?"

"On occasion. But more often by what is revealed to me within it."

"Do these revelations come during prayer?"

"If prayer is listening."

"Or ecstasy, perchance?"

"Never!" Her eyes flashed. "I have no time to swoon. My days are filled with work and prayer. My visions come when they will. Once, it was in the herbarium. I was blending the juice of grapevines and an extract of apple blossoms to cure a cataract. At another time, I was singing a lullaby to a blind pilgrim who bled from his mouth as he died in my arms."

"When your visions appear, are they troubling?"

"Often, my lords, since they contain messages I am commanded to share."

"And have you done so?"

"For years, I buried them, fearing I would not be believed. The fear imprisoned me, confining me to a bed of pain again and again. But the Voice that streamed from the Living Light never ceased: 'Write down what you see and hear!' And with a wildly beating heart, I finally conceded."

"We have come to hear those messages from your lips, my lady," the bishop said, gently. "But be assured that we come with no fever for the marvelous. We ask only that you describe the voices you hear, the faces you see, the words that comprise the commands."

"Then journey with me," she said softly. "I will guide you."

Hildegard breathed deeply for several moments, trusting her soul as she began.

Closing her eyes, Hildegard embraced her visitors within her vision. Removing her slippers of felt, she placed them on the shore and waded into the water. Turning, she beckoned to the bishop and deputy to follow. Lifting her skirts as she waded deeper, deeper, she felt the sand slowly slipping away from the soles of her feet. Invoking the power of the Water, she whispered, "Dear Friend, I entrust each of us to your care, now." Then turning her face toward the heavens, she asked that the clouds guide them to the place where the sky would open.

As they floated, the visitors' robes rippled out like magenta sails in the azure sea. One of the men began humming; his eyes were closed, his hands like open cups upon the waves. The other turned his head from side to side fearfully, certain he would drown.

As they drifted, into the sky above them, a luminous figure slowly came into view.

Her body lay curved like a crescent moon, and in her womb, they saw the perfect form of an unborn babe. Floating far above its tiny head was a gossamer kite filled with the brightness of a thousand eyes. The eyes watched as a pinpoint of Light in their midst grew into a fiery globe; then warmed by the breath of the Divine, the eyes saw the globe descend into the babe. The babe's form trembled in the womb as it received this fiery globe, its own true Soul. Now the Soul's Light slowly streamed into the babe's tiny heart and brain and limbs, flooding the tiny babe with the knowledge of its immortality.

Reaching out now, the abbess touched the visitors' eyes.

"My brothers, can you see now how the Soul flows through this body like sap flows through a tree? The Soul's Intellect flows into the babe's limbs like sap flows into a tree's leaves and branches, while the Soul's Will has the power to make its flowers bloom. The Soul's Mind will produce the fruits of that growing life, while Reason will one day help sweeten that fruit to perfection; and by taste and touch and smell, the babe's Senses will distinguish that fruit by its size and shape.

"All these wonders flow from the Soul, for it is the Soul that gives the flesh freshness in the womb, nourishing the babe's body just as truly as moisture nourishes the earth and flourishes it with fruit."

As they floated, the sun glowed overhead. Lulled by the waves and gentle breezes, the bishop and his deputy pondered all they had heard.

"Speak to us more of this Woman whose body is curved like a crescent moon," *the bishop whispered.*

The abbess sighed. "She is Lady Wisdom, the Voice that first spoke to me in my mother's womb and guides me still. It is her face that I see on the screen of the Living Light. It is she whom King Solomon praises. She is the one poured forth before the beginning, the firstborn of God's ways. She was created before the heavens were sculpted and the depths of the earth hollowed out, and before the rim of the seas was set and the skies were expanded. She is God's Beloved who was at his side when the strands of the world were woven. She is the Creator's delight, night and day."

"You speak of the Woman who resides in the Book of Proverbs!" *the bishop cried.*

"Truly, and it is her Voice that explains what I hear and see in my visions. It is she who is our first cradle, our first food. Her heartbeat is the first sound to enter our ears. Indeed, it is she who has called us here."

"For what purpose, my lady?"

"Look in her eyes!" *the abbess replied, gazing heavenward. "She is also called Ecclesia. As Mother Church, her children stream from her with the dazzling light of diamonds."*

Now they saw towering above them in the sky the image of a Woman as large as a great city. A crown shone on her head and splendor hung from her arms like radiant sleeves, touching heaven to earth. Light clothed her, and music circled her, and her breast shone with a red glow like the dawn.

Slowly, her image spread, shaking its splendor out like a silken garment. "In this way, I conceive and give birth," she cried out.

Yet even as she gazed at her beloved children, she trembled. "In these times, I also conceive and bear many who oppress me, their Mother, by schism and heresy, by robberies and murder, by adultery and fornication."

Then her words rang out, splitting the heavens: "Let all those who seek the Divine welcome my mystical words with a kiss, for what proceeds from me is life itself!"

Hearing her, the humming man murmured no more, and his companion wept, spilling the unshed tears of forgotten years into the understanding heart of the sea.

The room was still.

When the bells for Sext sounded, Hildegard rose at once and reached for her Psalter. Closing the door behind her, she left the bishop of Verdun pressing the gilded cross to his chest as his heart leaped beneath it, while beside him, his deputy slumped forward, his elbows on his knees, his face buried in his hands.

Richardis could not tear her eyes from Hildegard. At Matins, she noted that though the magistra's lips were moving, no sound came forth. All through the Psalms, she kept gulping. Something was wrong.

Richardis stayed behind in the chapel as the others straggled back to bed. But she was too preoccupied to pray. Had something unpleasant happened at the meeting with the papal delegates? Had they censured her or condemned her writings? Had something momentous occurred that had thrust her into despair? The longer she knelt there, the more her imagination soared. She had to find out! A wild thought seized her. Imprudent though it might be at this hour, she could knock on the magistra's door and at least inquire if her mistress was ailing. But was it worth the risk? The magistra might unmask her concern as curiosity. Still, Richardis remained anxious: for her mistress not to sing was for her not to breathe.

Though the delegates had left at noon the day before, the mere thought of them still filled her with excitement. Those few moments she spent with them made her feel more alive than she had felt since arriving here. Their very presence was like a surge of fresh air, pushing back the walls of the cloister. Not even the mud from their journey could mar the sheen of their leather boots or dim the shimmer of the bishop's black velvet tunic with its cuffs of ruby silk. She could still see his half-smile and feel his eyes following her as she walked to the door. Once outside, she had pressed her ear to the door, aching to glean a hint of what was happening inside. Were the prelates disarming the abbess with their quicksilver questions, or was she unnerving them with her simple replies?

Richardis could bear it no longer. She raced from the chapel and knocked at Hildegard's door.

"*Deo gratias.*" The hoarse reply was more of a question than a welcome.

"*Benedicite.* It is Sister Richardis, my Lady Mother."

Hildegard was swathed in her woolen cloak, shivering. Her hand shook as she held the candle up to the young nun's face and drew her in.

"What brings you here at this hour, my daughter? Is there some danger abroad?"

"All is well, my lady." She bit her lip. "I was merely concerned when I saw that you were unable to sing at Matins." But at the magistra's stare, she felt like a fool. "I should have waited until tomorrow, but I feared that you might be unwell."

"And this is why you have come?"

Richardis' face grew flushed. "I will leave at once, Lady Mother. I should not have disturbed you."

She began to turn away, but then Hildegard spoke: "Sister Richardis, my throat closed at Matins. I summoned the notes, but they would not come." She drew in her breath. "It was an agony."

"Has this happened before, my lady?"

"Never." The abbess' eyes were wild. "My throat closed the moment the prelates departed for Trier." Clasping her hand on her mouth, she gasped, "Oh my daughter, what did I say? What did they hear?"

"You remember nothing, my lady?" Richardis asked breathlessly.

"I spoke of my visions, of course: Lady Wisdom's words and Ecclesia's warnings. But afterward, there was only silence: not a muscle moved; not a word was uttered."

"But surely their silence was their way of kneeling before your vision's magnificence just as my hands quiver when I record your words." Drawing the magistra into her arms, she whispered, "You must believe me."

"Yet why were they loathe to offer me a single nod, a kind word, a drop of mercy?" Her plea was like a child's cup, held up to be filled.

"My dear lady, these men were not sent here to console you. They came to test the things you hear and see. Instead, you revealed mysteries to them beyond their wildest imaginings. You enfleshed Lady Wisdom from the pages of Holy Writ and allowed them to gaze into the anguished eyes of Ecclesia, into the very mirrors that challenge their lives."

Hildegard was astonished. "Is my need for approval only my pride in disguise?" The abbess' voice was small.

"Such needs are human, my lady. But you must not let them blind you to the power of your gifts. These prelates came in strength seeking simple answers but left haunted by questions that they must begin to ask. On their return, they will describe your vision of a soul's rapture as it illumines a newborn's body!" Richardis cried. "How can this vision not remind them that the fate of such souls trembles in their hands every day?"

"What a blessing you are, dear Richardis," Hildegard wept with relief. "After they left, my heart was a desert. Now you bring the rain."

Together they knelt and gave thanks to the Virgin. Then Richardis helped the magistra to her bed and kissed her forehead.

But as Richardis strolled to the dormitory in the darkness, she felt both full and empty. Full, to have satisfied her curiosity about the magistra's meeting with the visitors, and empty, because, in the process, the brilliant flame of yesterday's excitement had been snuffed.

The cavernous Church of the Sepulcher was roaring with voices as the daily session of the bishops' synod was about to begin. Pushing their way past a group of arguing cardinals, the episcopal delegates from Mainz found their places and settled in.

"That's Bernard of Clairvaux, beside His Holiness!" Sigmund nudged Henry.

"If that's the hawk of Rome, as he's reputed to be, then it's a frail hawk indeed. He's dwarfed by his legends," Henry grumbled, glimpsing the reed-thin figure in white who sat at the pontiff's side. The abbot's face was drawn, his sunken cheeks having long since collapsed into his faded orange beard.

"It's said that, in his youthful passion, Bernard existed on vetch and beech leaves and roots in an effort to establish Clairvaux and return monastic life to its former simplicity and discipline," Sigmund murmured. "And because his belly still bleeds from that time, he insists that a hole be dug in the ground by his abbot's chair since he vomits constantly."

"His eyes are searing," Henry admitted.

"No more than his pen, which has shriveled many a sheaf of vellum," Sigmund said solemnly. "No regrets, then, that I dragged you from your bed this morning, Your Grace?" Sigmund grinned slyly.

"None," Henry conceded. Sigmund came to Trier knowing that the official burden of this synod was on his own shoulders. The archbishop had little if any interest in discussing disputes and land grants and the distribution of papal revenues. Once they arrived, as Sigmund knew, Henry would begin wandering off, "exploring," he called it, rarely returning before dawn.

As the session was called to order, the flurry of figures around the pope slowly dispersed. Bernard rose to kiss the pope's ring, but as he knelt down, his legs seemed to buckle under him. Instantly, the pope shot forward to help his beloved teacher rise to his feet. The pontiff's humility took Henry's breath away, reminding him of the rumors that Eugenius wore a hairshirt beneath his papal robe. Regaining his balance, Bernard opened his arms to offer the morning prayer. His thundering voice stunned the assembly. So much energy poured from his body, Henry feared the frail abbot would burst into flames.

"No wonder they call him the conscience of Europe," Henry flinched.

Now Bernard announced that the Holy Father wished to share an important message with the assembly before the synod's daily proceedings began.

"My sons," Eugenius cried out, "In our lands, famine has many faces. Floods and pestilence have rotted our harvests; our storehouses lie empty; our serfs starve. In far-off lands, famine also fells our valiant Crusaders as they seek to wrench the Holy Land from the iron grip of the infidels."

Bernard nodded.

"Yet in such times, when the Devil appears disguised as Fear, God sends us his prophets. One such voice has risen in our midst to give us courage.

"In a vision, this prophet saw nine choirs of angels whirling like dazzling crowns around the throne of the Divine. In each angel's eye, a mirror reflected a human form. As Holy Writ teaches, humanity is created more perfect than the angels, for men and women mirror the entire universe, which is sealed within each one of them.

"Remember these choirs of angels when you gaze into the eyes of your brothers and sisters, for each must be received as another Christ."

As a hum of assent spread across the assembly, Henry became aware that Sigmund's face was gray and his jaw slack.

"My sons, listen well!" the pope's voice shouted. "The prophet from whom such visions and revelations flow is Lady Hildegard von Bermersheim, magistra of Mount Saint Disibod in the Diocese of Mainz."

A hush descended as heads slowly turned to seek out the prelate in whose province this prophet resided.

Feeling Sigmund's fingernails stab his arm, Henry bolted to attention.

"I trust you will agree to read the magistra's writings now, will you not, Your Grace?" Sigmund seethed, his voice edged in ice as he nodded to the curious prelates around them.

The winter of 1147 would be remembered as the time the first frost descended on the heels of the harvest, stripping the land of its gold and scarlet, leaving the fields and trees to mourn in gray and brown.

When the Christmas octave began, half the monks and nuns were wheezing the days and nights away in the infirmary with chest colds and fevers. Hildegard spent most of her days and nights in the herbarium preparing remedies, pausing only to stamp her feet against the cold. Despite all the clay pots simmering on the braziers, the chill still seeped through the stones, numbing her toes. Yet she dared not stop. Calls kept coming for more anise and fennel poultices to relieve stuffy noses and for extra flasks of cough syrups concocted from figs, pears, and rosemary.

Each day by None, Hildegard's arms were already aching from pounding and mincing the herbs in her mortar, yet despite the demands, the work filled her with a rare satisfaction.

I have been buried too long in my ledger, she thought. I had forgotten how the mere pinch of my finger can release the fragrance of basil or the sharpness of quince.

Steeped in this world, she frowned at Hiltrude's interruption: "If you please, my lady magistra, His Grace, Lord Henry, wishes to see you."

Turning, she was astonished to see the archbishop of Mainz in the doorway. "Greetings, my lady," he said, smiling exuberantly. His ruddy cheeks glowed above his smoke-gray cloak and matching robe trimmed in turquoise and embroidered in gold. As he drew near, his smile seemed to swallow her. Hildegard drew back, almost toppling a flask bubbling on a brazier behind her.

"Your Grace, you delight in surprises," she said, as she wiped her hands on her apron.

"The first of many, I suspect," he replied, his eyes flitting over the shelves of salves and ointments as he bent to sniff the seeds and roots heaped in the rows of wooden bowls.

"You are amazing, my lady," he sighed as he inhaled the scent-laden air. The old excitement flooded her. His smile was as slow and suggestive as his manner was bold. Though pain pierced her temples, she could hear herself breathe.

"You are privy to secrets to heal both body and soul," he declared as he stooped to avoid the clusters of dried herbs swinging from the wooden beams.

"Our Creator is generous, Your Grace," she responded.

"I know," he replied solemnly, peering at the key hanging from Hildegard's neck and then at the flask of poppy syrup resting on the table above the unlocked cupboard.

"The earth has many secrets, has it not, my Lady Abbess?" he queried obliquely.

"Indeed, Your Grace. Which is why great care must be taken in dispensing those secrets lest what proceeds as a blessing from the hand of God might, in man's hand, become a curse."

Folding his arms, he stared back at her. She felt him shiver.

"I have arranged a meeting with the abbot in his quarters after None today," he announced abruptly. "Please join us, my lady."

Then he was gone.

When Hildegard entered the abbot's quarters, she was surprised to see Volmar there. The monk's eyes were lowered, and his hands were clasped behind his back. And though Henry looked at her directly, he was chewing his lips.

Why is everyone so nervous? Hildegard wondered. And why am I here? *For a moment, she sensed Lady Jutta's presence.*

Kuno cleared his throat, then gestured to the archbishop.

"My Lady Magistra," Henry intoned, "I have been commissioned by His Holiness, Pope Eugenius, to convey his personal greetings to you." A strange smile curled his lips.

"I am honored, Your Grace," she replied simply. Why was she filled with such feelings of dread?

"His Holiness wishes you to know that he has blessed your writings, a portion of which he read aloud to the synod of bishops in Trier."

Hildegard covered her mouth with her hand and glanced at Volmar. His eyes were shining with tears.

"His Holiness described you as a prophet," Henry announced, "and..."

"Spare me, Your Grace," she protested. "I share only what I see and hear and am commanded to say. In this way, I merely respond like the strings of an instrument to God's touch."

But Henry would not be denied.

"I must convey, as well, my lady," he continued, "that Abbot Bernard of Clairvaux rose to confirm the pope's decision by proclaiming that the light of your visions must not be dimmed."

Kuno stepped forward. His hands were shaking, and the blood had drained from his face. "The abbey is deeply honored, Your Grace. Would you not agree, my lady?"

Before she could answer, Henry had crossed the room and stood so near to her that she felt his breath on her cheek. His nostrils were flaring while elation poured from his body like summer heat. "I am your servant from this moment on, my lady," he announced, his eyes glinting with light and his lips slowly parting. Then bowing his head, he whispered softly, "In more ways than you can imagine, my lady, you have changed my life."

Part Three

1148–52

*In time, the abbess became able to read
their desires, intentions, and thoughts
and would perceive in spirit
the story of people's lives,
and for some, she could foresee
the end of their present life.*

–Vita Sanctae Hildegardis

Spring had come early to the Rhineland. Paradise must be drenched with the scent of apple blossoms, Kuno decided as he strolled past the abbey orchard and gazed down at the curves of the Nahe River in the valley below. Throwing his head back, he bathed his face in the sun's warmth. He had never felt so ecstatic.

In the joy of the moment, a memory surfaced. A boy of six stood in a courtyard, squinting in the sunlight. The bodies of his two oldest brothers were slung across the backs of their approaching horses, their arms and legs flopping, their blood dripping down the horses' flanks. The boy felt the weight of his father's callused hand on his small shoulder. "You will avenge them, my son."

Kuno shuddered. From that moment on, he had failed test after test, fleeing from the threats of bullies and violence. The father's hopes for his son turned from rage to relief on the day Kuno became an oblate at Mount Saint Disibod. He was ten years old.

Kuno wrenched himself from the memory. If only that lad could have seen ahead to this day and the fame that his efforts would bring to this abbey. It still seemed like a dream. Since the synod, prelates and abbots from Trier and Eberbach had arrived to pay their respects to the lady magistra Hildegard, while donations from nobles in Bremen and Cologne continued to swell the abbey's coffers. Of late, it was not uncommon to have twenty noble guests at meals.

There were challenges, of course. Daily chapter meetings roiled with concerns about feeding the growing number of pilgrims who settled in clusters outside the gates or camped on the mountainside.

"Calm yourself, my Lord Abbot," Archbishop Henry had cautioned when Kuno complained. "You are a pilgrimage site now. Ask and you shall receive! You have only to voice a need and your benefactors will fill it. Trust me. You need only mention the magistra's name."

Henry had certainly acted on his own advice. Since the synod, he had exploited the magistra shamelessly, ingratiating himself with his brother bishops and cardinals by urging them to fully avail themselves of her counsel. The abbey's prestige had soared. Henry had triumphed at every turn: Kuno was indebted to him, as were his brother prelates. Indeed, without Henry, Kuno would not be unveiling plans for the new women's monastery at Saint Disibod's feast day celebration. His cup was full. The Virgin had answered his prayers.

"We must stop now," Hildegard announced suddenly. Volmar and Richardis looked up in surprise. The work had been proceeding well, and there was still at least an hour before Vespers. But the magistra had already slipped from her stool, clearly restless. As Richardis put her wax tablets away, Hildegard clasped the young nun's hand.

"Please excuse us, my daughter," she whispered. "I must speak with Father Volmar alone."

Volmar frowned as he cleaned the quills. It had happened again: the magistra's need to explain her every move to Richardis. It disturbed him.

As Volmar put his quills away, the magistra began pacing. What was it this time? he wondered.

"I have been commanded to leave this abbey," she announced.

"Leave this abbey?" The monk laughed. "Banished perhaps?" he teased.

"I have been commanded by the Voice of the Living Light." Her mouth was grim. "I must obey."

Volmar drew back, suddenly tense. "What are you saying, my lady?"

"I must build an abbey for my daughters."

The monk's jaw dropped. "But you have an abbey here, an abbey that protects you."

"From what?" her eyes flashed. "Full knowledge of how my lands are managed, a list of what my endowments purchase, a record of how my donations are spent? I have forfeited everything!"

"But all your needs are met. You want for nothing. Your daughters are housed and clothed and fed, and the monks serve your spiritual needs. Is that not a blessing?"

"A blessing? Is it a blessing to eat and sleep and work in quarters so cramped we stumble past one another? To beg for access to the library and account for every candle we burn?" Her eyes were wild now. "I can abide it no longer! We have outgrown this monastery; it no longer meets our needs."

"But, my lady, father abbot agrees. Plans are already in place to enlarge..."

"It is too late!"

"Be reasonable, my lady. What will you do? Where will you go?" Volmar felt an overwhelming need to protect her.

"To the place I was shown in my vision: Rupert's Mountain, a day's journey from here." Hildegard's voice was defiant.

"But there's nothing there except barren hillsides and some scattered rocks!" Volmar shouted, consumed now with fear for her. "And the Roman bridge where the Rhine and the Nahe meet."

"Exactly," she nodded.

"That scarcely matters, since my vision revealed that the land is holy ground." Folding her arms, she added, "Would you have me disobey?"

"You ask an impossible question, my lady," he said, turning away.

Her shoulders sagged. "I had hoped for support but hear only scorn," she sighed.

Volmar's voice was harsh. "My lady, what you propose is utter folly."

"In your eyes, not mine. Further, I would dispute who of us is the greater fool: you for pretending to be my friend or me for believing you."

Her words pelted him like stones. "My lady, you would need an army of architects and tradesmen, not to mention hordes of workmen and horses and shelter for every kind of animal. It would take years to build."

"So you take me for a fool as well? You forget that I have kept scrupulous ledgers for years for the abbot's convenience. But I have had enough!" she cried. "I must set the rules for my own house, establish my own library!"

"As abbess?" he asked, holding his breath.

"Why not? I am supremely qualified."

Volmar paled. "My lady, I cannot support such recklessness."

"Are you mocking my vision's command or expressing your lack of confidence in me?" she challenged.

His heart sank. What was she thinking? Without protection, she and her nuns would starve.

"Will you stand with me or not, Father Volmar?"

"I wish you well, my lady," he said. His eyes were burning.

"You have not answered my question!" she challenged him.

"Think of your daughters, my lady. . . ."

"Their loyalty will be tested, of course," she said serenely. "But those who have faith in me will persevere."

He opened his mouth to speak, but paused to weigh his words. "Have you informed Abbot Kuno of your plans?"

"You need not trouble yourself," she fumed. "He will be told in due time. But his approval is of little concern to me now since I no longer need him."

"You are wrong, my lady. Trust me! You will never break free of this abbey."

"Is that your hope or your fear, Father Volmar?" she seethed as she turned from him. But her knees felt weak beneath her, and her eyes were blurring. She must do this without him. Gripping her rosary, she prayed not to slide down the shaft of her self-doubt again.

"I will walk alone then," she announced, warning him. "I will find a way. I will build my abbey, and nothing will stop me. Not even my provost."

Whipped by her words, he stepped back from her, sick with confusion. Validating her visions was one thing, but supporting this plan was another thing altogether. For the first time, he questioned the Voice. Why would it command Hildegard to place herself and her nuns in such danger? Her desperation alarmed him. Where was her recklessness coming from? If only he could calm her, hold her hand, and beg her to reconsider, to not act in haste. But when he met her gaze, he felt himself plummeting.

Turning from him, Hildegard said with a sudden softness, "Never fear, my friend. I will go my way alone, if need be. Lady Jutta will guide me."

"As will I, somehow, some way," he heard himself saying. "I will honor my promise to stand at your side until the day I die."

Safe outside her room, Volmar flattened his back against the wall, his body captive to the tremors of his longing. "Until the day I die!" His promise impaled him. Despite all his restraints, he had bound himself to her without hesitation.

The circle of flags snapped in the wind. They splashed the sky with color above the guests who sauntered through the abbey gates for Saint Disibod's feast day celebration.

The air was crystal clear and sweet with birdsong.

The feast day event had taken on a deeper meaning this year. Many had journeyed here hoping to catch a glimpse of the illustrious magistra, Lady Hildegard. Once she appeared, the guests surrounded her with questions.

Richardis stood to one side, viewing the display with fascination, aware that her mother, the margravine, was strolling to her side.

"Each of your gowns is more beautiful than the last one, my Lady Mother," Richardis sighed, fingering the ivory lace on the cuffs and neckline of her mother's saffron gown.

The margravine offered her cheek, conscious that not even the drabness of her daughter's faded robe could dull her beauty.

"You seem quite content, my dear," she smiled.

"And why not? As the magistra's assistant, I'm the envy of the abbey!" Her eyes were shining. "Each day, she asks my thoughts and values my judgments and has gained access for me to the abbey library, despite the monks' objections. Now we can sit and discuss Saint Augustine's writings and plumb the riches of Rabanus Maurus." Still, her hand lingered in her mother's clasp.

"And how fares your work with her in the scriptorium?"

Richardis moved closer. "Astonishing, my lady, beyond description. Yet nothing compares with the magistra herself. She is a constant surprise."

"I could not agree more," the mother blinked, still stunned by the secret the magistra had shared with her earlier and her prompt response to help in every way. "Her plans for the future are extraordinary," the woman ventured cautiously. "Would you not agree?"

"Completely, my Lady Mother. She shares all her dreams with me. And I, in turn, will be with her until the day she dies." Her eyes were glistening.

Nearby, the crowd surrounding the magistra was stirring.

"My lords and my ladies, I beg your leave. I must pray before Mass," Hildegard announced to the crowd as she edged toward the chapel. As she mounted the steps, Archbishop Henry appeared in the doorway.

"Greetings, my Lady Magistra!" he said. His greeting was a little too loud. He lowered his voice. "Your letter delighted me, as did the opportunity to serve you. I attended to the matter at once and have brought you the documents you requested."

Hildegard stared at the scrolls in his hand.

"It was a simple matter," he added. "There were no impediments, and all the parties were agreeable."

"I am indebted to you, Your Grace."

"No more than I am intrigued with you, my lady," he murmured. "As your trusted courier, may I know on whose behalf I acted?"

This time, her smile was as cryptic as his.

"Of course, Your Grace, and soon," she said, taking the scrolls from him as she disappeared into the chapel.

The abbot's table had been placed on a raised platform for the midday feast. "So you may be seen by all!" Kuno enthused as he seated Hildegard beside him. His blessing before the meal was equally buoyant, ending with a promise to announce "great good news" before the guests departed.

Though the feast day fare was sumptuous and Hildegard's stomach churned, she had no appetite. As the chattering rose around her, she closed her eyes, hearing the splash of wine being poured and inhaling the zestful aroma of ginger and cloves that rose from the platters of rabbit and pheasant. She, however, tasted nothing, barely nudging the food in her trencher and feigning a few sips of wine.

Finally, Archbishop Henry rose, and a hush descended on the hall. With consummate skill, he enthralled the guests with a vivid account of the Synod of Trier, skillfully underplaying his role in bringing Lady Hildegard's visions to the pope's attention and carefully noting that his efforts were also rewarded by the subsequent affirmation of Abbot Bernard of Clairvaux.

As Henry flourished his cup to toast "our famous magistra, Lady Hildegard," the guests leaped to their feet to join him, while Abbot Kuno's hand shook with such excitement that his wine splashed over the rim of his cup.

"It is with deep humility that I receive your kindness," Hildegard smiled in response, "as I, in turn, lift the cup of my heart to my spiritual mother, Lady Jutta, of blessed memory, under whose wing I first nestled on this mountain as a small, frightened bird." She bowed her head before plunging on.

"In my childish innocence, it was with Lady Jutta that I first shared my visions, a confidence she chose to share only with Father Volmar on her deathbed, evoking from him his promise to be my spiritual guide. In faith and by God's grace, it was he who encouraged me to obey the Voice in my visions that commanded me to 'write what you hear and see.' With trust and humility, I have obeyed that command."

She paused as eyebrows arched and heads turned toward the monk.

"Yet of late," she continued, "I was awakened at night by a second command that set fire to my heart, almost shattering me." She swallowed. "In this amazing vision, I was shown a barren hillside, which was revealed to me as holy ground. Upon that soil, I was commanded to found an abbey for my daughters. When I protested, stating that this abbey was my only home, I was told that I must leave without hesitation and not look back."

Hildegard caught her breath, visibly shaken.

"I beg your prayers that I may be graced again with the courage to obey this second command with the same trust and humility as I obeyed the first."

No one moved. Beside her, she heard a gasp. Kuno's face swelled with fury. Next to him, Archbishop Henry stared straight ahead, his neck twitching as he moistened his lips furiously.

Hildegard's eyes searched for the margravine. Their eyes locked as the barest of nods passed between them. The deed was done: they could proceed now. Then the shriek of wood scraping on stone as Kuno pushed back his chair and stalked from the hall. Closing her eyes, Hildegard envisioned him running blindly until he sank to his knees in the orchard. Pounding the ground, he cursed heaven at Hildegard's announcement; then he retched from rage until his strength was spent.

Within the hour, news of the magistra's announcement had reached every person on the mountain.

"Did you know?" Hiltrude asked Richardis breathlessly as they filed into Vespers. "Did she tell you first?"

"She told me nothing," Richardis snapped.

"How could she do this to us? We should have been told before the others," Hiltrude whimpered.

"Ask her yourself, why don't you?" Richardis shot back.

At chapter the next day, the air was thick with friction. After the daily business was concluded, Hildegard rose from her chair.

"My daughters, I understand your distress about my announcing my plans to the benefactors. I grieve that I was unable to share the news with you first. But until the land was purchased, I felt impelled to proceed with the utmost caution. To my utter surprise, the final deed of sale for the land was placed in my hand moments before the feast day Mass yesterday. I felt it was a sign of God's graciousness that I was given this chance to announce my plan to our benefactors in person.

"It is critical that you know that, were it not for the Voice of the Living Light guiding me, I would never have dreamed of undertaking this move. But my vision assured me that great good would be accomplished there, and we would be showered with graces. I ask for your understanding and beg your forgiveness for any unrest I may have caused."

She waited for the usual sound of sighs and shuffling, but there was none.

"I welcome your thoughts, my daughters," she said softly.

But no eye would meet hers.

Finally, she dismissed them.

As she sat alone in the empty room, one ache consumed her: Where was Richardis?

"Is the magistra mad?" Kuno growled, peering at the speck on the map before him. "There's nothing there!"

"So it appears, my lord," Volmar said calmly. "But Brother Librarian insists that a document in the library proves that the site is, indeed, holy ground."

"Then why have we never heard of it?" Kuno demanded.

Volmar shrugged. Opening the book, the monk pointed to a page of faded script. "The site is referred to here as Saint Rupert's Mountain," Volmar noted, ignoring the abbot's sigh.

"Go on."

"It states that Rupert was the grandson of a prince in Charlemagne's court and the son of Duke Robolaus, who owned vast vineyards close to Bingen. At fifteen, Rupert converted, and after a pilgrimage to Rome, he returned to Bingen to build churches for the poor and deeded his lands to them. When he died five years later, his mother founded a monastery on the site of his tomb. It stood for a hundred years but was destroyed by the Normans. Brother Librarian maintains that a few remaining walls still survive to mark the site."

"The evidence is slight, but it's enough to support the magistra's request for a meeting," Kuno conceded ruefully, as he slammed the book shut. "Let's be done with it," he grumbled. "Go and get her and bring her here."

Kuno fumed as he waited, then sneered as Hildegard entered the hall: "You must be pleased that your dramatic announcement met with such success, my lady. A brilliant plan since it precluded any discussion with us beforehand." He turned to Volmar. "Would you not agree, Father Volmar?"

"It was a memorable day in many ways, Father Abbot," the monk agreed tonelessly.

So be it, Hildegard thought. I must stand alone.

"Plans are already underway for the move, my lord," Hildegard said, seizing the offensive.

"Not so quickly, my lady. As your abbot, I find any 'command' suspect that instructs a magistra to take her nuns and depart to a wilderness, with only stones for their weapons."

"But that will not be the case, my lord."

"Do you think you need only pack up your trunks and camp on this land to make it yours?" he thundered. "The rashness of your decision embarrasses me!"

"So be it, Father Abbot." Hildegard's voice was serene.

"My lady," he sighed patiently, "since you arrived here, you have been shielded from a brutal world. A single road in the valley below holds more danger than you could meet in a lifetime on this mountain."

"Danger wears many masks, my lord," she retorted, "not the least one of which is the mask of rash judgment. All the necessary preparations for my daughters' safety and well-being have, of course, been made. To proceed otherwise would be unconscionable."

"Then tell me, pray, how do you plan to feed and shelter them on a barren hillside that does not belong to you, my lady?"

"You do not understand, my lord. I have planned to purchase the land."

"Of course," he purred, "and your nuns would saw the wood and quarry the stones."

"We will not labor alone. Offers of help come each day."

"From the serfs in the village, no doubt?" he taunted.

"No, my lord, from the abbots of Trier and Eberbach, who have offered me the services of their architects and builders, and from countless benefactors who have pledged their help, as well."

Kuno sat back. How could this be? Then he remembered all the prelates Henry had sent after the synod. Still, without the land, such offers would remain merely gestures of good intentions. Smiling, he thought, I will play with her now.

"Do you plan to negotiate for the land yourself, then, my lady?"

"There is no need now, my lord. The deeds to the land will arrive any day now, bearing the signatures of the brothers Hermann and Bernard of Hildesheim."

"Take care, my lady," he smiled, "such deeds can be easily forged to trap innocents and fools."

"Too true, I fear. But Archbishop Henry of Mainz is neither, and it is he who acted as our official liaison."

A smirk twisted Kuno's lips. "All you lack now is my permission to leave, my lady," he smiled, "and as your abbot-protector, my conscience forbids it."

The custodian of the abbey's coffers was Arnold, the subprior. The spindly monk's robe seemed held aloft by the knobs of his bony shoulders; no matter how raw the winter chill, his tonsure was always glistening with sweat.

Arnold took exquisite, if not unnatural, delight in describing the sound each coin made as it dropped inside the abbey's coffers. His brothers would wink as he approached, rapt with news of some new donation, his appreciation palpable. When word reached him that the abbey faced the loss of the nuns' dowries, he grew so distraught that he refused all daily food. Despite their prayers, the brothers' efforts failed to console him. Day by day, Brother Arnold withered before their eyes until the abbot, in despair, sent word to his family to take him home to die.

It was an omen, the brothers muttered. The Devil had twisted Lady Hildegard's fame into a curse on Mount Saint Disibod. If her visions were truly of God, how could they plunge the abbey into such despair?

Tension between the abbey and the monastery was rising daily, heightened by Kuno's feeling of entrapment after his meeting with the magistra. As his anger rose, he began to harbor doubts about Volmar, fearing that he might be a traitor.

The rumors forced Volmar to forgo his brothers' company before Compline. Accusations of divided loyalties had become a burden he could no longer bear. The abbot's outburst at a chapter meeting had only worsened matters.

"My sons," Kuno had thundered, "as your abbot, how can I face my God if I subject these nuns to disgrace by letting them leave to risk the dangers of rape and starvation? How can I betray those noble families whose daughters have been entrusted to our care? I cannot abandon my sacred duty to protect these innocent women from harm!" Stirred by his passion, the monks had shouted their assent as they decried Hildegard's ingratitude.

Torn between his defense of the magistra and his loyalty to his brothers, Volmar now felt his soul was in shreds. In a fit of desperation, he retrieved the leather whip from beneath his bed, hoping the discipline would numb his body. He dreaded the night even more now, knowing he faced the agonies of temptation. He prayed to close his eyes and not feel the magistra's sighs on his cheek and the heat of her body as she stood by his carrel. Perhaps her leaving would be the answer after all, he had to admit. But at the thought of it, his heart crumpled. He prayed not to squander whatever time he had left with her. He must cherish each day, each hour, each moment. He must memorize the way her fingers grasped her stylus as she inscribed the words on her wax tablet, the sound of her voice when it soared in song, and the sight of her lips parting as her notes pierced heaven. And he must never forget the sight of sudden tears brimming in the violet sea of her eyes. Tears had flowed at all the important moments: tears of awe in the scriptorium, tears of joy in the chapel, tears of pain as she teetered on the threshold of death and his prayers reached out like arms to catch her. And now, he must find a way to remember and to forget.

Kuno leaped from his chair when Volmar entered his room.

"I've had enough!" Kuno shouted, thrusting a sheaf of vellum in Volmar's face. "Enough, do you hear! Read this letter!"

Volmar looked down with mounting dread:

To Abbot Kuno of Disibodenberg:

We rejoice with you at the news of the wondrous vision shared by Lady Hildegard at the recent feast day celebration. Confident of the graces it will shower on our daughters who are vowed to her community, we deem it our privilege and duty to assist the new abbess in every way.

You will understand, then, our decision to transfer all the Sponheim family's future donations from the Abbey of Mount Saint Disibod to the aid and sustenance of Lady Hildegard's new foundation at Rupertsberg, which she will ably lead as abbess. In this way, we honor the memory of Blessed Jutta, our sister and cousin, whose spirit, we are certain, already hovers over the site of her spiritual daughter's future abbey on Holy Rupert's mountain.

Richardis von Sponheim-Lavantall
The Margravine von Stade

Volmar opened his mouth to speak, but no words came.

"Have you nothing to say?" Kuno demanded.

"A grievous loss, my lord," he stammered. "A great shock, a sad, sad day."

"Loss?" Kuno screamed. "It is a disaster. The magistra is bent on ruining us. She has taken advantage of us with her visions long enough. I will silence her, indeed imprison her, if need be!" Storming from the room, he commanded Volmar to accompany him: "Come. You will officiate as my witness. This woman must be stopped before she brings further ruin to this abbey."

The magistra's room was lit by a single candle. Richardis was kneeling at the foot of her mistress' bed, her head in her hands, while Hiltrude sat at Hildegard's side praying. A cluster of sad-eyed nuns knelt nearby.

Kuno and Volmar looked shocked as Hiltrude came forward.

"Thank God you've come," she whispered. "Mother Hildegard collapsed and can no longer hear or see. Moments ago, she called out your name, Father Volmar, and asked to see you. We were so grateful. They were the first words she spoke."

Kuno sucked in his breath. No wonder the nuns at the door seemed so relieved to see them. Volmar was already at the magistra's bedside. His hands were shaking.

"How fares she?" he stuttered at Hiltrude.

"Her breathing is faint but steady, my lord," Hiltrude reported.

"How did it happen?"

"For three days now, we noticed that she seemed to falter when she stood in chapel. We thought at first that she must be fasting. But when we saw her stagger toward her chair at Matins, we knew she was ill. Still she refused our help and pleaded fatigue, assuring us she needed nothing. But when she failed to appear at Lauds, we found her collapsed here at her bedside where she had fallen. When she groped for our faces, we knew she was unable to see."

"Had she no complaints?" Kuno demanded, frowning.

"Lady Hildegard?" Hiltrude looked away. "If only there were, these occurrences would not confound us."

Kuno coughed nervously. "Is she with fever?"

"Not the usual kind." Hiltrude winced. "But her body is weighted with such a heaviness, it is as though her flesh had turned to stone. We cannot move her, yet dare not leave her alone."

"We will pray that this illness passes quickly," Kuno murmured, as Volmar looked up abruptly. "I will inform the brothers at once. The abbey will pray for her day and night," Kuno said awkwardly, as he edged away, nodding to Volmar to precede him out the door.

"Please do, Father Abbot," Richardis called out to Kuno, and as the door closed behind him, Hiltrude added softly, "And we will pray for you, as well, my lord."

"How can you?" Richardis sputtered, shaking her head in disbelief.

"Do you find father abbot unworthy of forgiveness, Richardis?" Hiltrude quickly responded.

"I don't know what I think anymore," she moaned. "Yet to judge him is to judge my own bitterness at being denied Lady Hildegard's confidence regarding the move."

"Perhaps now you'll understand how hard it's been for us to watch you being showered with special privileges," Hiltrude replied as tears sprang to her eyes.

But Richardis had already disappeared into her own tears, confronted with a truth from which she could no longer hide.

The letter arrived at noon the following day. Brother Porter delivered it himself, already saddened at the news he knew it contained. Seeing the seal of Arnold's family, Kuno too was certain that word of the pitiful man's death had come.

To Father Kuno, Abbot of Mount Saint Disibod:
Greetings.

May the grace of God bless you for all you have done for our dear Brother Arnold when he was among you.

After leaving you, we set out to bring him back to the castle of his birth, but aware of his constant pain, we doubted he would live to see it again, which has proven true. We traveled slowly, as every jolt caused him pain. And at day's end, we spread out our cloaks in a meadow.

As we prepared for sleep, a shower of stars fell across the night sky. Seeing it, our brother groaned suddenly, clutching his throat.

Crying out, he begged us to bring him to that place he had so fiercely maligned: Rupert's Mountain.

Leaving at dawn, we arrived at dusk only to find a few crumbling walls at the ruins of Blessed Rupert's crypt. Our Brother Arnold asked us to place him on the crypt, then stretched out his arms like Christ on the cross. Weeping, we knew his moment of death had come and prayed that he might receive the peace of God and the Virgin's comfort.

Then, like a miracle, our Brother Arnold arose, crying out, "*Deo gratias, Deo gratias!*" Weeping with gratitude, he began to kiss the ground, swearing to stay and to prepare the land for the new abbey's foundation, which he said would come. Within days, his strength returned, and he bade us leave him. When we saw him last, he was kneeling in radiance as he cleared the vines and brambles from the ruined walls with his bare hands.

It was his fervent wish that you know of this miracle and his need to serve Lady Hildegard there until the day he goes home to God.

Kuno knelt at the Virgin's feet in the chapel. He could barely breathe. Since the magistra's collapse, he had become obsessed with her illness, inquiring hourly about her progress. The longer Hildegard lay motionless, the more frantic he became. He feared that her death was imminent and that he would be blamed for refusing to grant her wish to leave.

Heightening the tension was the news of Brother Arnold's amazing conversion and its effect on the brothers. As the days passed, more and more monks rose at chapter to confess their envy of the magistra's fame and their anger at losing their prestige as her protectors.

But Kuno remained adamant. As abbot, only he could fully gauge the impact of the magistra's departure. The loss of the nuns' donations and dowries concerned him greatly, but the abbey's loss of revenues as a pilgrimage site troubled him at least as much. In truth, the bulk of his hopes and dreams for the abbey now hovered above the magistra's bed. He must remain firm: she must not leave!

"Help her to rise!"

Kuno looked up. Where had the words come from? They came again, clear and distinct, filling him. The bells for Compline began ringing. As he rose, the words filled his body again.

"Help her to rise!"

When the chanting at Compline began, Kuno sank into the comfort offered by the promises of the time-smoothed prayers:

God, come to my aid....

Lord, make haste to help me.

Night holds no terrors for one who sleeps under God's wings, ...

My refuge, my stronghold....

It is He who will free you from the snare of the fowler who seeks to destroy you!

Kuno wondered: Am I the fowler, caught in my own snare of pride and ambition? Is it my own stubbornness that is devouring me and this abbey? If Brother Arnold were here now, would he unclench my fingers from the abbey's coffers? He glanced around at his brother monks with whom he had chanted these psalms year after year. They had humbled themselves publicly in chapter by confessing their shame and anger. As their abbot, could he do any less?

> You will not fear the terror of the night
> Nor the arrow that flies by day
> Nor the plague that prowls in the darkness
> Nor the scourge that lays waste at noon....

In his room after Compline, Kuno heard himself pleading: "Holy Virgin, help me to help her to rise! And give me the grace and humility to let her go with my blessing!"

"Now let your servant go in peace."

For the first time in weeks, Kuno felt at peace. He fell on his bed and slept until Matins.

In three days, the magistra's strength had fully returned.

After Matins, Hildegard stayed to pray in the chapel, then slowly made her way back in the darkness to snatch a few hours of sleep before Lauds. As she strolled, her step slowed when she glimpsed the splashes of moonlight on the roof of the monastery, and next to it, the towering outline of her beloved tree. Its massive branches all but obscured the tiny courtyard beside the former hermitage. Over thirty years had passed since Lady Jutta knelt at her side and helped her plant it as a sapling.

For decades, she had watched it stretch and expand as it soared into heaven.

During that time, she had returned to the tree again and again, much as one would seek out the comfort of a trusted friend. But when she hugged it now, it had expanded so much that her arms could only span half its trunk. Undeterred, she still hoisted her skirts and climbed up into its sheltering arms when she needed to be renewed after hours in the herbarium. In this leafy bower, she was able to quiet her mind and reflect more deeply on the healing secrets of plants and herbs, which she was discovering at an awesome rate. The earth's generosity staggered her. She drew delight from knowing that her fragile sapling still nestled within the heart of the giant tree that loomed before her in the moonlight. By now, she needed only to glimpse it from afar to be refreshed.

"Flood me with courage tomorrow, my friend!" she cried out fiercely in the moonlight. "I will need your strength as never before!"

During Lauds, Hildegard began to feel the pools of fire in the palms of her hands. Pressing them together, she prayed, "Not today! Please God, not today!"

It was her forty-eighth birthday.

After Terce, the nuns filed into their stalls in the dim chapel, their eyes glinting like fireflies. Today, in preparation for their move to Rupertsberg, they must officially elect an abbess to head the new foundation.

The abbot would conduct the election on the nuns' behalf; Father Volmar and a brother monk would serve as witnesses. The doors were locked.

As he surveyed the rows of rapt faces on either side of him, Kuno nodded his greeting and stepped forward to call the official roll. One by one, the nuns stood, calling out "*Adsum*" (Present). The time-honored ritual to elect an abbess had officially begun.

Hildegard felt numb; the fiery pain in her hands was unbearable. She stared at the tabernacle on the altar, not daring to let her eyes stray in any way. Though she struggled to pray, she was tormented by her racing thoughts. So many resented the impending move, they could use this election as an act of rebellion. Why hadn't she made the announcement to her daughters first? What if the abbot's fears about failure proved true in the days ahead? If her daughters came to any harm, how could she bear it?

In the background, the ritual was proceeding as the abbot and his witnesses swore secrecy and the nuns vowed to vote for the one most worthy of the office, "having made no compact with another, nor accepted a compact from them."

Hildegard hoped they would elect Hiltrude. They know the skill and devotion Hiltrude lavishes on them as prioress, she thought. She attends to every detail of their needs while I sit in the scriptorium, steeped in my visions.

One by one, the nuns repeated the oath: "Item testor et juro" (So do I swear and testify).

As Hildegard spoke the words aloud, they felt like drops of hot oil burning her throat. She was unable to swallow. How dare she proceed with her plans for Rupertsberg when they would surely crash at her feet!

The vote was swift as it rippled from stall to stall. The abbot walked forward and cleared his throat. He proclaimed: "Domina Hildegard von Bermersheim Abbatissa electa est" (Lady Hildegard von Bermersheim is elected abbess).

"For the rest of your life," she felt Lady Jutta whisper. "Life, life, life, ... " the echo quivered as the pools of fire in her hands began to flame.

The next thing she knew, her darling Hiltrude was bowing before her, extending her hand to escort her to the foot of the altar, supporting her as she knelt.

Abbot Kuno stood on the step above her.

"In the name of His Holiness, Pope Eugenius," his voice rang out, "I confirm you abbess."

Lifting her hands, she accepted the symbols of her office: a plain gold ring, the seal and the symbolic keys to her prospective abbey, and with a gasp, Lady Jutta's small wooden cross, the sign of her office, a surprise that filled her eyes with tears.

Pressing the objects to her heart, she mounted the steps of the altar. Her hands trembled as she raised each object at the foot of the cross, then laid each one before the tabernacle.

A firm hand helped her descend the steps and guided her to the abbess' chair.

For a moment, she saw Lady Jutta sitting there, caressing a small blond head resting in her lap.

Edging back in her chair, she thought, "Dare I attempt this, I who have sat at the edge of my life for so long?"

Then the words, surging with Light: "Do not look back!"

Like a thunderclap, pealing bells split the air with a riot of jubilation as the nuns' *Te Deum* soared and blended with centuries of voices that had uttered the church's ancient prayer of praise and thanksgiving.

One by one, the nuns stepped from their stalls and approached their new abbess.

Once again, she watched them come, remembering the sound of their worldly wings flapping in confusion as each exchanged her jewel-toned plumage for the midnight robes of blackbird and crow. But now as they came toward her, they were the ones fluttering with joy. This time, she was the stranger being lowered into an unfamiliar nest.

They knelt before her, placing their hands between those of their new abbess, vowing faith and obedience as Hildegard bestowed the kiss of peace on the cheek of each new daughter.

"Your hands are so special," Lady Jutta *whispered again, "What secrets do you like to hold in them?"*

Hildegard nearly forgot to breathe as each one rose and bowed to her. Gisla, her head bobbing with gasps of joy, "For you, anything! Yes, yes, whatever you want," as the tears plopped down on her wimple. Dutiful Kunigunde, speechless as she squeezed her hand, while Ilse kissed her hand again and again, her blue eyes brimming. Only Gertrud surprised her with a sudden sob, ever mindful that her twin would have died had Hildegard not cured Gisla with devotion and almond powder.

Then came the flocks of birds who had nested after the first flock, especially Richardis. Her eyes were dancing: "But of course! of course! This is the chair of your destiny!"

Hiltrude was last in line, her step slow as she walked toward Hildegard. Hiltrude's lips quivered as she forced back tears of joy, though she knew that from this moment on, they would never hug apple trees as sisters again, as they had done for so many years before.

Hildegard's shoulders shook as she gazed into Hiltrude's eyes and sobbed with gratitude: "Dear Hiltrude, you share this chair with me. I beg your help. I need you so much!"

Hiltrude took her hands in hers and kissed them. "I will be there, my Lady Abbess," she promised.

I write by the light of a single candle flame that sways in the night wind on Saint Rupert's Mountain. Overhead, the full moon's radiant womb glows, illumining the sights and sounds I must not forget.

I hear Gertrud's determined footsteps falling for the last time on the abbey paths at Disibodenberg, the hesitant tap of Gisla's slippers on the chapel floor, Hiltrude's muffled sobs at the last Matins, the last Lauds, the last Prime. Then, as we depart, I watch each of them pause for one last look at Disibodenberg while Ilse sobs openly, scanning the garden walls embroidered with roses, remembering how she had secretly pressed the velvet petals to her lips like forbidden kisses in the fevers of each aching spring.

Again, the sweep of sighs, Richardis' the loudest among them, as the carts are piled high with all our belongings. Then only the complaints of squeaking cartwheels as the horses lurch forward past the rows of monks with folded arms and averted eyes.

Lastly, the specter of Volmar, his eyes glazed with pain as he looks but refuses to see us depart. Abbot Kuno nods and mumbles "Godspeed." The monks are silent.

My heart crumbles as I feast my eyes on my tree for the last time.

The clang of the abbey gates rings behind us, as joy and terror alight on the cart, like a dove and a crow. Now there is only the clop of the horses' hooves chopping our memories into little pieces as we spiral down the mountainside. I recall my parents' descent on this path and my terror as I watched them growing ever smaller, leaving me behind. Now, like them, I look up and wave to that small child one last time.

At every curve in the road, my daughters' moans of discomfort grow louder as their trickles of sweat mingle with their tears. We reach the flatland and travel on, each clop of the horses' hooves echoing the footfall of my fears.

As we travel, I marvel at the streams that curve their way across the landscape and am startled by the sad eyes of the ragged children, peering out from clusters of wattle huts that dot the valley.

And now we camp here in utter chaos on Rupert's Mountain, our belongings tossed around us like stacks of new-mown hay. I keep vigil amid the whimpers of my daughters' dreams, deafening my ears against claims that I am gripped by evil spirits. Why entrust a woman to found an abbey when powerful and learned men can better serve? they ask.

Two swords duel behind my eyes, exhausting me: one slashes at my doubts and fears, defending me, while the other pierces my dream until it bleeds. With a thrust, one sword thunders, "Madwoman!" The other glows with Light as it urges me forward to embrace a command I neither understand nor dare distrust.

I drift and dream as the Virgin's eyes flicker in the star-fields above me and pray to trust the moss-covered stepping stones that have led me here. And my first act must be to plant a tree at my door.

The margravine was impressed.

Three years had passed since her first visit to Rupertsberg, shortly after its founding. Then, the chants had risen through the open ceiling of the unfinished chapel, the nuns standing on planks on the muddy ground, surrounded by blocks of granite and stacks of wood.

Since then, swarms of workmen and architects had descended on Rupertsberg, dispatched by no fewer than five prelates and aided by a series of noble benefactors who, at the margravine's behest, had pledged their aid to the abbess. The progress was evident. The fledgling buildings had transformed the barren hillside into a thriving settlement. A cluster of swaying saplings now greeted guests at the gatehouse. Ahead was the shell of the new church of Saint Rupert, rising above the saint's seventh-century crypt. The cloister to the left was bordered by a ring of scarlet poppies and blue cornflowers. Nearby, scaffolding surrounded the dormitory, the refectory, the chapter room, and the abbess' quarters, clearly marked by a thriving maple sapling.

As the bells for Terce were rung, the margravine sighed, recalling the beloved sound from Mount Saint Disibod. Slipping into the shadows of the abbey church, she stood unnoticed; when the chants rose, she was transported. The notes were suffused with a crystalline beauty she had never heard before. They were rapturous.

As she stood there, she had a deep sense of satisfaction. She had been wise to offer Hildegard help in the beginning. Looking around, she knew what a vital part she had played in the progress that surrounded her. She reveled in the alliance, basking in the glow of the visionary abbess. What excited her even more was the chance to invest in such an outrageous venture: an abbey whose abbess owned her land and managed her own abbey, free from the yoke of the monks' control. Had she done nothing else, Abbess Hildegard would have been the talk of the Rhineland for this act alone.

Lost in her thoughts, the margravine realized that the chapel had emptied, though Hildegard had stayed behind to pray.

When she saw the abbess rise, she stepped from the shadows, surprising her. When they embraced, she felt the bones in Hildegard's body. She had grown painfully thin, and her skin was as pale as alabaster.

"Your gifts have showered us with blessings," Hildegard exclaimed, "but your latest one cannot be surpassed. It has truly established us as an abbey. Come, let me show you!"

Linking arms, Hildegard guided her to the oratory.

The margravine gasped. "The choir stalls have arrived at last!" she exclaimed, awed and excited as she ran her hands over the gleaming rosewood carvings. "I could not be more pleased. The woodcarvers carried out my wishes perfectly!"

Hildegard led her forward. "First you must sit in Richardis' stall and then in Hiltrude's so that they will feel your presence and you will be reunited as a family here, day by day."

"That was my hope," the margravine nodded, "knowing that it was from these stalls that prayers rise."

"And tears are shed," Hildegard said softly.

"Have there been many?" the margravine asked, frowning.

"Sadly, more than I could have imagined," Hildegard replied. "I was naive to think my daughters would forget the comforts of Disibodenberg: the wine cellars that were never empty, the storehouses full of candles and linens. All this, plus the treasures of the library we left. I grieve for Richardis, knowing how much she misses it."

"But surely, these things will come with time."

"For some, not soon enough. Sad to say, the complaints are often louder than the praise. I foolishly thought that once the altar was built and the stalls were in place, the grumbling would subside. But six are still threatening to leave."

"Six?" The margravine froze.

Hildegard lowered her head. "All I can do is pray. Many chafe with uneasiness at the abbot's refusal to transfer our dowries. He also balks at releasing Father Volmar to be our provost." Seeing her guest's frown, she caught herself.

"Forgive me, my lady. I regret that my welcome has soured into a complaint." Impulsively, she clasped the woman's hand in her own and kissed it. As she did, the margravine felt a surge of heat that startled her. What had passed from the abbess' hand into her own?

"Your generosity overwhelms me, Your Grace!" Hildegard blushed, hearing the gasps around her table.

"The mill is located at Lorch on the shores of the Rhine," Archbishop Henry explained to her. "The deed includes all the land nearby, as well."

She caught her breath. "Surely not the island too?"

"But of course." His eyes danced with her. "Little enough for the abbey whose name is on everyone's lips, as is the name of its abbess."

Hildegard's grew crimson again. "Your gift will allow us to begin constructing a guest house, Your Grace," she announced, "a hope I have long nourished."

"And I will be one of your first guests," he murmured. "I am eager to sleep beneath your roof, my lady."

"How clumsy of me," Sigmund interrupted, groaning loudly as he fumbled with his overturned winecup.

Henry ignored him and moved closer to the abbess. "Your *Sequence to Saint Rupert* was thrilling, my lady." She looked up in surprise. "I am certain that even my lord chancellor would applaud your spiritual passion, not to mention your musical genius. Your description of Saint Rupert's body as a chalice whose wine can never be drained..." He let the words hang in the air.

Hildegard felt strange. Henry made her words sound profane when he recited them, even blasphemous.

Sigmund cleared his throat loudly. "I find your description most reverent, my Lady Abbess," he said pointedly.

"For the pure of heart, my Lord Chancellor," Hildegard replied.

Henry sat back and drained his winecup.

"I spoke your name often at Aachen, my lady, when I attended the coronation of Frederick, our new king."

The room grew still.

"As I sat in Charlemagne's chapel, I could only imagine the ecstatic heights to which your chants would rise if you were to describe how the king's silver and hyacinth robes trailed him as he ascended the steps to lay claim to Charlemagne's marble throne."

No one breathed.

"But since you were not at my side, I found a way to bring you there," he announced loftily. "When I called King Frederick's attention to your visions, he commissioned me to bring you his greetings and assigned me to serve as your protector."

The room hummed with awe. Seizing the moment, Henry stood

and blessed her. He then expressed his regrets as he and his chancellor departed.

Neither man spoke until Rupert's Mountain lay far behind them. Henry broke the silence with a smile. "Were you jealous?" he whispered, brushing his fur-cuffed glove against Sigmund's cheek.

"Hardly, my lord," his chancellor scoffed, kissing the proffered hand without turning. "It was clear that you were drunk with desire, but not from wine, and not for her."

Hildegard pushed back the bedclothes and reached for her shawl. Thoughts of Henry had been stalking her since his visit. She felt nauseous, still repelled by the way he had mocked her by investing her description of Saint Rupert with his own desires.

She could not decide if he was a curse or a blessing. While one hand reached for his help, the other instinctively pushed him away. Though his land grant dazzled her, she felt suspicious. In her heart, she knew it would prove as useful to him as her visions had been in gaining him access to Pope Eugenius and now to King Frederick. The fear that she had become Henry's willing pawn sickened her, as did her growing awareness that she had become snared in the web of his intrigue. Yet since she was officially accountable to him as her archbishop, she could not risk alienating him.

Sinking to her knees, she prayed to Saint Rupert for prudence and vigilance, especially now that King Frederick had named Henry as her protector. Her head began aching again. There was so much to protect and so few she could trust.

"If only Volmar were here," she whispered.

Richardis placed her quill on her carrel and folded her arms. For the third time that hour, the abbess' dictation had faded and she had lapsed into silence. Richardis sighed. There was nothing to do but wait.

What could be distracting the abbess this time? Thoughts of architects or petitions for burial rights or simply the clattering of passing wagons? What happened to those days when no force on earth could have interrupted the abbess from their work?

Perhaps she was thinking back to this morning's chapter. Ilse had burst into tears, complaining that her hoeing chores in the garden had bruised her hands so badly that they bled. Gertrud, not to be outdone, stuck her feet in the air to show the calluses from her rain-shrunk boots, while Gisla complained that she could see through her threadbare blanket.

Richardis wished now that she had complained about the ache in her knees from the cold draughts that came through the cracks here in the workroom.

In a glance, she saw that the abbess was still motionless. For the first time, she wanted to shake her mistress and scream.

"Sister Richardis?"

"Yes, Lady Mother?" She bolted upright.

"We have not made much progress today. Perhaps we should rest."

Richardis stiffened. "As you wish, my lady." Flustered, she dislodged her pages of vellum, which scattered across the damp floor. As she bent to retrieve them, Hildegard saw that Richardis was close to tears. "There is always more vellum, daughter," she said softly.

"But little content, it appears, to record on it today," she simmered.

Hildegard looked away.

"Should we alter our schedule and not try to work every day, my lady?" Richardis ventured.

Hildegard sat up briskly. "No, no we must keep working. I shall try again."

Closing her eyes, she breathed deeply and slowly for several moments, then began to speak.

"A Virgin betrothed to My Son will receive him as Bridegroom, for she has shut her body away from a physical husband, but in her Bridegroom, she has the priesthood and all the ministry of my altar."

Priesthood and ministry for the Virgin, eh? Richardis thought, raising her eyebrows. So be it!

"The soul strives toward good but at times cannot prevent the body from sinning. Therefore, O human, believe in the power of your soul when tempted to lay aside your good mind and behave like a brute.

"For man's desire is like a brushfire and woman's desire like a warm sun. So it is that when a man feels this great desire in himself, he is like a stag thirsting for the fountain. He races swiftly to her and she to him. Tossed by the winds of desire, the man's need sweeps down to his loins, finding its way to his testicles, inflating his penis.

"And when a woman is making love to a man, her brain is on fire with sensual delight and summons forth the emission of the man's seed. And when

the seed falls into place, the powerful heat from her brain draws the seed to herself and holds it, and her sexual organs contract. She is like a threshing floor pounded by his many strokes and brought to heat when the grains are threshed inside her."

Hildegard's eyes were almost opaque now, her body crumpling with confusion.

Sweet Christ, for whom does she long? a voice screeched inside Richardis.

Standing abruptly, the abbess clasped her head in her hands and pressed her forehead against the wall.

"My lady, are you unwell? Should you take to your bed?"

My bed? Hildegard thought dully. But my bed is my battleground where I struggle against each night's drowning, as my body crests with every wave and my breasts ache with tenderness. And when I awake, I find my gown soaked to my flesh like a second skin, while my soul is caked with the salt of my shame. It is then that a man's eyes rise from the depths, smiling as he pours scented oils of praise on my shoulders. I have no bed that he does not invade, then flee, leaving me with a sleepwalker's stagger to mark the hours.

"We will try again tomorrow, my lady," Richardis sighed. "Another day, another time . . ."

And another drowning, the abbess thought.

The massive oak door closed behind the margravine as she entered the opulent quarters of the archbishop of Bremen.

"Good day, Your Grace!" The margravine bowed formally with lowered eyes, then looked up at her son with a sweetness he had not seen since childhood.

"My title still brings pleasure to your ears, does it not, my Lady Mother?" Hartwig smiled, taking her arm.

"Immensely, my son. I cannot deny it."

Hartwig rejoiced to finally see a flicker of light return to his mother's eyes. She seemed vague and weary, her shoulders hunched forward as though to protect her heart. It grieved him to see how her once famous eyes had grown dull and watery. And her words often trailed off, as though her thoughts fluttered like tatters of cloth on some faraway fence.

She was aware that she held more memories than loved ones in her grasp now. Her vacant stare unsettled him.

"Tell me, my lady," he said lightly, "do my quarters reflect my title? Are they grace-filled as well?"

"No less than their master," she nodded, glancing at the tapestried walls. "You have been seduced by the river-front market stalls again," she teased him, fingering the delicate Byzantine embroidery whose silken threads glowed in the afternoon light. Could she ever forget his childish delight as he roamed through the stalls of the Stade market, awed by the tinkling bells and the bolts of damask sold by turbaned, black-bearded men in their brightly striped robes? He had always been loathe to leave the world of their exotic tongues and the nearby smells of saffron and cinnamon. It seemed so long ago.

"Your father, the count, would not be surprised to see his son at the helm of the church of Bremen," she said. "But then, he always predicted your rise to prominence."

"And what wonders did he portend for my lady sister, Richardis?" he asked. "Surely he saw her bright light even as a child."

"Her curiosity intrigued him, of course, as did her quick mind."

"Both of which, I trust, have been nourished since moving to the Abbey of Rupertsberg?" Hartwig smiled.

"In many ways. But of late, she relishes her position as the abbess' confidante," the mother sniffed, "a role I find tiresome. As for a library, it will take some time to assemble a bounty comparable to that which she found at Disibodenberg. Perhaps now she will learn the merits of patience."

"She may not need to, my Lady Mother."

"Why?" She probed quickly. "Is the Diocese of Bremen considering the gift of a library to the abbess of Rupertsberg?"

"No, but the archbishop of Bremen is considering offering one to his lady sister."

"Surely not your personal library?" The mother was aghast.

"No, indeed. She would have no need of it, if she chose to preside over one of the most prestigious libraries in the land as abbess of Bassum."

"You jest, my son." The margravine paled. "What are you implying?"

"It appears that the Abbey of Bassum has been riddled for some time with internal strife. The nuns of Bassum have petitioned me to provide them with a suitable abbess from outside their ranks. Of course, I thought of Richardis at once."

The margravine was turning her ring now. Hartwig smiled. A good sign.

But she shook her head. "A magnificent hope but one doomed to failure, I fear. She is infatuated with Abbess Hildegard. She has imprisoned herself there. It grieves me to see it."

"I must give the Abbey of Bassum an answer within a fortnight," Hartwig said firmly. "I place the matter in your hands, my lady." He watched as her fingers began turning her ring again.

The margravine looked warily at the two carrels tucked in a corner of the scriptorium.

"We have finally decided which visions will be illuminated in the abbess' book, *Scivias,*" Richardis exclaimed eagerly, still pleased at her mother's visit.

"Another blossom to add to the abbey's budding bouquet," the margravine noted, peering at a vellum sheet dominated by a large blue initial "S" bordered by delicate scarlet ribbons and embellished with lilies and violets.

"And this will be the library one day," Richardis announced as they entered a small, adjoining room that was empty except for some books stacked against the wall.

"Soon, I suspect, with you in charge."

Richardis shrugged. "The assignments were just released, and Sister Radigunde was appointed librarian."

"Impossible!" the margravine flared.

"I was crushed, too, my lady," Richardis confided, "But I dare not show it. Too many already resent my appointment as the abbess' assistant."

"What assignment have you been given then?" the margravine asked, incredulous.

"I shall oversee the new house for poor women," Richardis shrugged, "a challenge that will at least allow me some measure of independence. Come," she said, anxious to distract her mother, "I'll show you the building." She knew that as they crossed the grounds, their voices would be drowned out by the warning shouts of laborers hoisting blocks of stone up to the scaffoldings. Finally, she pointed to a cloud of dust where workmen were shoveling dirt from an excavation.

"That's the site," she said. "The house will be close by the gate so the women can enter with ease."

"And your daily tasks?" The mother's voice was hollow.

Richardis inclined her head toward a pair of pregnant women with sagging bellies whose children were eagerly snatching bread from Sister Almoner's basket. "Look at them. There are sores to be treated, babes to be birthed, teeth to be pulled, and, always, corpses to be buried."

"I don't understand," the margravine complained bitterly. "With your knowledge of books and music, and your exquisite gift of embroidery..."

"And my vow of obedience, my lady." The nun's smile was thin with irony. "We were taught that the Rule asks us to obey with our hearts as well as our lips."

"And what of your work in the scriptorium recording the abbess' visions?"

"It will go on."

"Without you?" The margravine's voice was shrill.

Richardis' glance was impatient. "Have no fear, my lady. I will reap extra blessings by working with the poor. Almsgiving is central to the abbey's work. I must take my turn."

"You sound more resigned than accepting."

"What choice do I have?" the daughter snapped. "I asked for a challenge, and she provided one. What more can I say?"

"The very sentiments I conveyed to your brother when he announced his decision," the margravine sighed, "though he chose not to listen to me."

Richardis turned. "What decision?"

"He has not informed you then?" The margravine looked pleased. "Perhaps I did convince him."

"Of what?" Richardis sputtered, kicking a stone in her path. "Clearly nothing of any importance to me."

"On the contrary. I regard it as no small matter to be considered for the position of abbess of the Abbey of Bassum. He believed the position would suit you well."

"Bassum is the most prestigious abbey in Bremen," Richardis gasped.

"Indeed. But I told him of your devotion to the abbess and your pledge to stay at her side."

Richardis nodded. "You answered well, my lady."

"Why leave your coveted role here and burden yourself with a staggering staff and enormous duties?" the mother agreed. "The hospitality at Bassum is so extravagant, every king in Christendom and his retinue find reasons to rest there as often as possible. The dining hall alone is the length of your church, and the staff for the stables is the size of a small army."

"You have guested there yourself, then?"

"Often, when your father, the count, was alive." She paused, remembering fondly, but then shook her head. "But no, you would be well advised to remain here. You have a brilliant future at the abbess' side, and her fame will continue to open doors for you, especially as she grows older and weaker."

"She is stronger than you think," Richardis retorted. Leaning down to brush a leaf off her robe, she barely mumbled, "When did Hartwig speak to you of the position at Bassum?"

"Bassum?" The margravine squinted. "It's hard to recall since I dismissed the matter so quickly."

"Yet it was kind of him to consider me," Richardis mused.

"Kind, my Lady Daughter?" The margravine laughed. "You underestimate the depth of your brother's confidence in you. Bassum's history demands the leadership of an outstanding abbess. The archbishop of Bremen could scarcely risk appointing his sister if he feared she would not excel."

"Your flattery is wasted on me, my lady," Richardis retorted sharply, "as would be any offer from my brother."

"I am sure he was merely tempted by the thought of his sister following in Lady Jutta's footsteps. . . . "

"As you continue to be, my Lady Mother."

"How can I not, knowing your gifts as I do?" the mother protested. "But, as we both agree, it is not to be."

"A grievous loss for you," Richardis quipped, "since the prestige that attends the abbess of Bassum would gratify you more than challenge me."

The margravine shrugged. "If that's your surmise, then we should retire the matter. I regret having mentioned it at all."

"And my brother?" Richardis persisted. "Did he seek your permission before asking mine? Or was that part of your strategy?"

The margravine stopped on the path. "Of what am I accused? Of repeating your words of devotion to Lady Abbess Hildegard? Or have your feelings for her changed?"

Richardis felt the trap snap at her heels. "Certainly not. She is dear to me beyond measure."

"Then I don't understand."

"I think you do. I have foiled your plans by refusing to be your puppet, and you are angry. When will you accept the fact that your ambitions are not mine?"

The margravine's smile was bathed in sadness. "My ambition, my Lady Daughter? Ambition, like time, pours through my fingers now like sand in an hourglass. I hasten to admit that, had I your gifts when I was young, I would have journeyed through the night, without stopping, to be able to kneel and receive the abbess' crosier and staff at Bassum. But that opportunity was never mine, just as, unlike your sister Luitgard, I never had the opportunity to wear a queenly crown. If you choose to interpret my belief in you as my ambition, so be it. You will do as you please, as you always have. We will not speak of this matter again."

At None the next morning, Richardis learned that the margravine had departed from Rupertsberg at dawn.

The afternoon sun flung steepled shadows from the choir stalls onto the gray stone floor of the chapel. Richardis slumped in her stall, too listless to pray. As the shadows lengthened, she welcomed the sound of approaching footsteps, grateful for the diversion.

As she leaned from her stall, she saw the abbess bowing to the tabernacle at the altar. Hildegard lifted the scroll she was carrying to her lips and kissed it, then opened the tabernacle and placed it inside.

Even from a distance, Richardis could see that the abbess was weeping. When she went to her side, Hildegard clasped her hand.

"My daughter, Abbot Kuno has finally released Father Volmar to be our provost," she said, as tears of gratitude poured from her eyes. "I placed the abbot's promise in the tabernacle to protect it. My heart can rest now, knowing he will be back at my side in the scriptorium!" She was glowing. "Once Father Volmar arrives, I will be inspired anew to continue the work that he and I began long ago."

"He and I?" Richardis cringed at the words. And what of me? she thought. Have you forgotten the months I spent recording your description of the creation of the universe and also your vision of the passage of history and the last days? Have you no memory of the awe we felt when you were shown how the inner harmony of the universe is reflected in each human being?

"And you will, of course, join us when you are free, my daughter," she heard Hildegard add. "You will see, it will be the same as before!"

Richardis felt faint. Did Lady Mother know what she was saying? How could it be the same? Once the provost came, everything would be different. The special times they shared together would cease. Father Volmar would rank first in the abbess' life, while she would fade into just a voice and another pair of hands.

The memory of an incident in the scriptorium now rose and overwhelmed her. Heartsick, she recalled the abbess' description of the different ways that sexual passion affected the bodies of women and men. The graphic details had shocked her. It was not that she doubted the abbess' ability to see into the human body or to discern the emotional cause of a bodily illness. But this was different. Now she knew why. That dictation was inspired by the abbess' true feelings and fantasies about a man. How could it be otherwise? It was to Volmar alone that the abbess had given her heart, not to her. What a fool she had been not to see it.

Once he returned, whatever time she spent with the abbess would be subject to interruption by the sound of Volmar's voice or his knock on the door. She would no longer be privy to news and gossip from the abbess' table. And worst of all, she would be forced to defer to the monk when he visited the poor women's house, though it would be her domain.

"Stay and pray with me on this great day so we can thank God together, my daughter," the abbess begged. "Blessed Jutta is sending Father Volmar home!"

Richardis' eyes clouded. Kneeling, she fumbled with her Psalter, incredulous at the words of the first psalm:

> Do not cast me off, O God my savior.
> Though my father and mother forsake me...

The next day, Richardis awoke bathed in sweat, her hands still pressed against her ears. The scream had receded, but her limbs were still cramped with fear.

The scream had pervaded her dreams for several days. Each time, she stood in the doorway of the poor women's house, which appeared so clean and inviting. The benches and beds were arranged in neat rows, and the table was spread with food for the women and children. But the house was filled with the stench of death.

The scream began as a whimper then grew louder, tearing through the house, ripping linens from the beds and hurling food against the walls.

Before long, everything was in a shambles. What did it mean? Was the scream a curse, warning her not to enter? Or a blessing, releasing her from the stench of death?

The bells for Lauds jangled Richardis. Dressing quickly, she snatched her cloak and dashed past her yawning sisters. She was gasping for breath and sobbing, anxious to inhale the chill morning air and brace herself. As she stepped outside, a gust of wind buffeted her, pinning her against the building as her knees buckled and she slid to the ground. She could barely breathe.

As she stared through the morning mist, the distant autumn trees seemed to be moving toward her, startling her with their magnificence. As they loomed up from the somber gray fields, their branches lavished the sky with firestorms of color, splashing the heavens with patches of vermilion and streaks of blood-orange and gold. Now, a rush of wind swept through the trees as the branches swayed gracefully, and like arms with trailing sleeves, the breezes released the leaves to carpet the earth with incredible beauty.

The spectacle made Richardis dizzy. Why had she never allowed herself to be overcome by the earth's power before? Why had she blinded herself to its extravagance? It had always been at her fingertips. Why had she only lifted her eyes to this mountaintop? Why was she limiting herself to this place?

Now the wind rose, sweeping her forward into its dance of strength and gentleness, of holding and yielding. She too could rise from the grayness of her fields; she too was throbbing with possibilities. "Learn from us!" the trees seemed to cry out to her. "Your fields lie fallow beneath the frost of your desperation and choke with the weeds of your despair! Make haste to harvest your bounty of scarlet dreams, as we have. Fling your wonder to the winds with abandon, as we do, reveling in our season of splendor. So now must you, before your colors fade."

All through Lauds and Prime, Richardis felt as though she were standing in a furnace.

The trees had seeded her soul with their embers: they smoldered now, emboldening her to leave. Now she need no longer wait her turn to speak, to plead, to rule; she would no longer have to record another's words when hers would be law. Clenching her fists, she pounded her ribs: There is nothing more for me here, she decided. Inside the safety of her sleeves, her hands shook with a violent tingling: my fingers sob, she thought, since I dare not weep.

Nearby, the voice of the abbess soared with joy, piercing her heart, making her weak. How can I leave her? she wondered.

Then another voice rose, even more compelling, lifting her up, placing her on the crest of the wave: "Had I your gifts when I was young, I would have journeyed through the night, without stopping, to be able to kneel and receive the abbess' crosier and staff at Bassum."

To the Lady Margravine Richardis von Stade, from Hildegard, Abbess of Rupertsberg:

> Greetings.
>
> I hold up my heart to you so you may know how deeply my soul is wounded because of my loving daughter Richardis' departure.
>
> As I write, I see her radiance glowing before me, her virtues glistening in my sight like a necklace of pearls. Take care, my dear lady, lest by your schemes and manipulations, you rob her soul of that grace.
>
> Painful though it may be, you must accept the fact that the position of abbess that you so greatly desire for her is not the will of God nor will it gain the salvation of her soul. Of that, I am certain.

Hartwig handed the letter back to the margravine.

"I received a similar letter," he said, wearily. "The abbess wept at my feet, begging me to 'send my daughter back to me so that I may be consoled by her and she by me.'"

"And your reply?"

"A firm refusal, of course. But her letter still disturbs me. She hinted strongly that our family, indeed that I, had purchased the abbacy for Richardis," Hartwig reported hoarsely. "I can ill afford to have such a rumor abroad in my diocese, much less within the Abbey of Bassum itself. I have gone to great lengths to assure the nuns that Richardis will bring them the spiritual integrity that they so desperately seek."

But the margravine was still chafing. "I find it intriguing that an abbess who claims to see into the soul of her devoted assistant blinds herself to Richardis' ambition. Does she really think that any efforts of ours could have forced her to leave against her will?"

"Come now, my Lady Mother, surely you can see that it is easier for the abbess to think ill of us than to face the thought that Richardis would leave her. Still, when she speaks from her visions, her words have un-common strength. I feel it unwise to simply dismiss them as sentiments flowing from a broken heart."

"Then why did her far-seeing gifts not prepare her for Richardis' departure?"

Hartwig winced. "Take care, my lady. These are not simple matters. As a visionary, the abbess draws from a well whose depths we will never plumb. It behooves us to act with great discretion."

The margravine's smile was indulgent. My son is young yet, she thought. He will learn soon enough.

"Do not distress yourself about the abbess," she said, smiling. "In time, she will see that the mirror she holds up to warn me reflects her own face as well."

The archbishop of Mainz was livid.

"Calm yourself, Your Grace," his chancellor advised sternly. "Abbess Hildegard's demand that you rescind your approval of Sister Richardis' appointment to Bassum is nothing but an act of desperation."

"How dare she threaten me?" Archbishop Henry stormed, shaking her letter as he circled the room. "The woman's audacity staggers me!"

Sigmund shrugged and handed him a winecup to distract him but Henry was in no mood to be playful and shoved the cup aside.

Sigmund became impatient. "Your Grace, enjoy your dilemma. You have both an abbess in Rupertsberg and an abbey at Bassum at your feet, both pleading with you for Sister Richardis. You need only to affix your seal and the deed is done. What is your pleasure?"

But Henry only crumpled the letter and flung it away.

"Why have you allowed her to upset you so, Your Grace?" Sigmund asked calmly. "What dominion does she have on you?"

"I wish I knew," Henry grumbled. Retrieving the letter, he smoothed it and thrust it at Sigmund. "Read it to me again."

To Henry, Archbishop of Mainz, from Hildegard, Abbess of Rupertsberg:
    In the name of the Living Light that never leaves me, I repeat: your reasons for approving this girl's appointment to Bassum shrivel in the sight of God. Therefore, since it springs from the malice

of greedy hearts, we must ignore all your warnings and malicious threats.

May God's fiery flame sear your soul with this warning: Shepherd of God, lament and mourn now for, in your blindness, you squander God's offices for financial gain and give your support to those who mock God. Remember that Nebuchadnezzar fell and that his crown perished.

Arise and repent, Your Grace, for your days are short!

The letter slipped to the floor as Sigmund sat forward and buried his face in his hands. When he finally spoke, his voice was thick and his eyes were like bits of charcoal: "She must be humbled, Your Grace," he bristled, sharpening his quill.

Henry bolted from his chair.

To the Lady Abbess Hildegard of Rupertsberg, from Archbishop Henry, Prelate of Mainz:

By our authority as prelate and spiritual father of Mainz, we command you to release Sister Richardis von Stade at once so she may assume her official duties as abbess of Bassum. If you refuse, we will use our official power to convince you. Be advised: our decision is final.

During the months that Abbot Kuno had debated the wisdom of releasing Volmar to Rupertsberg, Volmar had been careful to guard his tongue. He was divided within regarding the move: despite the rancor in the air at Disibodenberg, he knew that leaving the mountain would mean forgoing the daily companionship of his brothers in exchange for the constant company of women. Despite his years as a provost, the prospect was daunting. Like many oblates, Volmar had spent his youth defending himself from impure thoughts by comparing all women with the Virgin. Only Lady Jutta had succeeded in lifting that heavy stone from his heart by her utter trust in him. Now that trust would be put to the ultimate test.

But now the fear flared anew. At Rupertsberg, not only would he be the only monk in an abbey of women, but he would be with the abbess constantly. Since she left, he had tried to subdue his flesh by fasting and taking the leather lash of discipline. But by now, the ache in his heart had spread to every bone in his body.

His only solace had been to reflect on those astonishing days he had shared with the abbess in the scriptorium where Lady Wisdom's Voice had left them breathless long after they had recorded her words and described her images.

When he least expected it, Abbot Kuno had announced his release at chapter.

For the first time in months, Kuno had felt he could breathe.

"A thousand welcomes, my lord!" the porter called out as Volmar rode through the gates of Rupertsberg.

"*Pax tecum!* [Peace be to you!]" the girlish novice added, blushing as she came forward with a pitcher of water and linen cloth.

"*Et cum spiritu tuo!* [And with you!]" he replied. "I am Father Volmar, your new provost."

The novice's eyes sparkled. "Ah, Sister Prioress will be so pleased!"

As he handed the groom his reins, Volmar saw Hiltrude running toward him, veil and skirts flying, like a blackbird in flight.

"How I've prayed for this day," she said, hugging herself. "Thank God you've come!" As she knelt for his blessing, she lowered her eyes. Her hands were shaking. After the blessing, she rose and faced him. "Mother will be reborn now that you've here," she gulped, her eyes glistening. "Come," she said, "let me show you your new home."

His house was footsteps away from the chapel. It was flanked on either side by newly planted trees. The two rooms were small: the parlor had a good-sized table with two chairs and a bench; a door opened to a second room with a bed and a prie-dieu. It was palatial to him. Hiltrude seemed both excited and nervous. Volmar noted how thin she had become and that her rosy skin had turned sallow. The flickers of joy he had seen upon his arrival had vanished. He saw, as well, that her once-firm chin had sloped into her neck now and she squinted. Yet her glance remained fastened on him as if she feared that he might disappear.

"Every stone here has a story," she explained as they toured the abbey grounds. "In the beginning, food supplies were so low we ate once a day, and the cold was so intense that we were always wrapped in blankets. But I always managed to find a way to keep us going."

"You have continued as prioress then?"

"At lady mother's request. At first, she was so busy meeting with the workmen, we only saw her at chapel. What made it worse was that we were unprepared to perform the most menial tasks, which made the abbess impatient. Most of the nuns abhorred the thought of soiling their hands with planting and cleaning. Though all had agreed to support the new abbey, few truly adjusted to the challenges here. Even after a year, many assumed that one day soon, steaming platters of food would arrive or that servants would appear at their elbows as they did at Disibodenberg. The last three women who entered disappeared within weeks." Pausing, she forced a smile. "Most of those times passed, thank God!"

"Has it all been drudgery? Were there no successes?"

"There were for those willing to work: for them, every brick laid was a triumph. But now, even more are threatening to leave."

"I don't understand. You have accomplished so much. Surely life is easier now."

Hiltrude frowned. "Surely mother has written you."

"Not for some time." Then he realized that he had been there almost an hour and had not seen her. "Where is the lady abbess now?"

"In her house, which she leaves only to sing the Divine Office and sometimes for daily chapter." Hiltrude looked away.

"Sometimes? Has she been ill?"

Hiltrude looked stricken. "In a way."

Volmar's stare demanded an answer.

"Sister Richardis has left to accept a position as abbess of Bassum. Our lady mother has been inconsolable."

Volmar paled. "I was not told."

"Father Volmar," the prioress gasped, "if I may so bold: though we never spoke of it openly at Disibodenberg..."

Volmar felt sick, as though he had lurched to the edge of a precipice. "Sister Hiltrude," he interrupted, "please announce my arrival to the abbess and my request to see her without delay."

When Volmar stood in the doorway, Hildegard uttered a wail that shivered him. "You have come too late! Why weren't you here to intercede for me? Have you no pity? My heart is cracked with grief."

Volmar recoiled at the sight that greeted him. The abbess sat crouched in a corner, her arms wrapped around her chest as she rocked back and forth. Her violet eyes were black pools now and flashed with a wildness that frightened him. Wisps of hair straggled from beneath her sweat-stained wimple. Her skin was gray, and her cheekbones nearly pierced the skin above her sunken cheeks.

"If only you had come sooner, you might have convinced her to stay," she accused him, flailing with one hand, while the other yanked at her rosary.

Could this be the homecoming he had dreamed of, had envisioned day after day for the past year? What had become of the luminous nun whom Lady Jutta had entrusted to him, the cherished abbess whose first thought once would have been to offer a Mass of thanksgiving for his safe arrival?

"Be seated, dear friend," she said, as her eyes darted about as though she was unable to focus. Then with the plaintive cry of a lost child, she whimpered, "My darling Richardis has abandoned me."

"My Lady Mother, I..."

But she had begun licking her lips distractedly. "Did you write and implore the margravine for me?" she asked. "I wrote her, of course."

Hoisting herself to her feet, she went to a table littered with papers and baskets and began scattering rolls of vellum in a frenzy.

"No. I remember. Of course. The letter has already been sent to her."

"And her reply?" Volmar asked, hoping to join in her flow of concern.

"None. She thinks I'm blind and unable to see how she has beguiled my precious daughter."

"And her daughter, as well, my lady," he offered gently.

"No longer!" she roared, her eyes wild. "We are her family now. She vowed obedience to the Rule and stability to this house."

"But not to your heart, my lady," Volmar replied firmly.

"She is vowed to the work," she cried, wringing her hands as she began rocking back and forth again.

Instinctively, Volmar stood and raised his hands above her head. *"Ave Maria. Gratia Plenam!*... [Praise to the Virgin!...]" he said, blessing her. At the words, the abbess sank to her knees, withered with sobs.

Volmar knelt beside her, repeating the prayer to the Virgin over and over, until she grew still. When the bells for Vespers rang, they rose and, like sleepwalkers, strolled to the chapel together as they had done a thousand times before. Once inside, he felt her step falter as they passed an empty choir stall.

Let us pray for each other, Sister Richardis, Volmar cried out inside, for each of our souls treads on the edge of a knife.

For days, Volmar felt overwhelmed. Nothing could have prepared him for the chaos that prevailed here as the abbess withdrew more and more into her grief. Were Hiltrude not so capable, he was sure that the abbey would have collapsed. Volmar woke up exhausted each day, still reeling from the shock of the abbess' condition. Yet he was determined to provide a sense of spiritual stability and to refuse to let the abbess' erratic demands interfere with his duties as chaplain.

On the first day in chapel, Volmar asked the nuns to pray for him so that he might be guided by God's grace in every way. The sea of wary faces before him had dismayed him.

"Many are bruised with regret," Hiltrude later explained. "After what they've been through, they are slow to trust."

But later still, as the nuns prepared to receive their monthly Holy Communion, the floodgates burst open in the confessional.

"It was so unfair. Richardis was denied nothing, . . . nothing!"

"Lady mother taught us that such friendships were strictly forbidden by the Rule."

"No one else dared enter the scriptorium while Richardis was there."

"Why was she assigned a plum like the poor women's house when senior sisters were far more qualified? But since Richardis wanted it, lady mother gave in."

"Since Richardis left, lady mother has ignored the rest of us."

"The Rule says, 'Let the abbess not love one more than another,'" and further states that she who breaks this rule will be severely punished."

"But who will punish the abbess?" Volmar sighed.

As the days passed, the abbess grew calmer. Volmar persuaded her to stroll with him each morning after chapter. At first, they walked in silence. In time, after the rains had softened the earth and a green sheen covered the hillsides, Hildegard seemed to come alive.

"Viriditas. The greening power of God, the kiss of the Holy Spirit," she sighed, inhaling the moist life rising from the earth. "Lady Jutta is here." She smiled and fell silent again; it was a day to remember. She had finally parted the veils of her self-pity and allowed the light to return to her eyes.

With the weather growing milder, Volmar carefully began to guide her down the slopes to the river's edge where the sound of the flowing waters refreshed her; then he chose the steepest way back in order to tire her body and help her to sleep.

As the weeks passed, she paused to pick dandelions for wine and to pluck grapevines whose juice she would blend with an extract of apple blossoms "to treat the stonemason's cataracts." One day, she gathered fennel to blend into a tincture for Hiltrude's forehead and temples, to soothe her headaches. She began to stop in the middle of a sentence to close her eyes, then trot off in a different direction to secure a much-needed herb. Volmar suggested to her that she might consider compiling an herbal compendium to share her healing remedies with others. "That would surely serve a need," she agreed.

"But *Scivias* comes first," he advised, and for the first time, she nodded excitedly. Then the spark died.

He knew that Richardis' shadow had fallen over her heart again, at the mention of *Scivias*, and with it, the desperate hope that perhaps today there would be some word from Bassum. But her disappointment only grew.

One day, as Volmar sifted through the mass of correspondence, his eyes caught sight of the papal seal. Since the abbess had made no mention of it, he assumed it had arrived while she was ill.

My dear daughter in the Lord, Hildegard:

To you whose eyes have been blessed to see great wonders, we send our greetings.

Regarding your request that your spiritual daughter, Lady Richardis von Stade, return to the Abbey of Rupertsberg, we have placed the matter in the hands of our son Henry, archbishop of Mainz. If he determines that the Benedictine Rule is not being strictly observed at the Abbey of Bassum, we have every confidence that he will recall Sister Richardis and arrange for her return to the Abbey of Rupertsberg.

Until such time, my daughter, I ask that you must reflect carefully upon the desires of your heart and soul. Remember that the serpent of old Paradise seeks to tempt us and destroy the great, such as Job. But we have every confidence that you will proceed with the greatest humility. To this end, be assured of our prayers.

Volmar was stunned. Although he could only infer the pleadings and demands of Hildegard's letter from the response he held in his hand, he could scarcely believe the lengths to which the abbess' desperation had driven her.

Yet at the deepest level, Volmar's soul wept for her. Now he truly understood why the Abbey of Rupertsberg had become a house of whispers, a rising chorus no confessional could hope to contain.

Hildegard braced herself against the wind as she hurried through the cloister. The snow had been falling for days, the layers hardening overnight into crystalline blankets that covered the hills with silver ice. The abbey had settled into a great sigh. The guest house was empty except for two widows muffled in layers of woolen shawls and memories. The world had never seemed so still.

Volmar had set aside time before None each day for spiritual counseling. He realized that the nuns still simmered with resentment about Richardis' access to the abbess' visions, a privilege they had been denied. With great care, he presented a possible solution to the abbess.

"Would you allow me to share my memories of your visions with them?" he suggested. "And thus invite them into the scriptorium by another door? It could also serve as an instruction," he added.

She seemed relieved.

The nuns were jubilant. The word spread quickly, and the hall was always full when Volmar spoke of the visions. Over the weeks, he guided them through the labyrinth of the abbess' revelations, describing the vision in which she saw Lucifer plunge into darkness through a shower of stars. In another, he traced the vision of the earth whirling in space, encircled by flames and whirlwinds and swirling layers of ether. And in still another, how the abbess had recoiled at a vision of the Devil in chains: a putrid monster covered with ulcers, its human hands clawing at its eyes which bulged with burning blood.

But there were also visions of radiance. The monk's face shone as he disclosed the abbess' vision of the Redeemer as he walked through a thousand sapphire worlds to reach his destiny.

The nuns were mesmerized. "There were times when I forgot to breathe," Gertrud admitted.

Then slowly, over the weeks, Volmar introduced Lady Wisdom.

"Does Mother Hildegard see her face?" Gisla asked.

"Indeed!" Volmar exclaimed. "She has appeared to the abbess in many forms on the screen of the Living Light. But she can come alive for us, as well, in the books of the Old Testament where we read that, even now, she circles the world, protecting it with her wings of compassion. 'For she is fairer than the sun and is more glorious than all the constellations of stars," Volmar quoted from Holy Writ, 'even surpassing the light as she passes into holy souls from age to age, birthing friends of God and prophets.'"

"Do you pray to her as one would pray to the Virgin?" Ilse asked.

"Indeed, if you need counsel and understanding. We are told 'Seek Wisdom! Love her and she will protect you!' Solomon himself proclaimed that he preferred her to his scepter and throne and said his riches were like sand when compared to her, just as precious jewels faded in her presence."

The nuns greatly rejoiced in their provost, nudging each other whenever he praised the abbess, unaware that she often sat listening alone outside the door.

In time, at Volmar's urging, the abbess appeared to share Lady Wisdom's legacy in her own, unique way. Using jewels as a symbol, she fashioned, with her words, a necklace of precious gems to emblazon Lady Wisdom's legacy.

The jewel closest to Lady Wisdom was Eve, who birthed the first human face of God and in whom the whole human race lay hidden. Beside Eve was the jewel representing Synagoga, the passionate woman who rose to great heights, like the tower of a city. The prophet Abraham glowed in her heart; Moses was at her breast; and the rest of the prophets resided in her womb.

The next jewel signified the Virgin, who blossomed like a fragrant branch and is eternally unfolding. Uttering her *Fiat*, the Virgin opened her womb to the wedding of heaven and earth and brought forth the Redeemer.

A pearl nestled between each gem, the abbess explained, to connect the gems with the majestic Ecclesia, Mother Church, her womb ever-pregnant with the seeds of compassion, her ears alert to the faraway cries of her abandoned children, her heart a nest, a cavern, a resting place.

Hildegard described other visions of Lady Wisdom, some of which clouded the abbess' countenance. She warned of an unspeakable fate that was drawing closer to Ecclesia. And she spoke of the hurricanes that would rend the last days with a tumult and of earthquakes that were destined to birth the new heaven and earth. But in the end, the abbess promised them, Lady Wisdom would be there.

As the nuns listened, their faces softened. At times, watching this, Volmar was so moved with joy that he was sure his heart would break.

He had come home at last.

The night sky was studded with diamonds as Volmar knocked at the abbess' door. He had come as usual to accompany her to Matins, lest she lose her step in the dark.

At his third knock, the door swung open. In the glow cast by a sputtering candle, he saw the abbess slumped forward in her chair. Alarmed, he rushed to her and was relieved by the flutter of her steady breathing. She must have fallen asleep while writing; her quill still rested in her half-open hand. Looking down, he glanced at the greeting:

To Richardis, Abbess of Bassum, from Hildegard, Abbess of Rupertsberg:

My daughter, hear me, I beg of you. Your spiritual mother cries out to you: my grief consumes me! Why have you destroyed the great trust and comfort that I placed in you?

I fell prey to this weakness out of love for you, believing you to be a noble person. But since I have sinned in this way, God has made that sin clear to me by the anguish and pain I experience because of you. How can you not know this? Now I warn others to set their hope in God alone and not in a human person who fails like a flower's falling petals.

Again, I plead with you: Why have you abandoned me like an orphan? I loved the nobility of your presence, your wisdom, your chastity, your whole life, your soul! I loved you so much that others were emboldened to ask, "What has possessed you?"

Now let all who have endured such a sorrow mourn the great love I had in my heart and mind for you who were snatched away from me in a single moment.

I pray that the angel of God may precede you, and the Son of God protect you, and his mother guard you. Be mindful of your poor mother, Hildegard, and desert me no longer!

Volmar felt like a thief as he hurried to chapel.

When the margravine opened her eyes, the faces surrounding her were bathed in clouds of ineffable light.

"Is it you, my lord, my husband?"

"It is, my lady wife," he said, kissing her forehead, as his hand brushed back the silver strands into the tumble of auburn hair on the pillow.

"And our sons, as well!" she cried out in joy.

Standing beside their father were Udo, then the two Rudolphs: the child and the man. The men's red-gold hair was aflame atop their flashing armor.

"You must join us now," the count said gently. "We must travel ahead to Richardis."

"Oh yes, yes. To Bassum!" she exclaimed. "We must see her grasping her abbess' staff, her baculus, as she sits in her abbatial chair."

"Indeed," the count said tenderly. "And so much more."

"Shall we go then, dear cousin?" she heard Lady Jutta whisper. The face she had prayed to for decades hovered over her, and the hand that reached for her glowed with light.

Rising from her bed, she took the count's arm.

"I will show you the way," Blessed Jutta said, as the margravine stepped forward into the rapture and her soul exploded with joy.

There were so many doors at the Abbey of Bassum. After that night, Hartwig would retrace his steps again and again. The first door led into the chapel, where he went to pray on his arrival. The second door led to the refectory, where he drained one cup after another, before he realized that he had not eaten or drunk since the day before.

Finally, an elegant iron gate led to the abbess' house, where the prioress greeted him. Then door after door as she guided him to the threshold of the abbess' private quarters, then through the door of her private library, and, finally, to the door to the abbess' sitting room.

"Deo gratias," the prioress called out, loathe to leave the company of the archbishop of Bremen.

"Benedicite." The reply from inside sounded winsome. When Hartwig entered, Richardis squealed with surprise as she rushed to his side.

"Is it truly you, my dear brother Hartwig?" she cried. "Your presence is like an answered prayer!"

He held her close for a moment, disturbed that she clung so tightly to him. Breaking away, he indulged her excitement with a smile as he marshaled his thoughts, knowing he must not hurry.

He need not have worried. Richardis' words tumbled from her like a waterfall: all her doubts and dilemmas, crises and fears, shocks and surprises. Every regret and misgiving that she had encountered since seeing him: all that was too new, too much, too little, too soon. She could not share the problems fast enough. His head was spinning!

"My Lady Abbess," he murmured from time to time. "My Lady Sister!"

There were too many tears, he worried. Or could it be shock of his visit?

He let her talk until she was spent.

Contrite at her deluge, she shifted nervously. "How long may we have the pleasure of your company at the Abbey of Bassum, Your Grace?" she asked, attempting a smile.

"I grieve that I must leave within the hour." Hearing her protest, he held up his hand. "You will understand why I must return at once, my Lady Sister, when you learn that I have come to bring you the sad news that our lady mother is dead," he confessed. "I must prepare for her funeral."

For the rest of his life, his sister's scream would ring in his soul; it would echo seven times a day in every bell he heard ring in every abbey church where he would swear he saw their mother's face in the crowd, the famous blue-green eyes beneath the coils of copper hair entwined with pearls.

Each time, he would cover his ears, praying his own scream of disbelief would be lost in that of his sister: "No, no! Not our own lady mother!"

"If nothing else, our attendance at this event should lessen the sting of my refusal to return Sister Richardis here from Bassum," Archbishop Henry grunted to his chancellor as they joined the last few guests hurrying toward the Rupertsberg chapel.

As they neared the entrance, Henry grimaced and slowed his step. "Tell me again: What is this spectacle we are about to see?"

Sigmund glanced about nervously, fearing they might have been overheard. "The abbess has written a morality play entitled *Ordo Virtutum*, the Order of Virtues. It depicts the struggle of a human Soul caught between heaven and earth. God sees her dilemma and sends the Virtues to strengthen her with assurance that she does not journey through life alone. But the Devil plots to snatch the Soul by seducing it."

"Truly, my lord chancellor?" Henry smiled, raising his eyebrow.

"The Soul succumbs, then pleads with the Virtues to rescue her," the chancellor continued.

"Of course!" Henry said, frowning with impatience.

"But surely you can understand the Soul's plight, Your Grace?" Sigmund countered.

"But of course," Henry grinned, as he tripped over Sigmund's foot, forcing his chancellor to catch him. "Just as you rescue me, my friend."

"You take more risks than you should, knowing I am here to stop you," Sigmund said, tensing.

"Then I should take fewer of them, which is unlikely, or you should take greater pleasure in the ones I place in your path."

Sigmund lingered behind Henry as they entered the chapel. It was bathed in candlelight. The play was about to begin.

Henry stared dutifully as the procession of Virtues glided toward the altar in long, flowing gowns. Humility was first; Patience, Chastity, Wisdom, and Mercy followed, each carrying the symbols of her office. Victory was the last to appear, wearing a veil crowned with a circlet of snowy blossoms.

On the altar, the Soul stood with outstretched arms, her loosened hair tumbling like corn silk onto her slender shoulders. Soon after she descended to the earth, she looked up, battered and bleeding, after her fall. She begged the Virtues to rescue her, the Devil's voice roaring with laughter, . . . boasting of his conquest.

"Do not mock me!" Chastity's powerful voice thundered at the Devil, while a voice inside Henry screamed, "Your loathsome secrets writhe like eels across the skin of your soul."

Sigmund felt Henry flinch beside him as he twisted in his chair.

"Do not mock me!" Chastity cried out once more.

The words snapped like a lash across Henry's cheeks, making him whimper. Sigmund tensed again at the sight of the sweat that now drenched Henry's face and neck. Leaning forward, Henry gripped his knees to steady himself. Hearing him gag, Sigmund quickly slid the cloak off his shoulders, readying himself in case the prelate vomited.

"Do not mock me, mock me, mock me!" Henry stuttered hoarsely, as his limbs began to flail in every direction.

Seizing the back of Henry's neck, Sigmund forced Henry's head down to his knees so that all who passed would assume the prelate was praying. He knew the danger signs: once Henry began twitching, it was imperative that he be removed before he lost control of his bodily functions. The prelate's mind and body were out of control now. He must get him to the guest house before he made a spectacle of himself. Throwing his cloak over him, Sigmund grasped Henry by the waist and all but shoved him to the door.

They had risked too much coming here, Sigmund thought once he had gotten Henry into bed. Despite Henry's bravado, Sigmund knew that Henry was secretly tormented by the abbess' warning that his days were numbered. Sigmund already dreaded the nightmares that were sure to assault the prelate in the hours ahead: the devils with twisted faces leaping into his eyes and ears and mouth, making him crazy. Then the sobs and clutches and demands for comfort that his grace would need from him to reach the dawn.

Until then, there would only be the sound of the archbishop's agony. "Can God forgive me, Sigmund? You must bless me again! I must repent of my sins. I am so afraid!"

It would be a long night, Sigmund knew. By now, he had collected too many memories of Henry's averted eyes, lies, and evasions. In the hours ahead, he could only speculate about whose firm grasp had restrained Henry the last time and whose arms, like his, had held him fast until the prelate collapsed at last into a merciful snore.

October leaves crackled beneath Hildegard's feet as she walked to the cloister. The air was so crisp and the colors so striking, she paused to place her face against the bark of a great elm and encircle it with her arms.

"Thank you for shedding your glory at our feet," she whispered.

Brushing back the bits of bark from her robe, she saw Volmar hurrying toward her. "A messenger has just arrived from Bremen," he said, handing her the roll of vellum as the color rose in her cheeks.

To Hildegard, Abbess of Rupertsberg, from Hartwig, Archbishop of Bremen:

We write to convey the tragic news that our sister, mine by body, yours by soul, has followed the way of all flesh. I am consoled in the knowledge that she now rests in the company of our lady mother, the margravine.

After her heartfelt confession, she wept for her abbey as I anointed her with the last rites of the Church. Then, she blessed herself three times, in perfect faith, hope, and charity, before she breathed her last breath.

Since receiving news of our mother's death, our sister deeply regretted receiving the dignity of the rank of abbess, which I had personally conferred on her.

I beg you with all my strength to love her as deeply in death as you did in life, with the same fervor with which she loved you. Those who attended her can attest to the countless tears she shed after departing from you and can witness to her intention of returning to you as soon as she had received permission. Alas. She was prevented from doing so by her death.

Hildegard felt her knees buckle, and she collapsed at the foot of the tree. Gasping, she reached out for a crimson leaf and pressed it to her lips frantically.

"My dearest Richardis! My darling daughter! I kiss the rose-blush of your cheeks for the last time!"

For three days, she lay in her bed, unable to speak. And though many tried, none could pry the scarlet leaf from her hand, even in sleep.

The icy winds of November were merciless, whipping the trees into submission until their branches swayed like captive skeletons. Inside the stone walls of the enclosure, it was so cold the nuns could see their breath as the chill pierced their skin like splinters. Their constant shivering only added to the pall that Richardis' death had flung across the abbey.

"Why did I judge Richardis so harshly?"

The question plagued them, each grieving as much about her own jealousy as she did about the loss of her sister.

"When I think of all the anniversary masses we've sung for our deceased benefactors," Hiltrude said, "who could have known that Richardis would be the first of our own whom we would mourn?"

And as the bells tolled, they could only speculate on how her death must be affecting the abbess.

Yet on the day of Richardis' memorial Mass, Hildegard appeared calm.

"I don't understand," Gisla murmured to Gertrud. "When I saw her last, her face was a waxen mask on the pillow. Look at her now."

From their stalls, their glances followed her as she walked to her abbess' chair, her chin high, her eyes burning like azure flames above her flushed cheeks, her manner almost triumphant.

"At the heart of her loss, does she also feel vindication?" Gertrud wondered, stunned at the mere possibility.

Volmar, however, knew differently, for he had already seen the change. He had seen it earlier when he went to bring the Host to the abbess' sickbed and found her fully dressed and kneeling at her prie-dieu. Applewood boughs were crackling in the fireplace, filling the room with a fragrant warmth.

Was this the same woman who had been blind and immobile for the past three days? he had wondered. Her face was glowing, bathed in a rare tranquillity.

After receiving Holy Communion, she had announced briskly, "I wish to send a letter to his grace, Archbishop Hartwig."

Volmar had blinked. "My lady, ..." he protested, but when her lifted hand silenced him, he reached for his stylus.

To Hartwig, Archbishop of Bremen, from Hildegard, Abbess of Rupertsberg:

My prayers reach out to console you at the loss of your sister and my daughter, Richardis. My soul still overflows with divine love for her since the Living Light first taught me to cherish her in a powerful vision. I was shown that God's love for her was so great, he could no longer abandon her to the worldly arms of a rival lover. Knowing that, she surrendered all worldly wonders.

Dear friend, be assured that my heart has banished any pain you may have caused me regarding my daughter. I entreat you to rest in that certainty.

Her face had been luminous. Lost in her thoughts, she had gazed into the fire, her hands clasped beneath her chin. Even with her back to him, he had been able to see the peaceful slope of her shoulders. Somehow, there had been a strengthening that had transformed her loss into triumph.

Aware of his observation, the abbess had turned to him and nodded. Though no words had been exchanged, in that moment, Volmar knew with utter certainty that Richardis had appeared to the abbess.

Part Four

1152–55

And my soul, as God wills it,
ascends upward in this vision,
toward the heights of the firmament
and into the layers of the atmosphere,
expanding over diverse peoples
in distant places and remote regions.

— Vita Sanctae Hildegardis

"Four guests and their parties are here presently, and four more will arrive within the week," Hiltrude informed the twins as they washed their hands at the lavabo before the midday meal.

For the past year, the guest house had never been empty. Whenever Hiltrude looked down from the cliff above the place where the rivers joined, guests were mooring their boats on the shore below. While life here was a constant challenge, she could not deny that Rupertsberg brought the world to their door.

These were exciting days because every guest at Hildegard's table was bursting with talk of their new young king, Frederick, the former duke of Swabia. His ties to two of Germany's most powerful feuding families, the Welfs and the Hohenstaufens, fueled hopes that he could effect their reconciliation.

"We have much to look forward to," the abbot of Eberbach announced at the abbess' table. "Our new king has proclaimed that his reign intends nothing less than the restoration of the Holy Roman Empire. And since Germany will be its centerpiece, he's already sent an expedition to Italy to reclaim Germany's long-dormant rights."

"I suspect he feels invincible after his overwhelming election," the archbishop of Trier explained. "He certainly lost no time in announcing that, since his head wears the crown, he is God's agent on earth, and therefore, responsible to God alone."

"He can surely count on the support of his clerics," a count from Magdeburg added soberly, "but the German princes are another matter."

Every head nodded. All present knew that resentment still simmered from the investiture controversy at the turn of the century. That clash between Church and Crown had created a political vacuum in which the German princes seized power. Backed by the papacy, the princes fought hard to prevent the royal office from becoming hereditary, knowing that royal heirs might thwart the princes' future plans to expand their own holdings.

"Our youthful king would do well to tend to his own house here in Germany before sending troops over the Alps to reclaim an empire," the abbot of Eberbach advised. "We must see if our new king Frederick honors the twofold agreement he made with Pope Eugenius at the Peace of Constance: first, to aid the pope in suppressing the Roman commune led by the fiery heretic, Arnold of Brescia, and, second, to support the Norman king of Sicily. Both conditions must be met before the pope will agree to crown Frederick emperor."

"In the meantime," the count added, "Frederick has already canvassed the kingdom to end the grievances between his warring princes and to test his bishops' loyalty."

"A matter that must surely concern you, my Lady Abbess, considering that your archbishop, Henry of Mainz, led the opposition to King Frederick's election," the archbishop of Trier noted.

Hildegard's voice was serene. "Is that his only encumbrance?"

"The only one we can prove," the archbishop said, frowning.

"I, for one, am intrigued with our new king's passion to vindicate Charlemagne's memory," Volmar intervened, hoping to change the subject.

"One of many passions about which, I'm sure, your gift could inform us, my Lady Abbess," the archbishop probed.

"Or might you tell us more about Pope Eugenius' swift consent to Frederick's divorce from Adela on grounds of adultery?" a baroness from Mainz asked Hildegard. "Or can you confirm that Frederick is already bargaining for her replacement in the courts of Constantinople?"

Hildegard saw the kingdom of Burgundy stretching out like a carpet at Frederick's feet while he clasped the hand of a young virgin.

"He will take another bride to bed," the abbess said, "and will discover love."

"Love in marriage?" the baroness laughed aloud. "For a king who seeks an emperor's crown? How quaint!"

The summer day was humid, the sun unforgiving.

Hildegard shook her head as she scolded the builders. Once again, they had failed to accurately follow her plans to enlarge the poor women's house. Eyes flashing, she stomped out the boundaries, her instructions drowned out by the sound of voices arguing at the gatehouse. The travelers were insistent; they must see the abbess without delay. Shielding her eyes, she saw that they carried the royal standard.

As she approached them, the messengers bowed deeply; then the older

one withdrew from his scrip a scroll that bore the royal seal. After blessing them, she instructed the porter to water their horses and provide them
with rest and refreshment.

Scroll in hand, Hildegard strolled to the chapel and knelt before the
Virgin as she read the letter.

Moments later, as Hiltrude passed through the sacristy to deliver some
altar cloths, she heard the abbess call her name. "Is there something you
need, Lady Mother?" the prioress inquired solicitously.

"Indeed," Hildegard whispered hoarsely. "I need you to accompany me
to the palace at Ingelheim. I have been summoned to counsel the king."

A week later, the abbess and her prioress boarded a boat on the shores
of the Rhine. From the moment she had passed through the gates and
begun her descent down the mountain, Hildegard found herself listening
for the bells for Prime and hoping that the copyists in the scriptorium
weren't dawdling and wondering if Gertrud was encountering problems
in chapter.

Only then did it occur to her that she could not recall a day in her
life as a nun that had been free of demands and duties. No wonder she
felt so strange and unsettled. Yet as she neared the shore, her excitement
grew as she realized that she had nothing to do in this moment but view
the houses that huddled together along the river's edge and listen to the
tradesmen shout as they unloaded their cargo and watch the fish wrig-
gling in the fishermen's baskets. For a moment, she was so overwhelmed
that tears sprung to her eyes. There was so much to see and touch and
smell. And time to do nothing but enjoy it.

As the boatman pushed away from the shore, she closed her eyes and
felt the sway of the boat beneath her body. She felt she was being rocked
and held in unseen arms. How easily one could drift for hours in this
watery world, forgetting time, she mused, full of a sweet confusion she
had never known. She felt so light and free, it almost frightened her, as
though she had sprouted wings but dared not fly.

"Do you think you will dine with the king, my Lady Mother?"
Hiltrude asked as she trailed her hands in the water.

The abbess stared back blankly. Both the question and the answer
seemed far away. She could only focus on the world of miracles unfolding
around her, like the pinpoints of light flashing on the water's surface. She
was as captivated by the river's depth as she was by the splash of the oars
and the whisk of fish swimming just beneath the water's surface. With a
sudden ache, she was reminded again of how little she knew of the out-

side world. But by midday, her eyes surrendered reluctantly to the lullaby of the lapping water and the rhythm of the oars, and she dozed.

The next thing she knew, Hiltrude was tugging at her. "Look, Lady Mother! There ahead!"

As Hildegard blinked, Hiltrude pointed to the distant outline of a castle, set like a crown above Ingelheim's rolling hills and dense woodlands. The closer they came, the higher the fortress loomed, each turret a bold testament to its former glory as Charlemagne's favorite dwelling. Little wonder that the new king had chosen it as his official palace.

After disembarking, the travelers and their grooms set out on horseback. The nearer they came to the palace, the more dwarfed they felt by its massive walls. The entrance was marked by massive pillars flanking a pair of towering iron gates that opened into the castle courtyard. Swarming around the gates was a crush of soldiers, merchants, and tradesmen seeking entry into the palace compound. Once inside, the travelers from Rupertsberg felt even more lost in the immense courtyard, which was reputed to hold more than a hundred knights and their horses.

From one side, they heard the shouts and laughter of soldiers lingering outside the colonnaded bathhouse, while opposite them, the spires of the royal church rose like graceful arrows amid the clustered roofs of its daughter chapels. Led by their grooms, the travelers pushed through the crowds inside the courtyard, drawing back as two knights with halberds passed them, the sunlight flashing on their ax-blades with their deadly picks and long, vicious spikes. Another soldier followed, carrying a scaling fork with a long shaft, its hook still encrusted with blood.

All around them, servants staggered under baskets of turnips and cabbages and squawking chickens while a pair of flaxen-haired serving maids struggled toward the bathhouse, their arms heaped with long linen garments held high to avoid the fetid straw that matted the muddy ground. Startled by the sound of screams and raucous laughter, the travelers turned to see a drunken soldier clasping a buxom servant girl from behind by her breasts. Her breadbasket tumbled to the ground as she kicked her heel back into the soldier's groin and elicited a stunned yelp of pain. Aghast, the abbess and the prioress lowered their heads and hurried on, grateful to see their groom point ahead to the entrance to the royal residence. At their approach, a pair of itinerant monks in tattered robes rushed forward with offers to accompany them, only to be roughly shoved aside by the royal guards.

Inside, the guards led the guests through a series of doorways to the entrance of the two-storied royal residence, guarded by large stone gargoyles on either side of its heavy oak doors.

Stepping into the cool interior and sudden quiet, the women sighed in relief. A handsome, young squire in a blue and silver tunic greeted them and ushered them to their quarters for rest and refreshment. When they entered the guest room, the women could scarcely believe their eyes. The room was the size of their cloister! One of the walls displayed a bear skin of immense proportions; its giant claws seemed large enough to circle a grown man's waist. Next to the bear skin, a jewel-handled knife shone in the half-light alongside a sword that Hildegard was sure could only be wielded by a giant. Glancing at a second wall, Hiltrude was drawn to inspect an immense, brightly colored tapestry. Its sparkling threads beckoned to reveal the forms of three veiled, half-naked women reclining beside a gushing fountain, while a quartet of swarthy men in turbans and satin robes hovered over them, one of them stroking the belly of one of the women.

Hiltrude's knees felt weak as she studied them. Were these the spoils their pious king had brought back from the Holy Land? She fretted, certain they would disturb the abbess.

But Hildegard had far different thoughts as she rested, recalling tales she had heard of Frederick's bravery in the Holy Jerusalem War when he was a battle companion to his uncle, Conrad III. On their return from the Second Crusade, Conrad had named Frederick as his successor on his deathbed, ignoring his son, the obvious heir. As events unfolded, Conrad's choice seemed fortuitous. In Frederick, the German nation had finally been graced with a decisive and dynamic leader. Times were ripe, as well, with circumstances conspiring in Frederick's favor. German towns sprang into centers of commerce almost overnight; in the process, they blunted the feudal power of the princes. The population was exploding, as well; and agriculture and the trades were flourishing.

Even as the abbess of Rupertsberg reflected on the future of her royal host, the glow of the Living Light brightened. Within it, a series of future events were revealed to her, explaining the reasons why she had been called here.

When the Light faded, Hildegard felt chilled. Turning from the future, she placed her hand on her heart and prayed for the grace to counsel the youthful king wisely while his ears could still hear and his heart was still open.

✠

When the doors opened and Hildegard entered, the chatter in the palace reception hall ceased. As she was escorted to the throne at the far end of the hall, curious courtiers turned to study her; a trio of women bowed; a group of clerics shuffled nervously. Her pace was unhurried, and the natural grace of her tall, slender form belied her fifty-six years. Her violet eyes arrested all who met her gaze.

"But she is beautiful," she heard a knight whisper to his lady.

The lord chancellor presented her. "Your Highness, the lady abbess of Rupertsberg, Hildegard von Bermersheim," he announced.

The aura of Frederick's royal bearing drew her forward: his red hair and beard and blue eyes, a vivid contrast to his fair skin. Crowned at twenty-eight, Frederick exuded energy and fearlessness. He wore a rippling emerald robe that seemed to serve as a foil for a diamond-centered gold medallion emblazoned on his chest. The cuffs and hem of his robe shone with bands of gold embroidery, and his belt was studded with pearls. Though he was of medium height, it was clear that strong shoulders and sturdy limbs enhanced his agility as a warrior. Confidence streamed from him like fire from the sun.

But Hildegard was unprepared for the shimmering presence that she now saw flaring behind him, bathed in the radiance of a silver flame. The majestic presence was unmistakable; a jeweled crown rested on the head of the great Charlemagne.

"We bid you welcome to our court, my Lady Abbess Hildegard," Frederick said, smiling.

The abbess was struck by the depth of his eyes: intelligent, restless, enveloping, as quick to challenge as to learn.

"Word has reached us of the magnitude of your visions. We trust your willingness to share their wisdom in matters pertaining to our reign."

"It is why I have traveled to Ingelheim, Your Highness," she replied graciously. "Yet know that though the visions flow through me, their messages are directed to those who have the courage to heed them and bring them to fruition."

The king's eyes narrowed as his lord chancellor leaned over to whisper to him.

"We extend the full hospitality of our royal domain to you during your visit," the king announced. "We shall meet with you privately on the morrow." Rising, he added, "Before then, we invite you to share Matins with us in our private chapel."

Behind him, the shimmering figure flared anew.

Seeing it, Hildegard wondered: With such a guide, what need has he of me?

"Trust," she heard Lady Wisdom whisper. *"It is I, not he, who have summoned you here."*

With a flourish, the manservant in the scarlet tunic placed the silver winecups before the monarch and his guest. Except for the royal guards, Frederick and the abbess sat alone in the king's private quarters.

"We are aware of the many pilgrims who honor your teacher, Blessed Jutta of Sponheim," the king began.

"She was mother to me in life as she is to countless others now in blessed memory," Hildegard replied.

"And your archbishop of Mainz, Henry Moguntin?" the king inquired, his eyes hooded as he lifted his winecup. "How fares he of late, my Lady Abbess?"

"I have heard little of him since his visit to the abbey at Michaelmas, Your Highness," she replied, aware of her throat tightening.

"I trust that, as your prelate, he visits with some regularity?" he probed.

"Indeed," she said. "More so since you appointed him my protector."

"Never!" The king's eyes blazed. "We not only protest such a rumor but deeply regret that you have been so cruelly misinformed, my lady."

Henry lied. The words shot through Hildegard's mind.

"However," the king continued, "it is our understanding that he has been exceedingly generous with donations of land and tithes to your abbey on Rupert's Mountain."

"As have so many, Your Highness," she acknowledged, treading carefully. "And none more than the Sponheim family, who gave us our dearest benefactor of recent memory: the Margravine Richardis von Stade, Lady Jutta's cousin."

"Stade," he nodded, thoughtfully. "Our greetings go to all at the Northmark who long for peace." His voice was crisp and official. "We expect to see Stade's future greatly expand as a center of trade."

Frederick looked away and remained silent for some moments, before finally lapsing into a deep sigh. In the fireplace nearby, a huge log glowed with an inner fire, as it sputtered and scattered the hearth with scarlet splinters. Watching the fading embers, Frederick turned and surprised Hildegard with a gentle request.

"Speak to us of your favorite way to pray, my Lady Abbess?" Before she could answer, he bowed his head. "We are eager to share it."

He did not stir when she began to sing, but his nostrils flared at the first flute-sounds of her chanting. Soon, the joy in her voice transcended the confines of the stone walls surrounding them, building a crystal bridge to other realms, filling the chamber with plumes of light:

> O current of power infusing all
> in the heights, in the deeps....
> O teacher of those who know,
> a joy to the wise
> is the breath of Sophia....

The king's eyes were blue pearls now. "Speak to us of this Sophia of whose breath you sing."

"My name for Sophia is Lady Wisdom, she who is described as the Beloved of God in the books of Proverbs and Ecclesiasticus and the Wisdom of Solomon: 'She who was poured forth at the first, before the earth was birthed, when there were no heights or depths, no mountains heaving, nor the span of skies made firm.'"

"But this is the Virgin, surely?"

"The two share much. For just as Lady Wisdom's womb births all living things in the cosmos, so her daughter, the Virgin, wedded heaven and earth in the womb of her human body."

"How did you come to know her?"

"I first heard her whispers in my mother's womb. All through my life, her voice has guided me through the labyrinth of my visions, instructing me at every turn."

"This Lady Wisdom of whom you speak," he asked, intrigued, "how does she appear to you?"

Breathing deeply, Hildegard closed her eyes and placed her hand on her heart.

"At the top of a pillar, I see a Light so bright, no human tongue can describe it. In its midst, a dove appears, holding a golden ray in its beak. A Voice from heaven cries out, 'What you see is Divine!'"

The abbess drew in her breath.

"A Woman dazzling with Light comes toward me now and is so glorious, my eyes can scarcely bear her splendor."

Pausing, she appeared to be listening again, then nodded.

"This Woman is as awesome and terrifying as the thunder's lightning and yet gentle in goodness as the sunshine. And in her terror and gentleness, she is

unfathomable to mortals, like the sun, which mortals cannot gaze at for long. But she is with all and in all and floods humanity with her compassion."

The abbess sat back, clearly awed at what she had just been shown.

"Your visions are both gift and burden, are they not, my lady?" the king asked softly, studying her. "Have you been allowed the consolation of knowing why you were chosen?"

The abbess shrugged. "How would knowing serve me? I merely announce mysteries just as a trumpet emits sound but does not cause it. It is the Living Light that breathes the sound into being. The visions are meant to flow through me to those who have been entrusted with guarding the earth and its treasures."

Now her eyes were drawn to a place above his head, and her mouth opened though she uttered no sound.

The king grew tense. "What is it that you see, my lady?"

Completely absorbed, she appeared to ignore him, her head inclined to one side, her body trembling. Now she turned to the throne. Her voice rang out.

"Hear my words, O King!

"The glorious Woman appears again, this time brandishing a sword as she shouts, 'O mighty God, who can oppose you? With your aid, no dragon will prevail over me, be he strong or weak, prince or outcast, noble or baseborn, rich or poor. Through you, I serve as a refuge for powerless humans, defending their weakness with a cutting sword. O merciful God, help me to defend them!'"

The abbess paled as she stared at the king.

"What is it, my lady?" he asked again, this time insistent. "What do you see?"

"Heed these words, O King! In the days ahead, dragons will assail you, and swords will stagger you, and the weak will cry out to God for your justice and mercy."

Her gaze impaled him. She could not speak.

"Share what you see with us, my lady!" His plea was a command. Slowly, she lifted her chin and stared at him.

"Listen well, I beseech you!

"In this vision, I see a king standing on a high mountain, observing all that lies in the valleys below. He desires to rule justly so that all dry things will become green again and whatever sleeps will awaken and the weak will be roused.

"But should the king fail to open his eyes, a dark haze will shroud the valleys, and ravens will tear whatever dwells in the valley to shreds. Be vigilant, O King, for robbers and vagrants are steeped in that dark haze and seek to

snuff out the light of justice. Seek to control the wild and slothful habits of men you have entrusted to act with compassion, for the idle morals of your kingdom's princes are base indeed and are often steeped in filth and negligence.

"O King, armor yourself to avoid temptation! Cast off all greed and choose moderation, so that when you stand before the highest judge, you have no need to blush with shame."

Now the abbess' eyes widened in astonishment. She had bitten her lip so deeply, it had begun to bleed. The king leaped to his feet.

"What is it, my Lady Abbess? What do you see?"

She turned away. "You will proceed to Rome and receive the imperial crown from the hands of a pope...."

He fairly shouted in jubilation, "It is the hope of our soul! Only then will we have the full power to restore the glory of the Holy Roman Empire of Germany, Burgundy, and Italy! Only then will we truly honor the memory of the great Charlemagne to whom we pray every day."

"You will not cross the Alps alone," she whispered, as the shimmering at his back flared in a huge silver flame.

"We will remember this day, my Lady Abbess," the king cried fervently.

Seeing him so stalwart and unafraid, Hildegard longed to touch his cheek, to caution him. But she could not, for his destiny awaited him.

"We beg your prayers in the days ahead, my Lady Abbess."

"Go in strength, Your Highness," she whispered.

And to the shimmering presence flaring anew behind him, she pleaded, "Do not abandon him!"

For the past three days, sleet had slashed at the mountain, leaving the paths glazed with ice and slick with peril. Desperate for shelter, more and more pilgrims straggled into the hospice, huddling together as they begged for a spoonful of porridge and a swallow of ale.

Gisla was so tired that every bone in her body was aching. "Thank God you've come," she said as the abbess approached her at a dying woman's bedside. "We need your healing hands desperately."

The room was packed with shivering bodies, their coughs and wheezes rising on every side. As Hildegard bent over the woman Gisla was attending, a yank on her robe startled her. Looking down, Hildegard saw a slack-jawed youth writhing in pain on a filthy blanket, his mouth contorted by a swollen lip.

Drawing closer, she saw that his lip was oozing infection: pus had already encrusted his chin. At her touch, his limbs flailed like sticks of kindling tossed in midair. The heat from his fever rose through his threadbare tunic as his bloodshot eyes implored her. The stench of his foul breath sickened her when she bent to examine his mouth. Signaling a novice, she ordered a tincture of wine and olive oil to quench the festering and instructed her to lance the infected lip with a fishbone.

Pausing to bless the boy, she turned away, only to feel the yank on her skirt again. When she looked down, she saw the boy lifting his trembling hands in gratitude. His gesture touched her deeply. This was the heart of the abbey's work.

She immersed herself in the hospice's needs, numbing herself to the news that the king had stripped Archbishop Henry of his rank. Two cardinal legates from Rome, Gregory of San Clemente and Bernard of Saint Angeli, had delivered the deposition to Henry at the episcopal palace. The official charge was gross misappropriation of church funds. No one feigned surprise.

The charges were all the more grave since Henry, as archbishop of Mainz, also held the title of imperial vice-chancellor, an office rife with opportunities for bribes and moral compromises. Seductions had beckoned Henry at every turn, threatening to compromise his episcopal office. When the whispers rose to a roar, the king acted swiftly.

Henry's disgrace stalked her. Night after night, Hildegard lay awake wondering how many of Henry's lavish gifts to her had been tainted. The true irony was that, by his weakness and greed, he had surely snatched bread from the very mouths of the desperate souls they were trying to feed here. But the deepest source of her anguish was her own self-deception. She had blinded herself to his obvious failings, falling prey to every flattery, allowing herself to be snared in the net of his charm. Even when she had confronted him with rumors of his indiscretions, Henry had cleverly distracted her by expressing anger at those who had caused her such needless distress.

She cringed now at the thought that she had expressed support for Henry in a letter to Pope Eugenius, begging him "to treat Henry with a mother's mercy, the better to mirror God's forgiveness since God desires mercy rather than sacrifice."

"Fool, fool!" she cried, scourging herself with the word again and again. "You chose to see his lies as fireflies when you knew they were wasps!"

As she twisted in her contradictions, she was confronted with an even deeper truth that she had long tried to ignore. Henry's greed was legion, his infamy, only a microcosm of the scandalous greed eating at the heart of the church. The truth sickened her as the bile rose, souring her mouth, making her dizzy.

Before her now, the glow of the Living Light flared into an ominous blaze. In the heart of the fire, she saw Henry's face rising above every sickbed: the symbol of the ravaging wolf let loose in the sheep-pen, the thief who soon deafens his ears to the rape of the earth as Greed strips the emerald shimmer from its breasts and hips and its flowing rivers are clogged with the stink of rotting fish, fouling the air with pollution, shriveling its branches of ripe fruit with poison-sweetness.

As the horror unfolded, a sob rose like a geyser from Hildegard's soul. The vision had unmasked him, revealing him as the King of Thieves, Greed's courier. Yet even as Hildegard recoiled, cursing him, Henry turned to her one last time, his eyes devouring her, still tempting her in ways that filled her with self-loathing.

Heartsick, Hildegard fled from the hospice, running blindly until she tripped on the roots of a giant elm. Crouching on the frozen ground, she flung her arms around the trees trunk as she pleaded with God to rescue all trees and all living things from the jaws of greed. The earth was too precious to die of thirst and gasp for breath and slide into extinction. It must never be!

Why did the vision assault her with such horror? she sobbed. Why was she destined to see it?

The sewing room was crowded. Ilse and the twins had settled in their usual corner where they could speak without being heard.

"How many days has it been since lady mother took food and drink?" Gertrud winced, as she smoothed out the white linen panel she was embroidering with pink and silver shells.

"Surely she's eating something," Gisla insisted.

"Crumbs, at best, Hiltrude claims," Ilse replied. "When she returned from her brief recent trip to Disibodenberg, she was already burning with fever. She was so weak, the grooms had to lift her from her mount and place her in Hiltrude's arms. She barely recognized Father Volmar."

"Her illnesses are always so sudden and mysterious," Gisla frowned. "Then she recovers just as quickly and dismisses our fears as nonsense."

"Until the next time," Ilse pouted. "It's tiresome."

"She tries to do too much," Gertrud commented, squinting as she threaded the needle. "Frankly, I'm not convinced that her decisions are always in our best interests."

Gisla nudged her, fearing that the novices nearby might have overheard her complaint.

"Frankly, I think that the unending stream of visitors tires lady mother most," Ilse muttered.

"Like our new archbishop, Arnold of Seelenhofen," Gisla added. "She could hardly refuse to see him after Archbishop Henry's disgrace."

"I don't think she sees the guests as a burden at all." Ilse shrugged. "I think she revels in every moment of it, though she'd be loathe to admit it."

"Are you jealous of lady mother's fame and her visions?" Gertrud asked, smiling.

"Hardly," Ilse sniffed. "How else would we learn about the new cures and medicines from Salerno or the scholars' quarrels in Paris or the arguments of the canon lawyers in Bologna? Mother shares the news with us, does she not?"

"Except the reasons why that trip to Disibodenberg made her sick," Gertrud scowled, as she pricked her finger.

But no one was listening.

"Come quickly! All of you!" the prioress was calling from the doorway. "Lady mother is dying!"

Hildegard heard her daughters' complaints as her spirit slipped from her body and hovered over her sickbed.

Looking down, Hildegard saw her daughters gathered around her sickbed, praying anxiously. Recalling their gossip earlier, she knew she must find a way to resolve their complaints and examine the feelings to which they, like her, had fallen prey.

As she watched her life parade past her, she saw a series of virtues and vices taking shape in symbolic forms, according to each one's nature.

Anger took shape first: its white eyes staring from a face that was human, except for the scorpion's mouth. Its body was shaped like a crab, with grasshopper thighs and snakes for feet. "I trample on all who wrong me," Anger shouted. "All should take care for my sword wounds swiftly, inflicting heavy blows on all who stand in my way!"

Then out of the mist, the virtue of Patience answered: "I resound in the heights and well up from the earth like balsam. Though you construct a tower of rage, I cause it to fall with a kind word and scatter your gains. For I am the air that nourishes all sprouting greenness; the fruits and the flowers of the virtues grow in me, and I transplant them in the human heart. I complete what I have begun: waiting and trusting. I destroy no one and surround all with peace. And while Anger dissolves into oblivion, I pass into eternity."

From the swirling mass, still more specters arose to confront her: grotesques like Cowardice, whose body trembled like a boneless worm while its human head was covered with a single hairy, flapping ear.

Sadness took shape as a raven–haired leper. It hid beneath wide leaves and tore at its breast, viewing death as happiness. And then, Deceit, the vice shrouded in darkness, approached. Though stuck in hardened scum, it kept oozing a slimy sludge.

Hildegard looked and listened with fascination to the dialogue between the virtues and the vices in her life. As each vice cried out, a virtue answered it, balancing the dance of darkness and light: Heavenly Love to Worldly Love, Discipline to Petulance, Dignity to Shame.

Only then did Hildegard come to see that each of those voices had struggled for dominance within her. Their rhythms rose and fell in shades of desperation and ecstasy, at times thrusting her dangerously close to the threshold of life and death.

Looking down now, Hildegard saw the outline of her own human body again. The blood was drying in her veins, and the marrow of her bones and bodily fluids were so parched that her soul seemed no more than the merest flicker in her body. Was she still alive? As she lay there, torches flared at the four corners of the bier on which she had been placed. Her daughters surrounded her, kneeling and weeping, certain they would witness her death within the hour.

Then, like lightning, a Voice coursed through her soul: "Ah eagle, why do you sleep? You will receive the knowledge you need to lead your daughters, and that knowledge will radiate from you like a splendid jewel. You will fulfill your destiny. Arise from your bed now for the time of your passing has not yet come."

In that moment, she felt the rush as she rejoined her body. Opening her eyes, she saw the grace of God in the eyes of her daughters and felt their relief and compassion as they lifted her from the bier and carried her to her bed.

The winter of 1153 was ending as news arrived of King Frederick's campaign in Italy. Before leaving, the king had ensured the loyalty of

most members of the German nobility through land grants and had secured the loyalty of the Church by appointing bishops who could provide
him with political and military support. Now he was free to concentrate
his energies on restoring the empire.

But the conditions confronting him in the Italian states quickly
daunted him. Since his royal predecessors rarely set foot in the cities
of northern Italy, the citizens had long since shed their political memories of imperial control. Feudal lords had been replaced by citizens who
had claimed the land, including its tolls, market profits, and the right of
coinage. Civic governments flourished, and merchants established powerful communes headed by consuls. The most notorious was the Roman
commune, headed by the fiery heretic, Arnold of Brescia, who fought
fiercely to secularize all church property.

From the start, Hildegard was uneasy at the news of Frederick's
sudden departure for Italy, especially since he chose a number of prince-
bishops to lead his armies, inspiring numbers of priests to follow by
exchanging the cross for the sword. How could so many priests have
abandoned their people? She sighed as she arched her back in the scriptorium. Her shoulders were beginning to ache again, as they had since
news came of Pope Eugenius' death.

By Terce, the morning's tasks had exhausted her, notably her response
to a letter from Eugenius' successor, Pope Anastasius, a weak and vain
prelate. Volmar had flinched when he recorded the abbess' letter, part of
which read:

O Shepherd, why do you neglect Justice, the heavenly daughter of
the king?

She was entrusted to your care, and yet you stand and watch as
she's hurled to the ground, her crown smashed, her jeweled tunic
torn from her body by the hands of immoral men. You cultivate
hypocrites who lust for gold more than righteousness. Instead of
reforming these shipwrecked people, you reach for evil with a kiss!

The world is already filled with deceit! Later it will be consumed
with a sadness so great, it will matter little to people if they meet
death. While there is time, I beg you, repent!

Volmar knew that since Archbishop Henry's scandal, the abbess' eyes
had been forced open as she saw how greed and corruption had seeped
like deadly mold into the cracks in the Church's foundation, weakening
it steadily.

"My lady, let us trust that your words to His Holiness will not go unheeded," Volmar had said when she signed the letter.

Hildegard shrugged. "It grows cold," she said, turning from her provost, leaving him wondering again what she saw and knew but must leave unsaid.

In the year of Our Lord, 1155, Frederick, Roman Emperor and permanent Ruler by Divine Grace, greets the Lady Abbess of Rupertsberg, Hildegard:

With great joy, we inform you that what you predicted for us during your visit to Ingelheim has come to pass.

In gratitude, we pray that we may always be pleasing in the sight of God the Almighty. Therefore, from the depth of our heart, we ask for your prayers and assure you that all matters that you call to our attention will be judged in justice and will not be influenced by the friendships or hatred of individuals.

Part Five

1155–70

For my own part,
I constantly experience a trembling fear,
but I stretch out my hand to God
to be sustained by him
like a feather borne on the wind.

– Vita Sanctae Hildegardis

The summer air was unusually sultry. Hildegard was certain the dormitory cots would hold more than their share of dozing nuns today and that few would stir until the bells for None. Today, even Hiltrude would rest.

Closing the back gate behind her, Hildegard pushed her way through the bushes and slipped through the narrow tunnel in the wall that opened onto the forested slopes.

The coolness of the woods calmed her. She rolled back the sleeves of her robe, tied her veil behind her head, and began her slow climb up the hill. The pungent fragrance of the forest drenched her senses. God is a spendthrift, she thought. Each step filled her with new energy. Climbing steadily, she paused and turned; she could no longer see the abbey. She was almost there.

In the distance, she saw the clearing and the lightning-gouged tree stump in its midst. From both sides of its blackened trunk, determined saplings had thrust their way out and up like a pair of muscled arms raised in triumph as their branches trembled with leaves. The sight never failed to thrill her.

Over the months, the tree stump had become a symbol of slumbering power surging up from weakness. Though fire had ravaged the tree's trunk, it had refused defeat and opened its battered heart to the Spirit's greening power, *viriditas,* the wellspring of new life. Now the time had come when she must trust that greening power within herself and embrace the summons that had flowed from her first vision.

"O human, you who are fragile like the dust of the earth, cry aloud about the corruption that is rising all around you! Cry aloud to those who, in their carelessness, choose neither to speak nor proclaim that corruption. Arise now and cry aloud, proclaiming what is revealed to you here!"

Sinking to her knees, she pleaded for courage. Chaos was everywhere. Sickened by church corruption, growing numbers of the nobility were joining the heretics to preach for a return to apostolic poverty. Rome was in an uproar. Only eighteen months after assuming the papacy, Anastasius had died. He was succeeded by an Englishman, Pope Hadrian IV, whose first move was to crush the power of the Roman commune by capturing the heretic Arnold of Brescia. Violence erupted in Rome during Holy Week. Hadrian acted swiftly, placing the city under an interdict that could be lifted only if Arnold were expelled and the Romans bowed to papal rule.

Seeing the advantage, Frederick marched on Rome, where Arnold was killed, thereby removing the final obstacle to his receiving the imperial crown, which Pope Hadrian was forced to confer on him in secrecy. When the Romans heard that Arnold was dead and that Frederick had been crowned without their consent, they rioted, forcing the newly crowned emperor and the pope to flee from the city like fugitives, leaving Rome in utter turmoil.

Rumblings of thunder signaled the approach of a summer storm. As surely as she could no longer delay her return to the abbey, Hildegard knew that the time had come to obey the command in her vision. She began her descent down the mountain, overwhelmed by a sense of relief and peace.

Hildegard spoke of her decision to no one, not even to Volmar. Since her return from Ingelheim, she was aware that the monk's anxious glances were following her, ever alert for further signs of illness or fatigue. But her silence, seeded by the grace of God with *viriditas,* dispelled her terror, preparing her for what lay ahead.

"I beg you to reconsider, my lady," Volmar protested, as he watched the abbess reach for her traveling bag.

"I cannot," she cried. "I dare not delay a moment longer, though God knows how much I dread returning to Disibodenberg for even a day."

"My lady, I beg you to wait."

"For how long? For five years, your brothers have withheld the final transfer of our legal rights to this abbey. Until that document is in my hands, this abbey will never be completely secure."

Grasping the arm of her chair, she pulled herself up and tried to straighten her shoulders. For the first time, he noticed the swollen joints on her once-graceful fingers.

"Surely there must be some other way, my lady, someone . . . "

"Who, Father Volmar?" Her voice was shrill. "You forget that, without my Lord Henry, I have no protectors left. I stand alone now. Utterly alone."

He whirled around. "You cannot be serious! What of your benefactors, what of your daughters, what of me?"

"Since none of you has risked challenging the abbot, I must. Until the book of benefactions is in my hand, the abbot's foot is on my neck and your brothers hold this abbey captive!" she shouted.

"My brothers be damned, then, and damned again," he answered. "Is that what you want from me? I offered to accompany you on your last trip, but you refused. Would you have me threaten the abbot personally?"

The abbess blanched. "Certainly not. All I have ever wanted was your understanding. Can't you see that unless I act now, this abbey could slip from my grasp at any time? Then I will have lost everything." Her teeth were chattering with fear.

Then he understood. Her fears are twin to her griefs now, he thought. She has lost Lady Jutta, then the margravine, then Richardis; and now, her once-trusted ally, the deposed archbishop of Mainz.

"My lady," he ventured softly, "I ask again: allow me to accompany you to Disibodenberg."

When she turned to look at him, her eyes with veiled with sadness. "I dare not, my friend. Once there, your loyalty to your brothers might be my undoing. I cannot risk losing you."

Her words seared his soul. He dared not look at her.

Seeing his hands flee to his sleeves, she was grateful for the knock on the door. "The grooms are ready, my lady," Hiltrude called out. "The horses are saddled and waiting."

"Pray for me, my friend."

But he did not trust his voice to answer.

The monks stood at their places at table, their arms folded, their chins on their chests. Prior Albert beckoned to Hildegard to enter, flinching with the same queasy courtesy with which he had greeted her at the gates.

The air in the refectory was stale with sullenness. Clearly this meeting was seen as a penance to be endured. As Hildegard walked past the rows of monks, only the scrape of their sandals greeted her. It sounds much like the kind of anger that grinds stones into sand, Hildegard thought.

The sight of Kuno startled her. His broad shoulders were stooped now, and his body was gaunt. She could not believe how the years had withered him. His skin was leaf-dry and flaking, his once blue eyes now watery.

He chose to look past her. His loss of hearing was evident in the volume of his speech.

"My Lady Abbess," he shouted, "as you know, the Rule states that all final decisions regarding the abbey's business must be made by the abbot alone. However, in deference to Lady Jutta, of blessed memory, I hereby waive the Rule and grant you, her obedient daughter, permission to speak in the presence of the brothers." Sitting down, he folded his arms and closed his eyes.

Hildegard stood and waited. One by one, the monks raised their eyes and looked at her, more out of curiosity, she knew, than interest. Only then did she raise her arms to bless them. But as one, they recoiled.

"My sons, in my plea for justice, I stand humbly before God and Saint Benedict," she began. "I come neither to barter nor to steal from this abbey but only to finalize the transfer of our book of benefactions, which is our legal property. It was bequeathed to us at the founding of the Abbey of Rupertsberg, whose site was legally secured by purchase fee and episcopal witness. Contained in the book are the records of our dowries, inheritances, and requests for family burial rights, which this abbey continues to withhold despite our repeated requests. I have journeyed here to secure it. The book must be placed in my hands at once!"

Kuno's mouth twitched wildly as he signaled to Prior Albert, who sprung to his feet.

"My Lady Abbess," the prior proclaimed, "your interests continue to be of utmost concern to us as they were during the decades when this abbey served with devotion as your personal guardian and protector...."

"A charge you accepted in exchange for our dowries," she interjected.

"But only in part," he snapped. "How can you measure the years of spiritual sustenance this abbey provided to you...?"

"Measure, my Lord Prior? Surely 'honor' would be the better word. The word 'measure,' however, could easily be applied to the profits from those land rents and vineyards and bridge tolls and mill fees that our dowries have continued to place at your disposal," she noted. "Is that not true, Father Prior?"

The prior squeezed out a smile. "Inform us then, my lady, of how you would have us divide donations from those families whose sons continue to honor their vows of stability to this abbey while their daughters tore up their family roots here to depart with you to Rupertsberg?" A murmur of assent swept through the ranks.

"We expect only those portions specifically designated for the Abbey of Rupertsberg," she replied impatiently.

"But clearly, my lady, you must acknowledge that we monks have labored in this vineyard since before you were born," the prior said, rubbing his hands. "Surely you would agree that in justice as well as charity, any portion we retain is well deserved."

"I do not agree!" she shouted. "Our records must be released without delay! You withhold them unjustly!"

The prior's smile was pitying. "My lady, you ask for a Solomon's decision here: to cleave the body of a child in two to satisfy the demands of both women who claim to be its mother."

"Beware, my Lord Prior. Do not mock justice by twisting Holy Scripture with specious arguments. In justice, you cannot deny us our rights simply to feed your greed. Our needs are great as well."

"Your needs, my Lady Abbess? For what, pray?" the prior snarled. "To purchase another mountain on which to build another abbey? To add to your abbey's elaborate aqueducts? To furnish your oratory with still more choir stalls and to double the carrels in your scriptorium? Your needs, indeed!" His voice was strangled with rage. "In your flourishing, you manage to forget that, even when you betrayed us by your departure, we surrendered one of our beloved brothers to be your provost. And yet, you come now, seeking even more while accusing us of greed. We have needs, indeed, far greater, I daresay, than any for which your recent fame might tempt you to plead."

"Enough!" The force of her fist lifted her to her feet, as her fury streamed from her. Both the abbot and the prior were aghast.

When Hildegard spoke, her voice was muffled thunder:

"My sons, heed my words well! In a vision, I was directed, at God's behest, to make my way to this mountain of Blessed Disibod, from whence, with your permission, I had seceded. In this vision, my gaze was directed to the person of father abbot."

Every eye widened.

"The serene Light declared to him, 'The women's alms do not belong to you or to your brothers! Further, if some among you unworthy ones attempt to take away some of my daughters' freeholds, then I WHO AM say: You are the worst of robbers. And if you try to take away their shepherd of spiritual medicine, Provost Volmar, then again I say, you are the sons of Belial, and in this do not look to the justice of God, for that same justice will destroy you.'"

The monks were dumbfounded. The only sound was the wheezing that issued from the husk of Kuno's body.

"I await your decision, Father Abbot," Hildegard concluded, turning to Kuno. His palsied hands were shaking wildly.

Behind him, in the Living Light, Hildegard saw the flaring tapers at the four corners of his plain, pine coffin.

"Repent while you can, my Lord Abbot," she whispered. *"Do not delay. Your days are numbered."*

As he heard her words, his eyes flared with an eerie gratitude. "At last," he murmured. "My burden lifted."

Surprising the prior, he breathed aloud, "Release the book of benefactions to the lady abbess of Rupertsberg."

Hildegard felt both humbled and overwhelmed at the trust people placed in her. Though there was no way she could sort through the baskets of letters that lined the walls, somehow, by the grace of God, the urgent ones always surfaced and found their way to her. The letter from the nun who walked toward her now was one of them.

Elizabeth of Schönau drooped like a willow as she floated toward Hildegard in the abbey cloister, her hands like wrinkled leaves pressed against her robe. Her nose was pinched, her lips, a thin blue line. Barely past her twentieth year, she appeared much older.

As she approached, her letter appeared in Hildegard's memory.

To the Venerable Hildegard, Superior of the Brides of Christ in Bingen, from Elizabeth, a simple nun:

As you may have heard, the Lord's mercy has been magnified through me more than I merit, by means of certain heavenly mysteries that are revealed to me. Through his angel, I was instructed to warn his people of what would befall them if they refused to repent of their sins.

Fearing I would be accused of arrogance, I kept these things hidden. Then, on a certain Sunday, I fell into an accustomed state of ecstasy whereupon the Lord's angel confronted me, saying, "Why do you hide gold in mud? The word of God was sent to earth through your mouth so that it may give glory to God and his people."

Then the angel lifted a scourge over me, striking me harshly five times in such great anger that for three days, my daughters attended me day and night as my body was shattered from this beating. I remained silent until the ninth hour, then confided in the father abbot who visited me. I told him of the angel's words and of the Lord's vindication that would soon descend on this world.

On the vigil of the feast of Saint Barbara, I fell into ecstasy, and the angel appeared again, instructing me once again to call the world to penance.

Again and again, my limbs have been loosened in ecstasy as father abbot tests my words among learned men.

My Lady Abbess Hildegard, I beg you to receive me so I may benefit from your counsel.

The letter still echoed in Hildegard's soul as she sat across from Elizabeth.

"You fast much, and sleep little, do you not, Sister Elizabeth?" Hildegard said, seeing the marks of the scourging beneath the nun's robe, some stripes so fresh, the blood was still visible beneath her robe.

"I cannot rest, my Lady Abbess, expecting that my words will be mocked at every turn."

"Is that what you fear most, my daughter?"

"I fear, as well, that my words will be dismissed as the temptations of the Devil. What am I to do? The angel of the Lord urges me on."

"Does this angel also reassure you?"

"Indeed, and reminds me that when the Fathers of Israel were given to weakness and apathy, the great women of Israel rose and prophesied, and governed the people of God so zealously that they enabled the people to triumph over Israel's enemies."

"You speak of Deborah and Hilda and Jael and Judith?"

"I do, my lady, yet I am reassured by an even more wondrous vision that I long to share with you."

Hildegard saw the light fill the young nun's soul like a sunrise.

"The face that I see before me," Elizabeth wept, "is the face of Mother Mary. I see her vested like a priest in a chasuble, wearing a crown of gold as she stands at the side of the altar in perfect peace."

The cascade of light flowing from Elizabeth's soul was enveloping her so completely, only the outline of her body could be seen.

"And now I behold the Woman Clothed with the Sun who sends out flames of lightning."

"Describe her to me," Hildegard whispered.

"My lady, her face bears the visage of the Body of Christ, weeping over the wickedness of the world."

"And the souls of both mother and Son, not a woman's nor a man's alone but both in one?" Hildegard asked.

Elizabeth's cry filled the room as her hazel eyes pleaded. "If you are both human and divine, my Christ, how could your soul not be both male and female? And if we are made in your image and likeness, how could our souls not be both male and female, too?"

✠

As he finished reading the letter, Volmar leaned back in his chair in the scriptorium, his smile filled with pride and wonder. "Another letter of gratitude, my lady," he said. "Your counsel has touched the lives of so many."

"I am blessed," the abbess agreed, almost to herself. "The lands are well managed; the storehouses are full; my daughters appear content...." Her voice trailed as a frown wrinkled her brow.

What was worrying her now? Volmar wondered. The abbey was thriving. There were forty nuns now, triple the number at Disibodenberg. And though there was always a stir somewhere, he knew from Hiltrude's easy laughter these days that life was proceeding smoothly.

"And so, since all is well," Hildegard announced loudly, folding her arms, and lifting her chin, "I am free to go now."

"Free to go where, my lady? And for what, pray?" The monk queried as he wiped his quill.

"On a preaching journey," she said, defiantly.

"A preaching journey, my lady? You?" Volmar puzzled. "Surely you jest?"

"Hardly." She drew in her breath. "In a vision, I was commanded to do so by the Living Light."

"I can't, ... don't understand, my lady."

"Then perhaps your hand will recall recording the command I received to cry aloud against injustice and corruption. Heretics swarm across this land, seducing the people with falsehoods, proclaiming that the flesh is evil and that we are the Devil's offspring. Since no man's voice has been raised against them, I must raise mine."

Flustered, Volmar let the inkhorn slip from his hand.

As he bent down to retrieve it, Hildegard shouted: "Look at me! Dare we delay warning the folk of the devastation at our door?"

"But you are warning them in your writings, my lady, ..." he began.

"It is not enough! I must go directly to the people," she replied, her eyes flashing. "I must travel to the abbeys and preach to the people in the market squares."

"I beg you, my lady, calm yourself," the monk pleaded softly. "Truly, I meant no harm. Would you not agree that it would cause scandal for an abbess to leave her cloister and face the dangers on the road in an effort to travel and preach?"

"Truly, Father Volmar?" she seethed, her nostrils flaring. "Then I suggest you acquaint yourself with my illustrious predecessors. The great Emperor Otto insisted that the famed lady canoness, Hrotsvit of Gandersheim, travel to preside at bishops' synods. He valued her so highly that he granted her the privilege of her own court and retinue of knights as well as the power of coinage bearing her portrait and..."

"My lady, please, I meant no..."

"As well, you surely must know how often the abbesses who presided over the double Abbey of Fontevrault traveled; those abbesses, you might recall, oversaw dozens of rectories and chapels and churches and nominated their own clergy."

Volmar ground his teeth but remained silent.

"My predecessors were fearless women," Hildegard insisted. "Their achievements hardly flowed from the stitches of sewing room embroidery."

Volmar turned away, drained by her outburst.

She began pacing, a sign that she needed time to think. Her face looked drawn, and the circles beneath her eyes were like dark smudges. She looked like her heart was cracking in a thousand places. She was terrified! For the first time, he saw the agony of a prophet who dreaded what lay ahead but could not turn back.

The travelers were grateful that Würzburg was only an hour away. The strong winds had made the horses skittish and in danger of losing their footing. Hildegard cautioned Gertrud and Gisla to keep their bodies bent low and their elbows pressed against the horses' necks to steady themselves. As the gusts whipped the trees along the river, they strained to hear each other's voices.

Until today, gentle weather had blessed the travelers' journey. Hildegard felt cradled in the soft breezes, her face soon dappled with the peach glow of the sun's warmth. Her body surrendered to the lazy sway of her horse's gait. As the days passed, her mind relaxed. For hours on end, she felt as though she were floating.

But now, as she braced her back against the rising wind, she became aware of her body's slipping back into the familiar tension of tasks and bells and rules that had been her life in the abbey for over fifty years. She realized how the decades of hard work and unyielding discipline had paved pathways of pain that now coursed through her body. Glancing down at her hands, she flexed her swollen fingers. And as she straightened up, she felt the ball of fire burning between her shoulders and recalled how often her head ached so badly that she felt as though it was filled with shattered glass.

From behind, she heard Gertrud's voice call out loudly, "Are you weary, my lady? Should we stop and rest?"

The twins' companionship on this journey had been invaluable. Ever vigilant, they had made every effort to protect her from the overwhelming demands made upon her during her visits at Eberbach, Kitzingen, and Bamberg. Though she was embraced heartily, she was unprepared for the tides of anger and distress she encountered in those she counseled. She soon found herself drained of energy, replenishing herself more and more through prayer and trust.

Once they returned to the open road, Hildegard's thoughts always returned to the mounting power struggle between the pope and the emperor. Questions about Emperor Frederick began to knock on all the doors of her mind.

Two recent events had benefited Frederick. The first was that he had been awarded his divorce from Adela on the grounds of consanguinity and had wedded a child bride, Beatrice of Burgundy. Her dowry included Upper Burgundy and five thousand vassals, swelling the ranks of Frederick's army.

The other significant event was the appointment of Rainald of Dassel as his new chancellor. Rainald's razor sharp mind reinforced his diplomatic skills, and he was fiercely committed to imperial rule. Though not highborn, he possessed a ferocious ambition that had catapulted him into imperial circles, leaving behind dim memories of his early life as provost of Hildesheim Cathedral.

"Rainald will flourish in the eye of the storm," Hildegard had confided to Volmar. "But his risks will alter Frederick's legacy forever."

Seizing the reins, Rainald quickly launched a propaganda campaign against Pope Hadrian in retaliation for the pope's treaty with William I, the Norman king of Sicily. The treaty had ensured that southern Italy would be closed to Frederick's ambitions for imperial rule throughout Italy, thereby overriding a former agreement between Frederick and Pope Eugenius. Hereafter, the action warned, Frederick would not be welcome in the Norman kingdom of Sicily, nor by the Italian communes nor by the papacy.

Tension between the pope and the emperor heightened at the Diet of Besançon, which Frederick convened to proclaim the unification of Burgundy with Germany. Two papal legates used the occasion to deliver a papal letter of protest to Frederick for allowing a crime against the Swedish bishop of Lund — his party had been attacked, robbed, and threatened with death — to go unpunished. When Frederick chose to ignore the crime, Pope Hadrian protested swiftly and unequivocally: a crime against a prince of the church was intolerable. His letter stated:

> You must remember, most glorious son, how graciously your Mother, the holy Roman Church, treated you last year by conferring upon you the imperial crown, the highest mark of honor and dignity and how she has always fostered you. Far from regretting it, we would be happy to confer even greater benefits upon you if it were possible.

Frederick was incensed at Pope Hadrian's implication that his imperial crown was a benefice, a gift granted by the papacy. Frederick raced to reply:

> We hold this kingdom and empire, through the election of the princes, from God alone, who by the passion of his Son placed this world under the rule of two swords. Recall that the Apostle Paul proclaimed: "Fear God, honor the king." Therefore, whoever says that we hold the imperial crown as a benefice from the pope contradicts the teaching of Peter and is a liar.

The line between the pope and the emperor was now drawn with blood.

"My dreams are filled with the wind-song from our abbey trees," Hildegard sighed, "and the sound our two rivers make when they blend at the foot of Rupert's Mountain."

The twins exchanged glances: the journey was taking its toll. Despite their efforts, the visit to Bamberg had exhausted the abbess. Surely they could convince her now to rest at Würzburg since they would be lodging there for a time.

Within the hour, the landmark tower of the Marienkirche appeared on the horizon, resting like a crown on the Marienberg near Würzburg. Legends surrounded the mountain, insisting that pagan fires still blazed in its heart, though the seeds of Christianity had long since rooted and blossomed on its slopes. Soon, the outline of Würzburg's ancient stone fortress came into view.

When the travelers reached the cathedral square, the noise was deafening. Work was being done on the cathedral, which seemed a teeming beehive with workmen clamoring all over it. Screeching hoists pierced the air as smiths and masons shouted instructions up to the artisans astride the scaffolding, while in the dust below, architects calmly bent over drawings of the cathedral's new facade.

A lively market fair was underway. Townspeople jammed the square and wove through the stalls. A dark-skinned stonecutter pushed past the travelers, his tools jangling from his belted tunic, his beard gray with dust. Nearby, a pregnant girl smiled in delight as she draped a fringed scarlet shawl across her shoulders, while behind her, two boys stole a handful of plums and dashed past a merchant hawking wide-sleeved woolen coats from his wooden cart. The air was sharp with the mingled odors of newly cured leather, while clusters of fresh leeks hung above slabs of salt pork and barrels of brine. Nearby, a traveling minstrel tweaked the chin of a thumb-sucking child as he passed while, behind him, the plaintive wail of a blind beggar rose above the sounds of squawking chickens and yapping dogs.

Scanning the marketplace, Hildegard grasped Gisla's arm firmly. "Finally," she muttered. "Look there. The Cathari!"

"The heretics?" Gertrud asked in alarm. "Where?" she whispered, craning her neck. But the abbess was already pushing ahead toward a large gathering of people at the edge of the market square. Every eye was riveted on an old man standing on the ledge of a fountain, his arms waving as the wind ruffled his long white beard. He looked like a patriarch: his face was creased like leather, and his eyes were as wild as those of a desert hermit. At his side stood a young woman whose blonde braids hung to her waist and whose radiance suggested a full-blown rose.

Both the woman and the man were dressed in simple homespun, the hems of their long robes spattered with the dirt of the road. Both were lean and their bare feet were knuckled with calluses. The man's wild passion provided a vivid contrast to the woman's luminous joy. "You have nothing to fear!" the man was thundering. "We come only to proclaim the message of the apostles: to beg you to repent of your sins and save your souls! Turn away, as we did, from gilded churches and false prophets who claim that heaven can be purchased with pieces of silver. These liars preached that the God of Light rules over this world when we know it was created by Satan alone, the God of darkness. And as Satan's property, we accept that our flesh is vile and corrupt and refuse to bring children into this evil world or to eat the flesh of animals. The flesh of Christ and the Virgin are only illusions. Our souls are spirits flung from Paradise imprisoned now on earth in decaying flesh."

When Gisla reached for Hildegard's hand, she felt only a fist.

But the crowd was mesmerized. The folk lingered, reluctant to leave.

Suddenly, a blood-curdling shriek arose, then the desperate, gurgling sound of choking. Nearby, Hildegard saw a man writhing on the ground, his head thrown back, his body jerking in spasms of pain. Pushing through the crowd, she rushed to his side as foam poured from his lips.

Bending over him, Hildegard blessed him with the sign of the cross. "In the name of Almighty God, I ask that this man's body be freed from his rack of pain."

For a moment, the man's twisting torso lurched and stiffened, then quickly went limp. The foam and blood from his mouth slowed to a trickle. Then a pitiful whimper issued from him like the cry of a lost child. Yet when he looked at the abbess, his eyes were flecked with light and he was still.

Hildegard felt the people pressing in around her, staring at the man whose seizures had long alarmed them and aroused their children's fears. Then their eyes shifted to the abbess. When she returned their gaze, they stepped back in awe. Ahead, an anxious voice parted the crowd as the dean of Würzburg Cathedral rushed forward, his bushy eyebrows flaring like the wings of a blackbird.

"She healed him of his frenzy," a dozen voices cried out to him excitedly. "We saw it with our own eyes!"

Sliding to his knees, the dean quickly glanced at the abbess, then at the man lying on the ground.

"Matthias! Matthias!" he cried, taking the man in his arms. "God has blessed you! This day will be remembered in Würzburg!"

"My Lady Abbess, though all our efforts failed," the dean rushed to explain, "Matthias' faith never wavered. He must have been waiting for you."

Hildegard reached for Matthias' hand and kissed it as the townspeople lifted him. Hildegard blessed him, then her eyes followed him until he was lost in the crowd.

"I hasten to offer you the full hospitality of this cathedral, my Lady Abbess," Hermann said, bowing nervously.

"I accept, my lord," Hildegard replied serenely. "Indeed, I would begin my work here and now, on the steps of your cathedral. There are messages I have been instructed to convey to your people."

"Instructed?" he stuttered. "Whatever you wish, my lady."

Every head turned to follow the abbess as she walked to the top step of the cathedral.

How elegant she is, the dean thought. He felt like a wide-eyed page in his uncle's castle again, noting the dignity with which the lady abbess carried herself, the folds of her black robe rippling behind her. And when she turned and lifted her chin, he saw her eyes close for a moment in prayer. "How radiant she is," he sighed, "How brave!"

Now every man doffed his hat. The women hushed the whining children clinging to their skirts.

Hildegard paused and explored the faces.

"People of Würzburg," she began, "Though you hear my words, know that the messages I bring are not mine but have been revealed to me in visions. I have been commanded to share these messages with you.

"In a true vision of the spirit," Hildegard cried out, "I was shown that you, people of Würzburg, and indeed, all people, were created for glory, not for shame!

"For it was revealed to me that, in the beginning, the blessings of fire and air and water and earth that God poured out soon entered into each of us. For fire gives our bodies warmth; the air gives us breath; from water comes our blood; and from the clay of the earth comes our bodies. And I saw in a vision how, when all was complete, God created humanity, placing man and woman in the midst of the world.

"When the time came, male and female were joined together in such a way that neither of them could exist without the other.

"Looking on creation, God saw its goodness and called each of us to glory, for though we are small in stature, our souls are so powerful, they can travel

over heaven and earth to far distant places. For each of our souls, your soul and mine, is a mirror of God, who is eternal.

"People of Würzburg, remember these truths and teach them to your children!"

The people stared, not daring to believe what they had been told. Mirrors of God? How could that be, with only a patch of land on which to scratch for their food for their lifetimes? Yet, having seen the lady abbess cure Matthias, how could they doubt that she was inspired by truth and that her words were of God?

As they stood and stared, slowly, the women with babies at their breasts held them up to be blessed by the abbess of Rupertsberg while others placed their hands on their swollen bellies and wept as they felt the stirring of their unborn children.

It was a bold move, but Hiltrude was desperate. At the midday meal, she announced, "Today's reading will be from Lady Mother Hildegard's new work, *The Book of Life's Merits.*"

"In the fifth image of a recent vision, I saw a woman called Worldly Sadness.

"A tree stood behind the woman's back. It had completely dried up though the woman's body was imprisoned in the clasp of its leafless branches.

"Since her arms were pressed close to her body, her hands hung down from the branches, and her fingers were shaped like ravens. Her belly and legs were also captive, and because her feet were made of wood, her roots were hidden, and she was unable to move. Her only clothes were the branches.

"Thus entrapped, she felt evil spirits smother her.

"In her desperation, the woman lamented, for every consolation had been taken from her and every power stripped. But a Voice warned her not to despair but rather to rid herself of the bitterness of sorrow and to cling to the knowledge that God's joy was at hand."

Hiltrude took a deep breath and looked steadily at Hildegard, but the abbess' head was bowed.

"Lady mother goes on to compare dry wood to humans who have surrendered the green vitality of their virtues," Hiltrude continued, "and lack the sap of life and the greening power of their good deeds. Thus lady mother teaches us that when we allow the power of our souls to dry up and allow ourselves to be clasped in the lifeless clutches of Worldly Sadness, then we, too, spread that sadness around us, causing others to lose that moisture that lady mother describes as the dew of the Holy Spirit. Let us pray each day that any signs of such sadness will flee from this abbey."

Hildegard's eyes were closed as every pore in her body wept as her own words returned now to accuse her. Though fully aware of her daughters' stares and whispers, Hildegard had neither the strength nor the will to respond. Since her return from her preaching tour, the slightest effort drained her. She felt adrift in a sea of despair, with little if any interest in the abbey.

Later that day, she forced herself to go to the scriptorium. Volmar was sifting through the mail and was delighted to see her.

"Good news today from the abbot of Magdeburg, my lady," he reported cheerfully. "He writes that all the things you have predicted have now been fulfilled, and he begs you to reveal what dangers the future holds."

"A question to be addressed to the pope and the emperor since it is they who choose those dangers for us," Hildegard said wearily. "I only interpret the things I see."

"Still, my Lady Mother, these letters clearly attest to your great . . ."

"Enough, Father Volmar, if you please."

Such rebuffs had not been unusual of late. The abbess had returned from her preaching tour deeply depressed. She had little to say about the world she had experienced outside the walls of Rupertsberg. From the news the guests brought, it seemed many new towns had sprung up recently, and the sky was now marked with the spires of new churches and cathedrals. What's more, they reported, flourishing trade routes had been established since the Holy Jerusalem War.

Yet when Volmar pressed the abbess about what had pleased her most in her travels, she spoke of soft breezes swaying the grasses in sun-splashed fields, of the graceful curve of her horse's neck as it bent to drink, and of the flurry of butterflies rising from meadows, startling her with their blur of beauty.

Weeks were to pass before Hildegard could summon the strength to describe the emotional onslaughts she had survived on the journey.

"I heard of abuses that were beyond belief," she confided to Volmar. "The memories still gnaw at my soul." She spoke of the deep-seated despair among the monks in Saint Michael's Abbey in Bamberg, of her shock at the rebellious nuns at Kitzingen, and of the chilling fear she felt when the folk applauded the heretics in Würzburg. All this, Volmar realized, as the abbess rode at times in the rain and cold.

The more she unraveled the skein of memories, the sadder she became. "For years, visitors have sat at our table and shared news with us of the world outside. With each tale, the doors of my imagination flew open. But now I have seen the pain and chaos for myself and can put flesh on the bones of my visions." Her face grew gray again.

"Now I can understand the urgency of the warnings I have received. If you could see the fate that awaits the Church and the Crown, my friend, you would never cease praying."

But when he asked her to elaborate, she refused. "I dare not," she said.

Yet Volmar had no doubt that Frederick's second expedition into northern Italy had alarmed her. As emperor, Frederick was determined that he alone would enforce the peace of Italy and quickly appointed imperial governors to rule in his name. The tolls collected by Italian towns for the use of rivers and roads and marketplaces would revert to the emperor, and all private wars would be outlawed.

"Is Frederick mad?" Hildegard cried out to Volmar. "Does he think he can crush the power of the Italian communes in a single act?"

"He is already doing it, my lady. It's said that he need only breathe an order for it to be carried out by Rainald of Dassel, whom he has now elevated to the post of archbishop of Cologne," Volmar reported. "Rainald defends Frederick's imperial dreams at whatever cost."

Volmar said no more. The abbess was already despondent at the news that Arnold, the new archbishop of Mainz, had levied a tax on the city to help finance the emperor's second campaign into Italy. The citizens promptly revolted, whereupon Archbishop Arnold placed Mainz under interdict.

In utter despair, Hildegard had dispatched an ominous warning to Archbishop Arnold:

This has become a time of wars, for men have forgotten to fear the Lord. Begin now to release all feelings you have of anger and distress, my son, and prepare yourself to meet God, for your death is near.

Over the next year, Volmar was consumed with attending to the abbess' correspondence. Letters poured in from France, England, and Byzantium, as well as from seemingly every hamlet in Germany. Few letters had intrigued Hildegard more than one from Abbot Gedolphus of Brauweiler, which recounted the lurid tale of Sigewize, a woman who was possessed of a devil.

Hildegard's reply was brief. She explained:

In a true vision, I was shown that a demon, in its own nature, is unable to enter into a person, for if it did, the person's members would dissolve and, like stubble, scatter in the wind. Rather, the demon obscures its victim and twists it into insanity and shouts out through it as though through a window. The victim's soul is then stupefied in sleep and unaware of what its body does.

"My prayer was not helpful then?" Hildegard asked Abbot Gedolphus, who sat across from her now.

"For a time, my Lady Abbess. Enough for the crowds to praise God with their clapping and stomping. But suddenly, the possessed woman was seized with a violent hissing, and with a loud cry, she began raving more wildly than before. The folk were furious with disappointment. We read your prayer again, my lady, but now the demon protested that it would not depart until it was in your presence."

"So you have brought the woman here?"

"Indeed," the abbot replied sheepishly. "But we traveled on the prayers of all those folk who have witnessed her long misery. They pray for her even now, certain only you can help her."

Volmar was aghast. "My lady, what will we do with her? Where will we put her? She can only cause havoc in the hospice and the infirmary. The house for poor women is already filled with birthing mothers and destitute women. How can you accept such a burden?"

"How can I not?" she replied tersely, then shook her head. "You sadden me, Father Volmar."

"So be it then," the provost shot back.

When they heard the news, the nuns were terrified. "How can we work and pray with a madwoman in our midst?" they objected at the next day's chapter.

"My daughters, I plead with you to entrust your fears to Lady Wisdom," Hildegard said. "While Sigewize is in our care, we must not judge her. She has been sent to us as a teacher, a mirror to challenge us to confront the demons that sleep within each of us and that we also long to cast forth."

The weeks unfolded like a series of nightmares.

Each day, Sigewize stood at the chapel door shouting obscenities as the nuns entered the chapel. She called Ilse a whoring thief, berated Gertrud for her mewling weakness, and accused Gisla of lustful thoughts. But though the stench of her unwashed body sickened them, they did not turn away.

At chapter, the abbess took care to explain the possessed woman's plight. "I see that the demon within her suffers three tortures," she declared. "The first, the disgrace of being dragged from one holy place to another, the object of unending horror; the second torture, to be drowned in the stares and pity of common folk; and the third, to be pummeled day and night by the power of prayer demanding that the demon leave its hiding place. Are these not tortures to which we also have been prey, my daughters? Have we not, at times, felt imprisoned by others' words and judgments or been the subject of their pity? Have we too not been forced to reveal our secret thoughts and feelings? How then can we deny compassion to this tormented soul?"

As the heavy veils of Lent muffled the abbey, the nuns increased their fast, eating only meager portions of food at table. Yet as their faces grew gaunt with penances, their patience with Sigewize grew. Day by day, they listened as Hildegard refuted and challenged all the demon's lies. Despite their cargo of penances, Lent seemed to pass quickly.

On Holy Saturday, Father Volmar presided at the baptismal font and blew on the waters to commemorate the moment the Holy Spirit breathed over the waters of the first creation. At that moment, Sigewize staggered from the shadows, twisting with spasms, and began to claw at the nuns' stalls. As she uttered a monstrous scream, she was flung to the floor in a convulsion, her mouth dripping with foam.

Horrified, the nuns fled from their stalls and clustered around the abbess as Sigewize writhed in agony, rolling back and forth on the cold stone floor. As Volmar lifted the crucifix above her, she shredded the air with her shrieks.

Raising her arms, Hildegard implored the Spirit to help her to free Sigewize. Hildegard cried out: "Depart Satan! Depart from the tabernacle of this woman's body forever so the Holy Spirit may be restored to its rightful place within her and she may know the Spirit's joy at last."

In that instant, Sigewize was thrown forward on the floor as the demon left her body in a flood of blood-stained urine. Freed at last, Sigewize's limp form fell at the feet of the abbess. Kneeling, Hildegard gathered her in her arms and held her tenderly until she had fully regained her senses.

"Give thanks when you speak of her delivery," Hildegard called out. "For though God allowed Job's body to be filled with the stench of running sores and foul vermin, God refused to let Satan overtake him, and Job, in turn, never abandoned God in his faith. So do I thank God, my daughters, for choosing not to abandon Sigewize."

Volmar was stung by those words. Through my doubt, I abandoned my lady, he reflected, grieving.

"How can you be surprised?" Hildegard asked Volmar. "A schism was inevitable. Hadrian not only refused to meet with Frederick but threatened to excommunicate him. Our emperor's no fool. In order to rule Italy, he must first rule Rome."

Volmar slumped in his chair, badly shaken, as he continued his report. "They say that Hadrian's body was hardly cold before Frederick, aided by Rainald of Dassel, challenged the lawful successor, Alexander III, with his own antipope, Victor IV. But that was only the start. Frederick summoned both papal candidates to an assembly at Pavia, charging the council to choose the legitimate pope. To no one's surprise, the council declared for Victor, the emperor's antipope. Frederick promptly received Victor at the entrance of the cathedral of Pavia, taking care to hold his antipope's stirrup as he dismounted as a sign of reverence. Then, at the altar, Frederick knelt and kissed Victor's feet, as did all those in attendance."

"Incredible," the abbess groaned. "And what of Alexander? Was his lawful election completely ignored?"

"Hardly, my lady," Volmar said. "Midway through the event, a huge number of candles were lit in the cathedral. Then, with every flame flaring, an anathema was hurled at Alexander, excommunicating him and all his bishops. At that moment, every flame was extinguished, and the cathedral was plunged into darkness. The anathema was complete."

Hildegard shuddered. "Frederick has split open Germany's soul like a ripe melon," she said. "Can't he see that he crushes the very seeds he seeks to harvest by forcing the faithful to kneel to an antipope?"

"If you please, my Lady Mother," Hiltrude interrupted, as she rushed into the room. "We've just received news that Archbishop Arnold was brutally murdered by the citizens of Mainz."

"Your prophecy was correct, my lady," Volmar sighed.

But the abbess was already pacing, her arms clasping her torso, her face ghastly white.

Hiltrude was the last in line at the nuns' monthly confession. When she finally knelt before Father Volmar, her voice was a whisper.

"Before God, I confess to my feelings of rage at lady mother's impending departure," she confessed.

"Rage, my daughter?" Volmar paled.

"Yes, and abandonment," she answered, louder now. "I dread assuming all the abbess' duties and burdens while she travels again." Her words came in short spurts. "I know from times past that I'll have no rest until the day she returns."

"Nor, indeed, will she, Sister Hiltrude," Volmar sighed. "But ironically, she would hardly dare leave if it were not for you. All we can do is pray for her safety. . . ."

"And my patience!" she snapped.

"Indeed," Volmar sighed. "In place of a penance, I have a request," he said. "After None, please meet with me in the abbess' workroom." He then gave her his blessing.

The afternoon sunlight was streaming through the open door when Hiltrude arrived.

"Sister Prioress," Volmar began formally, "I am taking the liberty of sharing some letters with you to which few are privy. As the abbess has always maintained, her revelations belong to the people. I would like you to meet some of them."

He reached for a packet of letters. "This one comes from a priest who writes of a boy who was so inspired when he heard the abbess speak in Bamberg that one night when he was away from home he invoked lady mother's protection before he went to sleep. That same night, the priest writes, the abbess appeared in the youth's dream and warned him to leave or he would lose his life. He departed at once, leaving behind scoffing companions. At dawn, enemies came and attacked them, just as lady mother had predicted. The boy's life was saved."

Turning to the next page, the monk read:

My Lady Abbess, I send you gratitude from across the Alps for the miracle of healing I received here in Lausanne. As I wrote before,

I had been felled by a flow of blood and could not leave my bed. A priest read your words as he stood over me: "By the blood of Christ, I order you, blood, to check your flow." When the last word was spoken, I was overcome with strength and rose from my bed at once and have not faltered since. All who have known of my weakness continue to be astonished.

"The stories go on," Volmar said, holding up several more letters. "The next two letters attest to the healing powers of a simple plait of the abbess' hair, which a priest placed on the body of a woman close to death in childbirth; the same plait was pressed again to the foreheads of two deranged women in Sudernsheim. All three can produce witnesses who can attest to their cures."

Turning the page, he went on. "This one comes from a mother who writes that her infant's tremors were cured instantly by a sip of water blessed by the lady abbess Hildegard. And still another is from a man who swears he was unable to swallow until his son dipped his fingers into water that the abbess had blessed and wet his father's lips with the drops of water. For the first time, the father's throat was opened."

Hiltrude's face was ashen.

"It is for those folk who can neither write nor read that lady mother has been summoned to leave these walls again. They, too, must feel her touch and heed her warnings. But my daughter, the abbess' trust in you is the key that opens the gate. Time and again, she has reminded me that you are the angel that Lady Wisdom knew she needed to walk with her."

"My world is so small," the prioress whispered.

"But your arms are wide, and you have eyes in your heart. God is with you, my daughter. He will not forget you in lady mother's absence."

The travelers from Rupertsberg left Trier at dawn, riding without rest. For the third time in an hour, Hildegard arched her back and stretched her limbs. Shifting on her mount, she was assailed again by the smell of mildew now invading her robes. Her only prayer was that she would not grow ill before her return to Rupertsberg.

As the abbess' companion, Ilse had quickly discerned the mistress' preference for silence. At the sound of her sigh, Ilse idled her horse long enough for the abbess to gain on her. Ilse welcomed the respite, knowing that Hans, the handsome abbey groom, would soon catch up with her. The dalliance had become a daily ritual, a dance she reveled in starting and ending at her pleasure.

Hans had come to the abbey a year earlier. Within a month, he had impressed the others with his skills at the forge and at the stables. His steady good cheer and quick mind soon endeared him to the laborers, especially when problems arose.

Ilse had been delighted at being chosen as the abbess' traveling companion, and she had been equally delighted at the news that Hans would be one of the grooms traveling with them. More than once, she had feasted her eyes on his long-legged stride and glimpsed the sheen of sunlight on his wheat-colored hair.

"Careful," her sisters had scolded when she told them, but Ilse only flicked her hand at their forebodings, determined not to let them quench her joy.

At first, once they began traveling, Hans had been wary of speaking to the nuns. At Rupertsberg, after all, workmen like himself rarely spoke to the nuns and then only on matters of abbey business. After a few days on the road, however, Hans had become more relaxed around Ilse, and she both welcomed and encouraged his attention.

Riding beside him now, Ilse voiced the one concern she knew would draw Hans' eyes to hers: "It troubles me that my lady abbess has not recovered from her reception at Trier," she murmured.

Frowning, Hans turned to her. "Perhaps we should have left at once," he said. "After her sermon, those crowds were trampling each other to beg her blessing or her touch."

"Unlike the furious canons who shoved them back," she whispered, leaning toward him.

"The abbess was on fire with her warnings, was she not?" he said, his eyes flashing at the memory. "Brave she was," he said, his callused hands gripping the reins. "And her words were dangerous, if I may say so, my lady," he stated softly. "Indeed, I never thought I would see a woman threaten bishops in their own cathedral!"

"The abbess claims that it's because these men have grown so weak that she, a woman, has been commanded to chastise them," Ilse said. "Otherwise, why would she risk uttering such dire predictions?"

"The truth she speaks cannot be denied," the groom replied soberly. "And all who breathe know it. As I watched her, it was as though she was born to rule in that cathedral."

"Like Saint Paul, the abbess would argue that God often chooses the weak to confound the strong."

"The abbess, weak?" He laughed. "I don't believe it. You can feel her strength in every stone and plank in the abbey."

"But she is also tremendously vulnerable," Ilse confided. "She is subjected without warning to visions of future events that terrify her and that prudence bids her withhold. I have no doubt that, at times, the weight of them must be so unbearable that her only escape is into illness."

Hans whistled softly. "You deepen my gratitude to be in her service, my lady. I can only say that when she pleads for justice, I feel compassion stream from her eyes. . . ." He stopped and swallowed. "There's none that's lost their land and seen their kin die from hunger who would deny the truth of her words." Shifting abruptly, he straightened his shoulders and stared straight ahead.

"And when she challenges churchmen with her cries for reform, are you tempted to brandish your sword for her?" Ilse prodded, unwilling to let such a fantasy vanish.

"Of course," he retorted. "I am duty-bound to protect all on this journey."

"And would you shield her from the wrath of the prince-bishops, as well?" she persisted, breathlessly.

"I would give my life for her," the groom said stolidly, aware that she was baiting him. "But only if death threatened her," he was quick to add. "I would hardly dare raise my sword to a lord of the land otherwise. I do not share in your privileges, my lady. I am not a cleric, nor have I a title or freehold. I know my place."

"I know that," she replied softly, but her eyes flashed with excitement.

"Then why do you goad me to pursue challenges beyond my rank?"

"Because the abbess contends that in all her visions of Mother Church, laypeople have proven to be the most powerful."

"Do not mock me, my lady." His tone was fierce.

"I do not," Ilse insisted. "The abbess also praises the great goodness of marriage, wherein men and women bring themselves to fulfillment in their coupling, filling the church with *viriditas,* the blossoms of new life."

When Hans turned to her, his eyes were shining. "I know that power well," he said. "I've held it in my arms. I feel it still."

"I never have." Her tongue was thick, her voice a whisper. "I never will." She screamed inside, heart-stung by his twin revelation.

"Look, there ahead," Hildegard called out to Ilse, "the spires of Krauftal on the horizon."

"I must join the abbess now," Ilse said quietly, letting her horse slow, letting the distance grow between them, plummeting slowly into the truth that day by day, she must now learn to live without him.

Hildegard lifted her face to the warmth of the noonday sun as the travelers stopped to rest.

"The moment I lie on the earth, it sends strength up into my body," she said as Hans helped her dismount. Yet once she had stretched out, she found her thoughts turning to Hazzecha, the abbess of Krauftal, at their next destination.

Hazzecha's flurry of correspondence had summoned up an image of an imprisoned bird whose cage was littered with feathers that had fallen when the bird had attempted to take flight. In her letters, Hazzecha had, in turn, begged, cajoled, then pleaded with Hildegard to visit her. Unless she escaped to a hermitage, she wrote, she could not save her soul.

As the travelers approached, the bells for Prime echoed through the forest to welcome them. The abbey buildings appeared far-spread and solid, the high walls thick and forbidding, and badly in need of repair.

A sullen porter with a flushed face and bulbous nose studied them through the gates, then grunted as he opened them. Once the travelers were inside, he turned to the grooms and jerked his head toward what appeared to be the stables. Still staring at Hildegard warily, he gestured to her to follow him as he silently led her to the gate of a large house surrounded by an even larger garden.

"She would be in there," he growled, turning abruptly back to the gatehouse.

But Hildegard paused. Even more confusing than the porter's rudeness was the tremulous sound of the chanting voices coming from the chapel. Was it just that the voices were thin, or was it that there were so few of them? As she strained to listen, the door of the house inside the gate flew open.

"Is it truly my lady abbess, Hildegard?" a high-pitched voice called out excitedly. "I prayed and prayed that you would not disappoint me."

Running toward her was a slight nun of medium height, her arms waving wildly as she struggled to slip on her wimple and stuff her chestnut curls inside.

Her smile revealed protruding teeth and deep-set brown eyes that seemed too large for her pinched face. Bands of lace edged the abbess' collar and cuffs. Instead of a cincture, she wore a silken cord at her waist with elaborate tassels. Beyond her astonishment at Hazzecha's attire, Hildegard was even more amazed that the abbess was not in chapel chanting the Divine Office with her daughters. Hazzecha clapped her hands more in excitement than reverence as she knelt to receive Hildegard's blessing. Jumping up, she linked arms with her distinguished visitor. "You must be hungry. I have arranged for food to be sent to my quarters so that we might dine alone." Ilse stood gaping as Hazzecha spirited her abbess away.

Hazzecha's reception room left Hildegard breathless. Dim and musty, it was crowded with candles of every size and strewn with huge clumps of wild flowers. Most were dried up. Dust flew up with every footstep. Now Hazzecha was urging her to sit, though the seat of the chair was sagging badly. Hazzecha crouched at her feet, and though she maintained a frantic smile, her eyes spoke of desperation.

"Are you really here, my lady?" she repeated again and again. But when Hildegard attempted to converse with her, she held up her hand. "We must dine first," she informed her guest, as the smell of food now wafted toward them.

Hildegard could only gasp at the feast the servants brought in and set before them: a tureen of steaming fish soup thick with leeks and onions, a platter of lamb stew seasoned with garlic, and a pair of partridges stuffed with grapes and cinnamon.

"My daughters will wonder why they are fasting today," Hazzecha winked, at the sight of her guest's astonishment. But the next moment, she burst into tears. Between sobs, she hastened to explain that it had been her joy to arrange this feast to honor her famous guest and also that she planned to fast for two months after the abbess' departure. Watching her, Hildegard felt as though she was trapped in a whirlwind.

Over the next few days, each time the bells called them to chapel, Hildegard noted that half of the stalls in the oratory were empty. The pitiful chants of those nuns who did straggle to Compline soon surrendered to yawns. Some of the older nuns simply curled up in their stalls and snored.

As Hazzecha poured out her fears and frustration day after day,

Hildegard fought to keep from being strangled in the net of the abbess' needs.

"What makes you think that by escaping to a hermitage, you will have a better chance of saving your soul than you do here?" Hildegard asked sternly. "Believe me, a cell is not what you think."

"Could it be worse than the prison in which I am trapped here?" Hazzecha seethed. "As abbess, I am condemned to nothing but accusations."

"Of what sort?"

"I am accused of making my daughters ill by forbidding them access to the infirmary for extra sessions of bloodletting, when all they really seek there is a chance to shirk their duties for a week and eat their fill of meat. Yet when I challenge their motives, they argue until I yield to their demands."

"And are you quick to remind them of their vow of obedience? And of your sacred duty to correct them?"

"I do! I do!" she cried, gnawing at a fingernail.

"When was the last time your nuns honored the Great Silence after Compline?" Hildegard asked. "Or fasted during Lent? Or ministered to the sick? Or distributed alms?"

Hazzecha stiffened. "I have tried in other ways, my lady. When my daughters defy me, I take the discipline at night, flogging myself until my back runs red. When nothing changes, I try even harder, flogging my hips and thighs, as well. All this in the hope that, by my doing penance, my daughters would see the error of their ways and embrace the Rule."

"But as their abbess, you have sworn to lead them by your good example," Hildegard insisted.

"You do not understand, my lady." The words boiled from Hazzecha's lips. "I was not elected to provide a good example. My daughters foisted my staff and my ring on me because of my weakness, not my strength. They chose me knowing that I could be compromised in ways that would render me useless and thereby free them to do as they pleased. And as time has proved, it has been the only way I could hope to survive."

Hazzecha was rocking back and forth now. "Surely it comes as no surprise to you to learn how many came here under protest. Like me, Sister Hilda was placed here as an oblate when her father went to the Holy Jerusalem War, and on his return, he forgot that he had a daughter. Sister Monika is one of seven who languish here because their husbands needed excuses to divorce them. As for our twenty widows, each grows thinner by the day, soon to be forgotten in death as they have been in life."

By now, Hildegard's throat was so constricted that she could barely breathe. "Have you no faithful daughters, then?"

"But of course! A pitiful few who freely chose this life and still struggle to keep their vows. Two of them kept me alive until recently. But now, even they have turned away and no longer hold me or come to my aid...when I weep." Her words became a sob. "Their lives have become secrets I am no longer invited to share." She began to rock back and forth again, humming mindlessly. "Of course, there are a few zealous ones. They keep the Rule and pray for their sisters here," she continued. "But they are young, and time will defeat them. Surely you have seen them lying prostrate at the altar. They often sleep there, believing it to be the only safe place to keep their faith alive in this abbey."

Suddenly, Hazzecha ripped the wimple from her head, releasing a tumble of curls onto her shoulders. Pulling her hair forward, she covered her face with it like a curtain of shame. Hildegard heard muffled sobs. As she reached for Hazzecha's hand, the frantic abbess fell to her knees and began kissing Hildegard's feet. "Before God, I have no failures left to confess. Give me hope, my lady."

Sinking to her knees, Hildegard held the desperate woman in her arms. "My daughter, I beg you to persevere."

Hazzecha jerked back on her haunches and gripped Hildegard's arm. "You don't understand, do you? I must leave here, my lady. I must leave or go mad."

"Together, we will find a way...."

"Of course, I could go to Rome on pilgrimage," Hazzecha intruded again, her eyes brightening. "But no one will go with me. Will you go with me, my lady?" It was a child's plea.

"That is not possible, my daughter," Hildegard replied, aware of how carefully she must tread.

The abbess must not correct to excess. Take care that the bruised reed not be broken.

"What would you have me do, my lady?" Hazzecha pleaded, a beggar child again.

"Stay, my daughter, I beg you. And trust. Ask for small triumphs each day and build on them until your strength returns. Seek the company of those faithful daughters who cling together in hope at the foot of the altar. Your salvation is there."

"Stay?" Hazzecha repeated dully.

"My daughter, look in my eyes. You are not alone. Do you think others have not felt throttled with the same despair and frustration? Do you think others have not longed to escape? Who of us has not staggered under the cross that has been placed on her shoulders, only to be lifted by grace again and again?"

Hazzecha sagged. "But you...," she began. "Can you compare...?" Her eyes clouded.

"I can, for I, too, have been humbled by my weakness and have been betrayed by those who swore their love for me. I, too, have been mocked by fools. Even now, there are days when I drown in self-doubt and rage at God. I often feel crushed by the burden, never understanding how I will find the strength to go on. At such times, dear Hazzecha, we must trust the grace that flooded us when we took our vows as abbesses. That grace is always there for us to claim. Rest now, and tomorrow we will pray together and make a new start."

Hazzecha slumped in Hildegard's arms and placed her head on her shoulder. They prayed together until Compline. When Hildegard left her, she was calm.

At Prime the next morning, as planned, Hildegard made her way to Hazzecha's house to accompany her to chapel. At the door of the dwelling, she heard a clattering, then an ungodly groan. Hildegard struggled against the door until it opened, flooding the room with streams of sunlight. Hazzecha's body was swinging from the rafters. Her cincture was her noose. Dashing to her side, Hildegard stood on the stool and reached up. Loosening the noose, she removed it from Hazzecha's bruised neck as the desperate woman uttered a bleak cry.

"Why did you stop me?" she gasped in frustration, pushing against Hildegard. "Why won't you let me die?"

Struggling to keep her balance, Hildegard stepped down and staggered toward the bed while Hazzecha flailed in her arms. After placing her down, Hildegard pressed her hands on the abbess' shoulders for several moments to restrain her. Finally, Hazzecha's body crumpled into sobs. Now Hildegard saw that the room had been rampaged. Pottery had been smashed against the walls, and the bedclothes were ripped to shreds. Hildegard was in shock; her ears were ringing; her throat was closing.

When the others came, they found Hildegard still struggling to restrain Hazzecha's body on the bed.

"I will not leave this abbey until her madness passes," she promised them.

It was the first day Hildegard had come to the scriptorium since her return from her preaching tour.

"What news of our emperor?" she asked, wearily, still haggard despite her week of rest.

"The Italians now call him Barbarossa, Red Beard," Volmar said, shaking his head as he cleared the work table in the scriptorium.

"A mild jest," Hildegard sighed, "compared to the names he's called here at home, where every German prince is now warring with his brother and cousin."

"True enough, but Frederick Barbarossa dares not leave Italy now," Volmar warned. News had drifted back that Frederick had been merciless when the Italian communes refused to submit to the rule of his imperial governors. In Crema, imperial troops shot arrows at fugitives who were being lowered over the city walls in baskets, and then set their city on fire. In Milan, people dropped in the streets from starvation while the Milanese nobility trudged barefoot through mud to kneel and kiss the emperor's feet. They begged for mercy as their heads were heaped with ashes and their city was was burned to the ground around them.

Barbarossa, indeed, Hildegard thought. His beard was the color of blood. She was surprised to hear herself moan.

Volmar looked up and frowned. "Your sighs reflect the sad news from Italy, my lady?"

"No more than the news from Schönau," she replied, holding up a sheaf of vellum. "The lady abbess Elizabeth writes of a vision in which an angel warned her again of the rising strength of the Cathari heretics."

After Volmar read Abbess Elizabeth's letter containing the vision, his face was gray.

"Can't you see that all I seek is a place where I can rest my spirit?" Hildegard grieved.

Again, she saw the hairshirt Elizabeth wore beneath her robe and the pathway of scars across her back and hips from the chain she wore day and night.

After some moments, she reached for her stylus and wrote:

To Elizabeth, Abbess of Schönau, from Hildegard, Abbess of Rupertsberg:

My daughter, these words come not from me but from the clear Light. I beg you to embrace moderation toward your body in every way, for moderation is the true mother of all the virtues. Remember that when a field has not been properly plowed, it yields only weeds, not wheat. It is the same for one who lays on her body more strain and danger than her flesh can endure.

Therefore, those seeking to perfect God's works should remember that, being human, they are vessels of clay, and must take great care not to abuse the body with which God has graced them.

O daughter, may God make you a mirror of life. Since I tremble always in the cowardice of fear, pray for me so that God will help me to persevere in his service.

"These heretics eat at the heart of Mother Church," Volmar said when Hildegard had finished writing. "Their powers of persuasion must be formidable. Why else would so many noblewomen be flocking to join them, leaving their titles and castles behind?"

"For good reason," Hildegard retorted. "Because they hunger for leaders who seek to follow the path of the apostles, which means embracing the poverty of the serfs. Who of our own prince-bishops preaches self-denial or chooses to keep three Lents each year or fasts three days each week on bread and water?"

"True," Volmar agreed, "yet the heretics succeed on other levels as well. They have confounded our cathedral scholars; they have opened schools in Rome and formed archbishoprics in northern France. Their logic and reasoning have proved a powerful attraction to our clergy, who are converting in record numbers."

The slam of the abbess' fist startled him. "There are paths that transcend the scope of scholars!" she thundered. "Faith always triumphs over reason."

"Reason has taken up residence in Cologne, my lady," Volmar sighed. "It's said that heretics cluster on every corner, seducing the people at every turn."

Hildegard pressed her fingertips into her forehead; the thrumming in her temples was beginning again. She felt a wave of nausea.

Where could she turn? Not to the churchmen she knew. From all she had heard at her table, most prelates remained complacent, still regarding the heretics as a nuisance, refusing to see that they were crippling the Church. The emperor had all but abandoned the homeland, condemning the people to life in the abyss of the schism.

"I must go to the people of Cologne myself," Hildegard suddenly cried out. "I must proclaim with every breath in my body that God has not forsaken them."

Volmar blanched. "It may be too late for Cologne, my lady."

"Never," Hildegard cried. "We must go together and warn them without delay. There is so little time!"

The abbess would not be dissuaded. To Volmar's dismay, they departed on the day that Hildegard entered her sixty-third year.

They rode in silence, traveling northwest along the Rhine past fields long since bleached by the summer sun. Autumn's night chill had already tinted the leaves of the trees with ruby and orange and cinnamon hues, often blending all three on a single leaf.

"This is by far the most beautiful autumn God ever created," Hildegard exulted.

"You say that every year, my lady," Volmar teased. Yet as they rode, he noted how the color had risen in her cheeks since their departure from Rupert's Mountain. A rare serenity flowed from her, as though the beauty of these fields had seeded her soul.

Volmar felt a wave of relief as he studied her. With Mainz in an uproar, the timing of their departure had been fortuitous. To retaliate for Archbishop Arnold's murder, the emperor had placed Mainz under siege. The city's protective walls had been destroyed and its privileges revoked, and staggering fines were imposed on its citizens. The city was in shock. Rainald of Dassel had been posted there to ensure Mainz's unconditional surrender. Volmar was grateful that the abbess would be removed from the city's pain. Yet as the outline of Cologne's city walls appeared on the horizon, Volmar could only guess at the fate that awaited them there.

Located on the west bank of the Rhine, Cologne had an illustrious history that Hildegard began to reflect upon as they neared the city. The Celts had been the first to settle there. Later, the Romans camped on the spot. Then, four decades before Christ, the Romans circled their camp with walls, transforming it into an outpost that they managed to hold for over four hundred years. Christians had dwelled there since the second century. Despite the scars of time, the city had maintained its strength and dominance.

As they rode through the city gates, Hildegard remembered a recent warning that had been whispered in her ear by a visiting abbot: "Nothing in Cologne escapes the vigilance of its archbishop, Rainald of Dassel," he said, "be it the fevers of the body politic or the collection of the city's customs and tolls." The abbot looked about anxiously. "Indeed, there are many who claim that even *in absentia*, Rainald keeps count of every heartbeat in his domain."

Not exactly, Hildegard mused as they entered the city. She herself had been invited to come and exhort Rainald's own clergy in Cologne by Philip, the domdeacon of Rainald's cathedral.

The cathedral was immense, its pillars the width of six men and its main altar designed like a stone fortress. Though the dampness was chilling, Hildegard was cheered by the sound of chanting voices rising bravely from an unseen alcove.

As she neared the altar, she wondered if she had come to the wrong place. The prelates seated on the altar looked more like a council of princes in the emperor's court. Their splendor dazzled her. A vermilion cloak bordered in ermine flowed from a bishop's shoulder while its matching satin robe flashed with a ruby-studded cross. Beside the bishop sat a canon, the rippling folds of his silver cloak adorned with swirls of purple and magenta embroidery, which were repeated on the matching purse attached to his belt.

Hildegard recalled the oft-told tale that Rainald had swiftly denounced a decree at the council of Rheims that forbade clergy to wear brightly colored furs. Rainald had claimed that such finery was an important symbol of the prelate's rank and privilege. He would have gloated today in the sweep of damask and the shimmer of satin.

Scanning the men's faces, Hildegard wondered if curiosity or interest had brought these peacock prelates here today. She prayed that some had come longing for inspiration: a surge of hope, a plea for reform, a helpful revelation. Seeing their cascading jowls and their swollen bellies, she wondered if any had ever stood under the blaze of a noonday sun to renounce the city's heretics.

For a moment, she felt the wind lifting the long, white beard of the Cathari zealot in Würzburg and ruffling the hair of the radiant girl who stood at his side. Their passion was palpable.

Could it be matched by the priests and the prelates here? "Put the words in my mouth, Lady Wisdom," she pleaded. Then she began to speak to the men before her:

"In a vision, I saw your faces as I heard a Voice cry out to you, 'Shepherds of Cologne, feed my flocks! Feed my sheep! As my priests, I have placed you like the sun and the stars so that you might give light to my people. Yet I seek in vain for the light that should stream from your sermons. Alas, like the night, you exhale only darkness. You protest and whine loudly: "You ask too much of us! We can't do everything!" Yet you lust for honor without effort and expect

eternal reward without earthly denial. Are you deaf to the Devil's sneers as you feed him with your poisonous morsels? "*My veins bulge with your venom*," he purrs. "*My breast heaves with your depravities.*" *But I, the One Who Am, say to you:* "*My Sons, repent while there is time. Cast out the heretics who prowl the streets of your city, destroying your church. Do not let these deceivers become the whip for your punishment, for even now, their seeds sprout with far greater heresies to come. Expel them before they plunge you into a nest of vipers! Refuse to lie prostrate, my sons! Teach those Scriptures forged in the fire of the Holy Spirit while there is still time!*'"

She stepped down from the pulpit. The faces blurred as they surged toward her, their smiles masking contempt. They longed to strangle her, and each of them thought: *How dare she? How dare she?*

They swept past her now. She held her ground, hearing their whispers slur into curses, numb with rage as they shuffled to their waiting winecups.

Reeling from the force of their fury, Hildegard strained to hear the sound of Volmar's footsteps, relieved to feel him guiding her hand to his arm as they slowly moved forward.

The abbess was trembling uncontrollably. Recalling his promise to Hiltrude, Volmar informed the grooms that they would be returning to Rupertsberg without delay.

Part Six

1171–73

Still, I have always beheld this vision
in my soul, from my infancy,
when my bones and nerves
had not grown strong, until the present time,
when I am more than seventy years of age. . . .
And from the third year of my life,
I have seen a Light so intense
that my soul trembles.

– Vita Sanctae Hildegardis

Hildegard grew alarmed when her Psalter slipped from her grasp that morning at Matins and fell to the floor. It had never happened before. What was wrong? She felt a strange lightness invade her body. Once she reached the safety of her room, she fell on her bed, fully clothed.

Later, all she would remember was the feeling that she was drifting. And yet the air she breathed was pure, the colors around her intensely vivid, and the gentle warmth that suffused her being was unlike anything she had ever felt before. A soft hum surrounded her.

Her ears were tender drums now, the words of the Voice of the Son of Man dropping like crystal rain on her soul, reverberating in every vein, in every drop of blood.

> *In the beginning was the Word*
> *and the Word was with God,*
> *and the Word was God.*
> *He was in the beginning.*
> *Through him all things came to be.*
> *Not one thing has its being but through him. . . .*
> *And the Word was made flesh and dwelt among us.*

The opening words from the Gospel of Saint John.

But now, behind the Son of Man, the figure of Lady Wisdom rose, resplendent and glorious, flowing toward him through waves of silken light, blinding Hildegard with the fire of diamonds as Lady Wisdom cried out:

> *"Before time began, the Creator fashioned me,*
> *to be present forever.*
> *Then the Creator called forth a command to me:*
> *'In Jacob, make your dwelling,*
> *in Israel, find your inheritance.'"*

It was the Voice that Hildegard had heard in her mother's womb: Lady Wisdom's!

Now the figure of the Son of Man advanced, then merged with the figure of Lady Wisdom.

*"I come as Light into the world,
so that those who believe in me
may no longer be captive to the darkness."*

Behind His Voice, Lady Wisdom's echo replied:

*"Wisdom sings her own praises
and proclaims her glory in the midst of her people:
'I issued from the mouth of the Most High,
and covered the earth like mist,
and dwelled in the highest heavens,
and presided over peoples and nations.'"*

The Voice of the Son of Man rose again:

*"For the Father loves the Son
and shares with him all the things
that he has done,
and even greater things to come,
which will astonish you."*

Then Lady Wisdom's Voice answered again:

*"Wisdom abides with you, for she knows your works,
and was at your side when you created the world.
She understands what pleases you
and what is in accordance with your plan.
About you she proclaims:
'The One who comes from heaven
witnesses all he has seen and heard,
and though some reject his testimony,
all who accept it attest to God's truth.
For the One whom God has sent
speaks God's own words.'"*

And the Voice of the Son of Man cried out again:

*"Yes, you know me and from whence I come,
yet I have not come of myself,
but come instead from the One who sent me."*

Swept into the dance between Lady Wisdom and the Son of Man, Hildegard's soul streamed like tears of joy through the pores of her skin. She felt embraced by a diaphanous shimmering without substance or form, beginning or end, suspending her above the ground.

Hildegard awoke with a violent shuddering. Clasping her knees, she shook in her bed. Her limbs were sleek with sweat. Into what world had she wandered? How could the forms she saw blend and become one so perfectly? Why did each of their messages from Holy Writ mirror so much of the meaning of the other? How could that be? And what did it mean?

When Hildegard finally shared the encounter with Volmar, she swore him to secrecy. Though she longed to dismiss it as a dream, something stopped her. Her womb had trembled when she witnessed it. The memory left her spent.

For the next few weeks, the nuns began to comment on the fact that the abbess seemed unusually withdrawn.

"Lady Mother looks at me with the eyes of a frightened child," Hiltrude puzzled.

Volmar nodded but said no more. It was clear to him that since the encounter, something had shifted inside the abbess. The monk had no doubt that the experience had transported her to another realm. As in a daze, as if still addressing Lady Wisdom, Hildegard had over and over again repeated the words:

"O my lady, I am unworthy of the task! How can you ask it of me?"

The words haunted Volmar. What command had she received that had frightened her so? Volmar never knew, for she never spoke of the incident again.

Two months passed before she announced her intention to resume work. "The new visions must be recorded now," she said simply. Stylus in hand, she inscribed the title on her wax tablet: *The Book of Divine Works.*

In the mystery of God, I saw a wondrously beautiful creature. Its human form was of such beauty and radiance, I could have more easily gazed at the sun than at that face.

And the Voice of the figure cried out:

"I am Love, the supreme and fiery force who kindled every living spark, and I breathed forth no deadly thing, though I permit them to be.

"As I circle the vaults of heaven with Wisdom's wings, I ordain all things rightly. The fiery essence of God issues forth from me, whirling about the beauty of the fields and blazing from the moon and the stars.

"And with the airy wind, I quicken all things by the power of an unseen pulse.

"I flame above the beauty of the fields to signify the earth: the matter from which God made humanity.

"I shine in the waters to indicate the soul, for as water suffuses the whole earth, the soul pervades the body.

"I burn in the sun and moon to denote Reason, and the stars are their words.

"So it is that the works of humans shine forth as a sign of their divinity. For God loved humanity so much, God made humans heir to the angels and all the wonders the angels forfeited.

"Now humanity is called upon to complete God's glory.

"For Love is at work in the circles of eternity, like heat within a fire, binding humanity to all creatures in an oath of loyalty, like man to woman and body to soul.

"Let all who fear and love God open their hearts to these words, proclaimed not by a human voice but rather from myself, the One Who Am."

Hildegard turned at the sound of Volmar's sigh.

"My lady, is the creature you speak of divine or human, woman or man, Love or Reason?"

"It possesses all these," she replied slowly, "and Wisdom as well."

"My lady, could you have seen the face of God?" Volmar heard himself asking.

But Hildegard shuddered and turned away.

It was Helenger's first visit to Rupertsberg since becoming abbot of Disibodenberg. As she watched him from the open doorway, Hildegard saw his eyes glancing about as he chatted with Father Volmar.

The abbess' greeting was cool but civil. Though the abbey had surrendered the nuns' book of benefactions, there were still papers missing, which left the matter of Rupertsberg's legal independence unresolved.

"I have come to tell you that Pope Victor died at Lucca," he announced briskly.

"And will a second antipope succeed him?" she asked.

"To be sure. Cardinal Guido of Crema, who has chosen the name of Paschal III."

"What news, then, of our legitimate Pope Alexander?"

"He has fled to France in the face of these uncertainties."

Hildegard moaned. "So the schism widens and deepens. And with a second antipope, Frederick risks excommunication."

The abbot folded his arms. "You have no reason to fear, my lady. No schism would interfere with the imperial letter of protection that, I'm told, the emperor recently granted to Rupertsberg."

"Quite right, my Lord Abbot," Hildegard replied. Then she lapsed into silence as she waited for him to reveal the real reason for his visit.

"As your former protector, my Lady Abbess, the abbey wishes to make a simple request of you. We ask that you write a life of Saint Disibod for our archives. Not for ourselves, of course, but to honor the memory of Blessed Lady Jutta."

Hildegard's smile was tranquil. "I will delight in doing so, my lord, upon receipt of the agreement finalizing our legal separation from the Abbey of Disibodenberg."

To Hildegard, Abbess of Rupertsberg, from Elizabeth, Abbess of Schönau:

I am greatly consoled by your understanding heart regarding my visions and your assurance that I am not mad. Yet many events have occurred of late that have deepened my doubts. Still, as you advised, I seek the virtue of discretion to resist the temptation to mortify my flesh unduly and have shed my hairshirt since its gnawing teeth have caused my flesh to fester, distracting me from prayer.

Again, in a vision, I saw the Blessed Virgin presiding at the altar in a priest's robe, her arms raised in consecration. My daughters told me afterward that during that time, they feared that my heart had stopped beating, so deeply did the vision transport my soul.

After I saw this vision, you filled my thoughts for days afterward. I entrust you to the care of the Virgin and beg your prayers that I may not falter in faith.

Though Hildegard hastened to reassure her, weeks passed before she received a reply. It was written by Elizabeth's scribe, her brother Egbert, a canon from Bonn:

My Lady Abbess, I write to convey the sad news that Elizabeth's heart, weakened from fasting, has stopped beating. She died on the eve of the feast of Mary's Assumption into heaven. The last sound she uttered was a cry of joy.

At the news, a wrenching sob surged through Hildegard's body. Running from the scriptorium, she flung herself down in the shade of an elm tree whose shadow fell across the stones of the enclosure walls.

"My lady," Volmar whispered when he found her, "surely you know what comfort and strength your words brought to Abbess Elizabeth. She is at peace now. Her struggle is over."

"If only I had not blinded myself to the signs and listened more clearly," she sobbed. "She needed me and I failed her."

Volmar kneeled next to her, confused. She had not known Elizabeth that long or that well. Why was her grief so profound? Hoping to help, he bent over her, but the words he heard startled him: "Richardis, my dearest, darling Richardis! Why did you leave me? Why did you abandon me?"

For weeks, Hildegard's correspondence lay unanswered.

"My lady, the letter bearing the royal seal of King Henry Plantagenet of England begs your attention," Volmar reminded her. "All reports indicate that England is moving toward a new alliance with Germany, and it's clear that King Henry II desires your counsel."

"I shall attend to it presently," she assured him. "But there is a far more pressing letter that must go to England first," Hildegard said, as Volmar looked up in surprise from his carrel.

To Her Royal Highness, Eleanor of Aquitaine, Queen of England, from Hildegard, Abbess of Rupertsberg:

Greetings.

Gracious queen, your spirit moves through changing clouds that give you no peace. Refuse to surrender your heart to the confusion of those around you.

Remain steadfast. In all your troubles, God will guide you, ever at your side and in all your works. Seek only the peace of God's grace in the days ahead and your heart will be calm.

As Hildegard placed her abbey seal on the letter, she saw the royal figure pacing the length of her rooms in her prison tower, her graceful hands still deft at her embroidery, though her wings were cruelly clipped.

"Dear lady, I understand your plight, for, in my own way, I pace with you," Hildegard sighed. *"Only our spaces are different."*

Volmar put down his quill as Hildegard sat back and folded her arms.

"We are not finished," the abbess said briskly, folding her arms. "My conscience demands that I no longer delay sending this next letter to a different kind of prisoner," she continued angrily. "One who is held hostage by his ambition."

To Frederick, His Imperial Highness from Hildegard, Abbess of Rupertsberg:

I plead with you: as God's servant, you must be vigilant! Take care that the jaws of death do not devour you. Pride has blinded you in your decision to elect a second antipope. Why have you succumbed to the snares with which evil spirits seek to trap you? Why are you betraying your people?

Repent, I beg of you! God's love never condemns but embraces the truly repentant person. Again I say: accept in your heart that all true power comes only from God. But also remember that all who flaunt justice will be avenged!

The roofs of Rupertsberg groaned under the weight of the February snow. No sooner had a footpath been cleared than it was swallowed by a new downfall. One could scarcely move now in the crowded calfactory as the nuns competed to get closer to the fire's warmth.

Nearby in the scriptorium, two lone braziers — set beside the carrels where Volmar and Hildegard were laboring on the *Book of Divine Works* — tried bravely to defy the stinging chill. Pausing to rub the stiffness from his fingers, Volmar cupped his hands around a brazier, trying to warm his body and unscramble his thoughts about what was happening.

The abbess' visions were changing dramatically, becoming more intense and far-ranging, yet somehow clearer than the others. In the section they had just concluded, the abbess had described a vision of the unfolding universe. Volmar listened, transfixed.

Her body swayed. She seemed to lean into the path of the winds that kept the universe in motion by their blowing as she described the relationship of the planets to the journey of the sun and the moon.

Now a figure of a human being came forward in the innermost circle of the swirling winds and revolving planets. The figure spoke:

"In the center of Love's embrace is the circle of the soul and the body. For just as the Word of God penetrates all creation, so does the soul penetrate the whole body like wind flowing through a house or like a sower seeding fertile ground or like a mother soothing her crying babe. Yet all these wonders are held in the arms of Love and are linked in a delicate balance in a universe created to be of service to humanity so men and women can work with it."

Volmar felt uneasy. Somehow, he felt as though the abbess was lifting the veils of the universe and peering into its secret soul. It frightened him. The old fear rose: What if she lost her way in this awesome terrain and chose not to return? Frowning, he turned to her and was met by her smile, then realized that she had been studying him. He blushed as he dipped his quill in his inkpot.

"Have no fear, my friend," she assured him. "We are protected and are never alone. We need only call for help and our angels will reply." A smile lit her face. "Heed my words," she said and then detailed a vision to him:

"As you watch how all creatures emerge from God's will, you can see how divine order spreads its wings to reveal the very essence of this ordered creation: angels and human beings.

"Some of these angels are seen in their fiery nature, others shine brightly, and a third group gleams like the stars.

"The fiery angels stand firmly in great strength before the face of God. In contrast, the angels of brightness can be moved by the deeds of human beings, who are also God's work. For these angels constantly gaze at our good deeds and carry their fragrance into God's presence.

"The angels who shine like the stars feel sympathy for our human nature and place it before God's eyes as though it were a book. These angels attend us! They speak to us in a reasonable way, just as God intended them to do. In the sight of God, they praise our good deeds but turn away from those deeds or those people who are evil.

"And because God has prepared the angels for various offices, God has also decided they should have necessary contact with human beings and show themselves to us under certain forms in accordance with God's will. However varied the tasks they carry out, all the angels revere God in devotion and knowledge.

"But even though God has provided human beings with the protection of angels, God has also endowed us, both in our wishes and deeds, with wings so that we can fly."

"Does that answer your questions, my friend," the abbess asked, softly, "and quiet your fears?"

In the dream, Hildegard lay alone in the cold empty hall. She was sur-
rounded by strange tapping sounds as though objects were falling onto a
stone floor.

The sounds grew louder, the falling faster. In the background she heard
the hushed cries, the scratching sounds like rats scurrying, then the racket
of rumbling cartwheels, the hordes of running feet, the walls tumbling
toward her.

Raising herself, Hildegard gasped for breath. She had willed herself
awake by refusing to be buried alive in the rubble.

Within days, news came that Pope Alexander had returned from exile
in France and was in residence in Rome again.

"He straddles a nest of scorpions," Hildegard warned. "On one side,
the fickle Romans; on the other, Frederick's breath on his neck. He must
take the greatest care."

"Have you so little hope for peace in Rome, my lady?" Volmar asked.

"One can have hope and still sleep with one eye open," she said.

Within a year, Alexander's position with the Roman citizenry weakened. Seizing the opportunity, Frederick crossed the Alps and headed
south to Rome for the third time. He sent Rainald of Dassel ahead to
devastate the Roman countryside, hoping to force the desperate Romans
to deliver Pope Alexander to him.

But Alexander had fled, leaving Frederick no choice but to force his
way into the Eternal City and decimate it with flames and thunder.

In the wake of the pillage, the citizens stood by horrified as their priceless Roman art was hurled from the walls to the ground to be trampled
underfoot by the hooves of imperial horses. A visiting abbot who had
been in Rome at the time swore to Hildegard that he actually had seen
soldiers prying the golden mosaics off the churches' most famous altars,
watching in horror as they splintered on the marble floors.

The tapping sounds from her dream resounded in Hildegard's ears again as
she saw the pieces fall and their flecks of gold disappear in the darkness, crushed
forever beneath the rumblings of cartwheels and scurrying feet.

"Did he ravage Saint Peter's as well?" Hildegard asked the abbot.

"He didn't dare, since he planned to enthrone his antipope, Paschal,
there the next day and use the occasion to extract a loyalty oath from the
Roman Senate, which would prevent Alexander from any future claims
to the papacy."

"A hollow victory," Hildegard sighed.

"Not quite, my lady," the abbot smiled. "Frederick also used the occasion to officially consecrate his wife, Beatrice, as empress of the realm. I

must say that she was glorious in her flowing gown of spun gold and her crown blazing with diamonds and studded with rows of topaz and pearls. Frederick could not tear his eyes from her, though others' eyes widened at the extraordinary length of his own ermine-edged silver cloak that he wore over a robe of white satin, belted with diamonds, while his crown was set with a hundred rubies."

Hildegard was stunned. How can an emperor glide from pillage to pageantry so easily? she wondered.

"Triumph surrounded the pair as they paraded in glory through the streets of Rome," the abbot continued. "Frederick exuded fearlessness, secure in the knowledge that his pope was ensconced on the throne of Peter."

"But at what price?" the abbess asked. "Rome is in such devastation!"

"One would never know of it, judging from the riotous jubilation resounding through the halls of Saint Peter's," the abbot said, shaking his head. "Guests swore that for the next two days, the crowns never left the heads of the emperor and empress."

"And the day after that?"

The abbot sucked in his breath. "It is as though divine revenge split the heavens! The skies poured down such a scourge of thunder and lightning that Rome became a swamp within hours, choking the people with a suffocating heat. Then, like a merciless scythe, a deathly plague leveled the city. In its wake, it is said twenty-five thousand soldiers of Frederick's army succumbed in a week."

"So nature defeated the emperor with neither sword nor flame," the abbess whispered.

As the Light glowed, Hildegard witnessed the frenzy as weak, breathless bodies tried to outrace the shadow of the pestilence: nobles and servants, priests and peasants, ancients and youths, covering the fields and heaping the streets with the stench of corpses. None could outrun the Angel of Death.

"And what of Rainald of Dassel?"

"Struck down, as well."

Hildegard nodded. Rainald had offered up his life in the service of an imperial dream, despite the spiritual schisms and political heresies of these anguished times: the Church's wealth, the thirst for power, the lack of faith, the absence of mercy. Yet Hildegard whispered a prayer for Rainald's soul.

"And what of the triumphant emperor and empress?"

"They escaped to the Tuscany hills, guarded by soldiers," the abbot said. "With Rainald dead and Alexander back in Rome, Emperor Frederick was reduced to disguising himself in peasant's rags and fleeing across the Appenines as a fugitive."

Hildegard announced plans for the establishment of Rupertsberg's first daughter-house within an hour of signing the deed of sale for the land at Eibingen.

With excitement and joy, she shared the news at chapter, only to watch her daughters withdraw into silence. Their reaction shattered her.

"I told them at once," she exclaimed to Volmar later. "What more could I have done?"

"It is understandable, my lady," Volmar said as they strolled in the garden. "For years, the older nuns have fed them with details of the hardships they endured when they came here to Rupert's Mountain. Now each one fears she will be chosen to undergo a similar trial."

"And what of their vow of obedience?" she asked sternly.

Volmar shrugged and clasped his hands behind his back. "I suggest that you announce your appointments for Eibingen as soon as possible, my lady. How many will you send there?"

"No more than thirty, including the novices," she said, "not counting the servants, of course, and the laborers whose daily work will need overseers."

"You have made your choices, then?"

"The important ones. First, there must be some older nuns, to provide stability. Certainly Ilse and Gisla..."

"And who will be prioress?"

"Gertrud, of course. It's critical that the Rule takes root from the start. She has a gift for leadership and has acted with prudence as subprioress. It has been no small task assisting Hiltrude in the supervision of our fifty nuns."

"Besides," Volmar noted with a smile, "Gisla would wither without her."

"You'll see. Gertrud's common sense will prove invaluable," Hildegard nodded, "and I'm certain she'll flower under your guidance."

Volmar drew back. *"My guidance,* my lady?"

Hildegard seemed surprised. "But of course. Who else could I even consider placing there as my provost?"

"Then you wish me to leave, too, my lady?" he stuttered.

"I would prefer to say that I need you there more than here at this time." She paused. "Surely you understand why I regard your presence there as crucial to the new foundation's success. Who could I trust more than you, my friend?"

"And our work together, the writing, the correspondence?" Volmar asked.

Hildegard's smile chided him. "It will continue, of course. I will be crossing the river twice weekly to attend to matters there, and once a routine is established, I am certain we can devise a plan." Her frown begged for his understanding.

He nodded dully, a sharp pain ripping through his side.

When he returned to the scriptorium, he was in such a daze that he almost tripped over a messenger who was leaving a basket of mail inside the door. The man lingered in the doorway nervously, twirling his hat.

"If you please, father, I promised the village folk to inquire about the lady abbess' health. Is she well of late?"

For a moment, Volmar stared in confusion. "But of course," he said. Slumping back in his chair, he added, "She does so well, we often forget that she is approaching her seventieth year."

"The midwives will be relieved to hear it. They never fail to invoke her name at childbirth."

The man bobbed backward in gratitude and left.

Alone now, Volmar buried his face in his hands. He felt lightheaded, as though he was suspended in midair. The abbess' decision to assign him to Eibingen was still incomprehensible to him. He could hardly believe it! To think that all these weeks he had taken such care to shield the abbess from the anger that rose from the rumors regarding the mere possibility of a move. Now he had been placed in the midst of it. The abbey was swarming with gossip. The nuns sought every opportunity to sneak to the orchard to vent their shock and disappointment or to dawdle as long as possible at the lavabo, where they splashed their hands noisily to drown out their words.

As the tension mounted, the nuns hoisted their flags of rebellion even higher. One flash point was Hildegard's defense of the Church's condemnation of seven Cathari who were fated to be burned at the stake. The nuns confronted the abbess carefully at first. Then they more boldly challenged her on the grounds of her own stance and teachings about the value of human life.

"The decision was made by a conference of churchmen at Vézelay," Hildegard fumed one day in the crowded calfactory, tightening her shawl around her shoulders. "The Cathari were denounced as heretics at the Councils of Tours and Lombez, yet their numbers grow and their teachings spread."

"Then you would agree that they should be burned to death, my Lady Mother?" Ilse persisted.

"They are *ketzer*, heretics!" she concluded more steadily, seeing furtive glances skip through the room, as the novices drew back. "It's true that I have taught you that the murder of others is a crime against justice, my daughters, but it is also true that it is the duty of Mother Church to protect her children from false teachings."

"But by murder, my lady?" Gertrud challenged. "If I recall, you taught us that not even a warrior may enter a church if he has come from shedding another's blood in the heat of battle."

"But that's quite another matter."

"Is it, Lady Mother? I fail to see how one can reconcile that teaching with one that seeks the death of the Cathari who have drawn no sword and seek only peace with their sisters and brothers."

The abbess' eyes flared. "Like the venerable Bernard of Clairvaux, I believe that faith does not question but believes," she seethed, "and I would remind you that since Mother Church is the defender of our faith, we must trust her decisions. She has spoken: the matter is closed."

Volmar winced when Hildegard shared the exchange with him later. He knew the toll these growing displays of defiance took on the abbess. Old doubts rose, sending her fleeing into her labyrinth of self-questioning, holding each complaint up to the light lest any facet of their argument escape her. He knew it would always be her greatest challenge as abbess.

Once he departed, who would console her, who would understand her pain?

Volmar's head throbbed, as much because of his thoughts of separation from the abbess as because of the challenges facing him and the nuns chosen to go to Eibingen. As before, he must seek ways to shield the abbess from the nuns' complaints as they struggled to adjust to their primitive site across the Rhine. Though Hildegard planned to travel to Eibingen twice weekly, Volmar knew the abbess' time would be consumed with meetings with builders and workmen and conferences with her daughters. His chats with her would be brief and brisk and would deal with the endless details affecting the new foundation. With the Virgin's help, he would, he must, find a way to cope.

The throbbing in his head had become unbearable. "Help me not to miss her this much, this desperately," he prayed to the Virgin, "until I sleep at Eibingen."

Hiltrude was inconsolable. A month had passed since Volmar and the nuns had departed, leaving a hole in her heart that nothing could fill.

"But surely you agree that life is returning to normal here," Hildegard noted.

"Whatever that means," Hiltrude retorted.

The abbess herself was lost in her preoccupation with the news that, following Paschal's death, reinforcing the schism, Frederick had designated a third antipope, Calixtus III. She wondered if Volmar had heard the news and ached to share it with him. Knowing her visions so well, he alone could understand the depth and breadth of her concerns. She could not believe how much she missed sharing the simplest events of each day with him. What had possessed her to send him to Eibingen? Gertrud could easily attend to any crisis that might arise there and adjust to any provost she might have sent. Why had she released Volmar?

Mired in frustration, she turned her thoughts to Frederick again and soon felt her anger mounting. Though she knew she would risk forfeiting his letter of imperial protection, she felt compelled to denounce this latest act, in the name of justice.

To Frederick, King of Germany and Emperor of the Holy Roman Empire of the German Nation, from Hildegard, Abbess of Rupertsberg and Eibingen:

Heed while you may, the thunder of the words that He Who Is speaks through me now: "With my own hands, I destroy the stubbornness and rebellion of those who despise me. Woe to those malicious ones who ridicule me!" Listen to these words, O King! Again, remember that all who flaunt justice will be avenged. If you seek to live, you must accept in your heart that all true power comes only from God.

Frederick did not reply. But shortly thereafter, the abbey awoke one morning to a smoke-choked sky and air too thick to breathe. The nuns were terrified.

Word soon reached them that in retaliation for Mainz's ongoing rebellion, Frederick had ordered Count Ludwig of Thuringia to set fire to all the countryside around Johannesburg, Mainz, and Bingen. It was only by their imperial letter of protection that Rupertsberg and Eibingen were spared.

"At last," Volmar groaned in relief as he clutched Hildegard's message inviting him to accompany her on her fourth preaching tour. Volmar was ecstatic. After months of confronting decisions and challenges in establishing the daughter-house in Eibingen, he welcomed the chance for a respite. The nuns' resentments had begun to grate on him. They chafed under Gertrud's zealous leadership and made no secret of their discomfort with the lack of conveniences in their new home. Yet right from the start, Volmar's greatest challenge had been to adjust to his separation from the abbess. The prospect of seeing her day after day on the journey thrilled him. Once reunited, both slipped back quickly into that intimacy wherein one gave voice to the other's thoughts.

Hildegard nodded to herself as she looked ahead and watched how the grooms maneuvered to gain pride of place at Volmar's side. They revered him. It was the same wherever they went. Sensing his goodness, people approached him, noting that his smile was the same for a serf begging a blessing as for a cleric desperate to confess. She had forgotten how much comfort she drew from his blend of strength and patience, as eloquent in silence as in speech. Yet as they approached the fifth stop on their journey, not even Volmar could distract her from the stiffness in her neck and shoulders and the numbness in her feet and hands. She was so tired, her vision was blurring. Volmar's concern outweighed his pleasure at her company.

"My lady, I beg you to reconsider your plans. Let us return to Rupertsberg," he pleaded, as they departed from Kircheim.

Hildegard was tempted.

Yet even as Volmar spoke the words, Hildegard saw a huge boulder looming behind him, an image that she knew she must circumvent before their return.

"We must go on to Zweifalten," she insisted. "Perhaps after that..."

With a sigh, Volmar snapped his reins. Would she never be satisfied? She could be blind with fatigue, but if she met a beggar on the road or heard a plea for her counsel, she could not resist. Her compulsion to teach and to warn was depleting her. How many cries for reform must she utter to feel that she had done enough for one day? On this fourth journey, she had stopped to preach at twenty-one places: to serfs in market squares, to bishops and clergy in cathedrals, to monks and cloistered nuns across the land. And at the mere mention of the heretics, she felt compelled to warn every stranger who crossed their paths.

"Recall that it was your hand that recorded Lady Wisdom's command 'to cry aloud against injustice and corruption,'" she reminded him. For decades, that command had inflamed her words and ignited her prophecies. Even now, as she braced her body against the wind, Volmar saw how this burden had rounded her shoulders and how her swollen fingers could barely grasp her reins. Despite his frustration, he did not question his pledge to devote his life to this woman whose body had become a burning bush.

By midafternoon, the travelers heard the first muffled roar of waterfalls in the distance. The double Abbey of Zweifalten loomed ahead at the juncture of two rivers, its twin waterfalls serving as a barrier between the men's and women's houses. As they neared the falls, the sound of the crashing waters deafened them and the clouds of mist blinded them.

Passing through this formidable barrier, they reached the abbey gates. Hildegard stopped suddenly: her heart was racing.

"Every breath we take here must be a prayer," she announced. "Secrets mask these walls like ivy."

The travelers approached the gatehouse. A lanky monk with straw-colored hair and a pointed chin advanced to meet them.

"I am Abbot Berthold," he announced nervously. "I bid you welcome." Though he extended his hands, he stepped back, his watery eyes brimming. "I regret that our abbess is unwell and unable to greet you."

"And Sister Prioress?" Hildegard inquired.

"She is detained, as well, and sends her regrets, my Lady Abbess," the abbot flinched, pinching his nose to foreclose a sneeze. Hildegard saw that his fingernails were bitten to the quick.

"Your lady abbess' visit brings rain to the desert of my soul," the abbot murmured to Volmar as they strolled to the guest house. "I prayed to the Virgin to bring her here safely. Only her words can...help us now."

"Not my words," Hildegard spoke up firmly, "but those of the One who speaks through me." But Volmar knew that her whitened knuckles betrayed her fear. As they toured the grounds, Volmar's frown deepened. Not one of the brothers they passed had raised his eyes or uttered a greeting.

"Surely they see us," he muttered.

"Too well," Hildegard replied grimly.

Later, when the bells rang for Vespers, Hildegard retreated into the shadows behind the nuns' oratory. The rows of bent backs told her that only the older nuns were in their stalls. During the reading of the First Psalm, a few nuns drifted in, but more to whisper than to pray in their stalls. The chanting was pitifully thin, as tentative as it was off-key. Few of the nuns made any pretense at following the readings. One chanted much too loudly, surely to cover the voices of those arguing beside her.

Before long, Hildegard realized that she was the only one singing. All the others were leaning from their stalls, staring at her. Yet the moment she stepped from the chapel into the sunlight, a dozen nuns flew to her like bees to a hive.

"Oh, my lady, your voice is wondrous, so utterly clear, so truly beautiful!"

"How long will you stay?"

"Will you teach us your songs?"

"And tell us how your daughters spend their days and nights at Rupertsberg?"

As the questions pummeled her, she felt herself being propelled down a path and into the abbey hall where she was gently but firmly seated. Several nuns rushed to place her feet on a mound of pillows, while two others appeared with silver cups of mulled wine and a tray of apples and honey-cakes covered with almonds. She could barely catch her breath. As the stream of questions continued, every answer she uttered was applauded. Holding up her hand, she begged for a pause. She scanned the gathering. Her eyes were drawn to a trio of nuns on the fringe of the hall. As one of the nuns shifted in her chair, her shawl slipped from her shoulders and was quickly retrieved by the nun sitting next to her.

Hildegard saw instantly that two of the three nuns were pregnant; the one in the middle was the abbess of Zweifalten and the one on her right, her prioress.

Hildegard felt faint. No wonder the others took care to crowd her with distractions. And no wonder Vespers had been such a mockery!

Hildegard awoke the next morning after a nearly sleepless night. Still shriveled with disbelief at what she had found here, she hurried from Terce to meet with Abbot Berthold in his quarters. But before she could open her mouth, the abbot poured out a litany of his woes and grievances, insisting that he was powerless to enforce the Rule. Since his authority was ignored, his leadership was seen as irrelevant.

"And why is that, Father Abbot?" Hildegard demanded.

Cringing, he sank to his knees, choking with such gulps of emotion that Hildegard feared he would vomit. Raising his trembling hands in midair, he begged her to hear his confession. His breath was sour and his sallow skin was tattooed with scars.

"As abbot of Zweifalten, I confess that I preside over a virtual brothel," he blurted out. "The monks' and nuns' hands slide over one another's bodies freely, their glances and gestures brazen with lust. At night, the trysts are shameless. Even the novices vie for the best view of the moaning couples as they writhe in the high grass behind the orchard." As he spoke, he picked at a half-healed scab above his lip, his eyes glazed with a vacant stare.

Hildegard grasped the arms of her chair to contain herself. "And your prior? Is he equally impotent? Or is there any shred of discipline in the midst of this chaos?"

"Ah-h-h-," he moaned eerily. "'Discipline'? A threadbare word here, rarely heard and barely remembered." Now his body began to crumple before her eyes as his arms curved around his chest and his shoulders caved forward.

"I ask again: Where is your prior?" Hildegard demanded.

"My arch-traitor?" he whined. "I rarely see him since he barely suffers my presence. But the brothers and sisters see him often, for they have been snared in his net, poor wretches. He need only sniff their hunger to bait them with unspeakable temptations as he applauds their appetites. I shudder to think how he might be engaged at this very moment." His body swayed as he began to cackle, "One on each arm, three in one bed..."

"Enough!" Hildegard shouted fiercely.

Cringing, the abbot began to claw at his scab again. "I forget that not everyone dwells in hell as I do, my lady." A light singed his eyes before it disappeared in his hairshirt of self-loathing.

"My failure gnaws at me like leprosy," be sobbed, falling at her feet. "Help me, my Lady Abbess! Help me to crawl to God!"

Hildegard strolled through the abbey garden in the darkness, struggling to marshal her thoughts. The abbot's confession had revolted her. Were there monks or nuns among them who still had the strength to struggle against the quivering of their loins or the rush of desire that swelled their breasts?

Yet though trapped in this morass of corruption, the abbot had received the grace to cry out for help. Evil had no need of a mask here: there were no pretenses, no lies or denials, no attempts to gloss over scandals. Only a fragile hope to restore the Rule. Yet Hildegard wondered what penance the Rule could impose on this abbey that could match the torture now consuming the abbot and degrading all those in his care.

As she walked, Hildegard's lips moved more in prayer and less in judgment. For some reason, she had been called here. Kneeling on the path, she pressed her brow against the earth.

"Lady Wisdom, in this place of monstrous pain, I place my faith in your miracles: the fertile soil, the cleansing rain, the gift of tears, the psalm that you brushed like a feather across my cheek at Compline: "God's mercy is from everlasting to everlasting...."

She was only an instrument. Tomorrow she would receive all that she needed. Tomorrow belonged to God.

By Prime the next morning, a blood-red sun emerged from the gray mist like a burning, weeping wound in the heavens. In the doorway of the abbey church, Hildegard turned and watched as the sun slowly released its crimson tears into the gray morning mist.

As Hildegard proceeded down the aisle, an ominous hum arose as though there were swarms of hornets on either side of her. But her stride was confident and her gaze unflinching. At the foot of the altar, she lifted the hem of her robe and knelt, then prostrated her body in an act of humility.

She lay there until the hum subsided and the church was silent. Then, after mounting the steps of the altar, she turned to face the abbot and monks of the Abbey of Zweifalten. When she turned, she saw that they had come forward as a body now and stood with folded arms at the foot of the altar.

Looking up from the stares that lashed her with contempt, she saw the red, bleeding sun now hovering above them.

"The famous abbess, eh? Still regal enough for one so old," the prior nudged the monk beside him.

"Take care," his brother warned, "she's one of the far-seeing, and her ears hear words before they're spoken."

"Come now, brother," the prior smirked. "How can she harm us?"

A moment later, the prior met the abbess' eyes. He felt as though his spine was melting.

"My sons, listen well," her voice rang out. "For the vision that summoned me here commanded me to forswear my own words so that I might allow the clear-shining brightness to speak through me. In your vows, you were once hailed as 'the mountain of the Lord,' God's mighty warriors. But now, each day and night, you spit these vows from your mouth!" she cried. "Your spirits have become storm-pregnant clouds that dissolve into sloth and shame, inflaming you with a lust that mires you in the filth of animals.

"Why have you forfeited your dignity and allowed yourself to be stripped of your manly strength?" she challenged them. "Only cowards whine that they can no longer deny the ache in their groins or the cravings of their human natures. If these are your words, then flee from this cloister before you pollute it further. You have squandered your right to preside at the altar.

"My sons, do you doubt that God watches as you race to wallow in some ass's stall to fornicate with the brides of Christ, turning your sisters into prostitutes, swelling their bellies with bastards whom they are forced to abandon or suffocate. Yet once relieved of your lust, you rush to don your priestly robes with soiled hands, smearing the Church with further ruin. Do not deceive yourselves! Without the grace of God, your priestly vows are a mockery!"

A hiss rose and swept like a wave across the assembly.

"Spare us your pious scoldings!" the prior called out. "And amuse us with one of your visions!"

"If you dare!" a voice mocked, a cleric wiggling his fingers in midair.

"Or can you remember them, old woman!" another shouted.

At their taunts, Hildegard began descending from the altar. Startled, the monks stumbled over each other as their ranks parted to admit her.

"Listen well!" she cried out as she stood in their midst. "For this prophecy is unfolding even now in each of your souls and bodies."

Some stepped back, though every eye dared her.

"In a vision that inflamed my soul, my eyes were graced with the image of a woman of such indescribable beauty and radiant tenderness that her presence dazzled my human mind.

"Her body bridged the earth and the sky, and her face streamed with the light of the sun and the moon, and her eyes pierced heaven. From afar, I saw that she wore a robe of ivory silk, and her mantle flashed with sapphires and emeralds while her shoes were fashioned of priceless onyx.

"Yet as I drew closer, I saw that her face was spattered with dust, and her robe had been ripped from her shoulders, and her mantle was smeared with filth, and her shoes were caked with mud.

"Now I heard her Voice cry out, 'Hear me, heaven, and mourn me, earth, I have been stripped of my glory! For though the foxes have holes and the birds of heaven their nests, I have no comforter or staff to uphold me. For my priest-protectors have abandoned me. Far from honoring my beauty and purity, they have left me desolate, spattering my face with their impurities. Steeped in the lust of their greed, they sink to unspeakable deeds of fornication and adultery, stifling the breath of those priests who plead before God for the strength to continue.'

"As I drew closer still, I saw that this woman stood here at your altar trembling uncontrollably, for her skin was ripped and torn. Her body was scarlet with rape at the places where she had been beaten and where her blood ran down her legs onto her feet. Parts of her had been stripped naked from her waist down to the private place where her woman's sex could be seen. Surrounding that place, her skin was black and purple with bruises, and her ravaged flesh was raw.

"Now to my horror, I saw that in place of her private parts, there protruded a monstrous black head with fiery eyes and the ears of an ass and the gnashing teeth of a lion. It was the head of the Antichrist!

"Then that monstrous head began to move from its place between her legs with such great force that the woman's limbs shook as though loosened from her body.

"Horrified, I watched as a great mass of excrement clung to the top of the Antichrist's head as it sought to raise itself up to the height of a mountaintop close to heaven.

"But then a thunderbolt struck the monster's head with such force that it exploded, releasing a stinking cloud that polluted the mountain it sought to ascend. And the cloud rained down such filth on the Antichrist's head that the people who saw it were terrified.

"Swirling, the cloud circled the mountain again and again as the people cried out, 'Alas, wretches that we are, we have been deceived! For Mother Church has been raped by her foster fathers by whom she conceived the Antichrist!'"

No one stirred.

When she spoke again, Hildegard's voice cracked like a whip across the gathering:

"Make no mistake! In this abbey, you strangle your Mother with your greed, and by your lust, you rape her. Repent, for my vision warns that the hours grow short before clouds will cover the sun and your day will become an endless night!"

Now thrusting her arms out angrily, she pushed back the monks on either side of her, even as their ranks fell back.

"We must leave here at once, my lady," Volmar gasped, as she crossed the threshold. "Your life could well be in danger, I fear!"

Hildegard did not protest. Within the hour, the travelers rode past the twin waterfalls. Volmar prayed ceaselessly for the tortured abbot while Hildegard prayed for the abbess and prioress of Zweifalten and their unborn babies.

For days after their return from the preaching tour, Hildegard steeped herself in the abbey's familiar sounds as though they were caresses.

"Lady mother always seeks solace in the earth after she returns from a preaching tour," Hiltrude whispered to the novices in the orchard as they saw Hildegard leaning against the trunk of an apple tree, her eyes closed, her head inclined. Their footsteps roused her. Seeing their puzzled looks, Hildegard explained that she was marveling at the rippling melodies she could hear in the waters of the abbey's aqueducts and in the rhythmic whip of the scythes in the fields.

"Wonders, all!" she told them. "But no more than the light in your eyes and the gift of your laughter." How young they look, Hildegard thought, and how eager.

Basking for a moment in the softness of their smiles, Hildegard felt their blend of awe and compassion for their wrinkled abbess as she neared her eightieth year.

"Do tell us a tale about your preaching tour, my Lady Mother," a freckle-faced novice enthused.

Hildegard paused.

For a moment, all she saw was Hazzecha's body through the open door, swinging in the sunlight, then the pregnant abbess and her unborn babe.

"As I mounted the pulpit in Trier," she rallied, "a small boy sitting astride his father's shoulders reached out to me for my blessing. And when I looked in his eyes, I saw glittering star-fields and soaring eagles and hills of silver sand. And his cheek was like satin and his kiss like a drop of morning dew. That moment hallowed every footstep I took on that journey, and the child's kiss will never leave my cheek."

The young women moved on. Hildegard thanked God that the novices had stumbled on her today. Yesterday she had sat here, recalling the moments on the journey when her heart had splintered into shards at each new scandal. There were so many thoughts she needed to talk over with Volmar. She was already counting the days.

A week later, she paused to say a prayer as she pressed her cheek against the gates of Eibingen. "How good God has been to us!" she exclaimed, seeing that the library and scriptorium were near completion and that the vegetable garden was almost ready for harvest.

Gottfried, her new secretary and current traveling companion, agreed, as he set down a box of books he had carried up from the boat. A kind man, his smile came easily and often, but today he seemed distraught and preoccupied.

Peering through the gates, Hildegard looked about for her provost, impatient to surprise him with her plans for his return to Rupertsberg.

Hildegard went first to meet with Gertrud and to examine the ledgers. She asked where Volmar was. "Father Gottfried is visiting with him," Gertrud reported, as she and Hildegard examined the ledgers. Shortly after they finished, she went to Volmar's house. As she knocked on the door, it swung open. In the half-light, she saw Gottfried kneeling by Volmar's bed. When he saw the abbess, Gottfried quickly rose.

"Forgive me, my lady," he said cryptically.

Drawing closer, Hildegard saw the mound of blood-soaked cloths on the floor beside the bed.

"In God's name, what is happening here?" she choked, chilled with fear.

"My lady, at first Prioress Gertrud was sure that Father Volmar was just exhausted from the preaching tour," Gottfried swallowed. "He kept to his bed for a week and then appeared to recover. But then..."

"How long has he been this way?" Hildegard demanded.

"He refuses to say. He has insisted that he was able to keep working. But I found it alarming today when he coughed up more blood than usual."

Crouching down, she saw the monk's gaunt face on the pillow. His eyelids drooped, and his lips were cracked, and his pulse was faint. Then she heard the ghastly rattling.

"My dearest friend, why did you keep this from me?"

There was only a gasp, then a groan as he tried to answer. Blood began trickling from the side of his mouth, and his tears spilled over.

The tears did not, however, obscure his gaze, which impaled her. Volmar searched her face with a tenderness he had never revealed in all the years she had known him. His eyes warmed her like the rays of the sun, holding her close, humbling her, giving all, asking nothing, filling her with an unbearable sweetness. Ever so slowly now, Volmar's hand reached up, free at long last to caress the apple cheek of the shy young nun, filled with uncertainty, finally able to brush back the spun-gold tendrils that had so often escaped from her wimple.

Now, with a trembling hand, he lifted the proud chin of the famous abbess, she who was known to defy popes and emperors and to exorcise demons from tortured bodies. At last, with a pitiful cry, he brought to his lips those fingertips that had held the stylus through which the words and music of other worlds had flowed onto vellum. He kissed her palm, feeling the warmth there that rushed too late to heal him. The moment he had dreamed of for almost forty years, the moment he could speak his heart to her, was finally his: a tender triumph, the harvest of aeons of desperate prayers and shattered dreams and stifled yearnings from the desert of his barren bed.

"You, . . . *you* are my Lady Wisdom," he whispered.

Then there was only the sagging back of his shoulders, even as the blood trickled through his lips.

Gathering him in her arms, Hildegard placed his head on her shoulder, allowing the warm blood to seep through her robe and the stain to spread dark and wide and deep until it reached her heart and kissed it.

Looking up, she saw Lady Jutta standing beside the bed.

"How truly and dearly you have kept the promise you made to me," the anchoress whispered to him. *"Now it is time to claim your glory! Come,"* she said, reaching out to him. *"She will never be far from you again."*

In that moment, Hildegard glimpsed the twin flames in Volmar's eyes flare one last time from the darkness. But it was not until dusk that her arms would surrender him, and then only because she realized that her shivering body could no longer keep him warm.

Stepping outside the guest house, Hiltrude's eyes ranged over the canopy of stars that had been flung above Eibingen. Father Volmar's soul is brightening the night sky tonight, she thought, still incredulous at the truth of her words. Thank God she had finally been able to calm the abbess; for a few hours, at least, her mistress could escape the shock of her loss and sorrow.

From the moment the breathless messenger had raced through the gates at Rupertsberg with the news, Hiltrude had refused it. It was only when she arrived here at Eibingen and saw the Disibodenberg monks guarding Father Volmar's body that her defenses crumpled.

At the memory, she felt dizzy again. Everything seemed unreal except for the sharp smell of resin from the newly hewn wood for Father Volmar's coffin. For the hundredth time, she grieved at the toll his weeks of secret agonies must have cost him.

Her thoughts turned to an earlier conversation with Father Gottfried. "Were you shocked, as well?" Hiltrude had asked him.

But he had only stared at her dully. "I must speak to your lady abbess at once," he had said abruptly, excusing himself and leaving her more confused than before.

The funeral procession reached the gates of Disibodenberg just before noon. The sky had been gray and overcast when they crossed the Rhine, but a fine mist had fallen within the hour, refreshing the air.

Abbot Helenger stood at the gate while the monks moved forward in waves toward the coffin, followed by flanks of servants and workmen.

Standing aside, Hildegard watched for several moments as the monks, one after another, knelt to touch the simple pine coffin containing the mortal remains of their beloved brother. Then she slowly made her way to the chapel.

"You and Lady Jutta are together now," she prayed to Volmar. "After all these years, my friend, you will see the visions before I do and hear Lady Wisdom's whispers first." Kneeling there, she longed to hold both Lady Jutta and Volmar close to her. She prayed to leave her body but was answered by a spasm of pain from her aching knees. "Hold me in your arms, my Lady Jutta. I am crouching again in terror in my corner in the hermitage. Sing me the songs that once stilled my sobbing. Reassure me once more, for I am an orphan again."

From the shadows of the chapel, Gottfried watched the abbess praying as he uttered his own plea for courage.

"Dare I approach her now?" he agonized. "Is this the time?"

"Who is there?" she called out clearly. Gottfried stumbled forward. "What is it that burdens your soul, my son?" she asked gently. "Your sadness has trailed my steps since we left Eibingen."

"My lady, I must confess to you that I knew of my brother Volmar's illness soon after his transfer to Rupert's Mountain, when he became stricken. But he bade me swear on Lady Jutta's soul to tell no one until his time came."

"Then he was already ill when he accompanied me on my journey? How could he have kept it from me?"

"He claimed that he pleaded with Lady Wisdom to spare him pain on the journey and promised to embrace his fate on your return."

Hildegard grasped Gottfried's arm to steady herself. "How soon after that was he confined to his bed?"

"Almost immediately. But it has been only in the last week that I heard the choking and stumbled across the blood-stained cloths that he hid in his trunk."

"He knew he was dying, then?"

"We spoke of it often toward the end."

"Yet he suffered in silence," she mourned. "Was he fearful?"

"Not of death. Only of a life he no longer had the strength to live."

"But his faith. Surely he knew God would..."

"Understand? Of that he was certain. It was his trust in the compassion of God that made him the brothers' most cherished confessor."

"Yet he chose not to seek their prayers in return?"

"He sought mine, my Lady Mother, unworthy as I am. He confessed to me that he had no more strength to go on. I learned that, for years, he had been offered bribes by those anxious to curry your favor and by others who wished to steal your prophecies for material gain. But most of all, he confessed his despair at the scandals that were revealed to him during your last preaching tour and the nights he went without sleep to hear confessions. By the end of the tour, he admitted, the pain in his body had become unbearable."

"He never told me," she moaned.

"I know, my lady. He wanted nothing to spoil the weeks he spent traveling with you. And when it was over, though his flesh was spent and his soul was threadbare, his heart was brimming over with love for you, my lady."

For an instant, Volmar's face appeared to her and then disappeared.

To Helenger, Abbot of Disibodenberg, from Hildegard, Abbess of Rupertsberg and Eibingen:

On the twenty-second day of May in the year of Our Lord 1172, an agreement was signed by our two abbeys and officially witnessed by Arnold, the late archbishop of Mainz. It stated that the Abbey of Disibodenberg would be required to provide provosts chosen by the Abbey of Rupertsberg.

As stated in that agreement, I request yet again that the monk Gottfried, my secretary, be officially transferred to the Abbey of Rupertsberg.

With renewed urgency I ask that you confirm his timely transfer to the Abbey of Rupertsberg.

The reply came two weeks later. Gottfried held his breath as he handed it to the abbess.

To Hildegard, Abbess of Rupertsberg, from Helenger, Abbot of Disibodenberg:

We have received your request for the transfer of Father Gottfried, our son and esteemed brother.

We will take the matter under consideration when time permits.

Hildegard flung the letter to the floor. "We will make short work of this arrogance!" she announced. "Take note, Father Gottfried."

To His Holiness, Pope Alexander, from Hildegard, Abbess of Rupertsberg:

I write to plead for your intercession on my behalf with Abbot Helenger of the Abbey of Disibodenberg, who has, for the past year, defied our official agreement to provide a provost for our abbey and a spiritual father and confessor for my daughters.

Though I greatly regret that my pleas go unheard, I tremble for Abbot Helenger, knowing he must one day stand before God and Blessed Benedict, as must we all, to answer for the care he has refused to provide to those entrusted to his care.

I entreat you, the fountain of all spiritual offices, to come to our aid.

Hildegard saw Gottfried swallow as he put down his stylus. "Now," she said firmly, "we must resume our work."

Does her mind ever rest? the monk wondered. Since Volmar's death, she had driven herself to complete those writings she had begun with him, especially the *Book of Divine Works*.

Sighing to himself, Gottfried watched her fingertip tracing Volmar's neat script and careful notations, as though by touching his words, she could bring him back.

Seeing him, Hildegard blushed and began shuffling the pages.

"Will an hour ever pass when I won't miss him?" she asked Gottfried. "It's as though I keep expecting a hand or a foot to be there, only to realize that it's gone."

Last night, she had longed to share news with him of Frederick's troops defecting in Italy, forcing the emperor to recruit mercenaries. But such news could never be shared with Volmar again.

Gottfried coughed loudly, jolting her from her thoughts.

"This letter should pique your interest, my lady," Gottfried said cheerfully. "It bears the seal of a Belgian abbey."

As Hildegard read it, she seemed amused. The writer identified himself as "Your humble and most devoted servant, Guibert of the Abbey of Gembloux." He claimed to "burn with questions regarding your visions that appear so clearly to flow from you like water poured from a pitcher."

Hildegard cast the letter aside. "He questions my claims to be unlearned since my knowledge of Scripture is so impressive and asks if my knowledge is infused and if I relay my visions in German or Latin. He asks whether, after I have dictated my visions and they have disappeared, my memory can recall them."

The torrent of questions made her head ache. She had neither the desire nor the energy to deal with them. How easily Volmar would have dispatched an appropriate response, she thought, sparing her further effort.

A week later, Gottfried was grinning when she entered the scriptorium.

"The white monks of Gembloux will not be denied," he said, holding up a sheaf of vellum.

"Still more questions, I trust, from the irrepressible Brother Guibert?" Hildegard inquired, as she removed her cloak.

"More of an appealing plea than an irksome request. How many letters do we receive whose words sing on the page?"

Hildegard looked away suddenly, as though she was listening. Her face softened. Without thinking, he reached for the wax tablet and stylus.

To Guibert, monk of the Abbey of Gembloux, from Hildegard, Abbess of Rupertsberg:

O faithful servant, the words I speak come from God, who works where he will, to the glory of his name, and not for that of mortals.

As a woman, I am never unaware of who I am and often tremble with fear since I am seldom confident of my own ability. But I hold out my hands to God, that I might be supported by him like a feather that has no weight or strength yet flies on the wind. For I cannot fully understand what I see while I remain in my human body.

Yet since I was a child until now, in my eightieth year, this Vision has never left me.

In its clasp, my soul climbs through the changing atmosphere to the top of the firmament and spreads itself out among different people in faraway places.

And since I see these things with the eyes of my soul, I see them through changing clouds and other creatures.

The Light that I see is not confined to one place. Though I cannot discern its height or length or breadth, I describe it as "the reflection of the Living Light." For just as the sun, the moon, and the stars are reflected in the waters, so do the Scriptures and sermons and virtues and certain human works shine on me brightly in this Light.

Whatever I see or learn in this Vision, I see and hear and understand simultaneously and hold them in my memory.

But what I do not see, I do not understand, because I am unlearned and was not taught to write in the way of philosophers. The words I write are not like those from the mouth of man, but like a trembling flame, or like a cloud stirred by the clear air.

I also have no way of knowing the form of this Light, in the same way that I cannot look directly at the sun. But within that Light, I often see another Light that I call the Living Light, but I never know how or when it will appear.

But truly, while I am looking at it, all sorrow and all perplexity are drained from me, so that I become an innocent girl again and not an old woman.

In this state, it is as though I am in a shining cloud, from which I can answer questions about the Living Light. It is also where I saw that my first book of visions should be called *Scivias*, Know the Ways of God.

But when I reside only in my body and my soul, I rely completely on the living God, who has no beginning and no end, knowing that by leaving all things to him, I will be kept safe from evil.

When Gottfried placed the letter in the messenger's hand, he was trembling, certain that he was entrusting a stranger to deliver a handful of stars.

Part Seven

1173–79

Angels attend us!
They speak to us in a reasonable way
just as God intended them to do.
They have necessary contact with human beings
and show themselves to us under certain forms
in accordance with God's will.

−Book of Divine Works
Vision Six, 2–5

No matter how often Hildegard stepped into the boat at the shore of the Rhine to cross to Eibingen, her delight in the brief crossing never dimmed.

Even before her horse turned onto the road leading to the ferry, her heart began beating with excitement. From the moment the oars splashed down, she was oblivious to everything around her: the boatman's hoarse shouts to the other ferrymen, the rattle of merchant's carts on the river banks, even the travelers' chatter and the fidgeting children sitting next to her.

Closing her eyes, she surrendered to the motion of the boat as it rocked in the water like a cradle. Those moments calmed her, like a prayer. It was a time to spiral within, to thank God for her blessings. Glancing at Gottfried sitting opposite her, she knew he was one of those blessings.

After Volmar's quiet competence, Gottfried's brisk efficiency had at first been a shock to Hiltrude and Hildegard, but they soon came to depend on it. The younger nuns were quick to note that, in spite of Hiltrude's stiff knees and swollen feet, and in spite of how often she asked them to repeat what they just said, she laughed more often in Gottfried's presence, and seemed much more relaxed, for which they were grateful.

Glancing at Gottfried now as they crossed the Rhine, Hildegard was grateful too.

She was never to step into the boat again without remembering that, within days of that crossing, Gottfried was felled by a raging fever. Though still weak, he chose to stay in his house by the chapel to convalesce. Hiltrude insisted on bringing his broth and bread to him each day and always stayed to chat with him. As the days passed, she found herself waiting impatiently for the midday meal so that she could see him. The visit was the high point of her day. After several weeks of nursing him back to health, she arrived one day to find him collapsed on the floor, his hand reaching out toward his prie-dieu. His body was still warm.

Seating herself on the floor, Hiltrude drew him close to her and clasped his body in her arms. As her tears flowed, she kissed his cheeks and forehead, knowing that only in death could she have done so.

Some time later, she looked up to see Hildegard standing in the door-way. The prioress was still rocking the dead man in her arms, his head cradled in the curve of her neck and shoulder.

Bending down, Hildegard blessed him. "How we will miss you, dear friend," she whispered to Gottfried.

Then gently, she loosened Hiltrude's arms from the monk's body, hushing her cries, silencing her explanations.

"There is nothing to grieve but the loss of our friend, dear Hiltrude," she reassured her.

The incident was not mentioned again.

Shortly before Vespers, Abbot Helenger appeared with four of the brothers from Disibodenberg.

"I've come to bring our Brother Gottfried home for his burial," he said solemnly. "He will sleep in the grave next to Volmar."

It was first time Hildegard had seen Helenger since the abbot had received Pope Alexander's letter instructing him to release Gottfried to Rupertsberg. As he walked toward her, she saw how deeply the abbot's head had sunk into his shoulders.

"News came last night that the imperial army was decimated at Leg-nano," he said, jolting her. "Emperor Frederick has agreed to make peace with Pope Alexander. The schism, it appears, has ended."

Hildegard stared, amazed that she was hearing this momentous news from the abbot of Disibodenberg. "How did it end?" she asked.

"During the imperial cavalry's defeat by the Milanese infantry, Fred-erick was wounded and thrown from his horse. Certain that their leader was dead, the remaining troops vanished, and the emperor was forced into hiding." Helenger's voice cracked. "The shame of it!"

Hildegard's head was suddenly throbbing, and her vision was blurring. She managed to reach the chapel and fall on her knees.

Before her eyes, armies of wounded soldiers staggered past her.

Dazed, she asked aloud, "How does one celebrate the ending of a bloodbath? With gratitude that newborn babes would be spared the fate of their skull-crushed brothers? With relief for widows whose husbands' heads were impaled on the end of a pike? With stoicism for those women who prepared the burial sheets for bodies whose ribs were crushed and whose limbs were scattered?"

Now the emperor's haggard face rose before her. Behind it, she saw the fire in the blue eyes of the young king who had prayed at her side in his private chapel. How full he had been of youth's breathless certainty!

And now as then, she saw the sudden shimmering behind him: the towering figure, the crowned head of Charlemagne. His hand now rested on Frederick's shoulder. Only he could console his passionate successor now, grieving with him as the shattered dream sifted like sand through both their fingers.

The schism was ended, but who could heal the hemorrhaging heart of the imperial dream?

The newly arrived monk exuded a boyish excitement that belied the fact that he was middle-aged. As he strolled through the orchard toward Hildegard, his eyes danced.

"My Lady Abbess, I must confess that your letter describing your visions was hardly what I expected," he said. "It was much more than I had hoped for!" A sunny smile crinkled his round face.

So this was the persistent monk Guibert from the Belgian Abbey of Gembloux, the one who wrote that "I cannot visit you for I am a cloistered monk."

"Who opened the gates for you to slip through?" she queried.

His laughter delighted her. "I must admit I held father abbot hostage with a promise to inquire about our abbey's future." The glint in his eye was triumphant.

"Ah, so that's why you've come," she said playfully. "To pursue prophecies, not answers."

"Both, my Lady Abbess," he assured her promptly.

"And the questions?"

"They are those that whet the appetites of my brothers at Villers," he grimaced. "They wish to know your thoughts on Moses and the burning bush and the nature of Pentecostal fire."

"Are those your questions, as well?"

"Hardly, my lady." His eyes took on a deeper glow. "My prayer is to find the best way to share your visions with others. After your letter, I could not sleep for days as I reflected on Lady Wisdom's messages in your visions." He suddenly grew embarrassed. "Do you find God to be a series of unending surprises?"

"Surprise is another name for revelation, my son."

His glance was uncertain. Then he reached in his scrip.

"I speak of surprises like this," he announced. "I stumbled over it while I was riding and it dazzled me."

Opening his hand he revealed a small stone covered with emerald moss.

Hildegard was sure her heart had stopped beating. Why has God sent this monk to me? she wondered.

Guibert's visit lengthened, the monk seizing every chance he could to be in the abbess' presence. Sometimes it was only a few moments as they walked together to chapel. But as the days passed, it was clear that the abbess was captivated by Guibert's blend of sincerity and intelligence, and she spent time after the midday meal to converse with him. His challenges intrigued her.

"My lady, if Lady Wisdom is who you say she is, why has she not spoken to us before?" Guibert asked.

"It was not time," Hildegard replied. "She is like the woman in Holy Writ who lit her lamp and searched in the corners of her house for her lost coin."

"And finding it," he recounted, "her neighbors rejoiced with her that she had found what was lost."

Hildegard nodded. "Lady Wisdom's Voice is like that coin: though lost, it was not forgotten. There were always those few who remembered...."

"And restored her to her rightful place at the Creator's side where she stood in the beginning," Guibert beamed. "Rejoicing in the knowledge that Synagoga came forth from her womb, and then Ecclesia."

"They return to remind us to cherish our own souls as ever-fertile wombs from which to birth our creativity," the abbess agreed, "be it building a castle of stone or siring a child or birthing it... or being a midwife for the visions that flow through me."

"I am awed to think that Lady Wisdom speaks to you, my lady," Guibert insisted. "You hear her Voice."

"As have others before me and as will countless others in future times. For her witness will always be everywhere. Reflect for a moment, my son: if Lady Wisdom was described as God's companion in the Hebrew Bible, and as the Shekinah, the feminine presence of God who guided Israel

on its miraculous journey, how could such a presence simply disappear?
Could she not take form in the New Testament, as well?"

Guibert threw up his hands. "My mind whirls with these new
understandings, my lady!"

"Yet I predict that, in time, people will listen for Lady Wisdom's Voice
in all their endeavors. For she is both gentle and challenging, shocking
and compassionate."

"Lady Wisdom has placed great trust in you."

"She has placed great trust in each of us. Yet for reasons unknown, she
has chosen to reveal to me, an untutored woman, those commands that
appear in my visions and that, I confess, exhaust me."

"Prophets always arise when the need is great, my lady."

But Hildegard turned away from his praise.

The news sped on the wind, and for months tales of the reconciliation
between Pope Alexander and Emperor Frederick, cross and crown, were
recounted again and again as guests displayed their tapestry of memories
at Hildegard's table. After nearly two decades, the fighting was over.

The pageantry began on Sunday when Frederick disembarked from the
Doge's galley at the Lido in Saint Mark's Square. He was met there by
several of Alexander's cardinals, who witnessed Frederick's oath to accept
Alexander as the true and rightful pope. Then Frederick was escorted
to the steps of the papal throne where, in a gesture of magnanimity, he
threw off his purple mantle and knelt to kiss Pope Alexander's feet.

Overcome with tears, Alexander raised Frederick up and bestowed the
kiss of peace as a roar swept through the crowds and every bell in Venice
began ringing.

During Mass in the cathedral, Frederick recited the Credo, the confession of faith, then prostrated himself before the pope once more, to
emphasize his loyalty.

And lest a shred of doubt remain, the emperor offered the ultimate
gesture of submission by holding the pope's stirrup when Alexander mounted, even offering to lead his horse. But in an exchange of
courtesies, Alexander refused.

By these gestures alone, the people were convinced that the schism
had ended.

As Hildegard listened to accounts at her table, she marveled at how easily the wrenching divisions between cross and crown had been glazed over and their cracks concealed.

Not so with Ecclesia's heart, she knew. For all time, it would bleed for her sons whose bones lay bleached now in sun-baked fields in Italy, their flesh long torn from their bodies as carrion, this final time, by winged predators.

Hildegard found herself waiting eagerly for her daily conversation with Guibert.

It was as though they sat before a loom of knotted threads containing thoughts and ideas, all of which they delighted in untangling. Their exchanges filled her with a rare exhilaration. How could this virtual stranger open her heart with a moss-covered stone for a key?

Seeing her joy, the nuns began nudging each other when they passed her. She had begun to sing aloud again as she strolled through the cloister, smiling at them with her eyes as she sang.

"Does that light in her smile reveal something of the proud mother delighting in her gifted son's devotion?" Hiltrude wondered. Seeing them chatting together happily, Hiltrude felt an old, dull jealousy arise within her.

Hiltrude could not, however, deny that a second springtime was flowering in the abbey. Yet in the midst of the blossoming, she found her steps felt heavier, and at night her sleep was so sound she had to rely on the novices to rouse her for Matins. In the midst of her rounds, she began to long for quiet hours in the chapel, a thought she quickly dismissed as a temptation to laziness. As prioress, she knew her work was her prayer.

To Father Bovo at Gembloux, from Father Guibert:

Greetings, dear brother.

To my great joy, I remain here at Rupertsberg in the company of the holy abbess, Lady Hildegard, each day a glowing page in the book of my life.

How can I describe how inspired I am by the nuns' efforts as they strive for virtue? I deem it impossible to say whether mother or daughter exceeds in devotion.

Harmony abides everywhere, and all serve the Rule so admirably, one can see how, with Christ's help, these women have conquered much.

On feast days, the nuns sit quietly in the cloister and practice reading and singing while they spend their workdays copying books or weaving clothing or embroidering linens for the altar.

As you might expect with such an abbess to lead it, the abbey is as rich in religious zeal as it is prosperous in income. All the rooms are large and beautiful and truly monastic in their simplicity. All the workshops have running water and are well equipped. The abbey supports fifty nuns, a steady stream of guests, and a number of servants.

What one feels most is the kindness and wisdom of the lady abbess, Hildegard. Were you here, you would see that the words that she writes and the notes her voice sings all flow out from her kind deeds and wise counsel. Since she is ever occupied, I cherish those moments I have with her.

As you might expect, her mind is keen, and while she insists on describing herself as "a poor little woman who is unschooled," you must believe me when I tell you that she is most conversant with Horace and Ovid and the Church Fathers, and I'm sure, through her visions, she converses with the Hebrew prophets.

Acting as her occasional scribe, I thank God each hour of the day for the privilege of serving her.

Snapping their reins, the clerics glared at the porter as he opened the abbey gates.

A short, flat-nosed rider flung out his black velvet cape as he dismounted. "Inform your provost that Lord Egbert, the choir-bishop of Mainz, has arrived," he barked at the gatekeeper, "and wishes to see him at once." The presiding bishop during Archbishop Christian's absence in Rome had arrived.

As Guibert approached, Egbert's eyes flicked over him.

"I have urgent business with Lady Abbess Hildegard," he informed Guibert sullenly.

Hildegard greeted him pleasantly in the reception hall, but the bishop's first words were abrupt.

"I regret that your burial of the body of the knight, Siegfried of Mainz, has summoned me here."

"Regret?" Hildegard puzzled. "But why? Lord Siegfried's family was one of the first to purchase burial rights at our founding."

Egbert's eyes glittered. "Yet you buried him knowing that, while he was alive, this knight was excommunicated on grave charges of fornication."

"Of course. And that the charge was lifted on his deathbed."

"We are not convinced of that, my lady," Egbert hissed. "We demand further proof."

"Proof beyond that contained in his burial papers?" Hildegard asked calmly. "Proof that clearly states that Lord Siegfried confessed his sins in a true spirit of repentance and received Holy Communion before being anointed with the last rites of the church?" Hildegard lifted her chin. "Were it otherwise, Your Grace, I would hardly have accepted his body for burial in our consecrated ground."

"A decision you may come to regret, my Lady Abbess," the bishop retorted.

Hildegard whirled around. "You underestimate me, Your Grace," Hildegard snapped. "The regret will be yours."

Snatching a parchment scroll from his scrip, Egbert thrust it at the abbess.

"As choir-bishop of Mainz, I declare that because Lord Siegfried's burial in your abbey gives scandal to the Church," he shouted, "I am forced to place the Abbey of Rupertsberg under interdict!"

The interdict fell like a hammer on Hildegard's soul.

Where had it come from? What did it mean?

Numb, she lapsed into silence, deaf to Guibert's outrage and Prioress Hiltrude's pleas. As her thoughts splashed against the walls of her mind, she felt adrift in watery depths she was unable to fathom. At times, she was sure she was drowning.

She made the announcement at Vespers. Though her voice was strong, her skin was ashen.

"My daughters, cherish the echoes of the chants we have just sung for they might well be our last. Hereafter, we must sing our praises to God in whispers."

Her hands were twitching as she unrolled the parchment,

Be it known to all, the Abbey of Rupertsberg has been placed under interdict. Hereafter, the abbey must cease to ring its bells or sing the Divine Office and will be denied Holy Communion.

This ban will be enforced until the lady abbess Hildegard exhumes the body of the knight, Siegfried, whose immoral deeds have caused grave scandal to the Church in the Diocese of Mainz.

At that moment, a cry spiraled through the chapel, plaintive and sorrowing, shivering the nuns. Heads spun and necks craned. Where did it come from?

For a moment, Hildegard saw Lady Jutta's face in the Living Light.

When news of the interdict reached the daughter-house at Eibingen, Ilse and the twins hurried back to Rupertsberg to comfort the abbess. The nuns were in shock. While they sat with her, she kept grasping their hands and touching their faces. Even during the worst of her illnesses, they had never seen her in such utter despair.

"What does Bishop Egbert have to gain by humiliating her with this injustice?" Gertrud asked Hiltrude later in the sewing room.

"It's his one chance to flaunt his power during Archbishop Christian's absence," Ilse suggested. "Silencing the famous abbess of Rupertsberg is an outrageous act, certain to attract attention."

"Perhaps," Gertrud mused, "but what does she have that he seeks?"

"Her spiritual power, of course," Hiltrude shrugged, "though I suspect he covets it more as a weapon to wield than as a gift to be used for the good of others."

"Are you saying that this bishop can only feel powerful if he takes lady mother's power away?" Gisla asked.

"It is one way, Father Guibert maintains," Hiltrude whispered.

"How sad!" Ilse moaned. "If men can only be strong if women are weak, then how strong are they? Can't they see how that fear keeps them hostage?"

"As we learned at Disibodenberg," Gertrud sighed. "But enough of that. How can help we help lady mother, Hiltrude?"

"By doing what we always do: storming heaven!"

"Why did I agree to this?" Guibert scolded himself as he dug his heel in the dirt at the abbess' door. The chiding passed quickly. In reality, he was so full of gratitude that the abbess had finally rallied after days of silence, he would have granted any request she made of him.

When Hildegard opened the door, she was wearing her cloak and hood, and she held her abbess' staff in her hand. Pointing it at the sky, she whispered, "See how blessed we are, my son? The moon will act as our celestial lantern!" Then scurrying past Guibert, she hurried down the path to the abbey burial grounds. Only the sound of barking dogs halted her. After scanning the landscape for a moment, she slipped though the graveyard gates. The rows of gravestones were tilted like weary sentinels in the moonlight. Guibert shivered as he passed them, not so much from the night chill as from the secrecy with which the abbess had clouded this request.

Scratching sounds in the grass alerted her. "Only rats," she reassured Guibert over her shoulder, urging him on. She stopped at a large beech tree, then turned to her left and walked forward six steps, before turning to the right and walking eight steps more.

By now, Guibert's throat was so tight he could hardly swallow. "My lady, you must tell me..."

"Soon enough," she mumbled, wrapping her skirts around her as she dropped to her knees.

By Christ's wounds, what is she doing? Guibert screamed inside.

"There is not much time, my son," she warned him. "You must kneel down and help me."

The monk obeyed, but when he felt the cold clumps of dirt beneath his knees, he protested. "My lady, I insist that you tell me."

But the abbess was already leaning forward, her arms outstretched as her open palms fanned across the moist topsoil.

"We must hurry." Her voice was brisk. "All signs of this burial site must be removed."

At last he understood. They were here to disguise the grave of the knight, Siegfried. These were the lengths to which she was willing to go to defy the interdict!

They worked until, at last, Hildegard sat back on her knees to survey their efforts.

"And now, my son," she said calmly, "you must finish our task by rolling over the ground. Your body will flatten the soil and seal the outline of the grave completely."

The monk's jaw dropped. "You cannot be serious, my lady."

"Do as I say, and do it at once!" she said sharply. "Only the voice of a priest can reassure the poor man lying here that his sleep is secure. Assure him, as well, that the Voice in my vision has vouchsafed for his innocence and has instructed me to ensure that his mortal remains are not disturbed."

Guibert was stunned.

Gritting his teeth, he rolled his body back and forth, then from side to side, as the abbess directed him. By the time she was satisfied, stones had ripped his robe and twigs had scratched his face and hands. He was furious.

"You may stop now," she announced.

As Hildegard reached down to help him rise, the monk pushed her hand aside. With a growl of disgust, he spit out the dirt that was gritting his teeth and shook off the mud and rotting leaves from his robe. His whole body was shaking.

"I understand your anger, my son, but there was no other way," Hildegard explained. "If they cannot find the grave, they cannot disturb him. I am merely obeying what I have been told I must do."

Guibert spit out more dirt but said nothing.

"Only one thing remains to be done now," she continued. Reaching for her staff, Hildegard walked to the head of the grave and, breathing deeply, raised her staff and lifted her face to the moon.

"I, Hildegard, abbess of Rupertsberg and Eibingen, do solemnly bless this hidden grave, in obedience to the command given to me by the Living Light."

Raising her staff, she made the sign of the cross above the grave: *In Nomine patris, et filii et spiritu Sancti.* Then, plunging her staff in the ground, she knelt on the grave and placed her cheek against the earth.

"Sleep in peace, my son," she whispered. "I will protect you lest any mortal seek to disturb your eternal rest."

In the moonlight, her eyes glowed like sapphires in her wrinkled face. Humbled by her tenderness, Guibert fell to his knees and placed his hand on his heart. This time, the abbess was risking everything in her passion for justice. As Guibert knelt there, his soul throbbed in the knowledge that by this act alone, he had bound himself to the abbess in a knot that could never be untied.

The interdict dragged on.

Though the bells were silent, the restlessness in the chapel was palpable, since every nun knew intuitively when the hours had come to chant the Divine Office. Glances were exchanged, and bodies shifted. After decades of raising their voices in praise, the silence seemed intolerable.

Trust!

The single word had become a full prayer, a final plea on each bead of their rosaries, a wordless signal when their eyes met.

Trust!

The days became endless corridors, lengthening into weeks, then months. All swore that they still heard the bells within, though now they tolled a lament to an abbey of fugitives adrift in a world of whispers.

Yet despite the silence, the chapel was crowded as never before as each nun bore silent witness to her faith in her abbess. Day and night, footsteps paused and knees bent to utter a hurried prayer before the altar. Often nuns prayed through the night in the darkened chapel, their sighs flung like silken scarves down the rows of stalls.

Trust!

To the Prelates of Mainz in Rome, from Hildegard, Abbess of Rupertsberg:

In light of the vision that was inscribed in my soul before my birth, I feel compelled to write to you concerning the interdict inflicted upon us by our superiors, a matter about which you have been fully informed.

Despite the injustice, we have honored our vow of obedience and have fully complied with the interdict's mandates. We have ceased singing the songs of divine praise, recite them now in the barest of whispers, and have denied ourselves Holy Communion. Yet you must be aware of the deep wound of sadness and bitterness that this interdict has inflicted on us and that chokes our spirits day and night.

Indeed, in a recent vision, I was chastised for accepting a decision that I knew to be unjust, since the burial in question was witnessed by all of Bingen's inhabitants, none of whom uttered a protest.

In this vision, I was also shown in awesome ways that by obeying you, I was guilty of silencing the voice of David, the Psalmist, who proclaimed that it is our destiny to praise God: "Praise God in the call of the trumpet, the lute, and the Psaltery. Praise God with the timbrel and with dance and with stringed instruments and organs. Let all that breathes praise God!"

Our praises serve to echo those praises we once shared with the angels in Paradise, and we know that the angelic Voice still lies dormant within us.

Listen well! As prelates, entrusted with the keys of the kingdom, you must know that in silencing those who praise God, you are opening what should remain closed and closing that which God wishes to be open.

"Believe me, I pleaded with lady mother not to proceed with this plan," Hiltrude had assured Guibert angrily, "but she would not be deterred."

"My sister, you must understand that this is the act of a desperate woman," Guibert had replied. "She is convinced that the interdict will never be lifted unless she speaks on her own behalf."

Hildegard had overheard that exchange, and their words echoed in her ears now as she and Guibert approached the episcopal palace in Mainz.

The canons were lining the steps of the palace to greet her. She heard their thoughts as Guibert helped her down from her mount.

"The Sibyl of the Rhine is far more than seventy years. She is a harmless old woman!"

"Look how she leans on her provost now, unable to walk on her own."

"Her fame is no more than a puff of smoke and will soon disappear. We will tolerate her."

Yet as she mounted the steps, every eye was lowered.

Inside, Hildegard surveyed the opulent reception hall, its tapestried walls and velvet-draped benches befitting a royal residence. Though it was midday, flames quivered atop the slender tapers. Silver cups gleamed on a huge table draped and tasseled in ivory silk. So these were the luxuries that had paved Archbishop Henry's path to his infamy, Hildegard thought. Could she have imagined during those frantic nights when she conjured up thoughts of him sleeping here that one day she would sit in a room below his bed to plead for her abbey with his peers?

When Egbert entered the room with two of his canons, his glance pressed down like heavy hands on her shoulders.

Both canons shuffled nervously as Egbert greeted her. Hildegard proceeded at once to restate her position and repeat her proof of Siegfried's innocence as she had done previously. The Abbey of Rupertsberg, she insisted, labored under no disgrace.

Egbert replied with a sneer. At that moment, Hildegard realized that the interdict had little to do with her. She was merely the instrument Egbert used to place his name on everyone's lips. It was unthinkable, he announced, to lift the ban at this time.

Heartsick, Hildegard signaled to Guibert to take their leave, but Egbert held up his hand.

"If you please, my Lady Abbess," he smiled unctuously. "We could be remiss if we allowed the famous abbess of Rupertsberg to leave our company without sharing one of her prophecies," he purred, casting a sideward glance at the canons.

"Regarding the outcome of this matter, Your Grace?" Hildegard asked, as her blood turned to ice.

"No, no, my lady," he replied, glibly. "Such a trifling matter would hardly do justice to your gifts. We would far prefer something more provocative, like a glimpse into our empire's future."

"I fear you would regret it."

"With all due respect, you err, my lady. Come now," he baited her, "do indulge us."

Glancing at Guibert, she saw that the veins in his neck were bulging. "My secretary will serve as my witness, then," the abbess began. The canons' eyes lit up while Egbert's tongue flicked at his lips.

Hildegard sat in silence, watching her hosts grow uncertain as the minutes passed.

"Can you hear them?" she whispered now, inclining her head. "The Voices?"

The canons leaned forward, their eyes darting over the room.

"Can you hear them calling you, the princes of this land? Can you hear them crying out your names? Ah…," she paused and cocked her ear, "their voices drop to a hush now as they whisper to one another: 'How long must we suffer these churchmen, these voracious wolves who pretend to be physicians, these priests who carouse with abandon and commit adultery while their every act shames the Church?

"'Yet while these churchmen ignore their sins, they condemn us without mercy. Like greedy thieves in their own household, they rape church property and devour all that lies in their path. While they betray their high office of trust, they subject the princes of the land to humiliation, leaving us destitute.

"'We will fall on them and cry out: "We can no longer tolerate such people to rule over us, wielding their estates and their holdings as weapons. Churchmen should have no more than their proper share and the laity should have its just apportionment. In no way has God ordered that a cloak and a mantle should be given to one son while another goes naked."'"

Egbert's face was crimson. "You speak of your benefactors, of course, my lady," he interrupted, "those princes of this land whom you stole from Disibodenberg and who now fill the coffers of your abbey and daughter-house."

Guibert leaned forward to object, but the abbess stopped him.

"Protest now, if you will, my Lord Egbert, but nothing can stop the prophecy that I see advancing toward you. For the perilous time draws near when the property and possessions of the Church will be seized and destroyed, just as vultures slaughter that which they trap in their talons and pinions.

"Heed these words: In days ahead, the emperor's grandeur will decline as will the power by which he and his appendages once held the empire. And once stripped of their glory, the empire will crumble into dust. Failure and scorn will assault them on every side, and these imperial leaders will be doomed to shame. Their dreams of expansion will be dashed, as tribes and nations look to new rulers to obey.

"And once shattered, the imperial rule will never rise again, and the bishop's office will be splintered forever.

"Then the princes and the leaders of the land will find little religious in the apostolic name and will form a low opinion of that office, turning instead to teachers and bishops with other names and from different places.

"The bishop's office will be ruptured forever, and the authority of the papacy will be diminished."

Outraged, Egbert sprang to his feet. "No more! No more! You have gone too far!" he cried, streaking from the room in terror, leaving his horrified canons with the task of escorting the fiery prophet to the door.

Blood that bled into a cry!
The elements
felt its touch and trembled;
heaven heard their woe.
O life-blood of the Maker,
scarlet music, salve our wounds.

Guibert shuddered at the cry that rose from the abbess' newest composition. How perfectly it mirrored the spiritual anguish the abbess had endured since the ban was imposed. Guibert added it to the abbess' song cycle that now contained more than seventy of her compositions. To Guibert, each one was like a leap to heaven.

In the last three months, the tides of tension from the ban had mounted, threatening at times to engulf the abbey. Following Hildegard's lead, the nuns took refuge in their work, redoubling their efforts to care for the pilgrims who crowded the hospice.

But the toll was great. The nuns' complaints of stomachaches and painful joints and stabbing headaches had doubled, and over half the nuns had ceased their menses in the past two months.

As Guibert sat down in the workroom to sift through the letters of support, the first one he read sent him racing to the abbess. The letter, from Archbishop Philip of Cologne, read:

Quite by chance, I came upon a knight who had been the companion of Siegfried of Mainz and swore that on the same occasion and by the same priest, both he and Siegfried had confessed their sins and received absolution. At my request, both the knight and the priest agreed to serve as witnesses and to swear under oath to the prelates in Mainz, augmenting the proof you have already provided.

In light of the witnesses' testimony, and knowing that Archbishop Christian would be detained in Rome indefinitely during mediations between the emperor and pope Alexander, I exercised my authority and removed the interdict myself. The matter is settled, my Lady Abbess. You need trouble yourself no more…

Hildegard sighed. "A thread on which to hang my hope," she said.

At the news, Guibert felt giddy with relief. Now they could return to normal.

"Still, the ban must be enforced until we have the documents in hand," the abbess insisted as she slumped in her chair.

As the days passed, Hildegard was drawn more and more to work in the poor women's house. She adored the children. Their sense of wonder and innocence nurtured her deeply while the utter trust in their eyes humbled her. "I have so much to learn from them," she confided to Hiltrude.

She was sitting outside in the sun with an infant in her lap when the letter arrived from Mainz. She hugged a child napping in her lap as she saw Guibert hurrying toward her.

"The letter is, as we hoped, from Archbishop Christian in Rome," Guibert reported.

"Go on!" she demanded breathlessly.

"He informs us," he paused, "of his distress upon learning that Archbishop Philip had attempted to usurp his jurisdiction. 'Your abbey,' he writes, 'must continue to comply with the terms of the interdict until I, Christian, the lawful archbishop of Mainz, inform you otherwise.'"

To Christian, Archbishop of Mainz, from Hildegard, Abbess of Rupertsberg:

We thank you for acknowledging our letter. In the name of justice, we kneel now and petition you to hear us! We have endured unspeakable pain and desolation by the ongoing scandal of the interdict, and you will understand our great distress upon receiving your letter informing us that we must continue to comply with the interdict's demands. We are plunged into even deeper pain and sorrow than before.

Since you have never displayed any doubt about my visions, I beseech you by the love of the Holy Spirit, do not despise the tears of your weeping daughters, for you too will one day long for mercy after the course of your earthly life is run.

Holy Thursday, in the year of Our Lord, 1179.

Prioress Hiltrude stepped outside the abbey chapel for a moment and breathed in the freshness of the dew-lavished earth. The soil was moist and yielding beneath her feet, and the trees in the orchard were tinged with scarlet-tipped buds. The earth was bursting with new life: a heady but dangerous time, she knew. Forcing her eyes away from the beauty, she reminded herself of the long day ahead.

"This has been the longest, harshest Lent in memory," she said to a wide-eyed novice who was polishing a chalice in the sacristy. "It feels like Lent began the day after Christmas."

As she spoke, her glance fell on her favorite gold censer, fashioned like a dove in flight. Its incense had scented Easter altars as far back as she could remember. But not this year. There was, however, one Easter ritual that the abbess would not relinquish: the washing of the apostles' feet, which symbolized Christ's love for the poor. The abbess had always performed the task and dismissed Hiltrude's objections that her eighty-one years were a deterrent.

"I will wash my daughters' feet, as always," Hildegard insisted. Then she added softly, "This year, above all, I *must*, my daughter."

As Hiltrude was about to leave the sacristy, she glimpsed a set of vestments lavished with silver embroidery that the margravine had donated on the day Richardis took the veil. How long ago that day seemed now! Suddenly, the decades of Lents and Easters and Holy Weeks blurred past her like a rushing stream, gone forever. Glancing at the shy novice, a sadness filled her. "Was I ever young?" Hiltrude wondered.

Good Friday.

Each year, the nuns felt the shock anew when they entered to find the chapel stripped bare. It was as though a blight had descended overnight, stripping it of every statue, denuding the altars of snowy linens and the fragrance of blossoming branches. And always, they gasped to see the door of the tabernacle, the holy of holies, open, revealing the emptiness inside.

The huge wooden crucifix had been placed across the steps leading up to the altar. It would lay there hour after hour as the nuns of Rupertsberg joined the multitudes over the centuries who had kept watch with Mother Mary and the Magdalene and those women who refused to flee when the bleeding began. For blood holds no terror for women, only power, only promises.

At Lauds, they found the abbess kneeling there, her eyes closed, her cheek against the nail-gouged feet of the crucifix, her breath as peaceful as that of a trusting child. She had been there since Matins, meditating on Christ's crucifixion, hearing her daughters' felt-slippered feet pause beside her. Seeing her, many wept, knowing how these past months had been the abbess' Gethsemane.

But during the last hour, the clouds in her heart began to clear as the Living Light grew brighter. Finally, the Voice she longed to hear: the whisper of Lady Wisdom, acknowledging the anguish of her soul's journey.

"Be comforted, for I see the shadows that cover you on the rack of self-doubt. I hear your plea for your long lost Mother.

"'O Mother Zion,' you cry, 'when I recall that it was you in whom I was meant to dwell, I feel the bitter slavery to which I am subjected. And when I remember the wondrous strains of music that dwell in you, I feel my woundedness. And when I recall the joy and brilliance of your glory, I am appalled by the scandals that have polluted your sound.

" 'Yet when I pour out my tears to you, O Mother, they are lost in the waters of wicked Babylon that roar at me and drown out my voice. So with great care, I seek the narrow path and a small cave in which I can hide and weep for the loss of my Mother.

" 'Then my soul becomes aware of a most sweet fragrance, and I recognize my gentle Mother's breath. What tears I pour forth then in the presence of that small consolation that flows from you. And I cry, "O Mother, O Mother Zion, how long will I be deprived of your maternal sweetness, out of which you formed me?"

" 'But hearing my cries, my enemies say, "Where is she, whom we imprisoned to do our bidding and fulfill our will? When she calls upon heavenly dwellers, we must be zealous lest she slip from our grasp."

" 'But I do escape, and scale a great height though my captors thwart me, lining my path at every step with thorns and thistles. But remembering the strength of your sweetness, O Mother, I am filled with power. Yet when I descend from that height, again I am attacked by serpents and scorpions that hiss at me. Shrieking, I cry out again, "O Mother where are you? Where is your help?"

" 'It is then that I hear my Mother's Voice answer my soul: "O daughter, flee! For the Most Powerful Giver whom no one can resist has given you wings with which to fly over all these obstacles!" And I, comforted, take wing and pass quickly over all these deadly and poisonous things.

" 'And I come to a tabernacle whose interior is of the strongest steel. And going in, I perform works of brightness, turning away from works of darkness for my sight has been restored and I am no longer blind.' "

Around her, Hildegard heard the footsteps circle and pause, as the whispers rustled above her. "Look there, lady mother's heart must be broken!"

But they could not hear the wheel of her plea, turning silently, her universe composed of four words: "Thy will be done!" Ceaselessly the wheel turned over and over again on the plea: "Thy will be done! If it be thy will, lift this stone of injustice from my soul, for it crushes me. Yet, not my will but thine."

She lay there until midafternoon, her lips parched, her throat constricted. Then placing her hand on her heart, she whispered, "Father, forgive them, for they know not what they do."

Aware that her strength was spent, the abbess now breathed forth her *Fiat:* "Into your hands, O long lost Mother, I commend the soul of this abbey."

Two weeks passed. "A letter from Rome from Archbishop Christian," Guibert announced, unrolling the scroll and bracing himself for yet another disappointment.

Greetings to Hildegard, the Abbess of Rupertsberg and Eibingen in the Diocese of Mainz:

I have written to the clergy of Mainz giving them permission to remove the ban if it has been proven to their complete satisfaction that the deceased man had, in fact, been received back into the Church. This must be established so no further scandal will be caused by this action.

My Lady Abbess, I wish again to express my utmost faith in your holiness. I regret any distress this matter might have caused you, especially if, in my absence, I have unwittingly contributed to that distress in any way.

Guibert's hand was shaking.

"And it bears Christian's signature?"

"Indeed," he said, "and he adds the words 'Good Friday' in his own hand.

To my Brothers of the Abbey of Villers, from Guibert:

I hasten to share the news that, by God's grace alone, the ban has now been lifted, and the voices of the nuns rise again to sing the Divine Office. As well, I thank God that I am able to say Mass again and distribute Holy Communion.

But the cost of the interdict has been enormous. The spiritual siege it imposed here has greatly affected the abbess. Buffeted at every turn by her superiors, she kept the faith and never failed to assure her daughters that the Spirit would not abandon them.

There are no words to describe how humbled I have been to witness all that the abbess has been forced to endure.

As you know, the Apostle does not permit a woman to teach in the Church. But, in truth, this woman is exempt from this condition. Anointed as she is by the Spirit, she fully obeys her visions' command to make public those things she receives in secrecy. Moreover, her heart is instructed by Lady Wisdom, and she has learned to value her experience.

Again, though the Apostle commands women to veil their heads, both for decency's sake and to show submission, this woman is free from the law. For she has transcended female subjection by a lofty height and is equal to the eminence, not just of any man, but of the very highest.

Yet being mortal, her body grows weaker. Of late, it often pains her to stand upright, and she must often be carried about. Yet, though broken, the instrument still gives out melody.

My brothers, pray for me that I may prove worthy, before God, to serve her.

The celebration for Saint Benedict's feast day was scheduled for July 11. The nuns from Eibingen had arrived the previous day amid great jubilation. Hiltrude was out of breath as she dashed to greet them. "Welcome, welcome home at last!"

Through the open door, Hildegard could hear the happy confusion as the footsteps hurried down the path to her room. Gertrud entered first and crouched at the abbess' knee while Gisla put her head in Hildegard's lap.

"Dearest mother, we've missed you so," they crooned, their wimples soon askew in a scramble of hugs. When did Gertrud's hair turn white, Hildegard wondered, and when did Gisla grow so plump? Everyone laughed as Ilse struggled to get through the door with her arms full of wildflowers. Plopping down, she squinted as she groped to smooth her skirts.

"Everything looks the same as when we left for Eibingen, but somehow it feels different," Gertrud said, peering at the sagging skin beneath the abbess' violet eyes and her maze of wrinkles. Seeing Hildegard, Ilse touched her own face and stifled a small cry. One by one, the nuns took their turns visiting, loathe to leave even when the others waiting outside chided them.

But when Hiltrude came to bring her to Vespers, Hildegard demurred for the first time.

"Daughter, my heart is so full of joy that if I try to walk, I will surely tumble over! That would cause a stir and disturb the prayer. Better to pray here," she nodded.

"As you wish, Lady Mother," Hiltrude said, brushing back the wisps of hair from Hildegard's forehead, relieved that she was conserving her strength for the celebration of Saint Benedict's feast day.

The next day, they carried her into the chapel for Sext and placed her in her chair. The abbess had asked them to include her favorite reading from the Solemnity of Saint Benedict: "The Lord loved him and adorned him. He clothed him with a robe of glory...."

Never before had the readings and chants sounded so new, so beautiful, Hildegard thought. Music must be the language of Paradise, she reflected, for what else could wed body and soul so perfectly? The reading continued: "He took care of his nation and delivered it from destruction."

At that moment, she saw the Light brighten and felt Lady Jutta's hand on her shoulder. But when she turned, her beloved teacher had disappeared.

When the chants ended, the abbess reached out her arms to her daughters as her glance moved up and down the stalls. "How my heart swells with love when I look at you," she said. "Each of you is an irreplaceable gift to me: a precious jewel! But now, my daughters, listen carefully, for I have words to share with you that I can utter only now, for our time is brief. As you well know, long ago Lady Wisdom's Voice whispered to me, 'I am the Living Light that illumines all darkness.'"

Now a hush swept up and down the stalls as eighty pairs of eyes fastened on her.

"My daughters, we read that when we were born, God concealed certain mysteries in us, for we were made in the divine image with respect to our knowledge and thoughts and deeds.

"For this reason, God discreetly caused Lady Wisdom to emerge from the divine Spirit. Lady Wisdom was sent forth under a shadow until God had completed the divine work. Before this achievement, however, God announced this coming with advance signs.

"In my visions, certain of these signs were revealed to me. I was shown how the Living Light was passed from Lady Wisdom to her first daughter, Eve; then to the great Synagoga, who held the prophets in her arms; and then to Mary, the Virgin Mother, the blossoming branch, the fruit of whose womb was the Word.

"Since that beginning time, there have been many who have heard Lady Wisdom's voice. In our time, I am but one.

"And now it is to you and all your spiritual daughters and sons that I bequeath Lady Wisdom, as I have been commanded to do by the Living Light. For the time draws near when the riddles of prophets and the writings of sages will be explained to you. Then as has been foretold, your daughters and sons will prophesy.

"The time will come when the world will seek to find that harmony that Lady Wisdom brings as she circles the universe: the harmony between the body and soul, the male and the female, the earth and its creatures.

"I place you now in Lady Wisdom's hands so that, with the Son of Man, you may walk with her and her daughters: Eve and Synagoga and Mother Mary. All are one, for everything in creation is a mirror of God."

They could not tear their eyes from her, though by now, few could see her through the glistening. This was, they knew, the legacy for which she had called them home. It was the only way she could leave them.

The last warm days of summer surrendered to autumn's crisp morning air. At Hiltrude's request, Guibert went to fetch the abbess lest she tire herself at the poor women's house. She went there each day now. With utter delight, she watched the children spin their tops and rock their wooden dolls. And after the women nursed their babies, Hildegard held each one and sang it a lullaby. Their blossoming fed her soul, she whose body grew thinner and smaller, closing in on itself like a secret, day by day.

As she rose and took Guibert's arm, she reached for her rosary, entwining it in her fingers like ivy, reassuring herself that the Virgin was nearby.

How quickly summer had come and gone since the ban had been lifted, Guibert thought. They strolled slowly until Hildegard stopped at the maple tree she had planted outside her door when she came here. Placing her cheek against the rough bark, she circled the trunk with her arms, "To thank it for its glory!" she explained as she smiled at Guibert shyly.

How can I not confirm her joy? the monk thought. The colors this year flowed from a spectacular palette: magenta hues blended into amber, and peach flowed into bronze on a single leaf. And at dusk, the sun's last rays set the trees ablaze before the darkness descended.

Each night, Guibert sat with the abbess after Compline, until Hiltrude came to prepare her for bed. As Hiltrude knelt to help the abbess to remove her shoes, Hildegard saw her brave smile and her attempts at cheerfulness. The abbess wept inside, knowing how often Hiltrude disappeared suddenly these days to disguise her tears.

"You are so good to me, dearest Hiltrude," Hildegard whispered. "You have blessed me with faith and devotion from the beginning. How could

I have lived this life without your love?" It was then that Hiltrude would gasp and turn away, her face contorted with pain and happiness. For it was to Hiltrude alone that the abbess had confided the day of her death and the hour it would come.

> O God, you are my God, for you I long;
> for you my soul is thirsting. My body pines for you
> like a dry weary land without water.

Each night, the abbess and the prioress recited the psalm together before Hildegard closed her eyes.

The abbess moved from her bed each day now to sit in the chair by the open door. "I must see the tree," she said, "and must take every joy in it while it can still display its wonder." And as she gloried in it, thoughts of the sapling they had planted in the hermitage courtyard flooded her, and again, she gave thanks for its flourishing.

"Lady mother knows the tree outside her door so well, she can tell which of the leaves fell on the ground in the night," Hiltrude confided to Guibert.

Over the next few evenings, when Guibert and Hiltrude came, Hildegard was full of memories.

"Remember the giggles in the dormitory at night at Disibodenberg?" the abbess asked her prioress. "And the first day that Ilse opened the trunk by her bed and spied her habit and swore she would never wear it?"

"I know my daughter Richardis will come soon, Guibert. We always shared a love for autumn."

"Richardis, my lady? Have I met her?"

"Not yet, but you will love her. She is my darling, the blossom of my heart."

"The lower branches are almost bare, Hiltrude. Look there! See how the few leaves left are perched like topaz birds against the sapphire sky."

"Has Lady Jutta enchanted you with tales of her pilgrimage to Compostela yet?" she asked Guibert. "She knows every stone on the road by heart!"

As Hiltrude made her way to the abbess' house with an armful of linens, the nuns clustered around her on the path.

"How is she today?" they asked anxiously.

"There is a certain sweetness now. She keeps kissing my hand," Hiltrude reported as her eyes brimmed. But they could see that the prioress' cheeks were gaunt and her eyes hooded.

"Look there, Hiltrude," the abbess said, peering at the tree. "Are the branches almost bare now?"

"A few still cling, Lady Mother."

"Hiltrude, my dear, I have need now of the brown wooden box at the bottom of my wooden chest. Would you bring it to me?"

The box was tucked beneath the abbess' old woolen shawl. As she lifted the shawl, Hiltrude hugged it, remembering when the abbess had worn it on their long ago journey to the palace at Ingelheim.

"Hiltrude," the abbess called out, "how many days will it take for Volmar to travel here from Disibodenberg? I watch the gate every day, but to no avail. Surely he'll be here tomorrow."

"If not tomorrow, then surely the next day," Hiltrude called back calmly, *not daring to face her.*

"Remember how beautifully he introduced the sisters to Lady Wisdom? Did he ever know that I sat outside the door, weeping with joy, as I listened?"

Hiltrude's hands were trembling when she handed the box to her and watched the abbess open it.

"Hiltrude dear, after my daughters, these are the dearest things in this world to me," she said, looking at them with incredible tenderness.

Looking down, Hiltrude frowned when she saw the three small, flat stones smudged with dust. "I knew they were gifts from God," Hildegard continued, "for they always appeared in my life to remind me to trust. The first stone was placed in my hand by my father. He taught me that everything God creates is a miracle, which is how soft, emerald moss is able to grow on a cold, hard stone.

"A village crone sent me the second stone to give me the courage to carry a burden I dreaded," she said. "And Father Guibert brought the last one as a sign that he had been sent to help me to finish my work.

"And so it is that I bless each stone again now, before I entrust them to you," she said, kissing Hiltrude on each cheek. "Now they are your stepping-stones, so that when the time comes, you can find your way home to me," she said, "and knowing that, you can let me go."

Sinking back on her pillows, she whispered, "I must rest now," aware that Hiltrude was unable to see that the room was already crowded.

So many hands reaching for her, so many faces, wave upon wave of unbearable bliss, lifting her into the scarlet music.

Outside, the wind rose, swirling through the bare tree one last time as Hildegard slipped into the arms of the Living Light on the other side of silence.

EPILOGUE

Hildegard's popular canonization began immediately. Huge numbers of pilgrims flocked to her grave and experienced healing miracles while others reported that they had lived to see her prophecies come to pass.

Pope Gregory IX opened proceedings for Hildegard's formal canonization in 1233, but because of mishandled documentation, his efforts were impeded. Although proceedings were reopened by Pope Innocent IV in 1243 and additional efforts were made in 1317, it was not until 1324 in Avignon that Pope John XXII announced her "solemn and public cult" by granting an indulgence of forty days to those who prayed to her.

Proclaimed now by three popes, the name and feast day of Saint Hildegard began appearing in the martyrologies, most notably, the prominent sixteenth-century *Roman* martyrology compiled by Baronius.

Reclaimed after almost nine centuries, Hildegard is heralded today as a foremother by modern feminists and as a saint by Pope John Paul II. Her prophetic writings include warnings of the Reformation; celebration and restoration of the feminine face of God present in the Hebrew Bible and the New Testament; the promotion of holistic healing; and forewarnings about the ecological peril that confronts our planet today.

Although the Abbey at Rupertsberg was destroyed by fire during the Thirty Years War, the ruins of the Abbey at Disibodenberg still stand and the Abbey of Saint Hildegard at Eibingen continues to be a flourishing Benedictine Abbey.

By permission of the Sacred Congregation, September 17, the day of Saint Hildegard's death, is celebrated in all Catholic dioceses in Germany as a double feast day.

SUGGESTED READING

Works by Hildegard

Hildegard of Bingen: Mystical Writings. Edited by Fiona Bowie and Oliver Davies. New York: Crossroad, 1990.

Hildegard of Bingen's Book of Divine Works. Edited by Matthew Fox. Santa Fe: Bear and Co., 1987.

Hildegard of Bingen's Scivias. Translated by Bruce Hozeski. Santa Fe: Bear and Co., 1987.

Illuminations of Hildegard of Bingen. Commentary by Matthew Fox. Sante Fe: Bear and Co., 1985.

The Miniatures from the Book of Scivias of St. Hildegard of Bingen from the Illuminated Rupertsberg Codex. Commentary by Adelgundis Fuhrkotter. Translated by Hockey. Turnhout, Belgium: Brepols, 1977.

Opera Omnia. In *Patrologia Latina.* Edited by J. P. Migne. Volume 197. Paris: J. P. Migne Editorem, 1855. The original of most texts written by Hildegard.

Saint Hildegard of Bingen and the Vita Sanctae Hildegardis. Translated by Anna Silvas, OSB. In *Tjurunga: An Australian Benedictine Review* 29 (1985); 30 (1986); 31 (1986); and 32 (1987).

Saint Hildegard of Bingen Symphonia: A Critical Edition of the Symphonia Armonie Celestium Revelationum (Symphony of the harmony of celestial revelations). Ithaca, N.Y.: Cornell University Press, 1988.

Scivias. Translated by M. Columba Hart and Jane Bishop. New York: Paulist Press, 1990.

Secondary Works

Dronke, Peter. *Women Writers of the Middle Ages: A Critical Study of Texts from Perpetua (d. 203) to Marguerite Porete (d. 1310).* Cambridge: Cambridge University Press, 1984.

Flanagan, Sabina. *Hildegard of Bingen — A Visionary Life.* New York: Routledge, 1989.

Lachman, Barbara. *A Journal of Hildegard of Bingen: A Novel.* New York: Bell Tower, 1993.

Newman, Barbara. *Sister of Wisdom: Saint Hildegard's Theology of the Feminine.* Berkeley: University of California Press, 1987.

Discography

A Feather on the Breath of God: Sequences and Hymns. Gothic Voices. Christopher Page. Hyperion A66039 (CD and LP).

The Lauds of Saint Ursula. Early Music Institute. Thomas Binkley. CD: Focus 911.

Ordo Virtutum: Sequentia. Barbara Thornton. Harmonia Mundi CD: 77051-2-RG; LP: IC 165-942/43 T.